LADY VIGILANTE

SEASON ONE

HAYLEY CAMILLE

LADY VIGILANTE

For my mother, Penny

CONTENTS

LADY VIGILANTE
PREQUEL

Winter, 1941. New York.

Three hundred men hustled in the pre-dawn chill, thin coats turned up against their ears, frost stealing their breath as it escaped their lungs. It was noisy, the dock lit with floodlights. The concrete was slippery with brine, too salty for the ice to take hold. A century of carriers waited to be unloaded; cargo ships that had sailed across the ocean to bring fresh produce to the Eastern Seaboard. It was the dead of Winter, 1941, and the longshoremen were edgy. They looked to the flashes of reeling gulls in the dark above, as they waited for the whistle that signaled the beginning of shapeup on the South Street Pier. Restless legs. Weathered hands. Tired eyes. Tense by the news that Pearl Harbor had been hit only days before. They were at war.

The overwhelming stench of gutted fish, oyster sheds and barrels of lobsters added a pungent pandemonium to the dock. Already, trawlers, draggers and scallop dredgers were being unloaded onto the pier by fishermen who never slept. Late-night fishmongers, in their long white aprons and rubber boots, were unloading thousands of black-backs and yellowtails, red snapper, and striped bass to the slipways. They were bound for the flounder-fileting houses that fed the Fulton Fish Markets, one of the oldest seafood wholesalers in the country. Soon, the peddlers and stalls would join them, with barrels of eels lining the docks and sand sharks strung up for display as the Wall-Street suits shuffled past on their way to work.

A bullish man with sharp eyes and neatly combed grey hair pushed through the crowd. He stopped beside an ice-chopper and leaned against the great steel frame, its rusted wheels reminiscent of an old colonial wagon. He watched critically as the mornings' team of dockworkers were selected from the milling crowd. He pulled a cigar from the breast pocket of his overcoat and lit it. Behind him, two goons in oversized suits flanked the wheels of the ice-chopper like sentinels, their eyes on the jostling men, watching for trouble.

One of the longshoremen in front turned away from the crowd. When he saw the man with the cigar, he stepped over, pulling off his hat, nervously. His red-checked jacket was threadbare.

"I didn't see ya there, Mr. Pinzolo," he said. He checked over his shoulder nervously. "You need somethin'?"

"Just waiting for Marco." Donald Pinzolo said. "You new? What's your name?"

"Landrey, sir."

"The boys tell you how it is?"

"Yes, sir."

"And?"

The man shrugged. "And I'm wearing my red jacket, Sir."

Donny's face split into a wide smile. "Well, Mr. Landrey, go tell Flannagan I said you looked good for the slings." He gave the man a hearty thud on the back. "We reward loyalty here, and you look like the kind of fella that I can trust."

"Thank you, Mr. Pinzolo!"

"Call me Donny. We're friends now, you and me. Aren't we Landrey?"

"Sure, sure! Say, you want me to go find Marco for you?" The young longshoreman was skittish, hardly believing his luck, unaware of the dark looks he was drawing from the crowd.

"Just get going or you'll miss the call."

"Yes, Sir!"

Donald Pinzolo nodded him off. He turned to the gunsel standing by the rusted wagon wheel over his right shoulder. They exchanged a grin.

From the back of the crowd, a heavy-set young man in an expensive overcoat pushed his way forward. The longshoremen let him pass, averting their eyes. As he reached the man with the cigar he stopped.

"What'cha doing here, Pops? There's no need – you know I got it all under control."

"Just checking in," Donny grunted. "It's good for me to show my mug every now and then. Keeps them on their toes."

"I got Jimmy on the crates. Nothin' to worry about – the shapes' like clockwork."

"You sure about that?" The older man flicked ash from his cigar onto the salted concrete. "A little pigeon told me Jimmy's been skimmin' the profits." He shot a side-glance at his son.

"Jimmy?" Marco looked over at the hiring boss. A middle-aged man with paunch belly and a shock of fiery hair was stepping up onto a platform in front of the crowd. "Get outta town!"

"He's taking you for a ride, Marco," Donny said. "And that shill of his, Rosco, too. We got eighty million a year rolling through here. You wanna risk that to some grifter with sticky fingers?"

"I'll kill the son of a bitch." Marco's face burned. "How'd you find out?"

"I'm a mind-reader," Donny chuckled. An old memory clouded his eyes and his mouth turned sour. "It doesn't matter how. Fix it."

Marco scanned the crowd. Up front, the red-haired hiring boss, Jimmy, sounded his whistle.

"I'll sink 'im." Marco's jaw was tight. "Me and the boys." A vein twitched at his temple. His ears burned and he pulled his hat off to drag a hand through his hair.

"Plenty more room for bones out at Dead Horse Bay." Donny muttered. The corner of his mouth twitched. He took another drag on his cigar.

The shouts intensified, as each laborer struggled to be heard. Jimmy scanned the crowd, his index finger jabbing the air as he singled out his favorites. A scratch, a nod, a red shirt – any covert signal that they were willing to pay for the opportunity to work. A couple of dollars kickback was the price to feed hungry mouths at home. Jimmy was hoarse as he called them. The men shouted back, elbowing their way forward, desperate to be seen over the carnival of corruption.

"Flannagan! Davis! Charester! Gullivan! Doyle! – You're in the hold. Appleby and Campion – winch drivers and hatch tenders – pick your men."

A look of relief and nod of recognition, as the chosen ones flashed their numbered tab at the hiring boss and took off toward the slipway and warehouses. The new one, Landrey, had made the cut. It was a cattle call. They did their jobs. Shut their mouths. Looked the other way. Gang bosses made sure their men were willing to pay for the privilege to sweat. But even a docked day's work could stave poverty for one more meal.

Then there were those uncalled for. Unwilling to pay off the union bosses or too guileless to know they should. Within an hour, more than half the men would be in saloons and flophouses, drinking their misery until dawn found them, again, jostling on the frozen dock.

"McMahon! Kilkenny! Roman! Churenski! You're boom men." Jimmy squinted through the crowd to catch a resigned hand flick. "And you, Barradale."

"Sack turners –Bellamy! Sharp! You there – Kreed! Jitney drivers – you know what to do."

It was treacherous work. Backbreaking. A winch too loose, a hand too sweaty, a footing misplaced – they'd be as dead as the glassine eyes staring out of the herring crates.

"Enough." Donny announced to his son. "Show me the stock."

Marco dragged his scowl from Jimmy's direction. He set off at pace toward the slipway where a fishing trawler was already being unloaded by a burly team of longshoremen. The floor of the vessel was a labyrinth of coiled ropes. A stack of crates on the slipway read *JT Vargus, Wholesale Fishmongers, Fulton Fish Markets, NYC.*

"I'm a goddamn genius, Pops," Marco boasted. "Fifty crates in the hold, full to the brim with crevalle jack. Gutted, stuffed and frozen in Colombia and port-hopped all the way from Miami. I'm in the fish business now – see?!"

"Fish business," Donny scoffed. "You're no genius until that *fish* is on the streets. I got five places lined up to hold it tonight." He exhaled and flicked the butt of his cigar into the East River. "Take care of it."

"And the winner of our *Annual Insurance Salesman of the Year Award* is... drumroll please, Mr. Kenealy –" a jolly-faced man tapped on the white tablecloth with his knife and fork as all the diners laughed. Close by, at a makeshift podium, a tall man in a tailored suit and moustache was unfolding the contents of an envelope. "Well – it's Mr. George Jones! Can you believe it? That's the third year running Mr. Jones has taken the prize – what a darb! Now, I don't know about you, folks, but I think I know who the butter-and-egg man is this Christmas! Pass him the cheque!" The room burst into laughter and applause.

At a table toward the back of the room, a young woman jumped to her feet. Her dark hair was curled in Victory rolls that fell over her shoulders. She was wearing a rayon cocktail dress that fell just below the knee, matched perfectly to her blood red lips, painted nails and high-heeled pumps. She pulled her husband to his feet, launching herself at him in a kiss that left a bright red stain on his cheek. The crowd laughed again.

"Oh, George, darling! You're a star!"

"Thanks, Jitterbug." George Jones grinned. He was about thirty years old, with wavy blonde hair parted with BrylCreem, dancing blue eyes and a boyish smile. His polished shoes shone as he navigated his way through the diners to the podium. Back at the table, his wife bounced on her toes, clapping. George winked at her from the podium as he was handed an ornately wrapped gift.

"Well deserved, George," the mustached man was saying into the microphone. "We're mighty lucky to have you."

"Well, gee, this is just swell, Mr. Weisenberg," George beamed, shaking the man's hand, "what a thrill. You know, there's nothing I like better than to sell my clients the best term endowment money can buy. In times like these you can't be too careful in your planning –" He trailed off, searching across the sea of applause for the one set of eyes he wanted to find. Betty blew him a kiss. George turned back and continued his conversation with enthusiasm, moving away from the microphone.

"You must be so proud!" The woman in the next chair grabbed Betty's arm and attention. "You know, my Morty says that George is next in line for a promotion. Maybe you'll get that new Hoover you wanted after all!"

"Wouldn't that be something?" Betty enthused. She dragged her eyes from her husband to sit. "By the way, you look an absolute dish, Nellie, darling. That powder I sold you is perfect for your skin tone. Didn't I tell you it would be?"

"What would I do without an Avon Lady in my corner?"

"You'd do perfectly well," Betty laughed. "But if I brighten a pretty face in these miserable war-ridden days, I'm a happy girl."

"And if I looked half the hep kitten you do, I'd be over the moon. So, tell me, Betty," the blonde woman's eyes narrowed, and she leaned in close, "what *is* that color your wearing?"

Betty looked around with dramatic intrigue. "Alright, you win, but it's our little secret – this is the only lipstick I own that's *not* Avon."

"Surely not!"

"*Victory Red.* Now, don't tell anyone or my reputation will be shot."

Nellie fell back, grinning as she reached for her champagne.

"Well, how could I resist, darling?" Betty said, in mock indignation. "Commissioned by Elizabeth Arden herself, just like the shade she created for our gals in uniform. You know she gave out thousands of red lipsticks to the suffragettes marching in 1912?"

"Really?"

"Oh yes, she's quite the *femme de résistance*. I must support that, it's patriotic! Besides, the color looks absolutely smashing on me, admit it."

"You slay me, Betty," Nellie laughed.

"One too many gin sours. Seriously though, I must drop by for a cup of tea, dear. There's a new perfume in the Winter catalog that's an absolute knockout. You'll adore it. But now," Betty stood, picking up her handbag, "you must excuse me before dinner arrives, the powder room beckons."

Betty wove her way through the tables toward the ladies' room. A brass band kicked into full swing. The bar was overflowing with hurricane cocktails and dry Manhattan's as couples kicked up their heels in triple step to the East Coast Swing. They dipped and spun as a crooner tapped his foot and brought a trumpet to his lips.

Beyond the red velvet curtains, the shoulders of Lady Liberty were heavy with the burden of war. But inside *Louis' Restaurant* on Lenox Avenue, tonight's party was all too keen to shed the shackles of reality for a few fleeting hours of freedom.

Betty skimmed the room and took a side door that she supposed led to the bathrooms. Instead, she nearly collided with two burly men, wheeling a stack of wooden crates on a metal trolley.

"Watch it, cookie!" one of them growled.

"So sorry." Betty stepped to the side to let them pass. As she looked up, her instinctive apology turned bitter in her mouth.

Ernie Miller.

Vito Ridgway.

Betty was too long presumed dead to be recognized by these men now. It seemed a lifetime ago. Someone else's life. Back then, her name was Susie. *Susan Polletti.* Betty suppressed a shudder. They pushed past her now, wrapped in their oversized zoot suits and sporting scars that boasted a lifetime of violence, raked their eyes across her blood red rayon blindly and turned their thoughts to foul fancies.

'Wouldn't mind a rough'ouse with that bird,' came Ernie's voice, as clear as day into Betty's mind. *'Show her pretty pins how us working boys like it.'*

Ernie had no idea his own thoughts had betrayed him. People never did. Betty didn't react, all the same. Instead, she gave a small smile, let them pass and walked on. She paused, then watched Ernie and Vito turn left at the end of the corridor.

Reading another's mind was not the most impressive skill Betty had, but it was certainly the most useful. Not that she didn't *try* to block them out of course, she was a lady after all.

Regrets. Loneliness. Depravity. Love. Selflessness. Lust.

She had heard it all. Betty had spent a lifetime listening in to, or avoiding, the thoughts of others. For the most part, she simply blocked the voices out. A silent mind was a blessing.

But then again, some thoughts, needed to be heard.

Betty made a snap decision. She followed Ernie and Vito back up the corridor. As she turned the corner into the reception room, she saw a door on the left wall swinging. She took it, pushing through the double doors to find herself down an almost identical corridor. It was deserted. She followed the sound of voices to a side door and pressed it open just enough to see through. Beyond, was the kitchen. Waiters were rushing to and fro amidst boiling pots and steaming frypans. Long benches covered in serving plates shone under bright lights. The room was a clamor of voices. But only one conversation piqued Betty's interest.

Ernie and Vito had stacked their crates by a silver bench. They were arguing with a man in a chef's hat. The crates had the words *JT Vargus, Wholesale Fishmongers, Fulton Fish Markets, NYC* burned into the wooden crates. From her vantagepoint, Betty could see the men perfectly well. Though she was too far away to hear, their quarrel came crystal clear through their thoughts.

"Maybe I oughta go get Marco to come give you a lesson in loyalty, eh, Louis?"

"But don't you see?" The chef implored, sweat pricking his brow. He pulled off his toque blanche and dragged it across his forehead. "I can't keep this stuff. What if one of my cooks tries to poach it?"

"Tell 'em to keep their mitts to themselves," Vito growled. "Marco's got a runner comin' after close tomorrow. So just stick the crates in the freezer, shut your trap and we're all good, see?" He stepped forward and took the chef's face in his hands, gently slapping the man's cheek. "Donny's been good to you, ain't he? We keep the Bowery Boys off your door for what? A grand a week? Now Donny wants a favor and you're gonna throw his generosity back in his face? I don't think he's gonna like that, Louis."

"I'm not, I swear! It's just – well, there's so much of it."

"This is only half. I got the rest in the truck waitin' to come up."

The chef's pallor turned grey. "There's more?"

"That's right, so you're gonna go make some room in your freezer, 'cause we don't want these fishies thawin' out. If they do, you'll have more than a bad smell on your hands, you got that?" Vito turned to Ernie. "You think he'd be a little more thankful."

"You'd think." Ernie shot his conspirator a wink. "Maybe we oughta go get Marco, anyways. Just so Louis here, understands what a favor from Donny really means."

"No! Don't do that," the chef cried. He fumbled with a ring of keys tied under his apron. "Just - just give me a few minutes. Right at serving time too –" He shot the men a terrified look and shuffled off into the chaos.

"What'd I say?" Vito grinned. "Come on, let's go get the rest."

Betty let the door slip shut and ducked up the corridor. She pressed herself into an alcove as Vito and Ernie pushed out of the kitchen with their metal trolley and disappeared back the way they had come.

She poked her head through the swinging doors. The waiters were preoccupied with the commotion of serving a hundred meals. The head chef was nowhere to be seen. Betty slipped inside. She pried the lid on the top crate from its cradle. Inside, a treasure of ice and scales glittered. Betty reached in, her mouth twisting in distaste as her fingers curled around a frozen fish. She whipped it out. Betty stuffed the fish into her handbag, snapped the clasp and turned on her heel. A few minutes later, she was safely seconded in a bathroom cubicle, digging it out of her cosmetics and cursing the wretched stench it had already left. She looked at the creature carefully, flipping it over. A pang of remorse hit her for its empty eyes and silver scales glistening under the light. It would have been dazzling in the water, vital and alive. A thin cut creased the underside of its belly. Betty ran her red fingernail along the slice and pulled the two halves apart. In place of entrails was a small wax-coated bag. Inside was white powder. *Cocaine.* Memories came rushing back.

💋

"Useless!"

Susie Polletti looked up from her book. She was sitting on a small brick fence about knee-high, at the edge of a derelict park. Her usual spot. Her clothes were threadbare, but tidy and meticulously clean. Her long hair was tied with a ribbon. She didn't look like the type of child you'd expect to be running drugs for the mob.

By her feet on the pavement was Susie's school bag, stuffed with homework she knew wouldn't get finished. After the snowbirds she was expecting had finished their business and scurried off to get high, she still had to prepare dinner for her father. An hour or two after that, he'd call back home to pick her up and drive to the place where her great uncle Donny did business each night. In a warehouse by the dock, she was forced into men's minds, a place no girl ought to venture. A nod was all it took to pass her judgement on to Donny. To expose his adversaries silently to their guilt.

Then came their punishment. Vicious. Remorseless. The pleas of grown men before they collapsed to the rug, a bullet to their temple. All at the word of a twelve-year-old girl. And in front of her as witness.

It hadn't always been her. Before, it was Susie's mother.

Ethyl had drowned in her gift, plagued by the inner demons of the criminals Donny had forced her to read. She had been a tool for him, a puppet. Donny had abused her mother's empathic ability, forcing Ethyl to listen in on the confessions of murderers and thieves. To pick out the truth within their lies. To steal the upper hand in a room of crooks. Susie's father, Roy, kept Ethyl compliant and degraded, feeding her dependence on the addictive white powder she craved. Each hit brought a few hours escape from the prison of her mind. Blessed silence.

When Susie was only twelve, her mother finally broke. Shelled by a silver teaspoon on the kitchen floor. Donald Pinzolo lost his secret weapon.

But miraculously, found a new one in her place. Stronger. More resilient. Susie.

Susie scrunched her face toward the setting sun. Her second cousin Marco, Donny's son, was only meters away, flanked, as always, by his thuggish sidekicks, Ernie and Vito. He was a few years older than her, nearly sixteen, but had the muscular, bullish frame of a boy much older. Susie hated him.

"You done 'em all?" Marco scowled.

Susie got to her feet, standing on top of the low fence. She looked him straight in the eye. "What's it to you?"

Crash!

Marco's palm barreled her chest. Susie fell backward off the bricks, bruised and humiliated. Marco straightened his shoulders and grinned at his laughing pals. He looked down at her, his eyes burning with resentment.

"Pop wants you, that's what."

Susie caught her breath. She tried not to let her fear show as she pushed up from the ground with grazed and stinging palms.

"Well I'm still waiting on Billy Jay and Streetcar. They're late."

"How much are they paying?"

"Six dollars each."

"Gimme the stuff. I'll have to do it". He thrust his hand toward her. Susie flinched, then realized he was waiting for the powder cocaine she had hidden in her sock.

"Bugger knows why he wants you there all the time," Marco growled. "What's a little brat like you gonna do that I can't? Nothin', that's what." Susie could hear the boy's thoughts churning with jealousy. Susie was Donny's shiny new weapon. She wasn't allowed to speak of her other work for Donny. Only her father and her uncle

Frank knew of Susie's gift to read minds. All Marco knew, was that this skinny, mouthy, twelve-year-old girl was more valued by his father than he was. He hated her.

Without taking her eyes off him, Susie climbed over the fence and held out the two bindles she'd pulled out of her sock. Marco snatched them from her fingers.

"Now, scram, useless!" Marco parked himself on the bricks in Susie's place and pulled out a crumpled pinup from his trouser pocket. "Hey Vito, check out the hot cake."

As Susie turned her back on them to walk to the dock, she almost wished she could stay.

At midnight precisely, Betty stole out of bed. She shrugged on her winter coat and toed into her Oxfords. It was going to be a long ride back to Louis Restaurant.

The cocaine she'd fished out of the frozen crevalle had been easy to destroy. Betty had simply flushed it down the toilet right there in the cubicle, then tossed the fish out of the window. Six crates were still hidden amongst the frozen food at the restaurant and Betty couldn't abide the thought of leaving it there. It was, no doubt, destined for gin mills and clip joints across the city, to be rationed out to the addicts that lined Donny's pockets with their addiction. *Not this time,* Betty thought. She pedaled faster and her bicycle wheeled through the dark night. Behind her, a garden spade rattled on the rack, tied with rope.

One o'clock found Betty breaking the locks of the delivery door behind overfilled skips and piles of trash. A satisfying *click* released the pins and Betty clipped her brooch back onto her jacket. The side door swung open. She slipped in. Betty allowed her eyes to adjust, then silently stole through the corridors, testing each closed door until she found herself back in the kitchen. The room was lonely in the unseen hours of the morning, sterile and cold, compared to the hustle and bustle she had witnessed only hours before. Soon, the bakers would arrive to warm the ovens with fresh bread. She had to be quick.

At the far end of the kitchen, heavy doors rumbled a low hum. Betty pulled one open. A splitting light broke across the room, stunning her. Quickly, Betty ducked into the refrigerator, holding the door ajar with her foot as she dragged an enormous ham across the floor to hold the door. She could see crates of frozen fish in the back corner, piled high with baskets of root vegetables.

Betty adjusted her gloves. It had been years since she'd used her *other* gifts. Since she'd used her strength for anything more than lifting the couch to Hoover underneath it. Used her speed for nothing more than sorting the washing in a blink. A little thrill shot through her at the thought.

Betty ducked inside. She picked up each crate in turn and trotted it out, as if the pounds of wood and ice and meat weighed nothing. Her muscles reveled in long-missed exertion. When she had all six crates piled by the kitchen door, she kicked the oversized ham back in. Making sure she was still alone, Betty carried the crates, three at once, back down to her bicycle.

What was I thinking? She eyed the thin bicycle frame beside her new cargo. *Now I wonder...* Betty rifled through the skips. *Perfect.* She pulled out an old metal step stool that had been tossed away. The fabric seat was torn and there was a crust of rust along the legs. *Make do and Mend,* Betty thought, happily. She set it down, considered it for a moment, then ripped the base of the chair from its metal pins. The metal squeaked and squealed as she bent it upwards, fashioning the legs out in either direction, like a short ladder. Betty lay the flat stool across the back rack of her bicycle and bound it with her rope. One by one, each crate was stacked on the now-wider carry rack until the bike wobbled under its weight. Betty bound them as best she could with her garden spade across the top, then took off through the night, a pyramid of drug-laden cargo behind her.

Out beyond Flatbush along Millstone Trail, Betty rode through the dark night until she reached the western edge of a marshland. She had been expecting the putrid smell that greeted her but had almost forgotten how forcefully it sucked her breath away and caused her stomach to boil.

Dead Horse Bay.

Until only a decade past, the shoreline had been encircled by horse rendering plants where the chopped-up, boiled carcasses of New York City's unwanted animals were churned to glue and fertilizer. The bay was a dumping ground for a century of scattered bones. Refuse from the garbage incinerators and fish-oil factories beyond the marsh added to the stench until the residents couldn't stand the noxious fumes any longer. They moved away. It became a landfill, swallowing decades of household detritus until the sand disappeared beneath the filth. Broken glass bottles, leather shoes and old telephones, mixed with eyeglasses, broken dolls and spoons and dead things. The bay had a squalid, apocalyptic air about it. It was a graveyard of *things*, once loved, then stolen away by malice, neglect, misfortune or time.

Decent folk stayed away from Dead Horse Bay.

But Betty had been here many times. As a child. With Donny.

Dead Horse Bay was one of her great uncle's favorite dumping grounds, though the bones he buried there were not horses, but men. Their deaths had been just as grisly. The irony of hiding Marco's shipment of cocaine-riddled fish in this place was not lost on Betty. Neither was she surprised, when she came across two bodies dug into a shallow grave in the dunes. Donald Pinzolo's legacy in the flesh.

Betty buried the silver treasure in a deep trench. She covered it over with trash. It had been a malodourous evening, but a productive one. She climbed onto her powder blue bicycle, tired to the bone, and began the two-hour ride home.

At six o'clock in the morning, Betty climbed into bed beside her oblivious husband, a small smile on her lips and her hair pin-curled neatly into a pink snood, smelling of lavender shampoo.

Outside the 68th Precinct of the New York City Police Department, a dark-haired detective stood by the open front door, chatting with a young officer in uniform. Above them, the three-story building rose like a medieval fortress, its corner tower grasping for winter sun.

It was a glorious day, despite the chill, and Betty watched a little wistfully as sunlight caught the detective's face. He was handsome, as he had always been, and despite the years that had passed, Betty's heart settled into a dull ache. A decade ago, Jacob Lawrence had been her world. But the night she had given up her old life and name, Betty had been forced to give Jacob up too. She sacrificed their future together. Her dreams. Her desires.

It had saved Jacob's life, of that Betty was certain, though the handsome detective did not know it. All he knew what that his childhood sweetheart, Susie, had been murdered, a victim of the arson that had consumed her childhood home. He had lost his heart that day.

Susie Polletti, Betty thought. *It's so long since I've been that girl.*

Jacob turned and looked out across the busy street corner. Betty quickly twisted away, letting the shadows and brim of her felt cloche hat hide her face.

Perhaps it's been too long.

Betty closed her eyes for a moment and let the chill breeze take her back.

***

She was fifteen years old, and Jacob had been her watchful shadow and only friend, for the past four. As she sat outside the general store waiting for him to finish his boxing lesson in the community hall across the road, Susie's heart was singing.

It was a training day. He was teaching her to fight.

Jacob was only a couple of years older than she was but had been training her for three years already. Ever since the bruises she wore from her father stopped fading. As the eldest son of a police sergeant, Jacob had access to classes that girls were never invited to join. Boxing. Fencing. Gymnastics. Karate. He didn't really like taking lessons himself, he did it for Susie. The better he got, the more he could teach. And Susie loved to learn.

Every afternoon after school, they would sneak down to an abandoned shed they had found at the docks, and Jacob would train Susie until her fists bled and he was bruised all over. She was unstoppable. Extraordinarily fast. Unnaturally strong. But only he knew it.

When it was time for her to go work for Donny, selling fet to the junkies in the park, she never let Jacob come along. A copper's son was bad for business. She knew that if her father or Donny ever found out that they were even friends, Jacob would end up at Dead Horse Bay. Susie was far too precious a commodity to lose.

Jacob waved to her through the streaked windows of the hall. He held up a hand three times, his fingers wide. Fifteen minutes and he was done. Susie waved back and smiled. Her heart skipped a beat. She didn't need to deny to herself that she loved Jacob. She had always known it. She only hoped that one day, she would find a way to show him just how much.

"Hey, useless!"

Without warning, Marco appeared in front of her.

Crash!

Susie fell backward as he pushed her, the chair upturning. Her head hit the sidewalk, hard. For a moment, sparks went whizzing in the black behind her eyelids. Nausea rose. Above her, she could hear Marco laughing. Ernie and Vito spurred him on. Susie grit her teeth and pulled up to her feet. Blood rushed to her face. Her arm was scraped and bleeding. She'd been so busy watching Jacob practice, she hadn't been paying attention to the sidewalk. She'd let her guard down. Something she'd promised herself never to do.

"Who're you waving at?" Marco asked suspiciously. He turned and squinted across the road toward the community hall. Susie shot a look of warning to Jacob and he scowled and stepped out of view. He knew the deal. He couldn't be seen to know her. But inside her head, Jacob's fury roared from within the weatherboard walls.

"No one," she said, stony-faced. "What do you want?"

"I wanna sit here and wait for Sally Moroney to come walkin' by with her big yabos, that's what. So that means you," he pulled a large paper packet from his pocket and slapped it into her hand, "are gonna do my run for me. Take it to Uncle Frank at the Capitol and tell him Pop wants him early tonight. Somethin' about the Bowery Boys." Marco picked up her chair and planted himself on it. Ernie and Vito jostled one another for the spare. "Get going, useless. You're blocking my view."

Susie held her breath for a moment, willing herself not to punch him. If she had wanted to, she could have snapped Marco like a twig. But it was no use, not yet anyway. Her second cousin was a bully, but he was nothing compared to her father and uncle. Until she was rid of them, there was no point in making her life harder.

Bitterly disappointed, Susie turned and walked away, glancing up at the streaked window as she left. She offered a tiny wave as Jacob watched her leave. There would be no training tonight.

"Oh, George, darling, you're so clever," Betty said. "*Insurance Salesman of the Year* again, you've outdone yourself!" The mahogany mantel clock ticked softly as Betty polished its glass face. She sat it on the telephone and switched the radio on. A lovesick melody warmed the small room. Betty turned back to her husband, glowing with pride.

"It's all thanks to you, Jitterbug." George winked and took her hand, pulling Betty into a slow waltz.

"You're a hopeless romantic, darling."

"No, I'm a hopeless case without you and you know it. Luckiest day of my life when I got caught in that snowstorm downtown. I found an angel in a white apron, holding a tin of Blosser's Cold and Flu Powder in one hand and my heart in the other."

"Oh George, it was just the drug store counter –"

"And I never saw a clerk as pretty as you –"

"Nonsense," Betty laughed. "The Blosser's does that you know, it's hallucinogenic–"

"Blosser's, my left eye! It was the girl of my dreams," George insisted, spinning Betty around and pulling her back in close. "Now look at us. Two beautiful children. Perfect home, perfect wife... I'm as happy as the cat that got the cream."

"Speaking of cream," Betty deflected, looking away. "There's a new night cream I promised I'd take over to Hattie after dinner. She's a flood of tears since the news broke. You know her Harold is in the 165th Infantry and they've already shipped him off to Inglewood to defend the West Coast?"

"An Avon appointment? At night?"

"I'll be perfectly fine, George. I do hate to see my ladies upset. Besides, we're at war now. You know, they say Hitler can't abide makeup on women, he's banned it altogether. So, I've determined it's our patriotic duty to be as glamorous as possible! *Beauty is Duty*, darling."

Betty hated to lie, but it was ten years too late to explain. George, so sweet and naïve, couldn't have imagined the horrors of her past. It was why she loved him – George was the living embodiment of perfect mediocrity. Uncomplicated. Simple. *Normal.*

Everything she could never truly be herself.

Over the past decade, Betty had allowed herself to be swept away by delicious, benign normality. Lace curtains and tea pots. Nylon stockings with white garters. Sunday roasts. Her picture-perfect children, Nancy and George Junior, playing knuckle-bones and skipping ropes in the front yard.

Betty reveled in obscurity. She painted over memories of bullet-holes and addicts with red lipstick and a splash of lilac perfume. Her dark past was masked by an incandescent smile. Her hands were busied by the to and fro of Avon appointments, serving cosmetics and charity in equal measure to any woman who crossed her path.

But seeing Ernie and Vito had brought the past rushing back. And that singular thought – that her demons were still hunting while her children played in the streets – brought a cold steeliness to her spine. Her maternal instincts spiked. Her senses sharpened.

Her paint was beginning to crack.

"Goodnight, my darling. Don't wait up for me!"

Betty wheeled through the lamplit streets on her powder blue bicycle. Her beloved cognac crocodile-skin Avon bag was securely tied on the back tray. Bottles of bath salts and pots of cream and nail varnish filled it to bursting. Underneath it all, in the false bottom of the bag, were some new acquisitions of a rather different nature. *Kitchenware.*

Betty slowed on the outskirts of the Fulton Fish Markets under the outstretched arm of Brooklyn Bridge. She let her bicycle tick across the frozen pavement. Two cavernous sheds were lit up like a circus tent against the dark harbor. Every night while the city slept, a hoopla of commotion rose in the night markets as buyers haggled with wholesalers amidst a spectacle of stacked seafood. Forklifts careened between walls of crates and fishmongers hacked with razor-sharp knives, cleaning and filleting en masse. Betty snaked past, down alleys toward the smaller warehouses, glad to slip back into obscurity.

JT Vargus, Wholesale Fishmongers, Fulton Fish Markets, NYC.

Peeling blue paint on the outside of a small concrete warehouse brought Betty to a stop. Betty wheeled her bike into a dark alley down the side of the building then leaned it against the wall near a side door.

She gently pried open the false bottom of her cosmetics case. The jars inside tinkled as they shifted. Betty pulled out her quarry and tucked them neatly into her garters. *Perfect,* she thought. *No one would ever suspect.* Betty picked up her bag by the handles and set it gently down on its brass feet. She straightened her dress and plumped her hair, smiling brightly to the deserted alley. Her red lipstick shone in the moonlight. She flexed her fingers and adjusted her gloves.

Betty closed her eyes and cast out her mind like a web, catching clues from within the walls. *Yes,* Betty smiled. *This is the place.*

Knock. Knock. Knock.

The side door rattled on its hinges.

Knock. Knock. Knock.

From inside, Betty heard a shout. Footsteps. A door flung open to reveal Ernie, his brow furrowing at the sight of her in the light that spilled from the passageway behind him.

"Yeah?"

"Avon Calling!" Betty trilled. She picked up her cosmetics bag and pushed past him.

For a moment Ernie stood there, stupefied. Then he came scrambling after.

"Oi! Lady! There's no broads 'ere! We don't want ya business
–"

With Ernie on her tail, Betty pushed through a second door
and found herself in a storage room full of crates. It was freezing.
The overpowering stench of fish guts and Lucky Strikes assaulted
her. Marco Pinzolo was sitting at a round card table. His upper lip
wore a frosting of white. Beside him, Vito dropped a playing card
in surprise, knocking his cut to the floor. A third goon looked up
with glassy, bloodshot pupils, the tell-tale badge of a snowbird.
Betty skimmed his hazy thoughts. *Freddie the shiv.* Another
enforcer for Donny, a lifetime of blood on his hands. *C'est la vie.*

"What's with the skirt?" Marco growled, kicking back his
chair to stand up. "I told ya not to bring anyone back here –"

"I think it's the broad from Louis' place, we saw 'er there."

"Well, what's she doin' here?"

"I dunno, do I!? Some kind of beauty queen sellin' powders
–"

"Good evening, gentlemen," Betty said, her tone light. "I was
just in the neighborhood and thought I might drop by and offer
my service." She placed her bag beside her.

Marco sized her up for a moment, then cracked a nasty grin.
"What's a bunch of good-lookin' fellas like us gonna do with
your beauty products, cookie?" The others guffawed.

Vito punched Marco's arm. "I can think of somethin' we
could do with her though," he wheezed.

"You really are making this too easy for me, boys," Betty
grinned, her eyes twinkling.

Marco sat back down. His eyes narrowed, as he studied her
critically.

"What do you want?"

"Want? From you? To offer my service, like I said. To give to
you," she stepped forward with a dazzling smile, "something
you've given to so many others."

Betty smoothed her red woolen dress, tracing the shape of steel against her thighs. *Comforting.*

"And what would that be?" Marco's jaw set as he stood up once more, his hands on the table. There was no humor left in his voice. The other men exchanged looks.

"A quick death. If you're lucky."

"That right?" he muttered. The scars on his face creased into hard lines. Marco's hand didn't move, but his mind flicked to the revolver he had hidden in his overcoat pocket. "Mouthy little cracker, aren't you? What did I do? Take your steady for a ride under a bridge?" More laughter.

"Oh, have I changed that much?" Betty said casually. "Yes, I imagine I have. Back when you knew me, Marco, I was nothing to you – just a scrawny little girl to be kicked around. A thorn in your side. Unworthy. *Useless.*"

Marco's shoulders straightened. Betty could see the light slowly coming on in his mind. She heard his thoughts rifling through years of violent memories for a name. His inner voice as he finally found it. *Susie?*

Betty smiled, cold and cruel. Her eyes flashed, dark amusement transmuting seamlessly into something else, something new and unnamed. Something a little... *unhinged.*

And right then, she knew.

It was time.

Smash!

Betty leapt forward, kicking off the chest of the glass-eyed thug beside Marco and landing on the table in front of them. The doper fell backward in his chair as Betty's laced-leather Oxford slammed under his chin. He crashed to the concrete, out cold.

Thump!

Her left fist knocked the gat from Marco's hand. It spun off, clattering beneath the crates. Betty drew back her right leg then burst forward, round-housing on the tabletop to kick Vito where he sat, his mouth hanging open in disbelief.

Vito smashed backward, triggering an avalanche of crates, ice chips and dead-eyed fish that shattered across the floor. A basket of eels came crashing down and he writhed beneath the slippery bodies, scrambling for purchase.

"You filthy little –" Marco lunged for her. With a roar in her heart, Betty met him halfway, leaping from the table in a dive, her hands closing around his throat before the floor hit his back. Somewhere behind, Ernie was reaching for his gun.

Slam!

She uppercut Marco's jaw with her elbow. He rolled, dragging her, as a bullet ricocheted off the concrete only inches away. Betty sprang up, grabbing split wood and sent it hurtling as Ernie let off another round. Marco dove behind barrels. The bullet pierced a stave and brine shot out like a penny fountain.

"I don't want no trouble, I swear," Ernie called. His hands were up, his eyes wide. The gun dangled from his index finger.

"Oh, but you've caused so much trouble already, Ernie," Betty admonished, turning to him.

"You know who *really* didn't want any trouble? Mr. Williams from the Dime Savings Bank. Nor did Harry Rooth or Samuel Squib from the Quaker House when you paid a visit to Old Gage because he owed you money."

"How do you know about –?"

"Oh, I know everything. I know where to find the bodies of Jimmy Byrne and Rosco Brackin out at Dead Horse Bay. I know all of your *dirty little secrets*," Betty said. "It's a rather useful skill of mine. And I have another, you know. Would you like to see?"

Betty raised the hem of her dress. Underneath, a shining row of kitchen knives gleamed in her garter. Her long, pale leg was bent at the knee, her skirt pulled high in bewitching fare.

"Pretty, aren't they?" she grinned. The reflection glittered in

Ernie's eyes. "And I am rather good in the kitchen. What do you think? Is it time to serve up?"

"Why?" Ernie stuttered, his voice rising. He was shaking, backing away. Another stack of crates stopped him short. At his feet, the doper was still out cold on the concrete.

"Revenge, darling," Betty breathed. "For all the lives you've taken these last ten years in Donny's name. The blood you've spilt for Marco's greed. For the children who've lost their fathers; mothers who've lost their sons. The *collateral damage*." Ernie slipped in the ice under his feet. The electric bulb above them reflected in a thousand fisheyes and diamond ice on the floor. Betty's breath turned opaque as it left her warm lungs. "It's quite fitting, actually, finding you here," she said. "After all, I believe this *is* a dish best served cold."

Faster than thought, she moved. Her body was lithe and disciplined, from years of training. At twelve, flicking a shiv at a barrel at the docks, over and again, until her fingers bled. At thirteen, countless hours learning to fight back against the demons that imprisoned her each night, committing murder in her name. At fourteen, training until her body ached, until her arms were more deadly than the weapons they held. At fifteen, a knife in her father's chest, as her final word against a childhood of abuse.

Murder him. Light a match. Walk away. It was a lifetime ago.

Now, her fingers found the steel again. *Comforting.*

Betty unsheathed three knives from her garter, fast as lightning, and flicked them, twisting her body with critical aim and deadly force.

Thud.

Thud.

Thud.

Each found its home. Ernie crumbled. The doper's chest stopped still. On the floor, Vito stared, the light fading from his eyes as he became one of the dead things around him.

"Well, you finally got what you wanted, Marco," Betty purred to the only man left alive. Marco was hiding, slipping between columns of crates, inching for the door. "Daddy's attention." She slipped into the maze. "I gave you ten years to make him proud."

Marco's breath was jagged, as he tried so hard not to give himself away.

A squeak. Footsteps. Betty pounced as he dashed for the door. Caught his legs and they crashed in an explosion of scales.

Crack!

Her fist caught his jaw. Marco fought back, his brute strength and aggression unyielding against her slight frame. Finally, she pinned him down, his arms splayed with Betty's final knife, slid from her garter, pressed against his throat. Betty looked down at him, grimy with sweat as he heaved.

"Did you do it, Marco?" she asked. "Made Daddy proud? After all, you got your dearest wish. You grew up to be *just like him*." With each word, Betty pressed her knife a little harder against his pink skin. "More's the pity."

A Harlem sunset, spilt red. And it was done.

Betty stood up. She straightened her dress, flicking off shards of ice and scales. Her nose wrinkled. *I'll visit Mrs. Schroeder at the drycleaner's tomorrow.* Betty wiped her boning knife on Marco's overcoat and slipped it into her garter. *Make do and Mend,* she thought, stepping delicately through the mess to retrieve the others. *For next time.*

Because there *would be* a next time, Betty had decided. A plan was forming now. This was bigger than Marco or Ernie or Vito. Bigger even, than her own revenge. The world was at war, not just across the sea, but right here, under her own feet. The city was diseased with crime and corruption, seeping like poison under the pavement and it all led back to a single man.

Donald Pinzolo. The head of organized crime in New York City. It was a family business after all. So, that made it *her* business. To step up and tear down.

Her great uncle Donny played the city like a chess board, profiteering from every wretched secret his army of thugs teased out of the sidewalk.

Every whisper of betrayal between bedsheets made its way back to him.

Every act of desperation by crumbling businessmen was seen.

Every empty purse that implored for mercy was counted.

And Donald Pinzolo was ready and waiting with sweet relief.

But relief was fleeting. All too soon debts were called in, secrets became blackmail and families were torn apart. He had his hand in the pocket of every politician and lawmaker in the city. *Favors* were Donny's price. And the debt was deadly.

I'll have to be clever, Betty thought, *to take them all down, one by one. Patient. Strategic. Ruthless. A lady vigilante, as it were. Oh yes.* She stepped over the bodies and picked up her beloved cosmetics case. *I do like the sound of that.*

Betty's heels clicked across the concrete as she let herself out of the frozen warehouse. *I may need help though. Someone I can trust to leave the evidence with. I can't keep hauling crates of drugs around the city on my bicycle, after all. And only so many secrets can be buried at Dead Horse Bay.* Betty's mind turned to the handsome detective she'd lost so long ago. *Could I? Things might get a little... complicated.* She sighed. *But if I can trust anyone in this city, it's Jacob.* A pang of guilt hit her as the side door swung shut. *Perhaps, after all this time, it was* time.

She turned her mind to the task ahead. *It could take months. Years even. And an awful amount of murder. Not at all ladylike, but still... rewarding, in its own way.*

Betty grinned as she strapped her cosmetics case onto her bicycle, swung her leg over and took off into the night.

Yes. It's time for a little anarchy. And who better than an Avon Lady to paint the town red?

1

————

A WOMAN'S WORK IS NEVER DONE

Fall, 1943. New York.

Betty Jones regained consciousness to the sound of scraping chairs and the smell of acrid cigar smoke filling her lungs. The skin around her mouth and nose stung like it had been burned. Her mouth tasted like copper pennies – the chloroform had left its mark. So, apparently, had her captors. Bruises were blooming on her cheek and collarbone, the telltale tightness of her skin suggested they were already swollen and darkening. Before she opened her eyes, she listened.

Shuffles found her ears from every direction. Heavy breathing close by, on her right. A whimper from her left. The crackling broadcast from a wood tube radio playing somewhere behind her. The hollow notes of a jazz clarinet piped from the speakers, echoing off a surface not far in front of it and bouncing around, distorting her sense of space.

Betty opened her eyes. A maze of heisted Army supply crates, old furniture and bric-a-brac were piled to the roof in all directions leaving no space bigger than a few meters wide, with the exception of the center of the room, where she currently sat. She didn't struggle against the chains that bound her hands behind her back. Just a gentle tug was enough to know that her wrists were securely attached to the chair. There was no need to move. *Yet.*

Betty looked up at the man sitting opposite her. He was on a chair similar to her own, with nothing between them. Betty's eyes were like shards of ice.

"You *will* die," she said quietly.

The man smiled and raised an eyebrow, his cigar in hand.

"The good wife speaks." He turned to the man beside him with a nasty grin. "She cooks, she cleans, she gets down on her hands and knees..."

His companion sniggered, his heavily scarred face gloating. He was missing the top half of his right ear.

To Betty's left, was a long table messy with interrupted packaging work. It was piled high with stolen military supplies of amphetamines that had been destined for the front. Wake up pills for pilots and soldiers. A dozen unkempt boys had been disrupted from their work, no doubt by her arrival, and now they stood behind the table, their eyes to the floor, too terrified to look up.

There was a movement in the maze of boxes somewhere behind her, and Betty closed her eyes. With a huge effort against the pounding inside her head, she pulled the thoughts of the room in from around her. *The shufflers.* How many?

Seven – twelve – nineteen – thirty – Yes. Thirty men hidden in the shadows of crates and makeshift furniture around her, all brought in to make sure she never made it out alive. Thirty-two, including the two in front of her. *Filth. Murderers. Mercenaries.* Every one of them deserved to swallow his own bullet.

"Let them leave," Betty said, nodding toward the group of orphans cowering behind the packing table. "They don't need to see this."

The man's eyes grew tight in thought and he looked to the boys.

"Maybe they do," he said, provocatively. "This lot are my finest and smartest – the *heirs to my empire,* so to speak. You take my own boys away from me – I take them instead." He stood up, letting his cigar hang from his mouth with his hands in his pockets as he turned toward the orphans, rolling on the balls of his feet. "Pay attention kids," he called out to them, his voice laced with dark humor. "I'm your family now, ain't I? Today's lesson is about trust. There are consequences for betraying trust in a family like ours." He lifted his hand and reclaimed his cigar from where it dangled at the side of his mouth, leaving a trail of smoke. "Family is everything, *Mrs. Betty Jones,*" he said.

From the shadows around her, the mercenaries began closing in.

"Shame. I always thought you had potential," the man continued. "I had my eye on you from the beginning, you know. Roy never saw it; he was too stupid. Even Frank never clued in. *But I did.* You were smarter than the rest, even my own boys, God rest their souls. You had potential. You were *useful.* Like your mother was, before she broke."

Betty caught his offsider's eye, and it narrowed, critically, in its ravaged frame.

"Well," she said, casually, "you'll find I'm not so easy to *break.*"

Her captor tossed his burnt-out cigar on the floor and leaned over Betty, one hand on each side of her chair, his thumbs pressing against the outside of her legs. When his face was only inches from her own, he spoke again. His breath was hot and dank on her face and every pore on his skin glistened with sweat.

"You've had the curse on me all these years," he murmured, with a dark grin. A tiny nerve under his left eye twitched.

Betty took a deep breath and straightened her shoulders.

A deliberate smile spread across her face, like a skilled artist painting on a mask.

Radiant.

Charming.

Betty's eyes flashed, a little too bright, as if something inside had suddenly come unhinged.

"Yes, I have," she said. "And I hope you're ready for that family reunion, Uncle Donny. Because I'm ready to give you one."

💋

Three months earlier...

"Now this delightful lipstick is everything you've ever wished for! It's as light as sheer silk on your lips, so comfortable and smooth and just look at the beautiful jewel-like appliqué on the top! Truly Mrs. Parsons, your husband will think you're a school-girl again! He'll be pleased as punch!"

A crisp one-dollar bill was happily exchanged for the promise, and Betty continued the three-story walkup lightly, stopping outside another brownstone apartment door identical to the hundred others around it. Children called up to her playfully from the street and she waved down at them through clothes-lines draped between the buildings.

Betty carefully placed her bag on the front stoop beside her, resting on its four large silver feet. She was as inordinately proud of her cognac crocodile-skin carry bag with its thick, tan leather-top handles and its precious contents, as she was of the title it afforded her.

She smoothed her red cotton dress down to where it hugged her waist and fell in a gathered skirt two inches below her knees. She adjusted her pale-yellow pill box hat with its jaunty red feathers and followed the curl of her victory rolls over her shoulders reflexively. Her bright red lipstick shone as she gave the closed door a bright smile, knocked sharply three times and reclaimed her bag.

"Avon Calling!"

The door opened and a woman, not much younger than she, appeared.

"Good Morning, Ruth darling," Betty said.

"Oh, Mrs. Jones, I forgot," the young woman flustered. She wore blue jeans and a pale blue sloppy joe sweater belted at her waist. Her hair was still in twisted rags from the night's sleep. From somewhere inside, a radio crackled with soft jazz and a woman's voice floated down the wire in a tale of misdirected love.

Beyond Ruth, sitting straight backed on the faded couch with her hands wrapped tightly around a teacup, another young lady sat.

Her twill skirt was neatly pressed, but barely modest. It was summer 1943 and with the war in full swing, fabric was strictly rationed to accommodate the soldiers' uniforms. New dresses were rare and barely made it past the knee. 'Mend and make-do,' the ladies encouraged each other daily.

Ruth cast her tea-guest an apologetic smile and turned back to Betty, lowering her voice. "It's not a good time Mrs. Jones, my friend Anna's sick, you see..."

Betty looked over Ruth's shoulder, to the other girl. She had the look about her of a startled cat, with red rimmed eyes and a pale, blotchy face. Her knuckles were white where they clutched the teacup too hard. A dark bruise stained her pale décolletage, disappearing beneath the neck of her blouse. Her yellowing cheekbone was poorly covered by pressed powder.

A sudden thought pushed unbidden into Betty's mind, and she heard it as clear as if Anna had spoken aloud. *Please Lord, no. Johnny'll flip his wig is anyone finds out.*

Betty's brow furrowed slightly at the girl's private admission, but she retained her bright smile. Anna had no idea her own thoughts had betrayed her, but regardless, it didn't take more than intuition to figure out where the girl's troubles lay. Anna swallowed nervously under Betty's scrutiny, lifting her chin. She pulled her dark cardigan protectively across her chest as the radio spun its final melancholy chorus.

"Sick, you say? Well that is a shame," Betty clucked sympathetically. "But what gorgeous kicks, darling!" Betty nodded to the patent red cork wedges the girl wore on her feet. "And such a honey, too. You sure must have the boys lining up to go with you!"

Anna's eyes softened a bit, and she gave Betty a watery smile.

"Only Johnny. He's my flutter." She twisted her fingers together wistfully, before her eyes filled with tears and turned resolutely back to her teacup.

Still blocking the doorway, Ruth's mouth set in a hard line. Flutter! He's not worth half of it, silly girl. Johnny's a rotten, dirty spiv and you'll end up a moll, or worse.

Betty's chest tightened and her heart hardened a little. A gangster's girl then. Well used to hiding her reactions to the thoughts of others, Betty instead offered Ruth sympathetic eyes.

"Well now, Ruth, how many times must I insist you call me Betty!" She patted Ruth's hand with her free one, offering her a meaningful look. "And trust me my darling, now is the very best of times. There's nothing that a nice cup of tea and some pampering can't fix."

Betty stepped inside the familiar sitting room and set herself on the couch next to Anna. Ruth hovered nervously for a moment, then disappeared into the kitchen to make a fresh pot of tea. Her thoughts jutted back indiscriminately. *As if I don't know! I should call the flatfoots, that'd teach him. Get him pinched for what he did! Anna's so stuck on him she'd never tell though, even for her own good. If only her Pop were still alive...*

In the sitting room, Betty placed her bag on the floor at her feet, then reached out to pat Anna gently on the knee. *Ow!* Anna stiffened and quickly stretched the fabric of her dress a little further over her skin. Betty drew back her hand delicately, clasping it with the other on her own lap instead, her red painted nails gleaming.

"You took a fall did you, doll?" She smiled kindly. "Never mind, bruises heal. We ladies are a little too clumsy for our own good sometimes, aren't we?" Anna eyes widened and she nodded emphatically, looking relieved. *He didn't mean it. It was probably my fault anyway. I'm such a bother to him, I know I am.*

Betty winked and continued without pause. "I did it myself on Tuesday- I entirely missed the steps and landed right on my behind, breaking two of my best perfumes into the bargain. My goodness, was I upset!"

Betty reached down and unbuckled her bag, pulling out a number of ornate bottles and lining them up on the coffee table. "Don't you worry, Anna; I've got the perfect concealer to hide those bumps. You'll be looking a dish in no time."

An hour later, Betty left with both girls smiling and Anna clutching a purse-full of free samples.

"And remember ladies," Betty turned back waving brightly, "There's always time to take time off for beauty!"

Unwittingly, the girls had told her all she needed to know. Hearing another's thoughts wasn't the most impressive skill she had, but it was certainly the most helpful. Not that anyone knew. Betty tapped in and out of people's minds selectively, for the most part leaving their private thoughts just that. She was a lady, after all.

No, Betty never *looked* for trouble, she'd seen more than enough already. Each night when she toed off her slippers and climbed into bed, the memories came roaring back. Empty syringes and dull silver spoons, broken plates and dark alleys. Blood. Fire. Revenge. And the very first whisper from another mind into her own when she was only twelve years old, *"I wanted so much more for you, Susan, my baby."* before that body too, was shelled by a syringe. That was someone else's life though. Now, Betty painted the darkness with a cherry red lipstick and a spritz of lilac perfume.

Her days were brightened by the simple things; laying a crisp New York Times by her husbands' breakfast plate in the mornings, braiding her daughters' hair, gently tending her little boy's scraped knee. They were her world, her eternal delight and devotion.

On occasions like these though, which seemed far too common, Betty had no choice. Some thoughts needed to be heard. Her hemlock heel pumps clicked against the concrete steps as Betty trotted down. She strapped her cosmetic bag onto the back rack of her powder-blue Schwinn ladies bicycle and rode home with plans whirring through her head.

Betty smiled benignly, turning the page of her copy of *Vogue* on the café table and sipping her tea. Behind her, oblivious to her interest, four young men preened themselves and catcalled passers-by from the street corner as they discussed their plans. Betty sighed at the predictability of it all. Although their conversation was too quiet to overhear, the words came clear as day from their minds anyway.

So, what's the word, Johnny? When do we hit the trucks?

I told you, Lou. It's sorted. All we gotta do is wait under 59th Street bridge at sundown and it's ours. The bennies, the fet, all of it.

What about the GI's?

We bump 'em like the Minton job. There's so much dope these days, the uniforms won't miss it.

Yeah, I 'spose, a third man said. But what about Frank?

Frankie's holed up at Capitol Palace, Johnny replied. His guys are gonna hit the truck near Harlem, so we get in first. Steal the stuff and bump the uniforms. Then we'll resell it to Frankie. He's got a gig full of buyers waiting to take it, so he's counting on this load. He'll have to pay to get it now, that's all.

Damn right he will, one man said.

A couple of them laughed.

I dunno, came a more hesitant, fourth voice. Frankie'll be mighty bent, Johnny. How do'ya know they won't get to us first?

They don't know where we'll stash it, do they? Besides, it's only a couple of days and I'll set up to meet him and do the deal myself. We get the cash, hit the silk and it's all done.

If you say so, Johnny. But what if-

Listen Willy! Just keep your stoolie mouth shut and we won't have to shut it for you!

No need to snap your cap, Johnny, you know I'd never!

The others muttered words of appeasement and their attention turned to a group of girls walking by instead. Johnny let out a low whistle.

"Check the gams on that dame, boys!" The others chuckled appreciatively. "I'm goin' fishin'!" Johnny took off across the street after the girls and the others disbanded, following him.

So, it was a heist. *Same old rubbish,* Betty frowned. The amphetamine benzedrine, or 'bennies' as the little white pills were known, were a staple for the men serving on the front. The government issued them to pilots, navigators and soldiers regularly, keeping the men alert, dulling pain and smothering their hunger in the cold, miserable trenches they kept. On the black market, bennies were crushed instead, mixed with whatever crack tonic was on the streets, and sold for a double hit. The white powder known as fet, heroin, was a little harder to come by, but got a top price in the jazz clubs of Harlem that saw addicts come and go like a tram stop. It was the perfect place to do business, as it seemed Frankie, 'The Smacker', Polletti was well aware. And these drugstore cowboys were already neck deep.

Betty sighed. She picked up her *Vogue* and handbag and dropped them in the front basket of her bicycle. The back tray was already strapped with a crate of groceries. She rode home with a heavy heart. *A woman's work is never done.*

💋

"How was your day, my darling?"

"Well enough, jitterbug." George stepped through the front door, passing his hat and coat to Betty, who hung them on the stand. He kissed her cheek and winked. "I sold four new trauma policies on my rounds, so that will keep us for a good while. Only the best for my baby-doll! I tell you Betty, this war is a blasted business, but it's certainly good for insurance."

Betty beamed and took his arm, leading him into the lounge. "You really are the cleverest thing, darling," she smiled at him adoringly. "My goodness you must be beat. Rest by the wireless for a bit, your pipe and slippers are waiting. Dinner's almost ready."

Betty called the children from their homework, humming to the music as she danced around the kitchen laying the table.

"My, you're a hep kitten, jitterbug," said George, leaning against the door frame with a smile. "You're as pretty today as the day I met you."

"Oh, shush," Betty blushed. From the day her husband had stumbled, endearingly snow-blown and sniffling with the flu to the drugstore counter she tilled, Betty had never once pried into his thoughts.

It delighted her. She didn't need to. The man was an open book, uncomplicated and kind. His genuine and perfect mediocrity was the very thing that kept the fires of her heart burning for only him.

"It's just this new moisturizer I have," Betty deflected. "It really *is* a miracle; all of the ladies love it. Actually," Betty turned away, biting her lip, "I have to visit the Seymore girls tonight after dinner to help them with colors. They're getting all dizzied up for the church social next week." She turned back, pleased the lie was done with. Inwardly, she forgave herself for it.

A small boy with nutmeg hair and freckles sat down at the table, stuffing a paper comic under his plate. He helped himself to the peas as his blue-eyed sister, six years older with her curls in ribbons, pulled up a chair beside him. Betty lay the pot roast in front her husband and handed him the carving knife.

"George Junior? Nancy? Did you wash your hands and faces, dears?"

"Yes, mom." They replied in unison, accepting meat from their father.

George Senior, turned back to his wife with a slight frown.

"You're going out after dark again?"

"Yes, darling, but I won't be long."

He chewed for a moment, then raised his fork mid-bite, considering. "You know, jitterbug, all this Avon business, it's not necessary. I pay the bills -"

"Oh, of course you do!" Betty supplicated, placing a hand on her husband's elbow. "It's not that at all! Goodness, no. It's just that, now that Georgie has started school this year," the youngest family member puffed his chest as they smiled proudly, "Well, I'm at a loss for things to do and you know how I love meeting my ladies. We girls will flap our lips at any excuse, and I just adore to make them feel a little ritzy. With so many boys drafted, they all work so hard to make do. I just - I couldn't imagine what I'd do if you were called up, George. There's talk of another lottery." Betty blinked back tears.

George nodded pitifully, patting her hand back. "Such a big heart, I understand, jitterbug." He turned back to his dinner. "Just don't overdo it. I don't like to see you put yourself out."

"Yes, darling."

After the children were in bed and George was settled in his favorite armchair with a pipe and newspaper, Betty kissed him goodbye, picked up her oversized cosmetic bag and left the house. She rode her bicycle along the quiet streets of New York and crossed the train tracks toward a darker side of town.

Knock. Knock. Knock.

"Avon Calling!"

There was a slight scuffle behind the door and the sound of men's voices. Above the voices, the sultry, fast swing of 'All the Cats Join In' rolled from the wireless. Betty smiled. It was one of her favorites.

Four. Five. Six. "Get it Ricky," instructed Johnny.

Make Willy get it, came the reply, growled too quiet to hear. A snorting sound and a sniff.

"Willy, get the damn door." *Just in case.* Instinctively, Betty knew Johnny was pocketing his gun. She smiled. *Seven. Eight. Nine.*

The door opened.

Ten. Eleven. Twelve.

"Yeah?" asked Willy. His face was scrunched in confusion as he looked at Betty, then past her to the dark street beyond the front steps, then back to her face. His fingers traced the cut edge of his oversized zoot jacket nervously. "What do you want?"

"Avon Calling!"

Betty stepped forward, past him into the doorway pulling him into the room with her and shutting the door behind them. She dropped her bag to the floor. Instantly, the game was clear.

Piled high on the enameled metal bench, plastic wrapped powder and tiny white pills were being counted by Johnny. He froze mid-count at the sight of her, dropping a bag that split into a puff of white dust on the bench. Behind him, ten crates of amphetamines were piled against the kitchen wall. To her left, two other men were wide-legged on the couch, leaning forward to the coffee table, cutting rows of whiz with a playing card. They looked up, startled with red-rimmed eyes as she bent forward lifting her lemon-scalloped skirt high above her knee to reveal a row of shining knives in her garter.

"Time to play, boys." She smiled, cold and cruel.

"What the hell?" Johnny rushed forward, his lip in a sneer and his right hand plunging into his pocket. Before the men could even blink, Betty pulled a six-inch blade and flicked it straight between one man's eyes, *thud*, and he fell, dead, against the couch, still staring.

Beside her, Willy lunged. With super-speed, Betty spun and leapt, cracking her knee against his jaw and sending a spray of teeth rattling to the floor. *Snap!* She brought the side of her flat hand against the back of his neck forcing him down, then kicked his backside hard, sending him sprawling forward into the closed door.

Without missing a beat, Betty ducked, *Bang! Bang! Bang!* - missing the bullets Johnny aimed at the back of her head. So utterly predictable, she thought. The bullets splintered the wooden door as *Crash!* Her heel shot out and around behind her, dragging the dainty hall table from the wall, sending it skidding across the floor toward Johnny who was one second from pulling the trigger again. One second was far more than she needed. Johnny stumbled. He righted himself, kicking the table from his path as he thundered toward her. The second red-rimmed doper from the couch was scrambling to his feet. He lunged at her from the other direction, his face frozen in chaotic fear as if his mind and body were at odds with reality.

Faster than thought, Betty stripped two more knives from her garter. She spun one in each hand and leapt for Johnny. She flicked the blades over her shoulders as her feet left the ground. They found their home in each of the junkie's thighs. The stench of blood and urine filled the room though Betty knew only she could smell it. She wrinkled her nose in disgust mid-flight.

Betty leapt into Johnny's outstretched arm, grappling for his gun. He grabbed her long hair, ripping it backward with his free one and Betty pulled her knee to his groin, hard. He crumpled. She wrenched the gun from his hand and flung it across the bench. Her elbow smashed backwards, gouging his ribs. Johnny swore, punching out. *Too slow.* Betty swerved away, pivoting on her left foot, spinning low. The ball of her right foot met Johnny's face, *crack!* and she round-housed again, slamming his chest, *crack!* He recoiled as she leapt high into the air, snapping her foot forward into his face. He fell to the checkerboard linoleum, chest heaving for oxygen. Carefully, Betty placed her heeled white gabardine across his pink neck.

Why? Johnny's mind begged of her.

It was instantaneous. The pleading, the *why? Why?* Once upon a time, she'd asked the same question herself. Memories came rushing back and bit her heart. Betty had been someone else then. A child. Torn by desperation for a picture-perfect life, a *safe* life, and the realization that there was no such thing. On the porch of her childhood home, she'd once held hands with her perfect life. He was two years older than her, fourteen, and his name was Jacob.

"Why? Why does it always fall off the edge right before it stops, do you think?" she'd asked him. Her voice was innocent, her suburban accent broad. A brass spinning top was whirring between them following the grooves of the wooden planks. A faded blue bicycle leant against the side of the house with pink ribbons tied to the handles.

"Dunno. Maybe the floor is lopsided." Jacob expertly caught the top as it spun toward the edge of the porch and flicked it to life anew. "When are you coming back to school?"

Susie looked down at her arm in a makeshift sling. "Maybe tomorrow. It was worth it though. Got Mom off the hook."

The boy scoffed. "Susie-pocket. Miniature defender of the Universe. You're mighty brave for a girl, I'll give you that. But you'll never win against that bastard."

"I did win," Susie retorted. "In a round-'bout way."

"I should tell Pop what he did."

Susie's eyed widened and darted to the open front door beyond the fly-screen. She grabbed his hand. "You can't, Jake. They'd take Mom too. She needs me."

Jacob sniffed loudly and swatted a fly near his face with his free hand. "'Spose. For now."

A dusty black Cunningham spun into the driveway and both of them startled. Susie jerked her hand away as a man in a striped slate gray suit with clover leaf lapels approached. He was slick and neat, and Jacob looked surprised as he jumped to his feet. The brass top spun off the side of the porch to land in the dirt.

"You don't look like a fortune teller, boy, so keep your mitts to yourself," the man growled.

"We were just -" Susie began.

"Did I ask you?" His eyes held a dangerous glint. He turned back to Jacob. "Got it?"

The boy pulled himself as tall as he could before replying. "Yes, sir."

The man studied him. "A kike, hey?" The words were laced with provocation. "What's your name?"

"My name's Lawrence. Jacob Lawrence." Jacob took a deep breath and jutted his chin out a tiny bit. "And my Pop said to let him know if anyone rags on me like that. He says it ain't American."

"Is that right?" Susie's father stepped forward with a darkly amused smile. "Well you can run back to your daddy and tell him I'll show him what a real American's made of, if he don't like it. And I'll give you a lesson on your mug if you don't watch your mouth."

Jacob shot a glance at Susie and her eyes flashed in silent warning. Despite it, Jacob stepped forward.

"My Pop's Chief Sergeant, sir. You sure you want to be sending him an autograph?"

The man's grin faded. "Get off my property, kid. You sound like you know enough of the law to figure I have every right to shoot you where you stand if you're gonna threaten me."

Jacob swelled in silent victory. It wasn't much, but he'd been waiting for the opportunity for months. Susie had never hidden the truth from him about where the bruises came from, but until now, Jacob had never had the displeasure of putting a face to the fist.

"See ya, Suz" Jacob muttered. He turned and kicked a pebble down the driveway as he left.

Susie quietly stepped back and picked up the brass spinning top from the dirt.

"Don't you move," her father said, without turning his head. Susie froze. Waiting for it was punishment enough. Jacob turned the corner of the street and disappeared out of sight. Her father turned around, stepping onto the toes of her shoes. The coffee spot on his shirt seemed to swell. "If I ever see that boy here again, I'm gonna make him disappear like a fucking magic show. And you'll get the front row seat. Do ya hear?"

Susie nodded, her eyes filling. Her father leant back on his heels, releasing her and took the steps two at a time, snapping open the flyscreen door. Susie followed him, shrinking into her dress.

"What the fuck, Ethyl?" he yelled, once inside.

A young woman in a crumpled day dress appeared at the corner of the kitchen door. Her pale skin was ruined and her eyes dark and dulled with some unfathomable pain. In another life, she had been beautiful.

"Roy?"

"What the hell are you doing, letting her bring a kid like that here? You want Donny to find out, is that it? You wanna see me taken for a ride under the bridge? And Susie winds up in a stitch with that boy?"

"No, I just- Of course not- I was just making them some cookies," Ethyl said nervously. She pulled a mixing bowl from the cupboard, clearly confused. "I forgot to turn the oven on- she doesn't have many friends - thought it might be nice..." Her voice wavered off pathetically as she found the flour canister.

"Cookies?" Roy crossed the floor in two strides and hit the mixing bowl across the bench. It cracked against the tiles. "You weren't even watching them. Off your face while a copper's boy is sniffing around the house!" Roy knocked her violently, sending Ethyl sprawling to the ground in an explosion of flour.

"They're only babies, Roy -" Ethyl whimpered from the floor.

"His old man's a copper!" Roy yelled. "If he dropped a dime, I'm done for!"

"He was nothing love. Just a kid -"

Roy rounded on the woman, glowering over her. From behind the kitchen door, Susie fought with her resolve to step forward. Tears made streaks down her face where the dirt of the spinning top had been smeared.

"You're sentimental! Weak!" Roy ranted, pacing the kitchen. "A chippy, just like your old man said. I did right by you, Ethyl, knocked up like you were. I could have left you with it when he kicked you out. I never wanted a kid. But I didn't because I'm a good man! I look after you Ethyl. And you repay me by bringing a copper's boy to watch you dope up?" He slapped her hard across the face.

"No! Pop, no!" Susie slid from behind the kitchen door and dashed over to her mother, cradling her hand in small ones. Track marks and bruises peppered the woman's arm.

"You keep out of this!" Roy roared at the girl.

Tears welled in Ethyl's eyes. "This life - I can't do it any more, Roy. It hurts my heart. They're in my head, the voices of the people Donny takes out. The ones you -" Ethyl looked away, too terrified to meet his eyes. "Every one of them. I feel it all too much, the lies and the shame. It's breaking me-"

"The shame?!" The words thundered from Roy and every glass

shook as if it might shatter. "You're ashamed of me now? You're ashamed I have a job to do? I gave you everything!" He pushed past her, yanking a sideboard drawer open and drew out a small paper packet of heroin and threw it down at her. "I give you what you need! And you won't get any of this if I'm in the cooler, you gowed-up bitch."

Ethyl picked up the packet. She clutched it to her chest. "It makes the voices go away."

"You just keep that door shut!"

"I will, I will! I promise."

They all startled as another man appeared in the kitchen doorway. He was smartly dressed with a hat and trench coat over his suit. He surveyed the room warily.

"Frankie." Roy said, stepping away from his wife and daughter.

"Donny's waiting," Frank said calmly.

Roy grunted in acknowledgment and disappeared into his bedroom. Susie looked up at her uncle standing by the door.

"You 'right Ethyl?" Frank muttered. Susie's mother looked up at him through bleary eyes.

"I shouldn't have - I made him angry. My fault." she mumbled, wiping dry the dark rings under her eyes. Frank's eyes swept the floor then caught Susie's. She glared, silently daring him to say something, anything, to show he disapproved of his brother's actions. Frank looked away.

Roy returned, shrugging his jacket over his shoulders. Underneath, a pistol was strapped to his body. He took an overcoat and hat from the stand by the door.

"Donny wants her tonight." Frank said, nodding at Ethyl, still slumped on the floor. She flinched. "He's got a deal with the Salleri boys going down," Frank continued. "He needs her to be there - do her mind reading crap and tell him if they're dirty. Can't trust those goons." He paused. "Better clean her up." Roy looked at his wife and took a deep breath.

"Get dressed," he said.

"Please, no Roy. Not tonight," she implored.

"You'll make yourself up and you'll get in that car. If Donny needs you, Donny needs you." He pulled the packet of heroin from her fingers and threw it back into the sideboard drawer.

Ethyl took a deep breath, tears slipping. Susie shot a dark look at her father, but helped her mother to her feet and into the bedroom to change.

Hours passed as Susie sat alone in the house. She had never been scared to be alone, it was a reprieve she cherished. She read a book, finished the homework she had left over from the previous week, then made herself a meager dinner from the contents of the refrigerator. Old magazines of beautiful women, stylish clothes and bright cosmetics were dog-eared upon her bed. A perfect life, frozen under glossy smiles that seemed always pleased to see her. Each minute, though, she worried for her mother. Susie had witnessed Donny's request many times when she was younger. Ethyl would be sitting in a smoky office somewhere, reading the minds of duplicitous men and secretly feeding their thoughts back to more corrupt and evil ones. Her payment was freedom, but not from her violent husband and his family. It was a fleeting freedom, carried on the wings of the heroin that muddied her blood and granted an escape from the overwhelming burden of the empathic super-senses that suffocated her every waking thought.

Ethyl was dropped back just after midnight and Roy and Frankie took off again into the night to continue their negotiations. The lines on her mother's face said it had been dark.

"I'm sorry, ma," Susie whispered once she'd tucked her mother into bed.

Ethyl looked up at her from the bed with a soft expression.

"You can't see that boy anymore, love. It's best not to let people get too close. It hurts too much."

"But why?" Susie asked. There it was again. Why?

"Because Donny will never let you go. I can feel it growing in you, just like it did in me. You're different, love. Special." She lifted her

hand, gently trailing her fingers down the side of her little girl's face. "But you're strong, Susie, so much stronger than I am."

Susie shook her head emphatically. "You could be strong Ma, it's this place, it's bad. We could leave together. Find a good place to live, with fancy curtains and lipsticks and perfume - just like in the magazines. You'll be so pretty mom, and I'll be good, I promise!"

Ethyl looked forlornly at her hands.

"They'd find me. They know everything, love. They're everywhere. Too many of them. I can hear them in my mind. Besides, I need them." Ethyl's fingers began to shake uncontrollably. She pulled herself out of bed and walked to the kitchen. Opening a sideboard drawer, Ethyl retrieved the paper packet of heroin and sat at the kitchen table in her nightgown.

"You don't need that stuff!" Susie cried.

"I feel things, love. All the pain, all the sadness in the world, more than you could ever imagine. The heartache of women, the loneliness of men on the streets. The burden is too much for me."

"Only pain?" Susie implored.

Ethyl took Susie's face gently in her hands. "No, not only," she said. "You were pure love." She shook her head, then stood and crossed the kitchen.

"Then just feel that and ignore the rest!" Susie cried. "Make it go away!"

Cutlery rattled as Ethyl raked through the drawer. She drew out a small silver spoon.

"I do make it go away," she said.

Susie tried to take the packet from her mother. She wouldn't force it though. Not today, when she'd already been through so much.

"Not that," Susie said, "Please don't. It's hurting you. I can tell." Ethyl pushed Susie gently away. She lit the stove and tore the packet open onto the spoon. As she held it over the flames, she pulled an old syringe from a high cupboard.

"You don't understand, love." Ethyl said. "I need this. I need the silence- to block them out."

"Please, ma. Don't -" Susie pleaded, as Ethyl slid herself against the cradle of cupboards doors on the floor. But the poison made its way into Ethyl veins as always. And for a moment, the woman looked peaceful. "He was right, I was weak..." she slurred, as she fought consciousness.

When she was done, Susie pulled the stick from her mother's arm and crawled into them herself, instead. With her ear pressed to the woman's chest, Susie heard her mother's heart slow, then, for the first time, something else.

Her mother's voice. Not aloud but inside her head, as if she were speaking through the deathly blue lips that remained closed.

I wanted so much more for you, Susan, my baby.

Through the thin nightgown, Susie heard Ethyl's heart stutter, then beat for the very last time. She clutched the gold locket around her mother's neck and cried until the morning sun, and her father, found her there.

Betty blinked, refocusing on the task at hand. A man was sprawled on the ground in front of her, boxes of amphetamines piled high against the wall and paper blocks of heroin spilled across the bench. Her white gabardine heel was pressed firmly to his pink neck as he struggled for breath against the checkerboard linoleum. Barely a moment had passed.

Why? Came Johnny's silent pleas again.

Betty looked at him, fluttering her thick lashes and pursing her red lips before she answered.

"Because darling, you're killing the American dream. My dream, that is." With a swift twist of her ankle, she broke his neck.

"Get back, lady! I don't want no trouble," came a voice from behind her. Betty turned slowly. The second doper was on his knees holding a shaking gun, pointed directly at her heart. Each thigh still bore a knife imbedded within it.

Thud! Thud! Thud! Betty added three more knives to his collection. He crumpled to the floor.

Plumping her hair and stepping over the bodies, Betty returned to the front door to retrieve her crocodile skin bag. She emptied each packet of heroin into a decorative glass jar meant for bath salts. She filled her bejeweled vitamin jars with bennies, then packed it all carefully under the false base of her bag. She layered the stash with her beloved cosmetics then dusted off her gloved hands.

Betty leant back against the sink, assessing the crates of bennies stacked against the kitchen wall. It was as she'd expected; too much to take home. They were large crates, each one enough for a single set of arms. Undeterred, Betty carried them out, three at once. She stamped down hard, dislodging a plank of wood from the front porch steps and ripped it from its place. She set it across the back tray of her bicycle, then strapped every crate to it in a pile, leaving the house empty but for its dead occupants and their incriminating white mess upon the bench. Betty popped her Avon bag into the front basket of her bicycle, balancing the apple she had brought with her on top. The enormous pyramid of crates wobbled behind Betty as she pedaled away. Her mouth twisted into a wry smile as she set off for a place to stash her cargo. Under a sliver of moon barely light enough to see by, she zipped down back streets and alleys before skimming the shadowy edges of Central Park. She was fast enough, and it was dark enough, that prying eyes wouldn't find her. Except of course, for old Herb, the tramp that slept on a bench not far from her destination. He sat up as she passed, mouth agape, with a paper-bagged bottle in his hand. Betty grinned, tossing the apple over her shoulder, smiling at the sound of a *crunch* as it landed between his open teeth, just as she'd intended.

"'Night Herb," she called as she rode away. Her destination was close now, and Betty slowed at a wire gate, passed through, then skidded to a stop outside an old tinkers' shop. The windows were boarded up. She pulled a bobby pin from her hair, jimmied the lock and entered with her cosmetic bag.

"Yes, this will do nicely," she said aloud to no one in particular, writing the address on the back of a card that read *'Avon Calling, Sorry I missed You!'* in cherry red script. Betty unstacked the crates and left them against the back wall in a neat pile, then jammed the door shut and left with a satisfied smile.

It had been an unfortunate end to the night, but nothing new. If anything, lately, Betty sought out evenings like this one with greater zeal than perhaps she should.

These men were just pawns in a much bigger game. Betty took them out, one by one, patiently, deliberately, strategically. And she'd begun her play months ago, with a single end in mind. *Donny.*

Donald Pinzolo's family of murderers and thieves were like an insidious disease on the city, with tentacles stretching far beneath the pavement. And Betty should know, given she was one of the family. Or rather, used to be.

He had politicians and militia in his pocket, thugs, prostitutes and pastors. From Stan the greengrocer to Dr Strauss at the clinic, politicians, gambling houses, even hospitals were indebted to his calculated generosity. Those naïve folks that lived their lives on the surface had no reason to question him unless desperate times dragged them below where he'd be waiting with a smile. There was no escaping the subtle manipulations that kept businesses humming in Donny's favor, or the constant reminder of debts owed. And God help the poor bastards if they couldn't pay.

Yes, a little anarchy was well in order.

Betty rode off into the dark night, humming happily.

I may even have time for a cup of tea before bed.

2

———

A DREAM TO CALL MY OWN

"Mom, are superheroes real?" asked George Junior the next morning. His Kellogg's Pep Whole Wheat Flakes were half eaten, and he was staring forlornly at the side of the cereal carton. 'Boy, it's Super!' was stamped in bold letters on the cardboard next to a brightly colored illustration of Superman.

"Of course they're not, you goose," said his sister, rolling her eyes. "Superheroes are just make-believe. People can't really do any of those things."

"Well now, Nancy, I wouldn't be so sure," Betty hushed. She turned to her five-year-old son. His moon-sized eyes were hopeful. "I happen to know that Superman is most certainly real, my little cherry pie. And not only that, he's quite the gentleman. Why, I spoke to him only last week on the telephone!"

"For real?"

"For real." The little boy gave her a dazzling smile and dug into his cereal with renewed enthusiasm. Betty tousled his hair and made her way into the sitting room.

She frowned. Nancy was eleven years old now. It wouldn't be long before her daughter would feel the changes in her mind she had once felt herself. Not long enough before her innocence was stolen and her head filled with the thoughts of other people. Once the voices broke through, Nancy's young heart would be moved by their sorrows as much as their joys, terrified by their secret fears and inflicted with their guilty pleasures. It was a terrible burden. The inside of a man's mind was no place for a young girl. Yet it couldn't be prevented any more than keeping the sun from rising. Nancy was sure to have other gifts as well, other burdens, but what they might be, were anyone's guess. Betty sighed. *It's time to have a quiet talk with her.* Whether the child could be trusted with such a secret, was another thing altogether. Then again, she had held the secret herself well enough.

Betty stopped in the sitting room by the telephone table. She held the wall lightly and closed her eyes as a memory came rushing back. Her mother was younger, prettier and Betty just a tiny girl, far younger than Nancy was now.

***

"And Grandmama too?" she'd asked as Ethyl brushed the girl's long dark hair. On the bed in front of her was a little silver box of trinkets. The child retrieved an old wooden clothes peg from the box and held it up for her mother to see. *"This one?"*

"Yes, that one was Grandmama's. Margaret, her name was, but everyone called her Peggy. She was my mother, just like I am yours. It's such a shame you never knew her, love. She was strong in her heart, just like you. She had the gift, like all the women of our family do. Mama taught me not to pry into people's minds though, it's not ladylike, she said. Sometimes you just can't help it of course, the voices get so loud. And sometimes you don't get to choose..." Ethyl frowned, lost in a dark cloud. The little girl on her lap twisted around to face her.

"Why did she put a peg in the box?" she asked. *"Because of her name?"*

The young woman looked down and gathered her thoughts. "In a way. It's best to put your gifts to good use, that's what your Grandmama always said. She washed bedsheets at the parish orphanage while Pop gave sermons in the church. She listened to all the women's woes and knew just what to say to cheer them up because she understood what loneliness or fear was inside their heart. There wasn't a woman in town that didn't love to yap over the washboard and soap with your Grandmama. She used her gift to help people understand themselves a little better." Ethyl smiled at the wooden clothes peg in her daughter's hands. *"That was just her way of helping me remember. 'Ordinary deeds can make all the difference if they're done right,' she used to say - or at least, I think that's what it was. I was only your age when she died. It's hard to remember now."*

"I don't think I'd like to spend so long washing sheets," Susie said, her little nose scrunched up. *"Even with Grandmama."*

Ethyl laughed. *"Oh, she did more than just wash the sheets, love. That's just how she helped people find themselves. She was strong, too, you know, she could carry a hundred-gallon tank of water in her arms. The townsfolk would've gossiped something terrible if they'd seen her filling the washing tubs each morning at dawn. Only I ever saw that."*

Susie's mouth dropped into an astonished little circle. She held her scrawny arms up, imagining how it might feel to have such strength in them. *I'd be strong enough to fight back when Pop takes you away at night. I'd stop them being mean. I'd fight all of them and we could run away forever.* Inside, the injustice of her own tiny size roared through her heart. She let her arms fall dejectedly to her lap, then tossed the peg back into the box.

Ethyl looked at her daughter, shocked at the sudden flare of anger that flickered across. She occasionally reveled quietly in the sweet joy of her daughter's imagination as she played, but for the most part, Ethyl left Susie's childish thoughts alone. But this was new. Anger and defiance practically leapt from inside of the girl in a tumble of emotion. Ethyl shuddered. It was not fear of her little girl, but for her -

and what she'd bring upon herself if she ever acted on the defiance and hate burning inside.

"You mustn't worry about me so much, love," Ethyl shushed quickly, pulling her daughter close. "For goodness sake, you're just a little thing. There are grown up problems in this world that you don't understand and you'll be in terrible trouble if you even try to. Everything will be alright as long as we're together and you're a good girl. There's nothing else to be done."

Susie picked through the box of treasures quietly again, not wanting to upset her mother further. These days, she was upset enough. Finally, the girl drew a silver hat pin out. She held it up to the light, squinting her eyes.

"What about this one?"

"Her Momma, my Grandmama, Viola." Ethyl said. "She was a very clever lady. She helped sick people. They'd come from all across the county to see her and she'd know just the right medicine to set them straight. She could feel their pain see, in her body and her mind. Then she'd set to work fixing them medicines to ease it. And this one -" Ethyl leant forward pulling a faded playing card from the box. "The Jolly Joker," she read aloud. "This belonged to Ida, her twin sister. Mama said that they were as different as the moon and sun those two, but close as biscuits and butter."

"Did she have the gift, too?" Susie asked.

"Of course," Ethyl smiled. She passed the card to her daughter to hold and began fussing with the little girl's hair. "But Ida was a bit of a lark, she didn't want to be pinned down like Viola, so she never married. She got into trouble at the euchre tables in Harlem. When she played, she could read cards as simple as reading her opponent's mind then made off with the winnings. She thought it was a right caper until they ran her out of town."

"Where did she go?" asked Susie.

"Grandmama never told," Ethyl smiled, wistfully. "She would've been in trouble with the law if they'd tracked her down. But Viola

found five dollars tucked under the wood pile every month until the day she died. So, I guess Ida kept up with her old tricks."

"I like the sound of that," Susie said. "I bet she had an adventure. Maybe the gift isn't so bad after all."

Ethyl's brow furrowed as she pulled a pink ribbon through the plait she had made of her daughter's hair.

"Maybe for you," she said. "You're strong."

Susie turned her cornflower blue eyes to her mother. "Will it hurt?"

Ethyl smoothed her daughter's hair back from her forehead. "Sometimes. Not in the same way that you might fall over or scrape your knee. It's different - like a hundred voices in your head, and as many feelings in your heart. But only one of them belongs to you. You have to learn to shut them out. To keep a part of yourself, only to yourself. Do you understand?"

Susie nodded, but then shook her head sadly.

"You're still little, love. You don't need to worry about this now. You'll understand when you're older," Ethyl said.

"But I don't want my heart to hurt," Susie said, her lip quivering.

"Love always hurts, my darling. You must be brave. Besides, there's something special waiting for you Susie, I promise. You've got a fire inside you."

The little girl layered the odd collection back into the silver box. "Can I put something in here too?" she asked.

"Of course," her mother said. "One day. And something of mine too."

Susie lay the box aside and circled her mother's neck with her arms, curling into her lap. She pulled one arm down and gently traced the engraved locket around her mother's neck with her fingertip. "Yours will be the prettiest," Susie said.

Ethyl kissed her daughters' forehead. "Only because there's a picture of you in it, my love."

***

Betty shook her head to clear it and smoothed down her periwinkle dress and white rounded collar. With the children at breakfast and George still getting dressed for work, she had a phone call to make.

"This is Frank," the voice answered.

"Good Morning, Mr. Polletti. This is Mrs. Ethyl Taylor. I'm the secretary for a new business man in town who would like to meet with you. His name is Mr. Jimmy Carson."

"Jimmy Carson? Never heard of him. What's this about?"

"Just business, sir. The usual kind."

"Is that right? Some big cheese from down south, I bet. Tell him I'm not interested."

Betty smiled as she spoke, making sure every word was clear. "I strongly recommend you meet with him, Mr. Polletti. Mr. Carson has a proposition for you."

"Yeah? Doesn't everyone."

"Please, Mr. Polletti, it will only take a few minutes of your time. I believe you may have lost something recently? A special delivery by some one-stripers?" Betty heard Frankie choke on his cigar. *Fuck! This is the bastard that knocked my deal!*

"Mmm," Betty smiled. "A simple exchange is all he needs, cash for shipment. Five thousand dollars." Again, Frankie spluttered across the line. "Where shall I tell him to meet you?"

"Capitol Palace, tomorrow night," Frankie grunted. "Tell him I'll be waiting with the cash." *And a fistful of lead.* "This boss of yours, lady, how will we - *I* recognize him?"

"Oh, don't worry, Mr. Polletti. He'll find you." *Click.*

Betty placed the receiver gently back onto its cradle and walked into the bedroom. George was in front of the mirror, his hair oiled down as was the latest fashion.

"Have you seen my tie, jitterbug? The blue one with the stripes?"

Betty smiled and cleared her throat gently. "You mean this one, dear?" She bent down, unknotting the tie that was close to the floor, holding the legs of their two single beds together to form one.

"My lucky tie," he winked, taking it and tapping his wife playfully on the backside. He slipped the tie under his collar.

"You rogue," Betty giggled. She took his shoulders, turning him to face her. With nimble fingers Betty fixed his tie and straightened his collar. She took a step back, delighting in the crisp, spicy scent of the Avon after-shower spray for men she had ordered for him only last week.

"Don't you look hotsy-totsy, today!"

"Thanks, jitterbug."

Betty stepped up to the mirror herself, smoothing her curls and preparing to pin her matching blue hat into place. A lady never left the house without her hat. "Say, George?" she turned back around as her husband reached for the doorknob.

"Yes?"

"What do you say to a night out tomorrow? I'll ask Mrs. Porter to look after the children. It's been such a busy week for us both."

"Mrs. Porter? Are you sure the old duck can manage it? She's as deaf as a post these days."

"Oh, she's fine, dear. She adores the children and they know to speak up. Besides, I've heard of a club in Harlem that's meant to be swell. The Seymore girls were raving about it - they said it was the 'Cat's Meow'!"

"High praise indeed!" George laughed. "Anything for you, jitterbug," he said. He tipped his hat and winked at her, then turned to head downstairs, where his breakfast lay waiting for him.

"Time to skidoo, Betty! The car's warmed up!" Betty gave the children an extra tight hug and thanked her neighbor once more for minding them, as George revved the engine in the driveway and pulled on his driving gloves. "Could you grab my wallet from the counter?" he called.

Betty ducked back inside and slipped George's wallet into her Avon bag.

"Now you be good, dears," she said, as she hugged the children one last time. "Mind your manners and speak up for Mrs. Porter."

The elderly woman leaned forward, cupping her ear, "What's that, dear?"

"Nothing, Mrs. Porter. Thank you again for watching them," Betty shouted, before sliding into the single leather seat beside her husband. Only three years ago, George had bought a brand new black Chevrolet with silver trimmings. He kept it shined and oiled and drove it around town each day for work, proud as punch. On the weekends that they went dancing, it still felt ritzy to sail past the crowded trams and trains on the way into New York City.

They passed the splendid houses of Park Avenue and skirted the East fringe of Central Park until they hit Lenox Avenue. Under its layer of grime and crooked smiles, the street was buzzing with energy and light. A dozen or more jazz clubs boasted the most talented musicians in New York. Every night the street was brimming with hep cats and zoot suits, brass and petticoats, all looking for a brush with fame. Cab Calloway and Willie Gant lent their weight to the heavy birth of the jazz scene where The Breakfast Club and big band orchestras would fan the flames for decades to come.

Betty and George parked the car on a nearby street. Her sleeveless, cherry red, satin dress swished at her knees as she walked toward Capitol Palace. Betty brushed her perfectly rolled hair back over her shoulders and took her husband's arm. Her lips and nails were painted bright red and her pumps were adorned with black sequins.

"Surely you don't need such a cumbersome thing just to go dancing?" remarked George, frowning at the large cosmetic case that Betty carried in her free hand.

"You know me, darling." Betty's eyes narrowed as she looked at the club ahead. "Never miss an opportunity."

Within ten minutes of arriving, Betty and George were kicking up their heels in triple step to Glenn Miller and his Orchestra. The crowd pushed against them on all sides, dolls and cats spinning and tapping the East Coast Swing. 'In the Mood' began, all trumpets, trombones, drums and reeds and Betty threw her head back and laughed as George dipped and spun her. Again, they surged into the smoke and body heat of the throng, reveling in glorious music.

The bar overflowed with hurricane cocktails and gin sours and in every corner, soldiers at port sat draped in adoring girls. Beneath the ritz and glamor though, Betty felt the undercurrent of the seedy world she'd once fought her way out of. At least twenty of the zoots skulking in the crowd were Polletti's men. She felt their eyes raking the newcomers and assessing the moves of everybody in-house. Betty knew they were searching for Mr. Jimmy Carson, the fictional new wise guy that had played Polletti for a fool. And if their behavior hadn't given it away, their thoughts certainly did.

There's no way that spiv's getting out of here alive, one goon thought, fingering the gun inside his pocket. Frankie could tear any mans' guts out.

Betty smirked. That suited her just fine.

"Goodness, I'm puffed, darling," she said, retrieving her Avon bag from their table and leading George to the bar. "Would you mind ordering me a drink while I powder my nose?" Betty leant in close, deeply inhaling his scent.

"You're a miracle, my George. So sweet and steady." She kissed him lightly on the cheek.

George smiled. "Not too dull for a diamond like you?" he asked. "Because I can dance a mean Lindy Hop!"

Betty laughed. "Perhaps later. Life should be sweet and steady, darling. That's why I love you." She smiled brightly, then made her way back through the crowd as he stood happily at the bar, nodding to the music.

The office was easy to find. An unmarked door past the lavatories. A narrow hallway. Another unmarked door with a thug waiting outside, arms crossed over his too-big jacket. The man let out a low whistle as she walked toward him. She set her bag down in front of him, smiling coyly as she pulled on her black leather dress gloves.

"Well, hey there Sugar, aren't you a sight for sore eyes! Are ya' rationed?"

Betty battered her eyelids as she drew close.

"Sure am." *Crack!* With a spin and a high kick to the temple, the guard was dead. "And you're doing a terrible job by the way," she muttered, stepping over his body.

Without hesitation, Betty picked up her bag and opened the door. She stepped into a small storeroom that had been fitted out as an office. There were ten men smoking and playing cards, each with a gun beside their hand. They startled as she strode in and jumped to their feet in confusion. The potent stench of *Lucky Strikes* sucked towards the door as she slammed it shut behind her. The lively music that had followed her down the hallway muted to a dull thud, like a metronome that kept pulse with her heart. Betty surveyed the men quickly. Everything was laid bare for her - their motives, fears, their weaknesses. Everything swept into her mind in a whirl of information which she assessed as a matter of reflex. It was a terribly unpleasant sensation, to stare down your enemy knowing full well what he was capable of. These weren't just goons; they were Frankie's closest. Betty knew every one of them by sight. They were trusted for a reason. Killers, every one.

"I believe you have some cash for me, Frankie?" Betty said, ignoring them and getting straight down to business. There was no point keeping George waiting. Behind a wooden desk at the end of the room, Frankie stood up fast, knocking his chair over. He stared at her in disbelief. It had been twelve years since Betty had last seen her Uncle Frank, but with the exception of gray sides and a paunch belly, the man looked just the same. Betty, however, was unrecognizable from the broken child he had once known.

"What's this? Carson sends a broad to do his dirty work?"

"Oh no, Frankie. Mr. Carson doesn't exist. But I'll be taking the money all the same."

Frank's face split into a wide grin and his men laughed. "Will ya now, doll? And how do you suppose you're going to do that?"

Betty looked thoughtful, then turned to the wall behind her and hit it with the side of her fist. She listened carefully for the hollow thud of vibration that traveled down the wall on both sides. Then she smiled, sharp and ruthless.

"With ease, Frankie. First, I'll kill every one of you slimy bastards in this room. Then I'll take the cash from the safe in the paneling behind that terrible picture of your cousin Donny."

Frankie glowered up at the monochrome photograph of a hawk-nosed man with oil slicked hair and a cigar hanging from his lips. A slow dawning of comprehension broke across his face.

"You dirty little whore! Get her boys!"

Before the words had left his mouth, Betty had dropped her handbag by the door and leapt. *Smack!*

Crash!

The first two men to arrive had their heads knocked soundly together and crumpled out-cold to the floor. *Joe and Lefty down.* Betty made a mental note to finish them off later as she caught the wrist of Fat Vito, twisting his gun up to the ceiling, spinning him around, then pointing it back onto the crown of his own head. He was strong. He twisted back around, his biceps bulging with the effort. But not strong enough. Betty forced him back, jabbed the back of his knees with her pointed toes. He collapsed to his knees as she forced the trigger down. A shower of blood sprayed the floor through his own face, away from her body. It wouldn't do to ruin such a splendid dress. *Three down.*

Two more men jumped her, one from each side. Behind her, Larry the Horse reached around her throat with long fingers, squeezing tight. His rabid breath on the back of Betty's neck was even more a violation than his attempt to strangle her. Betty ran him backwards, impaling him on the muzzle of Pozzy's gun as he took aim. *Bang!*

Betty had heard his intention long before the bullet left the chamber. Pozzy's bullet pierced Larry the Horse instead of her own gut as she shimmied sideways in frozen time, letting it continue past her tiny waist and into Rusty Salvatore, a gold-toothed bastard with his gun pressed into her bosom as he too, pulled the trigger and missed her moving flesh by a fraction. Both men collapsed. Released from their vice, Betty leapt high, spinning as she round-housed the head of the smoking gun left standing. In a split-instant of shock, Pozzy realized that he too, had received the second-hand bullet from Rusty's *Liberator*, before *Snap!* his neck lolled like a baby bird and he fell on the corpse pile at Betty's feet. *Six down.*

Three men were left. The youngest, a nasty little blight that Betty knew to be Cracker Charlie, was shooting erratically into the chaos of falling bodies. Lifting her dress high, Betty let the men take in the gleaming fence of knives in her garter. *Thud!* Charlie was down with knife to his jugular, spilling blood from his mouth. *Seven. Flick! Thud!* Betty finished off the two unconscious men she'd started with. She was nothing if not thorough.

"Well boys, it looks like it's just you and me..." Betty purred, spinning her final two knives lazily in her hands as she filtered the thoughts pouring in from their minds. "Oh, please," she sighed, grabbing a whiskey flask from the card table and flinging it toward the shortest man, who had his finger on the trigger of a gun. The bullet met the flask halfway and ricocheted off the metal rim, sending both objects to the filthy concrete floor. Their weapons gone, the fight was now down to guts and strength alone. Despite being burly and street-wise, the men didn't move.

Frankie was still behind the desk, staring red-faced and furious at the rapid failure of his best. Closer to her, the two remaining gangsters looked back to him for support, their legs shaking.

"What do we do, boss?" one man asked. She almost felt sorry for them. Almost.

"Yes, Frankie," Betty drawled, "What should poor Ronnie do? He's in quite a fix here and he can't possibly think for himself." She smirked. The men's minds betrayed their character in an agonizing montage of loyalty laced with murder, ambition stained by greed and sparks of love that told her they had once been so much more than they were now. Lost potential was an unhappy thing. But their hands were dirty and like their comrades sprawled on the floor behind her, Betty read no intent for self-redemption in their minds. Which made them equally as deserving of the death they so frequently dealt. She wondered what she'd do if she ever felt true regret in one of the murderers she faced. So far, it hadn't happened.

"Boss?" Ronnie asked again, his eyes darting between Betty and Frank.

Frankie's lip curled and he turned an ugly shade of purple. "You do what I told you to do, you useless son of a bitch. Kill her!"

The two remaining men looked at each other slowly, as if daring the other to act first.

"Oh boys, really," Betty clucked, shaking her head in mock amusement. "I don't bite you know." She ran forward onto a kicked-out chair and toppled it backwards, riding the height to the card table where she landed. She dropped her knives, spearing the wooden table on each side of her body. Reaching one hand up high, she grabbed the electrical cord dangling a bare light bulb onto the table from the roof. She yanked the cord through its hole, and grabbed Ronnie's collar, pulling his feet from the ground. In an instant, she shoved the light bulb in his stunned mouth and forced it shut, electrocuting him as he crashed to the floor.

Betty dropped down beside the remaining man, ignoring Frankie, who was now rifling through his drawers for the key to his safe.

"How would you like to die, darling?" she asked.

"I...I...I wouldn't," the man stuttered. His hands were dangling, and a wet stain bloomed on his oversized pants.

Betty regarded him coldly. "Is that so?" she said. "Well, I just happen to know there was a shopkeeper in Manhattan last week that had the same preference. And a baker in New Jersey. Remember old Mr. Chang? Or poor, stupid Davey Thomas at The Flourhouse? Simple men with families, over their head in debt until Frankie here stepped in to bail them out." Betty glanced to Frankie, whose lips twitched. She looked back to the goon remaining in her way. Sweat glistened in his pores. "And when they couldn't meet their obligations?" Betty lowered her voice to a whisper and leaned in close enough that her lips brushed his ear. "Bang." The man whimpered.

"I also know that you, Tommy," - his face drained - "pulled the trigger both times." Betty looked disinterestedly at her painted nails. "That being the case," she looked back to him, "I think it's fair to say that no one gets what they want." Betty's fist met his gut as she ploughed Tommy backward into a dusty cabinet of booze. The glass shattered behind him. Shards of it pinned him, like an insect, to the wall.

Betty took a deep breath and reclaimed her throwing knives from the card table. What she wouldn't give for a long, hot bath right now. She turned back to Frankie. He had his hands up above his head, the safe keys dangling from his fingers.

"You can take it all."

"Thank you, I will."

Frankie let out a nervous sigh of relief, eyeing off the carnage around him. "I don't get it. Why'd you do this? For the money?"

Betty surveyed him curiously. She always knew Frankie was smarter than the rest, but he was still a coward.

"Of course not, Frankie." Betty sighed. Sometimes, especially at times like this, the lines blurred. Her smile dropped and her eyes became as devastatingly sad as they had been twelve years before. Betty was suddenly unmasked, a ghost of vulnerability and anger. The ghost of Susie.

"You knew what he did, Uncle Frank. You knew what Pop put us through," she said. Betty's eyes turned hard and her muscles tensed under the delicate dress. Frankie grappled with understanding, his eyes scouring her body, searching for clues. "He used me, you both did," Betty continued, her resentment boiling higher with each word. "You let Donny use my mind, just like he did to Mom. Even after it killed her. What chance did I have, a twelve-year-old girl?" Betty stepped forward and Frank blanched.

Betty could see it finally hit him.

"Susie? Little Susie?" he choked out.

Betty tensed, so unused to that name now. Her chin lifted, and she continued. "He used her as a punching bag, Uncle Frank. And you used him to hide behind, to do your dirty work. You, Uncle Tony, Uncle Vince, Lucius, Marco, Joey, Tyrone, Carlos. All the boys. And they're still doing it now, aren't they? Well, except for Marco. He won't be doing anything anymore." A self-satisfied smile brushed her lips, then disappeared.

"That was you? You took out Marco?" Frank spluttered.

"Mmm," Betty brushed the fabric of her skirt down noncommittally. "I came across him last year hauling some coke at the docks. Let's just say he caught me on a bad day."

"Jesus Christ."

"And Donny up there," Betty continued, nodding toward the ugly photograph on the wall behind him, "Well, Donny uses everyone, doesn't he?"

Frank's eyes widened. "You're going after Donny? Holy hell, you can't do that! Let me talk to him, Susie. We can do it together. He'll be glad to see you kid. Hell, I'm glad to see ya. I mean, I was cut up when Roy died sure, but I never wanted to see you hurt. Nor your mother. It was just the way he was, see?"

"The way he was?!" Betty snarled. "You saw your own brother day in, day out beating his wife and kid, and it's just *the way he was*?"

"But I tried! I told Roy to cool his jets. He was hot-tempered, always was. I had my own wife, my own kids. I got to keep my head low. This isn't a game we're playing Susie. Donny was watchin' me too. I couldn't look weak or he'd lose me from the team. Anyway, your mother, she had problems Susie. She didn't have it in her. Not like you did. We had a good four years with you on the team, kid. And all these years I thought you were dead."

"I bet that was a loss for you," Betty spat back at him, vehemently. "Didn't have your secret weapon anymore did you? Had to deal with Donny on your own terms."

"I've done all right," Frank said. His eyes trailed the carnage in his office. "Seems you've done alright too."

"Better than alright," smiled Betty. She took another step forward and took the keys dangling from Franks hand.

"Now hang on a minute. I'm your family. It doesn't have to be this way. You got skills kid, I can see that. We can come to some arrangement."

"The last arrangement didn't work out too well, did it Frankie?" Betty said. "Not for Pop, anyway." Her mind flashed back to that warm night, twelve years before. The blood, the gasoline. Her father's limp body on the kitchen floor, with a knife hard in his chest. He hadn't even fought back. Never saw it coming. Susie was then sixteen, working for Donny from the day her mother died and they'd discovered the girl carried the gift and curse of her mother's line. Mind-reading. Empathy. Like her mother before her, the girl was an invaluable asset to Donald Pinzolo, whose world was based on knowledge, secrets and lies. But her mother had been right, Susie *was* stronger. She could control it and reign it in. That night, after she'd murdered her father and walked from the blazing inferno of her childhood home, she'd left her old life behind.

Frankie gaped, speechless, but his mind spoke for him. Memories of smoldering timber framing, a dead man under the rubble and a missing teenager, presumed burnt alive.

"You killed your own father?" Frank stumbled back a step, knocking the chair against the back wall. His skin was ashen. "Jesus, we blamed the Castelano boys. Thought it was a hit."

"It was a hit. My first."

"But you were just a kid. I never thought that you… that you could…"

Betty smiled coldly. "Surprise." Her shoulders straightened and Betty swallowed hard, glad for the confession. "This is revenge, plain and simple, Frank. I want a world where you don't exist. Each and every one of you."

Frank's eyes darted between Betty and the still-closed door. His tongue ran his bottom lip and a bright sheen of sweat illuminated his pink skin.

"Your security guard is dead," Betty said matter-of-factly.

"Jesus," he breathed. "I mean, of course he is. You had to, I understand." Frankie gingerly raised his hands and shuffled back, slowly lowering himself onto his chair. "You had it rough kid, I get it," he said, with a sigh. "Roy was a bad egg from the start, he was never any good to you and your mom, didn't deserve either of you, but especially Ethyl, she was too good for 'im. Too kind." Frankie's eyes were suddenly sincere, he dropped his hands down to his lap and shook his head sadly. "I liked your mom, Susie, I swear I never wanted her hurt," he slowly pulled himself in to his desk.

Betty stood in front of it, her resolve fading as Uncle Frank's words came. It felt so good, to be *heard*. No one had really *heard* her since she was a little girl. And Frank, he knew what it had been like for her. What she'd been through.

"Me and your Aunt Thelma, we took you home after the funeral, remember? I talked to Roy, tried to sort him out a bit." Frank's voice was mellow and his words dripped with sympathy. "He was past it though. Never could control his temper. I don't blame you, fighting back. He deserved it, didn't he, kid? You put up with it all for so long..."

Betty had hunched, almost broken down by that glimmer of understanding. Of kindness. Frank *was* sincere, she could feel it feeding into her thoughts from his mind. Washing over her like waves of compassion. *Drowning her.* She was standing so close now, in front of his desk, with her red dress soft against the wood.

"You don't need to fight anymore, Susie," Frank said. "You've got family again now. I'll protect you, keep you safe. I'll sort all this out," he nodded to the carnage surrounding them. "They'll never know you were here. Our secret, okay. I'll look after you, kid." The knives in Betty's hands gently touched the wooden table and the noise surprised her. She looked down at them, and let go, leaving the blades on the desk. She looked at her empty hands.

No.

Mistake.

Then she saw it. Frank's hand had shifted, so slowly she hadn't realized, as he'd retrieved the revolver strapped under his desk. His knuckles were white around the handle, held low on his lap. Pointed at her. She caught his eye and they both knew.

Frank leapt to his feet, gun cocked and grabbed her arm, pulling her chest into the barrel. Betty was enraged, more than ever. His betrayal was nothing compared to her own humiliation for letting it happen. Even now as an adult, she was weak.

Her eyes flashed flint and fire, her elbow smashed into his jaw and the gun spun across the room.

"Susie-" Frank groaned from where he fell.

Betty laughed, humorlessly. "No Frankie. Susie's dead. I'm just your local Avon lady. Making a delivery."

And with that, Betty flicked her two remaining knives into his heart together, buried to the hilt.

***

Betty collected her cosmetic case from the door and walked around the desk. She stepped over Frank's body and took the keys hooked around his fingers, emptying the contents of the safe onto the table.

She carefully packed the cash under the false base of her bag and layered the drugs on top in glass bottles amongst her cosmetics. She tore open a single packet of smack and spilled it across the desk and Frank's face, shutting her handbag, which was now considerably heavier. Betty plumped her hair. She straightened a lopsided picture on the wall, then walked over and slowly opened the door. Apart from the dead guard, the narrow hallway was empty. She dragged the guards' body into Frank's office, closed the door and jammed it shut. Betty removed her gloves and folded them neatly into her bag as she walked quickly back toward the noisy bar, regaining her poise with each step. Betty ducked into the lavatories as she passed by, to re-apply her lipstick. Not one step out of the ladies' room door, she bumped into George.

"But I just checked a moment ago, you weren't there!" he exclaimed.

"George, dear. Well, of course I was, where else would I be?"

"I don't know," he said. His eyes flicked suspiciously at her, then back up the hallway beyond the lavatories. "What took you so long?"

"Goodness, what a question to ask!" Betty said. "Ladies business, dear. And before that I was helping a lamb who needed a touch of color. She's going to hold a sales luncheon for her friends for me, so it was worth the stop."

"Working on your night off, dear?" George said, somewhat on edge.

"Guilty as charged. You know me, never miss an opportunity."

"Quite." He replied. "Always selling something, aren't you?"

"Yes, I suppose I am." Betty took a breath through her teeth and plastered a smile on her face. "Did you get me a drink?"

"My wallet is in your bag," he replied, sourly.

The realization hit Betty like ice. He'd been waiting outside the ladies' room almost the entire time. "Of course it is, I'm such a goose," Betty said. Her cheeks blushed. Acutely aware of the bloodbath she had left only meters from where they stood, Betty dropped her bag on the floor, opened it and began to shuffle the contents, desperately looking for the wallet she had dropped in earlier. "So many bath salts," she muttered with a nervous laugh. Her shoulders were unnaturally hunched, preventing too close a view at its contents. Betty closed the bag and stood up, handing George his wallet.

They walked back out together into the din. Betty sat nervously at a table with the bag at her feet while George bought her a Martini. She slid the olive off with her teeth and leant forward to kiss George lightly on the lips, but he turned his head.

"Thank you for the drink," she said quietly.

"I don't like this Avon business," George said. "You were gone for quite a while there. I thought I'd lost you."

"Never," Betty said, touching his hand. George shifted uncomfortably and Betty's heart sank. He'd never questioned her before; he'd never needed to. Her eyes glistened. She'd been selfish. She'd brought tonight's job too close to home.

The orchestra eased into "At Last" and Glenn Miller crooned softly from the stage. She took her husband's glass, placing it on the table with her own.

"Dance with me?" Betty asked.

"I'm not really in the mood..." he replied.

"Please, George." Betty squeezed his hand gently and he conceded. She led her husband to the dance floor and circled his neck with her arms.

They danced, slow and intimate, oblivious to the crowd around them. With every note that passed, Betty ached to feel herself slip back into the life she craved. The one she had built for herself on a foundation of blood and lies. The pretty life. Where walls of pearl and perfume sheltered her from the past. Her arms tightened around George protectively. *Nothing can take this life away from me. My dream. My own. At last.*

Betty looked up into George's eyes but for the very first time, was met with hurt and confusion instead of adoration. His jaw clenched and he looked away.

The shock quickened her heart. *He doesn't trust me anymore.* She felt sick.

As the song drew to a close, Betty held back tears and lifted her chin.

"I'm sorry George, I've upset you. I really didn't mean to; you know how I get carried away with my work, I do so love it. But not as much as I love you."

George's expression softened and he met her eyes again. "It's alright, jitterbug. I just - sometimes I feel like I'm a bit second-rate, you know? I'm not entirely sure you really need me at all."

Betty stopped still, while others around them began to sway as the band struck up a new piece.

"You must understand George," Betty said, earnestly, "*every-thing* I do, is because I need you. Perhaps not in the way you think, but, here," she pulled his hand up from her waist and held it over her heart. "More than you'll ever know. You saved me, you know."

"I don't know about that." George smiled. "You were doing quite well enough when I met you at that drug store counter. You sure saved me from that blasted cold I had. And every day since."

"Then we've saved each other," Betty said. "As it should be."

An intrusion to her thoughts stole her attention. One of Frankie's guards was heading downstairs. *Time to leave.*

"What do you say we head home, darling?"

"Already? Don't you want to keep dancing?"

"Let's dance at home," Betty replied with a soft smile. "Perhaps we can push the beds together..."

The twinkle returned to George's eyes.

And they left.

On the front steps of the New York City Police Department, Officer Malcolm Parker stood watching pedestrians. He was a bit huffy at the thought of being given such a menial task. There were plenty of others that could have done it, but his boss needed an extra set of eyes on the street. Specifically, his own, in fact, because Parker had proven himself to have a good eye for things not-quite-right. For that distinction, Parker was pleased, albeit currently bored. He'd been waiting an hour and a half and as yet, he'd seen nothing out of the ordinary for a Tuesday morning. No suspicious characters lurking the corners, no odd conversations close by, not even a stray dog. Parker sighed and stretched his neck, bouncing on his toes. It was almost break time.

"Excuse me, officer," a woman's voice called out, "but could you give me directions to the nearest subway, please?" The woman in question had soft brown eyes and a pretty face and was bouncing a baby carriage with one hand as she waved him over with the other. Parker puffed his chest, glad for the opportunity to show off his good manners and have a conversation. He descended to the bottom step and explained the route, gesturing as he did. Behind him, pedestrians continued walking by. A pair of brown leather Gold Cross pumps wove between the people. The woman wearing them swiftly stepped up to the building entrance, deposited a large box wrapped in brown paper, then continued on her way. By the time Officer Parker turned around again, not twenty seconds had passed, but he'd failed in his morning's duty.

"I'll be blowed," the officer said, pulling off his hat and scratching his head. He scanned the scene in front of him for any indication of who had left the parcel. There were businessmen, women shopping, soldiers and nurses in uniform. It could have been anyone.

"Darn it!" Parker cried, followed by, "So sorry, Ma'am," as his outburst was admonished by an older lady passing by. Officer Parker picked up the box and took it inside the station.

"Sarge, another drop!" He called as he passed his own workstation and continued to the office of his boss. Parker sidestepped a janitor scraping the name-paint off the glass door, in preparation for a new one. Sitting behind the desk, a neatly dressed man of barely thirty years old looked up from his paperwork. He was tall and handsome and had a thoughtful face, with the exception of a certain tiredness about his eyes. The walnut name-plate in front of him declared him to be Sergeant Jacob Lawrence.

"You see anything?" he asked hopefully.

Parker shook his head, ruefully. "I turned away just for a moment, and bam! there it was. Not a whiff."

"Darn it!"

"That's what I thought," said Parker. "Sorry Sarge." He sat the box on Jacob's desk. The sergeant pulled on some gloves, then gently tore the box open, fully expecting to find the same thing he usually did. Once again, he was right. Inside, was a neatly packed stock of amphetamines in decorative glass jars and thick paper parcels of heroin.

"Might have been from Polletti's crew," Jacob remarked. Whenever a homicide case opened up in his district, it seemed an anonymous delivery of drugs wasn't far behind. There had been a few hits about town lately. Some local thugs and corner sellers taken down. Known small-time dealers working in the same circle. All violently murdered and left with a mess of white powder on their faces to expose their appetite. The Polletti case was a particularly nasty one though. Twelve bodies in a small room at the Capitol and a bloody, gruesome mess. Polletti had always been on Jacob's radar, intently so, in fact, but he kept his books clean so was impossible to bring down. It seemed someone else was doing the new sergeant's job for him. And better.

"Golly, this is new," Officer Parker said, reaching in to pull out a small white card with red writing. Jacob frowned, taking the card from him. He ran his thumb thoughtfully over the writing on front. In cursive script it read, "Avon Calling - Sorry I missed you!" He flipped it over. In neat handwriting on the back was an address.

"Parker! Get the car."

Within twenty minutes they were breaking down the door of an abandoned Tinker's shop near Central Park.

"Mighty strange place to stash stolen goods, isn't it?" Officer Parker said.

It was a derelict fringe of the city with every second shop

boarded up, but still, there were people outside on the streets. Sergeant Lawrence looked around shrewdly, half expecting his mystery murderers to be watching, hidden around a corner. They certainly seemed brazen enough for such a stunt. The fact that once again, they'd slipped past Parker with the delivery told him they were bold and clever.

The officers fanned out behind Jacob as he burst into the shop with Parker on his heels, guns raised and loaded. The scurry of rodents gave the only sign of life.

Officer Parker let out a low whistle. Along the back wall, a dozen crates were stacked high, each one labeled with the tell-tale insignia of the US Army.

"Get me a crowbar, Officer Wilson."

A copper-haired policeman ran out the door.

"More of the same, you think, Sarge?" Parker said.

"I'd bet on it," Sergeant Lawrence sighed. "Wake up pills for the boys on the front. From the transport hijacking near Harlem, I'd say." *Ballistics would confirm it soon enough.*

Officer Wilson came back in with a shiny new crowbar and passed it to Sergeant Lawrence.

"From the hardware store across the road," Wilson explained. "The owner wants it back when we're done."

"Course he does," Jacob smiled. "That much metal probably needs a ration certificate. Make sure he gets it back Wilson."

"Yes, Sir."

Sergeant Lawrence pulled on one of the crates to shift it. "Blast," he grunted. "Make yourself useful, Parker."

"Sorry Sir." The two men lifted a crate down together and set it on the ground with a thud. Jacob used the borrowed crowbar to pry off the lid.

Officer Parker looked inside and let out a low whistle. "That lot'd be worth a greenback or two," he said. "How'd they get here then?"

Jacob thought for a moment before replying. "No one's going

to hijack a truckload of stuff just to return it a few weeks later. They must have been intercepted." And then, almost under his breath, "Someone out there paid the price for ripping off Uncle Sam." Jacob pulled the *Avon Calling!* card from his pocket and ran it through his fingers. "Our mystery men have been busier than I thought."

"But they're on our side, right Sarge?" Parker said, cheerfully.

"This isn't about sides, Parker," Jacob replied. "This smells a lot like revenge. Someone out there's got a score to settle and that's dangerous for everyone. We need to bring them down. All of them."

"Yes, sir."

"And we're going to need a truck for this lot," he said. "You'd better call it in."

Sergeant Jacob Lawrence walked back out to the street curb with the small white card in his hand. *Vigilantes.* It must be. A team of lawless, violent men loose on the streets were never a good thing, no matter who their target was. But why on earth would they leave the address on the back of an Avon card? Was it a diversion? Or just something they picked up from the trash, perhaps? Jacob studied the handwriting on the back of the card. A feeling of uneasiness settled in his gut. Something about it was familiar. Unable to put his finger on why, he tucked the card back into his breast pocket.

Avon Calling. At least now he had something to work with.

💋

3

CHOCOLATE CAKE & SANDWICHES

At six o'clock precisely, Sergeant Jacob Lawrence knocked on the door of a tall, handsome house in Borough Park, Brooklyn. A middle-aged woman with glossy, dark hair piled up elegantly, opened the door, meeting him with kind eyes and a wide smile.

"My bubbeleh!"

"Hello, Ima," Jacob said, her smile bringing light to his own tired eyes.

"Where is my neshika?" She pulled Jacob into a tight hug and kissed his cheeks affectionately. "I've barely seen you the last few weeks. You work too hard."

"It's just been a bit crazy at work," he said.

"Ah, you don't need to explain to me. The wife of a police commissioner, remember?" Golda Lawrence ushered her son into the house and shut the door behind him. "I'm just glad your father has retired and I finally get some time with him, even though he plays golf every other day." Jacob could hear voices coming from the lounge.

"Is Michael home?" he asked, keen to see his younger brother who had recently begun university.

"Yes, he's here," his mother said, a twinkle in her eye. "And I invited the Sonbergs for dinner as well. Adina has come with them.”

“Mother, please-”

“Oh, shush Jacob. She is lovely and such a beryeh for you. So smart and a good Jewish girl, what could be better?”

“I’ve told you mother, I work too much, I’m no good for anyone right now,” Jacob said.

“You are nearly thirty years old, Jacob,” his mother said, reproachfully. “You need to make a life for yourself and some grandbabies for me. Goodness knows your brother isn’t going to give me one anytime soon, he can barely string a sentence together around women.” She pulled her eldest son into another hug. “Just have some fun for once, hey? Take her out, see a show.”

With a reluctant sigh, Jacob followed his mother into the lounge. Amos and Esther Sonberg were talking animatedly to his father by the fireplace, while Michael sat awkwardly on the couch with a pretty young woman who seemed to be trying her hardest to elicit conversation from him. Michael’s face lit up in sheer relief at the sight of his brother.

“Jacob!” he said.

The others turned around at his name and within a moment, Jacob was wrapped in the warm embrace of his father followed by a sturdy handshake from Amos.

“My son, the newest Sergeant in the New York City Police Department!” said Abraham Lawrence proudly.

“Well done, dear,” said Esther leaning in to kiss him on the cheek.

“Just like your father,” Amos added. “And a better man couldn’t be found. The city’s in safe hands.”

“That’s very kind,” Jacob said, smiling, and moved over to hug his brother.

“Have you met our daughter, Jacob?” asked Esther, rushing forward. “This is Adina. You know, she is the personal secretary for General Brandway under the Women's Reserve. Such an important job!"

"Oh mother," Adina said, getting to her feet, laughing. "It's really not that important."

"I'm sure it is," said Jacob kindly, reaching out to shake Adina's hand. "It's nice to meet you." Their eyes met, and Jacob's heart shifted a little. "So, you're a SPAR then?" Jacob asked, impressed. The SPARS were a new reserve of civilian women, dedicated to administrative roles that assisted military operations. The Coast Guard had formalized the arrangement to replace men in recruitment, shopfronts, warehouses and communication roles, freeing them up for active service.

"One of the first," Adina replied. "I was a clerk for a few years, straight out of secretarial college. When the opportunity came up to help our country, well, I wanted to be part of it. In my own small way, of course."

Esther hovered nearby, beaming. "What a good girl. So responsible. You'll make a fine mother, one day. Don't you think so?"

"Ima!" Adina flushed and Jacob couldn't help but laugh. It seemed he wasn't the only one under duress.

"Well, I for one, will be happy when you leave that job, children or not," Amos growled. "There are other ways to serve our country, Adina. That General gets his pound of flesh out of you, that's for sure! Barely home before ten in the evening some days," he continued, turning to Jacob. "I know there's a war on, but a young lady shouldn't be out that late on her own. There are too many troublemakers on the streets nowadays. You'd know that well enough, Jacob, I'm right, aren't I?"

"I'm perfectly capable of looking after myself, Aba," Adina interrupted, with a frown. "It's only a short walk to the train station and there are plenty of night guards around the General's office. You worry too much." She nudged her father gently and gave him a reassuring smile, which softened his face.

"I still don't have to like it," Amos grumbled. "Young women out on the street at night, coming and going, it's not safe."

"I've heard of General Brandway," Jacob said, deftly changing the subject, "although I haven't had the pleasure of meeting him yet."

"Well, I'm not sure it will be a pleasure in all honesty," Adina said. "He tends to be rather abrasive. I think I'm the only one who can manage his temper sometimes."

"That can't be easy to work with in such close quarters," said Jacob, a flicker of concern crossing his features.

"Oh, I don't mind so much," Adina said. "I'm tougher than I look, despite what my father says." She raised an eyebrow to Amos and his brow furrowed again.

"Thinks she's unbreakable," he muttered.

"It's my job to make it a little easier for the General," Adina smirked and continued on, resting her head momentarily on her father's shoulder. "Arranging appointments, taking notes and typing, managing his personal affairs, that sort of thing. I'm sure it's rather drab compared to the goings-on of a police sergeant though."

"You'd be surprised," Jacob chuckled, "I probably have more paperwork on my desk than you do right now. And I'm probably half as good at managing it."

"I'm sure you're not," Adina replied. From the corner of his eye, Jacob noticed his mother exchange a look with Esther. If he wasn't so engaged in conversation, he'd have given her a look of his own. As it turned out though, Adina was far more interesting than he'd expected. She was lively and intelligent, with a pretty face, olive skin and coffee-colored eyes lit with good humor.

"In any case, the General is a busy man with a difficult job," she was saying, "especially lately with the- well, with some unexpected problems we've encountered over the past months."

Jacob raised an eyebrow, then nodded thoughtfully. He knew all about those unexpected problems. "Yes, I'm sure it has been difficult," he said. "My department has recently become involved with Brandway's logistics operation - not our usual area of expertise. The military tend to handle these things internally, but this time there are some boundaries crossed. To be honest, the General's problems have fallen into my lap as the newly minted workhorse at the station."

"Really?" Adina said, surprised. "Well, I suppose that means I'll be seeing a bit more of you then, Jacob." Her eyes twinkled.

Jacob felt a rush of warmth to his neck. He looked down at the roses woven into the green rug beneath his feet, then back to Adina and couldn't help but grin. It had been a long time since a woman had left him short of words. Perhaps there was, after all, something a bit different about this one.

"What is this, Adina?" Amos interjected. "What have the police to do with your work? I told you it's not safe for a young lady!"

"Nothing Aba," Adina cajoled. "It's just a small thing, but you know I can't talk about the particulars with you anyway. It's classified."

"Classified, my knee!" Amos muttered. Esther rolled her eyes and took her husband by the elbow. "Oh, let the young people talk, you old kvetch," she clucked, and led him over to the fireplace to pour another drink. Abraham and Golda laughed and joined them, beginning a new conversation.

Jacob grinned at Adina, who was watching her parents with affection. Beside him, Michael stood awkwardly, not sure which party to join, or avoid.

"We should worry when they *stop* worrying about us," Jacob said, nodding toward their parents. "Thankfully I have Michael here to absorb most of my parents' attention," he said to Adina, wrapping his arm around his brother's shoulder. "A clever plan I instigated when I reached twelve years old and decided a baby brother would be the best countermeasure for over-protective parents." He winked at Michael, who shook his head, red-faced and chuckling.

"All your idea, then was it?" Adina laughed.

"Unquestionably," said Jacob. "I can be very persuasive."

"You could never quite persuade them to let you have that motorcycle you wanted," said Michael, looking between them with a raised eyebrow.

"Now hang on a minute, I was stitched up!" Jacob objected, mock offense in his eyes. "I nearly had them convinced on that until the Drezner brothers ruined it for me. If David hadn't taken a flip over the dock under Brooklyn Bridge, they'd never have found out we'd been practicing until we already had our license!"

"All three of them ended up in the East River, including the motorcycle they'd borrowed off Charlie Banstein's pop," Michael laughed, shrugging off his brother's arm and picking up his drink. "I don't think I've ever heard mom scold him so loud. He turned up at the doorstep soaked to the bone, right on dinnertime, with Officer Tilley holding him by the scruff of his neck. I was awfully impressed, even at five years old."

"So you should have been, I was an unsung hero that day! It took me six months to pay back my share of that motorcycle, and I wasn't even the one that rode it off the dock. I jumped in to save David, and then Caleb jumped in after me! There we were flapping about in the water trying to keep the thing from sinking with an audience of fishermen laughing their pants off. There wasn't a chance mom would let me get my own bike after that. I never heard the end of it."

Adina laughed, holding her arms across her middle. Jacob regaled her with more tales of his youthful misadventures while Michael directed him toward the silliest memories and skirted others. There was always a shadow his younger brother was sensitive enough to leave alone. They turned to Michael's college classes for conversation, peppered with a few good-natured jibes about his reluctance to take out the myriad of pretty girls he was surrounded by on campus. By the time Golda called them into the dining room for dinner, the three of them were in high spirits.

"To these young people," Abraham said, raising his glass above the sumptuous spread of food laid before them, "a brilliant law student, a clever and unbreakable young woman and the newest police sergeant on the force." His eyes were nothing but pride.

"Mazel Tov!" they all toasted, and the conversation flowed across the table once more.

An hour later, as his family and their guests drifted back into the lounge room after dinner, Jacob stepped out to the back porch with his drink. It had been a good night. A great night in fact. But like always, Jacob couldn't seem to shake the cloud that followed him. He heard the screen door click quietly behind him and turned to see his father standing there.

"I hear there've been a few nasty hits lately," Abraham said, gently. "They land on your desk?"

"Yeah," Jacob sighed. "Polletti's crew and some others, street dealers mostly."

"Mmm." His father leant against the rail, looking up into the night sky. "Better that rubbish is gone. Been causing trouble for years. They were bound to end up cold at some point."

"Yeah well, they were certainly that," Jacob muttered, the blood-soaked image of the office all too easy to recollect.

"You think it's connected to the GI heists?" Abraham said, his eyes still sweeping the stars.

Jacob looked at him, surprised. "How do you know about that?"

"Please, son," Abraham said, turning to face him. "I haven't been out of the game that long. People talk. Besides, what else would Brandway have to do with it? Amos might not know what his daughter does every day, but I do. He's right, it's not safe at the moment. Not that anywhere is with this rotten war going on."

Jacob hesitated. "I think they're connected. Just not sure how yet."

"It'll come," his father said. "In the meantime, how about you start getting out once in a while? You need to have some fun, have a life, son. Adina, she's a nice girl."

"I don't know, Pop."

"Listen Jake," his father said, seriously. "I know what you've been doing all these years. I saw it too."

Jacob closed his eyes.

* * *

He was not yet eighteen when his father had answered that phone call, with a coffee mug in one hand, dressed in his uniform and ready to leave for the station. Abraham had rushed off, but not fast enough for Jacob to miss the look that passed between his parents and then across to him. Fear. As a seasoned police inspector, his father had never shown fear of anything before.

"Stay here", Abraham had yelled as he'd left. And immediately, Jacob had known that that fear was meant for him. But fear of what? He wasn't even finished with high school. The only thing Jacob had to fear was loss. And outside of his family, the only loss great enough was...

Cold dread washed over Jacob's skin and he sprang up from the breakfast table, defying his mother's pleas as she dropped a plate of toast in front of his five-year-old brother. Jacob dragged his bicycle from the front porch and took off, over flowerbeds and through hedges, taking every shortcut he knew to reach Susie's house. He skidded to a stop, throwing his bike aside at the end of her street. The entire road was blocked off by police.

Neighbors stood about in dressing gowns and pajamas, evacuated from their homes to the street before sunrise to keep them safe. With the immediate danger now gone, they stared at the flattened and smoking remains of Susie's house with morbid curiosity from behind police tape, waiting to be allowed back inside their kitchens and bedrooms to resume their lives. None of them had cared for the years that she'd suffered, but now, they stretched their necks forward, keen to see into the house they had so readily turned a blind eye to before. A group of old women uttered sympathies and prayers to each other, shaking their heads in shallow affectation.

"Go away!" Jacob yelled at them, as he pushed through the crowd. "Please! Just get away!"

Jacob stumbled across the gray-ashen bitumen yelling her name, blindly fighting against a web of arms that tried to restrain him. A terrible smell, burnt plastic and chemicals stung his nostrils, making the ground spin. The road was wet. The ash, the timber, the uniforms. Everything was sopping wet. From some far-away place, he heard the siren of a fire truck, clearing a path through the onlookers to leave. Their job was over. Others, just beginning.

"Let him through," a voice eventually called. It took every ounce of will to focus his eyes on the face of the man picking his way through the debris to reach him. The tiniest part of Jacob was aware and thankful that he wasn't alone. But the numbing fog in his head registered that same fearful look he'd seen only twenty minutes earlier at the breakfast table. It was a fear of telling his son a terrible truth. Fear of breaking his heart.

"I'm sorry, son," his father said. "She's gone. No one could have survived this mess."

"No." Every visceral part of Jacob's body twisted inside and he fell forward, vomiting onto the ash. He felt his father's strong arms supporting him. After a few minutes, his knees felt steady enough to sit upright. A singular thought broke through the shock.

"Roy?"

"They found him in the kitchen, what's left of him. Isn't much, I'm afraid to say," Abraham replied. "There were signs of violence. It looks

like the house was broken into first. He was already dead when the fire begthen."

There was something in those words that was uncomfortably satisfying. Not least for all the years Jacob wished he could have repaid Susie's father for the abuse he so readily handed out to his daughter. Someone had finally dealt him the death he deserved. There was no end to the list of lowlifes that might have wanted him dead. But Susie, though, she was just a girl trapped in a terrible life she couldn't escape. She hadn't deserved a death like that.

***

"How long are you going to chase ghosts, Jake?" Abraham asked, laying a gentle hand on his son's shoulder. "There's no revenge to be had. Nothing you can do now to change the way things turned out."

Jacob looked at his father, twelve years on and wearing that same thoughtful expression, now framed by grey hair and the lines of a difficult career.

"You need to live your life. It's good to work hard, I worked hard - I would never have made commissioner if I hadn't. But work for the right reasons, son. To build a life for yourself, to make a better world for your family, for the children you'll have one day."

Jacob took a deep breath and then smiled at his father, tears in his eyes. He blinked them away. "You are right, of course, Aba, you always are," he replied.

"Just give this girl a chance," Abraham said. "She's clever and has a nice smile. And I hear she can make a mean mandlach."

Jacob chuckled, finally convinced. "Alright, alright, I'll ask her. Let's get back inside, before they leave."

In the quiet of the house, Betty was finishing the last stitches to the underside of George Junior's mattress. She was sitting on the floor, half hidden behind the bed and confident that George and the children were distracted in the yard outside. She could hear the little ones playing tag and the occasional swish of newspaper as George turned the page.

Oops, an escapee. Betty smirked as she picked up a single hundred-dollar bill from the floor near her knee. She rolled it up and stuffed it into the unstitched gap where she had slit the edging of the mattress for what seemed like the millionth time. The cash she'd taken from Polletti's safe had a new home. In fact, the mattress had almost more cash than stuffing now, but little Georgie Junior couldn't tell the difference and George Senior was none the wiser either. She wasn't entirely sure of her plans for it, but it always paid to keep a little money aside for a rainy day. Or a lot, as it were. Betty finished her neat stitching and straightened the sheets.

As she worked, Betty's memory drifted back to the first time she'd picked apart the seams of Georgie's mattress. To the blood money she'd stuffed inside it.

It was over a year ago now, not long after she'd put Marco Pinzolo on ice in a warehouse near the Fulton Fishmarkets. At that point, her next step had still been unclear to her. The icing on the cake of course, would be taking down Donald Pinzolo himself. But Betty had decided, rather logically she thought, that the best way to eat a cake was not whole, but rather, to cut it away, slice by slice, until the last crumb was gone.

If she killed Donny first, one of his nephews or underlings would be quick to fill his shoes. But if she dismantled his empire piece by piece, there would be nothing left to claim when he was finally dispatched.

So, it was fortunate then, that one such nephew, Emilio Pinzolo, happened to cross Betty's path at the wrong time, and in the wrong place. For him, at least. Bringing down Emilio and leaving his gang of thieves leaderless, had been a piece of cake. And Betty loved cake. After that, her way forward had become clear to her. Slice by slice, crumb by crumb, she would eat Donny for breakfast. But that second slice – Emilio – she remembered like yesterday...

***

"Tell me, Gertie, *truthfully,* how are you managing?" Betty had carried a cup of tea over to a stained, threadbare couch, and passed it to the forty-something year old woman who was sitting back on it, feet up, with a baby at her breast. The woman sighed and shuffled into a more comfortable position, balancing the teacup on the edge of the couch, away from her newborn.

"I'm tired as old bones," Gertrude said. "I tell you Betty, if I have any more it'll clear do me in. Jean and Clara are good girls, but the twins are all sorts of trouble at the moment with their teething and I'm getting no sleep on account of this one."

"I can only imagine," Betty sympathized. "I don't know how you manage. I remember how hard it was with little Georgie when his teeth were giving him trouble, but two toddlers at once! You must be frayed nerves and a constant headache."

"And the rest," Gertrude said. "But I'll manage, I always do. Mend and make do, Betty. No point moping about it, that ain't gonna keep floors clean and mouths fed."

"Quite right," Betty said, gesturing to a large basket of bread and vegetables that she'd sat down by the open kitchen door. "Still, one of the Marigold ladies will drop by every other day with a basket, just for the next few weeks until you get on your feet again. And we girls don't mind putting in a bit of elbow grease either, to keep the moths out of the pantry." Betty looked around the tiny apartment, messed from corner to edge with the stuffs of Gertrude's brood. The twin toddlers, Elmer and Leo, were playing on the floor at Betty's feet with four-year-old

Agnes. Their hand-me-down singlets were grubby, but their faces scrubbed clean. The toddlers were sporting rosy cheeks and dribbling chins, the telltale signs of new teeth breaking through.

The small apartment was oppressively hot. The sweat of summer slipped under doorways and seemed to swell inside the room. Woefully small windows permitted no breeze. At night, children slept in their underwear to keep cool. By day they played under fire hydrants. The stinking hot summer seemed to roll on forever.

Seven children and a largely absent husband had burdened Gertrude Cole with a tough year. When baby Sarah had come along, Betty had drawn up a roster to make sure the poor woman didn't crumble under the strain.

With Betty at the helm, the Marigold Church Social Committee spent their spare time organizing charity fundraisers and lending a helping hand to families that needed it, often extending far further than the boundaries of church members. Between her volunteering as a Marigold and her Avon business, often combining the two, Betty never had a quiet moment. 'The Devil finds work for idle hands,' she recited to George when he protested her constant busyness.

"I'm like the cat that's got the cream, but I'm not gonna turn your gals away, that's for sure." Gertrude took a sip of tea. "I'll be hard-pressed not to get used to it though, having cups of tea made for me and all," she said with a put-on air and wide smile. "Next I'll be wanting one of them fancy maids they have out at The Surrey." She put down the teacup and adjusted her baby's head. Gertrude's eyes were circled with dark shadows but crinkled with love. The woman's face was careworn, like a dusting cloth used well beyond its capacity, color and softness washed out into thin lines and dry skin. Her day dress hung loose on her, and her apron, currently pulled down on one side to breast feed, needed replacing. Faded yellow daisies over navy poplin looked more like nondescript confetti after hundreds of washes against a corrugated board and ringer.

"I'm sure Bette Davis would gladly send a maid if we appealed to her, but then who would wash all those darling outfits she wears to sell war bonds and perform for the troops?" Betty laughed. "No, no maid needed, Gertie, we're bringing The Surrey to you. You just take care of these little angels and we'll take care of the rest."

"Little angels," snorted Gertrude, "try popping in around dinner time and you'll change your tune on that one." She looked down at the toddlers on the floor who were fighting over a handful of toy cars. "Leo, give it back to your brother, he had it first." Leo let out a wail as Elmer grabbed the toy back with a pudgy hand, then the latter began crying as it was stolen back again with a smack. Betty got up and retrieved a half-dozen colored wooden blocks from her Avon bag and made a show of handing them over. The tears stopped immediately.

"I've got a stash of Georgie's toys if they'd like them, Gertie, he's doesn't play with them anymore, now he's started school."

"They'd love that," Gertrude said, gently lifting the baby away and propping her over her shoulder.

"Oh, may I?"

"Sure, love." Gertrude passed over the newborn and Betty carefully set her against her own shoulder patting the infant's back.

"It feels like an age since mine were this small," Betty clucked, breathing in the newborn scent. "She's an absolute doll, Gertie."

"She is that," Gertrude said, a little sadly. "Wouldn't trade any of them for the world. But I can't do it again, I tell you that. We can't afford to feed them as it is."

The baby let out a small burp and Betty cooed at it, delighted.

"I was thinking of gettin' one of them new womb veils they were spouting off about at the new clinic downtown," Gertrude continued, "but Walter won't have a word of it. Thinks it's a sin. He don't like to see me struggle but he sure ain't gonna hold off on pleasing himself to save me from it. I'm only thankful he was off on the boat half the year or I'd have a clear dozen by now." She took another sip of tea, her mouth turned down. "He shipped out of Fort Hamilton last month so I suppose there's no chance I'll be getting pregnant again until the war is over anyway. I won't even mind so much as long as he can keep himself out of the way of the bullets. I'd rather have a hundred kids than lose him altogether." Gertrude let out a sad sigh, then seemed to bolster herself. "It's the way for all of us now, isn't it though. Losing our menfolk but doing our best."

"And what about the older ones, are they any help to you?" Betty asked.

"Jean and Clara are good girls," Gertrude said. "When they're not at school they'll do all sorts to help keep house. Right good little mothers they'll make one day, 'specially Jean. But not before she's married, or I'll have somethin' to say about it."

"And Joseph?"

Gertrude's expression clouded. She held her arms out for the baby and Betty passed Sarah back. "He's giving me a new grey hair every bleedin' day," she said, settling the baby at her other breast. "When Walter got called up it's like Joe turned into a little man overnight. Not in a good way, mind you. Sneaking out at night and skipping school. He was such a good boy before. Now he's gone all cagey and suspicious-like. Turns up with money and won't say where it came from. Lord knows what he's getting up to out there. I think he's fallen in with a bad crowd." The woman's face sagged and she looked tired far beyond her years. "I fished a knife out of his school bag a week ago and cigarettes every other day. And here I am with my hands full and no way of pullin' him home by the ear. I don't know what to do with my Joe. He just won't tell me anything anymore, the little bugger. Thinks he's the man of the house with his dad off in the army." She closed her eyes for a moment, as if drawing strength from the baby. "I'm worried he's going to get himself into trouble."

As if on cue, there was a sudden racket outside the apartment door. It swung open, and the three eldest children spilled in, tattered school bags thrown to the wall. Gertrude raised an eyebrow to Betty as Joseph slipped in last.

"Hello, Mrs. Jones!" Jean and Clara chirped, then descended upon the toddlers and the kitchen respectively.

"Got a kiss for your mother?" Gertrude asked her eldest son. He looked at Betty with shifty eyes then complied, tipped his newsboy cap to Betty, pulling it off his head and stuffing it into his back pocket. "What's that on your fingers?"

Joseph hid his hand, but not before Betty saw the black ink staining them.

"My pen broke again. Here," he said, thrusting the offending hand into his front pocket and pulling out a handful of notes. It's for you."

"Another twenty dollars?" Gertrude's face paled and her eyes were wide. "Where'd you get this, Joe?"

The boy shrugged. "I did a few jobs for one of the dock-workers on my way home yesterday, that's all." Betty felt the lie itching at his conscience. "He's got more work for me too, he says." Joseph gave his mother a wink. "Anyway, I gotta go, Tony's waitin' for me in the boneyard." He ducked past the women and grabbed an apple from the kitchen. Joseph was short for his age, which Betty guessed was about fifteen, and still had the baby-face and dimples that no doubt let him get away with far more than he should.

"I told you not to go in that cemetery," his mother growled. "It's disrespectful."

"I'm only meeting him there," Joe said, jumping over the toddlers to race back to the door. "Besides, no one gives a rats."

"You'd better be home by supper this time, or I won't keep a plate for you," Gertrude said. Her eyes narrowed and she sat forward, baby still attached to her nipple, as if she might jump up and fling the door shut to keep him trapped inside.

"Sure you will, ma," Joe laughed, and took off through the front door again. Gertrude's face burned.

"Little rascal," Betty smiled, trying to soften the blow. She got to her feet and collected the empty teacups, then walked through to the tiny kitchen. Joseph was lying, that was clear enough. But where his sudden windfall had come from, had Betty worried as much as his own mother. It was a quick tumble from mischief into danger when you were out on the streets.

A small window overlooked the courtyard of the tenement complex, where four great brownstone buildings backed up against one another with a communal square of grass between them. Down below, an elevated area of grass was littered with ancient headstones and above ground tombs. Neglected shrubs bordered the outside railings. Between the buildings, swathes of rope were looped from each fire escape to high metal pulleys bolted to the opposite building's façade, crisscrossing the expanse of sky between them like ship sails. A mass flutter of white shirts, trousers and unmentionables flapped in the wind seventy feet above the ground. Soon enough, Betty saw Joe pop out from the ground level and fling himself up and over the wrought iron fence surrounding the graveyard. A tall boy was perched on a concrete tomb, smoking. He waved as Joe appeared. Betty couldn't shake the feeling that the boys were up to no good.

It was the ink that worried her, but first, she needed to be sure of her suspicions. Teenage boys, after all, were frequently into misbehavior of one kind or another. From her vantage point above them, Betty cast out her own mind, so that she might catch the boy's conversation from their thoughts, like scooping fish in a net.

"He wants us on the Bowery tonight," the taller boy was saying. *"You gonna come?"*

There was a little hesitation in Joseph's mind before he answered.

"Course I am. What time?"

"Midnight."

Righto. Joseph dragged his cap from his back pocket, then pulled out a cigarette. He held it up to his friends' and took a drag, scorching it to life.

"We'll go early. Make the quota before we see him. If we don't, we'll cop it."

"Yeah, I know."

"You know what I reckon?"

"What?"

"I reckon he's gonna give us our own corner. You and me and Barney. We can handle it. I think he's seen we're up to the job."

"Yeah, maybe. What if he found out about the slots?"

"How could he?"

"I dunno. But what if he did?"

"Keep your head, Joe. Did you get your knife back?

"Not yet," Joseph said, resentfully. *"She's hidden it. But don't worry, I'll find it by tonight."*

"You better. Come on, let's get crackin'. Time to grease up our fingers."

The boys chuckled and stubbed out their cigarettes. They pushed off the tomb and jumped the wrought iron fence to join the pedestrian traffic of the street below.

Betty turned back to the kitchen and began to wash the

teacups absently. If she was right, and she always was, Joseph was already in over his head.

It was going to be a late night.

***

At eleven o'clock, Betty was waiting in the shadows of the ancient Jewish graveyard. Six floors above her, folds of dirty sheets and a small hand hung over the side of the concrete fire escape platform which was jutting out from the side of the brownstone apartment block. Gertie's apartment. Her half dozen children were sleeping on the fire escape above in their socks and underwear, tucked around each other like spindly jigsaws of hair and elbows, knees bent into spaces between little arms and backs. There was nothing but cold metal rails to keep them from rolling off. Even in the still night air, they would be sweating. Many fire escapes in the old tenement buildings cradled a similar precious cargo. Children escaping the heavy heat, spilled out above the city in slumber. Presently, one of the figures stirred, and Betty watched as Joseph untangled himself from his feigned sleep. Carefully, he stepped over his brothers and sisters and made his way down a half-dozen fire escapes, balancing like a cat along metal railings until he padded lightly to the ground.

He pulled on his cap, then adjusted something under his coat. Joseph took off across the forgotten cemetery, skipped the wrought iron fence and disappeared up the street. Betty was close behind.

She trailed him along St. James Place and turned left into Park Row, hugging the shadows to keep out of sight. Joe merged with a group of revellers as they stumbled between clubs. As he fell in step, the boy smoothly slipped his hand into the overcoat pocket of the man in front of him, slid out a wallet and tucked it into his own. He dodged past a woman who had her arm linked with her beau and apologised profusely as he knocked her off kilter, then turned away with the purse he'd slipped from her handbag.

He's good, Betty thought. Better than I expected.

When she'd seen the ink on his fingers, she knew instantly that Joe had been thieving. It also meant that someone was training him. The more talented the pilferer, the less ink they collect as they insert their fingers into the neck of a milk bottle that had been coated in it to practise. Clean fingers were a sign that the pickpocket was clever enough at it to steal wallets undetected. Someone was recruiting young boys to thieve, and Joseph had been caught up in the game.

"Sugar peanuts, five cents a bag!" screeched a vendor, the wheels of her cart rammed up against the gutter. Betty smiled and passed by.

Pickpockets usually operated in small bands. Betty assumed that Joseph and his friend Tony, along with the third boy they'd mentioned, Barney, had cliqued into such a team. For teamwork it was. While the best boy slipped his fingers into pockets, a second would distract the passers-by. A third boy was waiting to whisk the reward away. Crowded rail stations, busy streets and markets were their hunting ground. But always, there was a bigger picture. Someone pulling strings behind the scenes, allocating corners and terminals to work in, skimming a juicy cut of the steak before paying the boys their due. As Betty followed Joseph into Chinatown, she had her suspicions as to who that might be.

"Joe! Over here," Tony called, straightening up. He was leaning against a pie stall, licking his fingers. In the blaze of streetlights, he was all gangly arms and legs with a long face in that awkward stretch between boy and man. There was an air of nervous excitement about him as he stepped toward his friend and they spoke in low voices. Betty stepped in behind a throng of theater-goers to wait.

"Deadwood Dick!" growled a stout woman in the theatre booth in front of the lobby. "Twenty-five cents a ticket." She was propped up on a pillow-padded chair within the ticket box, her hair blowing back on account of the electric fan on the floor aimed up at her face, which was sagged and pale. Behind her, a stack of paperbacks lined a shelf, beside a rabbit's foot and a rosary.

Betty pulled a dollar from her pocket and handed it over, then waived away the ticket.

"How are things, Maize?" she asked quietly. She adjusted her handbag.

"Oh, alright, love. The usual. What brings you round here at this time 'o night?"

Betty inclined her head slightly toward Joseph and his pal, who were still hustled at the pie stall.

"Oh, them two've been up to no good, alright," Maize scowled. "Sticky fingers."

"Do you know who they're working for?"

Maize laughed. "Who'd'ya think?" Her voice was gravelly and seemed too deep for such a small frame, owning to the cigarette habit that kept her fingers constantly moving. "But they'd better watch themselves, because that rat's getting too big for 'is boots."

"What do you mean?"

"I mean these street urchins he's puppeteering are being weaned onto the hard stuff. And once they're hooked, they're more willing to flash a knife or take a stab to get what they want. Never ends well." She grimaced and shook her head. "Snatchers and muggers next, that's what they'll be. And after that, if they're not killed, I'll be scraping them up off the theatre chairs ev'ry night after they sleep off the booze."

Betty handed over another dollar. Maize stuffed it under a jar to the side of her till, and Betty knew that soon enough it would be passed out to one of the bums searching for a comforting bottle or bed for the night. The middle-aged woman at the ticket box had been a fixture in the Bowery for longer than anyone could remember. Despite her sharp tongue and tough exterior, she was one of the softest hearts Betty knew. There wasn't a breath breathed in Chinatown that Maize couldn't tell where it had blown in from and why.

"Where can I find him?"

Maize fixed Betty with a suspicious glare. "I wouldn't, love. You know what that little git's like."

Betty handed over another dollar. Another bum saved from a night on the streets. When Maize got off her shift, she'd begin her daily rounds, cleaning them up from the pavement and finding flophouses to take them in, usually on her own coin. Betty glanced at the two teenage boys who had begun walking again, bellies full and nerves alight.

"His mother's worried," Betty said. "She's got a newborn you know. And five others. Just putting her mind at ease, darling."

Maize hmphed and rolled her eyes. "Always pulling on my heart strings. Five Points. Try the tunnel under Doyer's. Watch yourself." Maize waved Betty off with a grunt, shaking her head.

Betty scanned the clock in the theatre as she walked past. It was a quarter past eleven, which meant she had forty-five minutes before the boys were due to meet their boss. Forty-five minutes wasn't much time to get to him first. She left the boys and headed back the way she'd come, along Park Row and across to Chatham Square into the Bowery. A few stores along, Betty slipped sideways out of the bright lights of the pedestrian and pickpocketing hustle. It was simply a doorway between closed stores. An unobtrusive hole in the façade of an otherwise unremarkable building. Steps took her down, down, down into a basement tunnel below Chatham Square.

It was time to re-meet an old acquaintance.

Though the infamous Five Points Gang had unraveled since the Prohibition had fallen, her great uncle, Donald Pinzolo and his men had stepped in to take over the territory. It was a family business, of course. And in the case of Chinatown, it was his nephew, Emilio, who had outshone the others in taking the reins. Emilio was the leader of a gang of thieves and professional hustlers in the Five Points neighborhood in Manhattan. Emilio's father, Aldo Pinzolo was Donny's younger brother. Betty had never known him. Aldo had been hit by the Castellano Boys before either she or Emilio could walk. A payback feud had erupted that was still firing over two decades later. It was this gang rivalry that Betty had used to her advantage the night she'd finally escaped Pinzolo's grasp. Her name was Suzie then. The Castellano Boys had been blamed for the murder of her father Roy and the arson that took their home, and presumably killed fifteen-year-old Suzie in the blaze along with it. No one had ever suspected that she had killed her own father in cold blood. Nor, that she had staged her own death. Betty smiled as her heels clicked dully along the tunnel floor.

The walls were concrete, with occasional signs written in Chinese hanging on closed doors that led off on either side into the dark. A flickering lightbulb every few meters gave the place an eerie feel. The tunnel was deserted.

A century of dust and grime coated the floor. The tunnel was a well-kept secret that had offered salvation to gangsters in need of escape for decades. At one end, was the unassuming staircase that Betty had stolen down on Chatham Square. On the other, a hidden flight of stairs up through the Chinese Opera House onto Doyers Street. Straight into The Bloody Angle.

Spurning the immaculate organisation of Manhattan's grid of streets and lots, Doyers Street was a notorious exception. It was a narrow, dogleg curve, buried deep in the heart of China-town between The Bowery and Broadway. Home to gambling houses, prostitution caves and opium dens. The street was noto-rious for gang warfare and criminal activity. Not long ago, the cobblestones had been stained red with blood. It was known by many names past. Murder Alley. Tong War Territory. *The Bloody Angle.* The latter had stuck. And bloody it was.

An almost ninety-degree angle, the road's middle allowed gang members to sneak up on one another unannounced. As one turned the corner, they were accosted with the slashing, stabbing frenzy of their rivals, and fell dead, soaking the road with blood. It was a fight to the death or escape through the tunnel.

Dozens of men had been cut down by hatchets in the Tong Wars, as rival Chinese gangs, the Hip Sings, the Four Brothers and the On Leongs, took upon one another with revenge in their hearts. *Hatchet men,* the term was coined forevermore. In the decade after, the Tong Wars gave way to the Five Point Gang and their Prohibition bootlegging, blackmarket and bullets. When the Eighteenth Amendment was repealed and the ban on alcohol lifted, Pinzolo's mafia of thieves and thugs took up the mantle of violence, with Emilio at the helm. And so, the bloodbath continued. It was old news to Betty. As a child, working for Donny, she'd witnessed the extortion and murders that fed that business. For her, Emilio was just another thug. Another slice of cake to cut away to crumble Donald Pinzolo's empire.

Betty crept along the tunnel. The walls were grey and oppressing, plastered with a history soaked in blood. Each locked door Betty passed, felt stuffed to bursting with old secrets and interconnected tunnels. A maze of dark opportunity. She crept on.

A dim light was shining from under one of the office doors.

Whispers. Betty pressed herself against the wall for a moment, listening. She threw out her mind to catch them.

"You been short-changing me, Hitch?"

"No boss, I wouldn't do that. I swear."

"That's not what I heard."

"I dunno what ya mean. I swear I ain't done nothing."

"Yeah? 'Cause Magsy says different. I gave you these slots because I thought I could trust you. I'm missing two hundred since last week. Where's it gone?"

"It wasn't me, honest."

"A nickel here, a nickel there. Emilio's not gonna find out, is what what you thought, Hitch? You think I'm some dumb meatball? That I don't have eyes on my own game?"

"No way, man, I didn't think that. Magsy's giving' me the bum rap! I gave him the takings, I swear. Every slot at the Quail."

"I don't believe you." There was a squeak of fright. The cock of a hammer. "I've warned you about this before. I already caught you with your fingers in the cookie jar last year. I told you what would happen –"

"This is different! Please, no please! It ain't just me this time. You're lookin' at the wrong guy!" There was a thud and a scuffle. "Please! Boss! It wasn't me. Let me – let me – wait, I got somethin' for ya, okay?"

"You gonna squeal now?"

"Sure, sure. It was them young one's that started it. That Cole kid, and the stretch. The ones you're training up in the square. It was their idea."

"The new kids?" There was a pause as Emilio drank in this new information.

"Yeah, he's brass as buttons that baby-face. A real cheek. They been comin' with me to do the pickup. He said his old lady needed clams real bad and he was gonna make it up on the street once you gave him his own corner. Pay it back, you know. I didn't wanna do it, boss, but I felt sorry for the kid. I thought he'd pay it back before ya noticed."

"You thought wrong, Hitch."

Crack. Thud.

The man called Hitch was dead. Betty closed her eyes. Her second cousin, Emilio, had always been hot-headed with an itchy trigger-finger. Standing only five-foot-five, he compensated for his bruised ego with a violent temper. His reputation for brutality had made him the perfect enforcer for Donny's business. Just like her own father, Roy.

Act first. Don't ask questions later.

A third voice spoke up. It was calm. Measured.

"We were gonna give that kid his own corner tonight, boss. He's been doing real good with the thievin'. He's a natural."

"That right? Where is he?"

"He's comin' in at midnight with the tall kid and the dumb one. The three of them make a good team. I been showin' him the ropes, but he's got it down pat. Kid's got charm, and stretch is quick. Dumbo's the lookout. I was gonna give them Chatham Square for a few months. Move the others downtown."

"Yeah? Well, plans have changed. I'm not having some smart-ass rookie takin' me for a ride. Next thing he'll be in cahoots with the Castellano's to put a bullet in my back."

"He ain't gonna do that, Emilio, I swear. The kid's not bad. He's got sticky fingers, that's all. Just teach him a lesson."

Smash! Something heavy shattered across the concrete.

"You know what 'd happen if I let him get away with this? They'll all be doing' it. Takin' me for a ride. They'll lose respect. And then what?"

"Okay. Let me rough him up a little. It was the other kid too, I think, they both need a good shake up. I'll get the lettuce off them and bring them down a peg."

"No, I'm gonna deal with this myself. Go find the kid. Bring him in."

"You're not gonna top 'im are ya, boss? The kid's alright —"

"What did I say?" Emilio growled. There was another thud. *"And get this stiff out of my way."*

A shuffle of feet. Betty turned and ducked up the tunnel, pulling two hairpins from her long Victory Rolls as she moved. She stretched one out, then bent the end of it up like a hook, folding the other over itself in half. Using the bent hairpin for tension, she inserted the hook into the lock of the next doorway. One by one she maneuvered the internal binding pins into place. *Click.* The door swung open. Betty slipped inside. Footsteps. A shadow passed by. The associate was gone.

Betty let herself out of the room. Her right-side garter was tight, steel bound by lace. She pressed the warm knife against her thigh as she walked. Comforting.

Click. Click. Click.

Betty quietly let herself into the room. Emilio had his back to her. He was sitting at a table. Pencil in his hand. A ledger in front of him. He had always been good with figures. Piles of bound greenbacks were on the desk. *Blood money.* The boys had chosen a bad person to steal from.

"Good evening, Emilio."

He spun around.

At the sight of her, his guard dropped. *Just a broad,* he thought.

"Who are you?" He glanced at the body slumped against the wall, thinking fast.

"Less than a memory," said Betty. She locked the door behind her. Slipped her handbag off her shoulder and dropped it neatly onto a box.

"What's that supposed to mean?" Emilio got to his feet, the chair scraping from under him. Betty glanced about the room. They were alone, with the exception of the snitch, who was dead.

"Using children as pickpockets, Emilio? *Tsk. Tsk.* That seems a little unsophisticated for a cat like you."

He stepped forward. Scraped her body with his eyes. "You been following me, lady?" he asked, chin lifting. He chuckled, uneasy. Betty felt his thoughts whirring. *The body against the wall. An unexpected witness. But she's not scared. Is she one of ours? Is she with the kids?* Emilio's right hand ghosted the pocket of his overcoat. A Colt .38 Super Automatic was buried deep inside the wool. "So what if I am? What are you – their mom?"

"Goodness no," Betty purred. "I'm a mother, yes, but not *theirs*." Disarming him with her smile.

"Who are you, then?"

"Ooh, what a fun game. Let's see," Betty began to count on her fingers, grinning broadly as she moved closer. "I'm the neighborhood Avon Lady. I'm a devoted wife. I'm President of the Marigold Church Social Committee – I take my charity work *very seriously*. I'm a mother, as you know – perhaps I should have said that one first –" Betty stopped, tapping her fourth finger. Immaculate painted nails gleamed cherry red under the bulb buzzing from the ceiling. "Mmm," she mused, lightly. "Now what was that other one? I'm sure there were five strings to my bow..."

Emilio stepped forward, not sure what to make of the beautiful woman that had stepped so assuredly into his lair. They were the same age, the same height. His tightly curled hair matched Betty's in color. A trifling family resemblance that Betty wished were not there.

"Ah yes, of course," she said, as if it had just occurred to her. "I'm a 'Lady Vigilante' as well. I really must type up some business cards."

"A lady what?" The corner of his lips curled. "What is this? Some kind of joke?"

"*Vigilante,* darling. A little sideline to my charity work. I lend a hand to the unfortunate wretches that can't defend themselves against people like you."

"That right?" Emilio slipped his hand into his coat pocket. He kept it there, curled around the revolver he had inside. Betty heard the hammer cock. Still, he didn't strike. "I know you, don't I?" he said slowly. Somewhere inside, he struck the right memory. "You're Uncle Roy's girl," he said suddenly. "That's who you are! Suzie Polletti!"

"Suzie Polletti?" Betty shook her head and dropped her counting hand. "No, that's one person I'm not. Not anymore."

"You are!" He exclaimed victoriously. He stabbed his finger toward her. "That's who you are! You were always in Donny's warehouse. Always at his side. I remember you now."

Betty smiled and slipped closer.

"I won't deny that I *used* to be that girl, but not anymore."

"They told me you died."

"Oh, I did."

"Doesn't look like it to me," His eyes narrowed as he pieced it together. "Donny was real cut up about it too. So what? You ran away, is that it? Too good for us, little Suzie?"

"I do wish people would stop calling me that."

"The one who got away..."

"Not far enough, I'm afraid," Betty sighed, theatrically. "It seems everywhere I turn, some little shadow of my past is there to haunt me."

"And that's me, is it?" He pulled his hand out of his pocket. Revolver raised.

"I'm afraid so." Betty looked over at the body slumped against the wall. Arms curled underneath him, face down. A black fedora thrown onto his back, like a pile of trash waiting to be picked up. Another one for the Hudson or Dead Horse Bay. She stepped past Emilio, taking no heed of the gun in his hand and ran her nails lightly down the ledger. "I recall you were quite good at mathematics in your younger days." Neat lines of calculations covered the page. Weekly takings from his network of thieving, gambling dens and protection rackets. The symmetry was lovely. *So organized. So clever.* Betty shook her head. "Such a shame you didn't pursue it in a less –" she glanced again at Hitch's corpse – "*blood-thirsty* manner."

She felt the cold muzzle of the revolver press into the back of her head. Apparently, Emilio had decided her opinions were unwelcome.

Smack! Betty spun around, her forearm up and ready. It slammed into the Colt. The gun spun across the room and hit the concrete wall above Hitch's body.

Bang! The bullet discharged as it hit. A puff of concrete dust spat from the ceiling above their heads. Betty ducked as Emilio's fist struck out. She swung her arm into his waist and forced him against the desk. He was bent backwards, arms flailing. Betty forced herself over him.

Crack! Her fist claimed his jaw.

Emilio recoiled. The back of his head smacked the desk and his eyes rolled back in his head. He slid sideways, dragging his bookwork off the desk as he fell, spilling papers and bundles of money to the floor.

"Christ!" He groaned, scrambling on his hands and knees, slipping on the sheathes underfoot. "What the hell, you crazy bitch?!"

"Sorry darling," Betty grinned, standing over him, "did you not expect a lady to fight back?"

"Aaargh!" Emilio stood, then ran at her full pelt, red-faced. He grabbed Betty's throat, forcing her back. They scuffled, punching and stumbling toward the wall.

Crack! An uppercut to the jaw and Betty's head spun. White sparks flew behind her eyelids.

Thud! Betty's head smacked against the concrete. She stumbled sideways, the soft body of Hitch underfoot.

"Now, I've got you." With a malicious grin, and one hand at her throat, Emilio slipped the toe of his two-toned wing-tip under the revolver that had landed to rest on an angle against the prone arm of Hitch at his feet. Deftly, he flicked it up with his shoe, catching the gun in his free hand. He pushed his weight into Betty, forcing her back against the concrete wall.

Click. He cocked the hammer. Pressed the steel into her chest.

"You should have stayed in the kitchen, *mom.*"

Smash! Betty head flung forward, smashing Emilio's forehead with her own. He ricocheted backwards, falling to the floor.

"And you should mind your manners!" Betty seethed. She threw herself on top of him. Ferocious fists flew both ways as Emilio clung to the gun, and Betty tried to screw it out of his grip. She sat astride him, pulled his head up and smashed it back down onto the concrete floor. Despite the blow, Emilio kept brawling, his eyes aflame and teeth bared.

He threw her over and they rolled. Betty grappled for the revolver and knocked him back, forcing him onto his stomach. She wrenched his gun hand behind his back and sat on him, ripping the Colt from his fingers. Finally, he stopped still, heaving for breath.

"Why?" He coughed. He began to tremble.

And there it is, Betty thought. *The 'Why?'* As if a decade of murder wasn't enough of a reason to end it. She leant forward, letting her breath ghost his ear.

"For the boy, Joe Cole. And whoever comes after him and whoever came before." Betty pulled the trigger, into Emilio's back, straight through his heart. And he lay still.

Betty got up, dusted herself off and pushed a tendril of escaped hair back into her Victory Roll. *I didn't even need to dirty my knife.*

"A bullet in your back," she said, wryly. "Perhaps it was the Castellano Boys again, after all." She stepped aside and picked up Emilio's pencil and ledger book that had been knocked to the floor. Betty pushed the ledger down on the desk, flicked through to a clean page and tore it out.

She looked up. Her hand suddenly frozen. There were footsteps outside, getting closer. Time had run away from her. The associate was back with the boys he had been sent to fetch.

Betty scanned the room, then bent over the desk and scribbled a note.

. . .

Go home, boys. Keep your noses clean. Consider this a warning.

Betty dropped the note onto Emilio's back. It was a little direct perhaps, considering she had no intention of harming them. *But shielding the boy from the truth will do him no favors*, Betty thought. *On the other hand, the fright may be enough to scare him away for good.*

She sprang up and scanned the room. The doorknob rattled.

"'Lio, it's me," growled a voice from the other side. "Lemme in."

A tall bookshelf caught her eye. Or rather, the edge of it. It was pushed up against a wall, heavy with old objects that held a thick layer of dust. Behind it, was the frame of a long-forgotten door. Betty ran forward, grabbed the bookcase with both hands and pushed with all her strength.

The doorknob rattled again and the associate hit the door with his fist.

"Emilio? I got the boys."

Crash! The bookcase came down, heavy timber splitting as it caught the adjacent wall in a shower of wrought iron and china, old fabric and dusty books. The tunnel shuddered.

"Emilio!" The associate was shouting now. Pounding on the door with his fist. Within ten seconds, a bullet would break open the lock and he would come flying in to find Betty standing over his boss's dead body. Ten seconds was more than she needed.

Betty pounced, grabbed the bundles of cash. Stuffed them into her handbag. She tore open the hidden door she had spied behind the bookcase and ran through it, slamming it shut behind her. Through the next door, and the next, in the pitch dark. Dust and haunted whispers stirred and danced as she raced through the tunnel. The walls did their job. Another fugitive escaped. Another secret kept.

Within minutes Betty emerged from the staircase deep within the Chinese Opera House. Stole through and melted into the seedy crowd shadowing Doyers Street. She slipped boldly through the Bloody Angle and whisked away. By the time the associate and his teenage proteges discovered Emilio's body, her warning note and the secret door, Betty was back in the crowds of the Bowery, casually strolling past the theater with a smile, handbag tucked tightly under her arm.

***

It was two weeks later that Betty had seen Joseph again. Another sweltering summer's day. She had come to deliver a basket of groceries to Gertrude, and to deliver a message to the boy. An hour of wandering along the Bowery first, browsing and delighting in the shops and stalls with little Georgie Junior, had put her in an excellent mood. A *two-scoops of ice-cream at the parlor* type of mood. With his treat dripping down his hand, her four-year-old son had been barely contained with excitement at the sight of the street-sellers shouting and singing their wares as they passed. Later, the lady selling corn-on-the-cob had given him an extra buttery one, and as they'd passed the theater, Maize had waved and smiled at them.

They'd purchased from a salesman with a rope of whisk brooms slung over his shoulder and his apron turned up in sewn pockets to keep change. Georgie had played hopscotch outside Senior Fabio's Fat Men's Shop, in front of an enormous painting of a portly man in his underwear on the brick façade, and beneath an even bigger advertisement for Extra Dry Beer. He had played marbles with some local boys while Betty shopped at Mr. Lim's Greengrocers, and petted a stray cat outside the milk depot. By the time Betty had reached Chatham

III

Square to visit Gertrude, her basket was twice as full, and Georgie's legs very tired.

As they rounded the corner, her son's energy had miraculously renewed. An eight-foot water sprinkler had been erected in the street, sending a shower of cool water onto the hot pavement. Two dozen children were stripped down to their underclothes and swimsuits, hands joined in a great ring, circling it like a maypole. They shouted and danced as the sprinkler rained down on them and it took only one pleading look before Georgie had flung off his shoes to join them.

Betty had found Gertie sitting on the front steps of her tenement building, bouncing her newborn on her knee. Six of her seven children were under the water, and Betty was surprised to see Joseph included, kicking around the edge of it with a few of his friends. Betty sat down and swapped her basket of groceries for a hold of the baby.

"How are you, darling?" she cooed, both to Gertie and baby Sarah at once.

"Pushin' on, Betty," Gertie said. "I got four hours of sleep in a row last night, that's a new record for this little bunny." The lines on her face were softened by sunlight. She beamed down at her children, watching them play.

"And Joseph?"

Gertrude turned to look at Betty. "You wouldn't believe it, but he's come good. He's quit working for whoever it was down at the docks, and besides the lost pay, I'm not complaining. He was up to no good, Betty, I can feel it in me bones. Now he's home ev'ry afternoon and helpin' with the housework an' all. Not a toe out'ta line. I don't know what changed 'is mind, but I'm pleased as punch about it."

"He's a good boy," Betty said. "Perhaps he just needed to remember it. You know, I was talking to Mrs. Levinsky at the bakery on Pearl Street yesterday – she's one of my Avon clients you know – and she said they're looking for a boy to help in the store. Saturdays and every other afternoon after school, for thirty cents an hour. I remembered how good your young Joe is with people and thought it might be just the ticket for him. Do you think he'd be willing?"

"Oh yes," Gertie said, looking across at her son. "I think he'd jump at the chance. I'm not gonna pretend we couldn't do with the money, either."

"Wonderful! Well, I told her Joe was the perfect boy for it. Let him know to call on her after school tomorrow. She'll be expecting him."

"I'll do that, thanks Betty."

"A problem shared is a problem halved, dear. Remember that."

They'd sat there for another hour chatting before Georgie had finally worn himself out, and Betty had carried him to the subway and home.

Betty brushed off the newly stitched mattress, shaking the memories out of her head. Joseph had done well at the bakery, and soon left school to take up an apprenticeship there. Baby Sarah was now over a year old. The cash she had taken from Emilio's lair that night, was still safely stitched into Georgie's mattress.

Emilio's network of thieves and thugs had been frayed, but not unraveled. There was plenty more work to do before she could allow herself a reprieve from the work she was now bound to with an almost religious zeal. She had accomplished a great deal in only one year, but she had barely scratched the surface of Donald Pinzolo's empire. The blood money she stitched into their beds while her children played, was a drop in the ocean.

Betty picked up her son's teddy bear and popped it on his pillow, then left with his dirty clothes basket under her arm.

A few minutes later, with the washing machine swishing and a platter of sandwiches, desserts and a jug of home-made lemonade in her hands, Betty joined her family outside. It was a beautiful spring day. Betty laid a picnic table where George read, as neighbors greeted each other over fences and children whizzed past on bikes. George was still reading his paper in a porch swing chair as the children rolled and giggled on the grass. It was pure, perfect domestic bliss. Betty hummed happily to the melody on the radio through the kitchen window.

"Your kisses are the sweetest things -" she sang along, twirling to get George's attention to feed him a sandwich.

George looked up at her with a wary smile. Betty beamed. The Frank Polletti job had been a setback. It had been too messy, and George had become suspicious at her absence from the dancefloor at the Capitol Jazz Club. Her husband had been unusually quiet since, and Betty was determined to entirely win him back from his doubts.

"What a perfect day, George dear!" she said. "Isn't it marvelous?"

"Every day is perfect with you, jitterbug," he replied. He caught her hand, looking anxious. "You are happy, love, aren't you? We have a good life, don't we?"

"The very best, George. All I've ever wanted is this perfect life you've given me."

His brow furrowed. "This old flat tire isn't holding you back then?"

"Never dear," Betty said. "I'd follow you to the ends of the earth."

George smiled and reached up to trace her face gently with his thumb. "And I'd carry you home again. What more could a kitten ask for, hey?"

"Not a thing, dear. In fact, perhaps," she added, lowering her voice to a whisper and leaning into him, "we can push the beds together again tonight?" Betty rose an eyebrow suggestively. "I'll put aside your lucky tie."

"You'll be the death of me!" he exclaimed with a broad smile.

"I certainly hope I'm not, darling."

"I knew I married the right girl," George laughed, giving her a light tap on the backside. Betty giggled and kissed him with genuine affection.

George, seemingly supplicated, returned his attention to his paper. Betty stepped over to finish the picnic and watch the children play. Her smile dropped immediately. George's words rung in her ears, but not for the reason he intended. *You'll be the death of me.* A darkness of mood fell upon her as she mulled those words over. Uncle Frank had been a symptom, just like her father and the many conspirators that swept a seething tide of violence underneath the city. Blackmail, addiction and death were their favorite side-effects. Treating the symptoms was all well and good, but to have a clean and healthy life, to have a *perfect* life, you had to remove the disease itself. And in this case, the disease was Donny. Donald Pinzolo, her father's cousin and boss of the family business for the past thirty years. Not an easy disease to eradicate, bound up as he was in political webs, dark business and silent watchmen. She'd been sloppy with Frank. It was time to play smart.

Betty began serving food distractedly as she watched the children run back and forth laughing.

"I'll do anything to keep our perfect life safe," she muttered. Her voice turned bitter and her features set as hard as ice. "Anything."

George looked up from his paper with a smile. "What's that, Jitterbug?"

Betty raised the enormous, gleaming silver knife in her hand and quickly plastered a bright smile back onto her face.

"Nothing dear. Cake?"

"Chocolate cake, sonny?" asked a portly woman in a black and white serving outfit to a freckled nosed boy sniffing around the table. In an expansive park in an otherwise derelict, industrial part of town, an elaborately laid picnic table was the center of attention for two hundred of the city's most influential guests. A fancy white marquee decorated with balloons and ribbons housed a packed dance floor and swinging jazz band, all enjoying the spectacle of an afternoon celebration in the sun. The boy took the plate from the serving woman greedily and ran back to his friends who were kicking a ball across the grass with none other than Mr. Donald Pinzolo himself. The man was putting in a good effort, despite the extra weight and more than sixty years he carried under his belt. He laughed as he gave a good-natured clap to the shoulders of a slightly awe-struck teenage boy who'd kicked a goal. The press lapped it up, flashing their cameras and scribbling into notepads, fighting each other for the best angle and biggest smile.

Government officials and businessmen were milling around with champagne and pork sandwiches, discussing current state of affairs with their chests puffed out in as much importance as they could manage. The press junket boasted an odd mix of poor and rich. The former were the residents of St. Augustine's Home for Unwanted Boys, an orphanage which rose in half-dilapidated splendor behind the marquee. Workmen and machinery scurried to and fro on the renovation site, painting and plastering under orders from the site manager to put on a good show.

A tall man with keen eyes and quick movements stepped up to a podium as the band finished. He waved away the applause that began for him.

"As Mayor of New York City, I'd like to welcome you to this auspicious occasion - a happy day for the many boys here today,

as well as we folks who care so deeply for their future." He let
the applause come this time, smiling broadly for the press that
had situated themselves in front of the podium. "Now, a little
over a year ago," the Mayor continued, "I received a proposal on
my desk that I knew would make a big difference to our city.
And not just because it came from a darb who can always be
counted on to pay the check!" He chuckled along with the scattered laughter from the crowd below him. "No, the offer to fix up
St Augustine's orphanage came from a big heart. A heart willing
to make a difference to our community. A businessman with his
finger on the pulse of our city. A family man with strong values
and a legacy to continue like his father before him. As the mayor
of New York City, I take great pleasure in expanding our partner-
ship with Mr. Donald Pinzolo." The Mayor gestured to the sixty-
something man who was holding a soccer ball behind the gathered crowd. "Donny," said the Mayor, "If you can join us now
and leave the fun to the kids -" the crowd laughed. Donald
Pinzolo, tossed the ball to one of the orphans he'd been playing
with and winked in good humor. He made his way through the
guests wiping sweat from his brow, playing to the crowd and
waving for the cameras. Two men in dark suits followed close
behind him.

The Mayor stepped away from the microphone enthusiastically and leaned forward to embrace his investor with a handshake and friendly slap on the back.

"Lose the gunsels, Pinzolo. It looks bad for the press," the
Mayor muttered through a frozen smile.

Pinzolo glanced to his offsiders. With the tiniest switch of his
head, the men stepped back immediately into the crowd.
Pinzolo took his place up to the podium.

"Kind words, Mayor Sutherland, kind words. There's
nothing more important to me, than giving today's youth something to look forward to, a life of opportunity. So as part of my
commitment as benefactor to the St Augustine's New York City

Orphanage I'll be personally ensuring that each boy gets an apprenticeship within my business network and gets the chance to contribute to the growth of this great city of ours. One day, I'm sure, they'll make fine fathers for a new generation of Americans." Donald Pinzolo smiled, then paused. His mouth dropped to a woeful expression. "Now, with Uncle Sam doing his part to keep our good country safe, we all have to pull our socks up to support our boys on the front. I know what it's like to lose a son, my own boy Marco was taken from me only months ago in an accident," he paused for a moment with his eyes cast down. "Our young men are more important now than ever before, and these orphaned kids have no one looking out for them. So, I'm going to pay the checks that need to be paid," a small wink went to the Mayor, "to mold a new generation of New York's finest under my own men."

A hearty round of applause followed as Mayor Sutherland and Pinzolo cut a symbolic ribbon circling a model of the renovated building.

"Now, please folks," Pinzolo announced, stepping back in front of the microphone, "enjoy yourselves at my expense!"

Another round of applause, laughter and champagne began flowing. Spectators dispersed into conversation as Pinzolo and the Mayor posed for photographs shaking hands. After a few minutes, they disengaged and began their individual ministrations through the crowd.

A heavyset man in a dark suit approached Pinzolo. He was one of the two that had been guarding him earlier. A jagged scar was left where the top of his right ear had once been. The man leant forward and whispered something to his boss, whose eyes narrowed. He gave the guard a curt nod and then watched him walk away through the crowd. Through a forest of faces, Pinzolo caught the eye of Mayor Sutherland who was engaged in conversation with an enthusiastic woman wearing gaudy pink. The Mayor raised an eyebrow at the guard's departure and Pinzolo returned him a meaningful look, tipping his champagne glass with a smirk. They both turned away and the band struck up a new tune.

💋

"Are you warm enough?" Jacob asked with a slight frown. "It's unseasonably cool tonight."

"That's the third time you've asked since I arrived," Adina replied, laughing. "You needn't worry, really, I'm a big girl-" but Jacob had already taken off his coat to drape across her shoulders. His fingers brushed the bare skin of her collarbone, and he stepped back, shoving his hands quickly into his pockets. Adina straightened the jacket over her velvet evening dress and short-sleeved shrug, careful not to dislodge the matching navy crocheted calot pinned to her hair.

"I don't bite, you know," Adina teased gaily, bumping her arm gently against him. They continued walking, navigating the pedestrian traffic of Seventh Avenue toward the Roxy Theatre.

"I'm sorry," Jacob smiled, "It's not often I get to take a beautiful woman out to dinner, and to be honest, I'm hopelessly out of practice. If you were a mugger or a scoundrel this would be much easier on me."

Adina's face lit up, then she pursed her lips in mock consideration. "Well perhaps I ought to steal something," she said, stopping by the windowpane of a jeweler. "I'm happy to become a petty thief to put your nerves at rest, in fact I could use a new watch anyway. Let's see, that one there perhaps," she said. She pointed at a square faced lapel-brooch hanging from delicate gold loops under an ornamental bow. "Practical *and* fashionable! What could be better?"

"It *is* very nice," Jacob said, "and I'll admit your mug shot would be far prettier than those I usually have to take, but I'm sure your mother wouldn't thank me for it when she bailed you out tomorrow morning."

"My mother would manage just fine, Jacob." Adina looked at him sideways, a little smile playing on her lips. "I was surprised you asked me out actually," she said, "given the lack of subtlety she displayed at dinner the other night. She's about ready to marry me off to the highest bidder. Most men would run a mile."

"She was rather enthusiastic, wasn't she?" Jacob chuckled.

"Yes, well, I've often wished for a brother or sister purely to share that enthusiasm," Adina said, with a small sigh. "I'm afraid she's taken up finding me a husband as a permanent vocation in life. I long for the days she used to play bridge, instead. Far less pressure."

Jacob laughed. "So you're not keen on her efforts so far?"

"Goodness, no. Although I have high hopes for this evening, of course."

"I'll do my best to live up to them, then," said Jacob. "Now the pressure is on me."

Adina hooked his arm playfully. "Not really. I just enjoy toying with Ima's fears, and she knows it," she said. "She also knows I'll settle down when I'm good and ready. The thing is, I really love my job and I'm not quite ready to give that up yet. Shocking, isn't it?"

"Shocking?" Jacob said. "Of course not. You're a modern woman. I wouldn't expect my wife to give up work immediately, unless we had children to care for -" Jacob stopped dead in his tracks, his face red. "That is - I didn't mean that *you'll* be my wife, or that - I'm not saying I wouldn't want you to be," he stammered, "or that you would want to be anyway, or that *we* should have children, I just meant - oh geez, I told you I was no good at this." Jacob looked around frantically, as if searching for a mugger to save himself from the situation.

By now, Adina was laughing so hard she nearly fell. "Stop, truly! You're the funniest thing. Of course I know what you meant. Don't worry, I'm not taking that as a proposal. You're still safe!" Jacob's embarrassed relief melted into laughter as well, and they stood for a moment, bound by the awkward connection with wide, silly smiles. Finally, Adina looped her arm through his again, and they continued walking.

"I did warn you," Jacob said.

"I'll filter everything you say," she said, "No getting married on the first date."

"Thank you," he said. "And I'll try to keep my foot out of my mouth."

"A perfect arrangement. Is this where we're going?" Adina said, stopping in front of the theater.

"It is," said Jacob. He patted his pockets then looked to her helplessly. "I'm afraid our tickets are in my coat." Adina shrugged it off her shoulders and passed the coat over with a smile.

"Voila'!" he said, pulling two tickets from the pocket. "I hope you like Don Ameche. My officer, Parker, suggested this film, he's rather a buff when it comes to theater. You wouldn't know it to look at him. Apparently, his girl insists on going once a month. He saw this one last week and said it was hilarious."

"I'm looking forward to it," Adina said. "Although, it's Gene Tierney I like. I saw her in Thunderbirds last year. She's absolutely divine." Her eyes wandered the Grand Foyer as they entered a milling crowd. The mezzanine was a masterpiece of marble columns and golden décor, attended by a half dozen ushers in crisp uniforms and courteous military bearings. A musician played a pipe organ to patrons as they sipped champagne and chatted in gowns and suits. An enormous oval rug spanned the floor in richly woven designs of blood red and each pillar framed carved statues in filigree painted alcoves. A night at the Roxy wasn't simply an evening out; it was a rare opportunity to put aside the shortages of war and indulge.

"It's nice to be out," Adina remarked. "Everybody seems so

happy. Sometimes I forget that life goes on outside of the office. I get used to war talk all the time; logistics and ships, troops and rationing. It's nice to forget about it for one night."

"It certainly is. Although I find it hard to forget, anytime. Especially the rationing. I'm lucky I have money enough to get by, but in my line of work I see a lot of people that don't. It was hard enough for them before the war."

Adina shook her head, sympathetically. "Everyone's doing their best to help out though. Meatless Tuesdays, Wheatless Wednesdays, that sort of thing."

"True enough," Jacob said, stepping up to the bar. "It helps, I suppose. Ima's planted a victory garden in the backyard. She says she's got more vegetables than she knows what do with. She's pickling them and giving them to all the neighbors and friends at the synagogue. She's always had a green thumb, though, which is lucky, because my father could kill a cactus through neglect."

"Oh, that was your mother? I found a jar of pickles in our cupboard yesterday. No vinegar - I was surprised because my mother said they were Kosher, but she doesn't have any cucumbers growing herself. I'll have to ask your mother for the recipe."

"Yes, that sounds like hers. I'm surprised a jar of cucumbers made it out though, usually my father steals all those ones on the sly. Champagne?" Jacob offered as he paid the barman, and Adina took the elegant crystal flute.

"They're making it here in New York, now, did you know?" Adina said, taking a sip. "California, too. Different grapes for different climates, but it's cheaper than shipping it in from France, apparently."

"Is that right?"

"Yes, I heard about it at work. The girls were complaining it wasn't as nice, but I don't taste the difference. What are you having?"

"Rum. Not my favorite, but it's bearable with Coca-Cola. I

prefer whisky, but it's almost impossible to get these days. The distilleries have been repurposed to make torpedo fuel."

"Surely you know some shady characters in your line of work? I'm sure you could find whisky if you really wanted it."

Jacob laughed. "I do know plenty of shady characters, but none I'd want a favor from. I'd never have the opportunity to drink it anyway. I'm always working."

"So am I. You know what?" Adina's eyes shone and she leant in a little closer. "Perhaps we ought to change that." Stretching forward onto her toes, she kissed Jacob gently on the side of his mouth.

Jacob stopped still. He closed his eyes for a moment as she pulled away. *How many years had it been?*

"I haven't overdone it, have I?" Adina said. "Shocked you too much? I could always steal your wallet so you feel more comfort- able-" She looked down toward his pockets with one eyebrow raised.

Jacob laughed and lifted her chin with his finger. Their eyes met and hers were dancing under the glittering chandeliers. "On second thought, I think there are enough scoundrels in my life right now. Shock me all you like." He bent quickly and kissed her once more.

The evening show began in splendor as they took their seats for the film. The theater itself was lavish and elegant, with soaring Spanish-inspired cathedral ceilings and intricate embellishments on every surface. A 110-piece orchestra pit sprang to life. Pipes and strings, brass and percussion rose in a sweeping harmonic as the Roxyettes took to the stage in a line of feathers and glitter. They were the most famous precision dancers in the country, and world renowned. Jacob had seen them perform twice before, but each week at the Roxy brought a new routine and pre-show lineup that took the audience's breath away. As they spun and kicked for a final time, they split away to reveal Vilaro and Ysabelle center-stage, who danced the riveting tango for which they were acclaimed. Juan Vilaro lifted his wife effortlessly and spun her upside down, then sent her flying across the stage where she landed on one knee with the other leg extended beneath the tassels of her sparkling red dress. The crowd roared with approval and they took their bow, quickly replaced by Jerry Colacci, the Master of Ceremonies for the evenings' spectacle.

"Good evening, folks!" He bowed extravagantly to their applause, "Would you believe last night I got out of bed, tripped over the bathroom mat and knocked myself silly? It was my darkest hour." His walrus-sized handlebar mustache and pop-eyed expression had the audience in stitches before he even hit the punchline. "Luckily my wife turned on the light!"

"We'd had canned tuna again for dinner - fresh fish is slippery to get a hold of these days. Say, what did the fish say when it swam into a wall?" He looked eagerly past the dazzling lights into the front row of seats, searching for any takers. "Damn!" he exclaimed, and the audience guffawed. Jacob laughed heartily, and felt Adina slip her hand into his. He squeezed it gently.

The comedian suddenly took on a somber tone and shook his head sadly, "But seriously, folks, the war has certainly taken its toll on all of us. I was thinking only the other day how an empty champagne bottle is much like an orphan – they've both lost their pop!" Amidst groans and laughter, the man dashed about on the stage, reeling jokes and anecdotes with fantastic zeal until the audience were breathless. When at last the red velvet curtains parted to reveal the movie screen and Colacci said his goodbyes, Adina and Jacob felt as if they'd already been served their full nights' entertainment. An usherette passed by with a tray of sweets, and they settled back into their seats to watch *Heaven Can Wait* with ice-cream, popcorn and a thrill that was owed to more than the entertainment alone. Jacob looked surreptitiously at his date's profile in the flickering darkness of the theater. *There was something a bit different about this one.*

"I'm losing patience here, boys," said the man with the scar-torn ear. "You know I don't like the smell of this place."

"Too much piss," scoffed his offsider.

The scarred man scowled. "Too many stripers."

He kicked one of the two chairs he stood behind and the man strapped into it whimpered. His pants were wet. Beside him, a second man's eyes darted between his captors. Both hostages had been severely beaten and were beyond struggling. The industrial warehouse they were trapped in was military property. It was past three in the morning, and the transport and storage facility was deserted, but for these two unlucky workers. There had been military guards of course, but they'd been swiftly dispatched at the entrance with a round of bullets. Two more goons were guarding the warehouse door. One sucked food from his teeth disinterestedly while the other watched him in disgust.

"I swear, I swear to God, Felix, we got nothing to do with this shit. We're sending the trucks out, just like we're 'sposed to!" the second hostage cried.

"That right?" said Felix, scratching the edge of his half-ear with a knife.

"Yeah! No one has the route but you. The papers come in from up high, I copy 'em for you and then pass 'em onto the drivers, just like you told me to."

"Just like I told you to?"

"Yeah, boss, for sure!"

"Mmm," said Felix. His lips twitched dangerously, but his voice was slow and steady. "So how is it boys, that someone's beating us at our own game?" He walked behind the men. "What do you think, Carl?"

Felix's off-sider chuckled and flicked out a knife. He began to pick his fingernails with it.

"How is it then," Felix continued, "that every time we jump a gig, some fucking wise guy turns up and steals all our shit? The bennies, the fet. All of it. Then kills our boys and gets away without leaving so much as a whiff."

Carl laughed darkly and cut in, pushing one of the hostage chairs back with the sole of shoe and leaning in to the terrified man's face. Felix narrowed his eyes, irritated.

"We're not getting' paid for all our hard work, see?" Carl growled. "Killin' GI's aint a pleasure cruise. Sam's sending more of 'em each time and we got nothing to show for it. We've lost good men to whoever you're selling us out to."

"- And I don't like being double-crossed," Felix cut back in, kicking the hostage chair forward again in line with the other.

Carl grinned and settled back on a table, swinging his legs gleefully. "Someone's got a blabber mouth, boys."

The second hostage shook his head so hard he almost tipped over. "It wasn't us, I swear!" He looked earnestly to Felix. "We never told anyone, on my mother's grave!"

"Your mother was a whore," Carl snapped back. His eyes gleamed. The man was unhinged. "I reckon' we make tiger meat of 'em."

"Please, no!" cried the first hostage.

Felix turned to his partner. "Shut it, Carl," he said. The scarred man then stood, staring at the two hostages, dispassionately. For a full minute, he just watched them without saying anything as they trembled. "The thing is kids," he finally said, quietly. "Whoever's cutting our grass, just got personal. They took Frankie, and Frankie was the big guy's nephew. Last year, some smart ass took out Donny's son, Marco, too. So, we've got ourselves a bigger problem than just the drugs."

"I don't know anything about that," the first hostage said.

"Donny's a family man, see," Felix continued, thoughtfully. "He doesn't like to see the missus cry. It's not good for the grandkiddies to lose their daddies. So we gotta sort this out."

In the doorway, the two guards caught each other's eye and smirked.

Carl, who'd been watching resentfully, flicked his knife from underneath his nail and leered forward. He scraped it swiftly across the knuckles of a hostage. The man screamed and Carlos looked at Felix greedily. Felix nodded.

"Let's start again, shall we?" Felix said.

The following morning, Sergeant Jacob Lawrence pulled up to the curb outside an industrial warehouse. Crime scene officers were scurrying to and fro and the grounds were crawling with military personnel and reporters. Jacob ducked under the police line surrounding the industrial transport warehouse, flashing his badge at the two soldiers standing guard. Ahead, two bodies were strapped around the base of a streetlamp with rope.

"It's a bloody mess!" Parker greeted him. The officer was already taking notes, standing by the dead men.

Jacob shot a stern look at his underling.

"Sorry, Sarge," Parker said.

"Who are they?" asked Jacob.

"Dave Thomas and Bob Castabel, sir" he replied. "A couple of pencil pushers. Civilians."

"I thought this was a military operation?" Jacob said, one eyebrow raised in surprise.

"It is, sir. These two were in charge of coordinating the transport trucks, hiring laborers for the loading docks, paper routes, that sort of thing. Outsourced, under contract. Strictly controlled, but still civi work."

"Destination?"

"The lorries? Fort Hamilton, sir. From there, the crates are shipped out to the front."

"Mmm," Jacob said, thoughtfully. "Where were the guards?"

"Killed, sir. At a guard station near the entrance. Single shot to the head, four of 'em at the start of graveyard shift. They hadn't done their rounds yet, no signature on the one o'clock time sheet. They must have been taken by surprise."

"Contents of the crates?" Jacob asked, already sure of the answer.

"Dunno. Classified, sir."

"Well," he said, leaning forward to inspect the bodies with a grimace, "thanks to our vigilante, I think we got the heads-up on that one anyway. These two must have been on the take. Someone made an example of them."

"You think it's linked to the Polletti case, sir?" Parker asked.

"I'm sure of it. Just don't know why. Whoever killed Polletti made sure we knew he was dirty. There's a lot of dope running underground since the war started. Now gangsters are turning up dead all over the city and crates are being channeled back to us instead of hitting the streets. With the red tape, it'll be months, maybe years, before those crates make it out of the legal system. They're evidence now." Jacob scratched his head, thoughtfully. "These two must have been part of Polletti's crew. There's no way the lorry routes would make it out without someone on the inside."

"But Polletti never got his crates," Parker observed.

"No," said Jacob, "We got them. Someone's cleaning up the streets."

"Maybe we should send them a card!" said Parker, brightly.

"Yeah, maybe we should," Jacob said dryly. He pulled the Avon Calling card from his pocket. So far, his inquiries to the Avon head office in New York had been fruitless. They knew nothing of the amphetamine crates. They'd crisply informed him that there were hundreds of Avon representatives in the city, all respectable women and they couldn't entertain for a moment the thought that one of their ladies was involved in such a thing.

They'd sent him away begrudgingly with a list of names and a harsh word to keep his thoughts from the press.

"Let's get this mess cleaned up," Jacob said. "I'm going to have the G-men on my back within an hour. Brandway included." He thought of his date with Adina and wondered how much she knew of his day-to-day work. The thought of her seeing this bloody mess and hearing about his inability to stem the recent flow of violence surrounding Brandway's operations brought a rush of frustration to his skin.

💋

"Alright children, it's time to go!" Betty shuffled them ahead of her out the front door and clicked it gently shut, balancing a honey cake in one hand with her handbag hanging underneath. "Now mind your manners for Mrs. Porter."

"Do we have to go?" asked George Junior. "She smells like old biscuits."

"George Junior! What an awful thing to say," Betty admonished, stifling a smile. "She's a darling and absolutely adores the both of you. We must always be kind, no matter what people smell like. Besides, you get to have cake if you come."

The little boy brightened at the mention of cake and skipped ahead down the path and through the open gate of their white picket fence, only to turn around and enter the identical gate next door. He began running across the lawn with his arms wide, mimicking the stuttering gunfire of a fighter plane. Nancy trailed behind, her face buried in a book.

"You'll have to put it away," Betty said. "It's only polite."

"But I'm nearly at the end of a chapter," Nancy sighed with a scowl. At the look on her mother's face, she reluctantly shut the book. "Laura's going on a sleigh ride with Almanzo. I think one day they might even get married."

"Laura who?"

"Laura Ingalls, of course," Nancy said, waving the book in the air. On the front cover, Betty saw a picture of a colonial girl with horse and carriage below the title *These Happy Golden Years*. "When I grow up I want to be just like her. I can't wait!"

"To marry Almanzo?" Betty teased, anticipating her daughter's response.

"Of course not! To go on sleigh rides, and to drive cars, seeing as buggy's aren't around anymore, and to chase wild horses in a paddock to break them in, just like Laura did. She was awfully brave. Did you know she left home at only fifteen years old to become a teacher? Imagine that. That's only four years older than me!"

"Yes, imagine," Betty murmured, not needing to imagine at all.

"Well, I want to be that brave. I want to have adventures like she did."

"I've no doubt you will, darling. But remember, adventures can be very dangerous. I'd rather see you safe and sound at home than zipping about with wild horses and fast cars."

"That's just because you don't like adventures," Nancy said, sullenly. "You never do anything exciting, just make cakes."

Betty pulled up her daughter and looked her squarely in the eye. They had reached Mrs. Porter's front door, which thankfully was still shut. George Junior was still spinning about on the grass, oblivious to his sister's mood.

"Listen to me. Don't try to grow up too fast, Nancy. I know it's hard to imagine, but the longer you're a child, the easier your life will be. Make it last. You may not understand why yet, but one day soon you will and I'll tell you adventures enough to make your hair curl. In the meantime, I think you'd be surprised at how exciting a cake can be." Before her daughter had time to respond, Betty knocked loudly on Mrs. Porters door then rang the bell for good measure, throwing Nancy an encouraging smile.

"Oh, what a delight," the older lady exclaimed, opening the door. She clasped her hands together excitedly, although she'd been expecting them all along. She shuffled her guests into the sitting room and set about collecting teacups for the table.

"Don't worry yourself, Mrs. Porter," Betty said, laying the cake on the table and giving George Junior a sharply disapproving look when he wrinkled his nose at Mrs Porter's offering of a biscuit, so that he took one with an overly-cheery 'thank you' instead.

"I'll make some tea." Betty walked into the kitchen, with which she was already well acquainted, and set about making a pot of tea. Nancy's turn of mood had upset her more than she let show. It was happening more frequently now, as the girl's books and friends led her to glimpse beyond the rosy veil of childhood into what may lay beyond it. It was only natural she would want to grow up of course, but Betty needed to resist it for as long as she possibly could. Nancy's childhood would end much more abruptly than the girl realized and could lead her into dangerous territory without careful guidance. Betty sighed as she let the tea leaves steep and listened to Nancy talking dutifully to Mrs. Porter through the open doorway. She was speaking loudly, to accommodate the near deafness of her audience.

"- and I had arithmetic with Mr. Whistler because my usual teacher, Mrs. Sampson was away ill with influenza. I made her a card and gave it to Sammy, because he lives four doors down from her and his mother is calling in on her on Sunday after church. But then Bessie's mother said she ought to be careful seeing her at all, because last week her cousin across the bridge died of influenza and he wasn't even that sick to start-"

She was a good girl. In her heart, Betty knew she owed her daughter a truthful conversation about what lay ahead, before she was caught unawares by the betrayal of her own body and its unnatural abilities. But truth be told, Betty, herself, wasn't ready for it. *Next week,* she thought. *Or perhaps the week after. When I've got all this business with Donny off my hands.*

She placed the pot of tea onto a silver tray, along with two glasses of milk and a large knife. She returned to the sitting room where Mrs. Porter was looking rather bewildered by Nancy's stream of conversation. Betty smiled at her daughter, silently relieving her of her efforts.

"I brought you some of my new Avon lotion, Mrs. Porter," Betty said, pulling a pink jar from her handbag. "It's the one I was telling you about, especially for skin that needs a little more conditioning than usual to keep its glow."

"Keep a beau?" the old lady repeated, cupping her ear. "Well, it's many years since anyone looked sideways at me, dear!"

"It's *glow*," Betty repeated louder. "For your skin. I think you'll find it helps with the dryness; you only need a little bit."

"Oh yes, I always need a little sit. I can barely make it to the greengrocer's anymore with this arthritis in my hips. I keep a chair at my dressing table for curling my hair each evening so I can sit in that if need be."

"Lovely," Betty sighed, giving up. She passed the jar across the table and poured the tea instead.

"How much money do I owe you, dear?" Mrs. Porter asked. "For the cream?"

"Absolutely nothing," Betty said, turning her attention to slicing up the cake and passing George Junior the first piece. "Although I do have a favor to ask." Betty avoided the curious gaze of her two children.

"I have a few more occasions coming up, where I might need someone to watch the children for a short time. I'll make you all dinner beforehand, of course. And they practically look after themselves. Would you mind?"

"How lovely!" Mrs. Porter exclaimed. "More time with the children. Well that'll be an adventure, won't it!" The old lady looked at Nancy, who managed a weak smile back. "We could even bake a cake!"

Donald Pinzolo sat behind his new mahogany desk at the orphanage. The front room had been converted to a spacious and decadent office overlooking the grassy park out front. A large cat lay leisurely across the top of his desk. The man stroked it distractedly as it flicked its tail. In front of him, Felix and Carl stood waiting for his response. When he finally spoke, Pinzolo's voice was quiet, like he was trying to keep it from hissing.

"So, you mean to tell me, you got nothing?" he said.

"They were blind, boss," Felix said. "Didn't have a fuckin' clue who was behind it. But by the time we gave 'em the third, they were too far gone. We had to cool 'em."

Pinzolo stretched his neck to the side. His jaw was clenched tight. He looked down at the newspaper on his desk. His own grinning photograph was on the front cover, shaking hands with the Mayor. 'Pinzolo's Heart of Gold' was printed above it.

"And whose idea was it to tie the bastards to a lamp post, boys?"

Felix stiffened and looked sideways to Carl. The other man was relaxed, pleased with himself.

"I thought we should leave a message, boss," Carl said. "To the ones stealing our shit."

"You did?" Pinzolo said.

Carl snorted, grinning. "Yeah."

"Mmm. Well that's your problem right there, Carl. I'm not paying you to think. I think. My cleaning lady thinks. My goddamn cat thinks. Not you. You follow orders." Pinzolo stroked the ginger cat with his left hand as Carl's grin dropped into a frown.

"I didn't-" he began. Pinzolo held up his right hand.

"That stunt just made my job a whole lot harder. I said make 'em talk, then make 'em disappear. Not turn the job into a flat-foot circus." As he spoke, Pinzolo used his free hand to open his desk drawer.

Carl followed Pinzolo's movements with his eyes. They widened. His whole body began to shake.

"You've got no class, Carl. Never did." And with that, Pinzolo lifted his right hand from his drawer, complete with revolver. Carl crumpled to the floor with a hole in his head as the cat screeched and fled from the desk. Two men in dark suits let themselves into the room from outside.

"Get him out of here before he stains my rug," Pinzolo said. The men gathered up Carl's body and dragged it from the room. Standing alone now, Felix looked unmoved.

"He wasn't right in the head that one," Pinzolo said. "It's dangerous, when they've got no control over themselves."

Felix shrugged.

"I need someone I can rely on," Pinzolo said.

"You can rely on me."

"Yeah, I think I can." Pinzolo stretched back in his chair, choosing a cigar from a tin box and lighting it. "I'm a business-man, Felix, and I have a business transaction for you. I've been good to you, haven't I?"

"Yeah, boss. So far."

Pinzolo chuckled. "I like your attitude, Felix. You don't trust anyone, even me. That means you're smart. I wouldn't trust me either."

Felix smiled vaguely. "What do you need?"

"Find out who's stealing my business. Whoever took out Marco, God-rest-his-soul, and Frankie and the boys on the truck jobs. Someone knows too much and they're making a fool of me. I want them buried."

Felix considered the proposition in silence, nodding. "What's in it for me?" he asked.

Again, Pinzolo chuckled.

"Your life, for starters," he said. "Ten thousand. And you get Vince Junior's spot at Kitty's Kat House."

Felix raised an eyebrow.

"I'm bringing him in to teach him the family business," Pinzolo said. "I'm running out of nephews here. Besides, I know you've got a shine in your eye for one of those dancers. Little red-head with an ass to die for." Pinzolo winked and Felix inhaled sharply. "How about I don't kill her either."

Felix shot a glare at Pinzolo, quickly re-evaluating the man. There was no one, save Tilly herself that knew of their love affair. No one that knew Felix beyond the cold detachment to life and death he showed; that only she could peel away. The girl bit his bones. And apparently, Pinzolo knew all about it. Even his hunters were hunted.

"She's nothing to me," Felix lied. "Just a bit of fun."

"We'll see," smiled Pinzolo.

4

KITTY'S KAT HOUSE

In the basement of St. Augustine's Home for Unwanted Boys, a wooden crate was being pried open with a crowbar at one end of a long table. Two dozen young boys stood around, fidgety and sullen. It was the kind of Saturday they would normally have raced into the dingy courtyard to play two-ball, swing on lamp posts and scuffle over turns on the old bicycle kept there. But recently, their lives had taken an unexpected turn. They now had a job to do.

The basement was almost as long as the building itself. Wooden crates were stacked to the ceiling, dividing the room into parts. Many contained ammunition and rifles, hijacked off the route to Fort Hamilton. There were field rations too, granulated sugar, celery salt, pork luncheon meat and fruit bars, boxed up together in peel-back tins, never to reach the boys at the front. Instead, they were now destined for an underground market where anything could be bought for a price. An open box of Hershey's Tropical Chocolate bars were used as rare incentives for the orphans to keep their mouths shut on what they saw. But the real incentive in working, was to avoid the punishment Pinzolo's men regularly dished out to anyone that opened their mouth unnecessarily.

Hidden behind one long wall of crates were two makeshift offices with grubby tables covered in cigarette butts, lewd magazines and playing cards. There was another table near the center of the main room, where Pinzolo's goons could keep an eye on their young charges. A few steps away, Vincent Carelli Junior spilled the contents of the crate he was opening onto a long table. Fist-sized packets of small white pills piled in front of the children.

"Same as yesterday, kids. Wrap each one in newspaper and string. Pile them back in the empty crate. When you're done, start a new one."

With their eyes down, the orphans scurried to begin. No one wanted the beating they knew was waiting if they disobeyed. The youngest boy, of about nine years old, looked at the pills warily. He turned his dirty face up toward Vince.

"What are they?" he asked. The others stopped and stared, mouths open. The sandy-haired kid closest to him elbowed the boy hard in the ribs.

"Shut up!" the bigger boy hissed.

Nearby, the table of men stopped playing their card game and looked over through a haze of cigarette smoke. One smirked.

Vince narrowed his eyes and stared at the boy, who shrank back.

"What's your name, kid?"

He hesitated.

"Samuel."

"You like to know what's going on, hey Sam? Don't like to follow orders?" Vince strolled casually toward the boy and leaned down. He dropped a heavy hand on Sam's tiny shoulder. The boy pulled himself straight, barely breathing. His eyes were like saucers. The kids standing around the table, shuffled back, subconsciously. Despite his fear, the dirty-faced boy lifted his chin slightly. He met Vince's eyes with his own.

"Not really. I just want to know what they are, that's all."

The others recoiled. Vince however, looked surprised. He bent down, face to face with the boy. Sam frowned back.

Finally, Vince laughed.

"I like you, kid. You've got guts. I was never one to follow the rules either, so I'll humor you." He straightened back up. "They're magic pills, Sam. You take one and all your troubles disappear for a while. You can do anything, like a fucking super-hero. These are what keep our soldiers fighting even where they've got their legs blown off and a dozen Krauts up their ass."

"So, why have you got them?" Sam asked, feeling a little braver.

"I'll tell you why," Vince smirked. "Because Mr. Pinzolo's a businessman and there are people out there that pay good money for 'em. It's all for the greater good kid. The city needs to keep on moving. We keep the troublemakers fixed up and under control, it's less trouble for Uncle Sam. And if we don't, someone else will do it and we miss out on the dough. Gotta keep the money rolling in to look after you kids, don't we?" Vince gave the boy a rough clap on the back.

"Yeah, I guess," said Samuel, eyeing off the pills. Vince followed his gaze to the table.

"'Course that stuff wouldn't work on you lot, you're too young. A kid like you would end up in city morgue if one of them got dropped in your pea soup." Vince smirked. "Don't make me prove it." He winked at Sam.

Vince walked away and sat down at the table with the Pinzolo's other men who had resumed their card game. "Now, get to work you lot," he yelled, over his shoulder. "And keep your mouths shut."

A few minutes later, Felix descended the stairs to the basement and wove his way through crates toward the table of smoking men. His mouth was set in a hard line as his eyes surveyed the room.

"What's this?" he said, nodding toward the table of orphans working. Vince looked up.

"New runners. Donny wants 'em trained," Vince replied. "No one's gonna stop a kid playing on the street corner are they?"

Felix grunted, frowning. "Where you gonna fit a gat? In their diapers?" he said.

Vince stood up, chest out. He didn't like Felix, the man was too hard to read. Dangerous.

"Don't burn me up," Vince said. "I don't give a shit. The boss says it goes, I do it. Donny has a way with kids you know. He likes 'em." He turned to look at the table. "They wanna do it, don't you kids?" The orphans shuffled together, avoiding the gaze of the men.

"Yeah," said a quiet voice. It was Samuel. "We wanna do it." The little boy looked at Vince and got a nod of approval back. The kid had nerve.

"See Felix," Vince said, "I'm good with kids, too." The other men laughed.

Felix wasn't amused. "There's a new truck arriving any minute," he said. "You lazy bastards are meant to be clearing a space for the crates, not sitting on your asses, babysitting. You want the boss to come down and catch you at it?"

Vince scowled. The other men jumped to their feet, butting their cigarettes. They disappeared into the mosaic of stolen crates, quickly filling the basement with the sounds of wood scraping across the floor. Vince stood up, crossing his arms.

"Now you listen to me. This is my gig, and I'll decide how to run it. How about you take a hike. The girls at Kitties need you to go powder their noses. Tell them I'll be over later to kiss 'em goodnight -"

With a quick snap, Felix's fist flew across the gap between them. Vince's head cracked back and he stumbled for balance. Blood streamed from his nose.

"Don't mess with me, Vince," Felix said, his voice smooth,

like ice. "I don't care who your daddy was. If you mess with me, you'll lose." He turned to leave. "By the way," Felix said, over his shoulder. "Donny wants you." He left.

Betty leaned her bicycle against a concrete building but stayed on it, one leg resting on the ground, with her shoulder to the wall. She bit into an apple, taken from her handlebar basket. The last rays of the sun were disappearing behind a long, decommissioned railway shed some distance in front of her, but she stayed out of sight. She'd be down there soon enough. It was a run-down industrial area, frequented only by the women that ran the great hydraulic presses in a metal factory closer to the main road. Betty was quite safe, for now, and could easily have talked her way out of a tight spot by claiming she was peddling cosmetics to the workers. But there was no one around at this time anyway, and she was quite invisible in the shadows.

The dirt road at the base of the hill below her ran parallel to empty railroad tracks. Traffic had been diverted many years ago, to newer, asphalt roads and this route was rarely used. Except of course, by Army supply trucks. Betty had followed their routes often, from the various storage warehouses and ammunition factories into Fort Hamilton where the ships waited for cargo. It was easy enough to read the minds of the drivers to determine their ever-changing routes through the city. There were only so many diversions they could make, which made them vulnerable to tracking. Clearly Pinzolo's men had tracked them too, no doubt with less savory methods. The best Betty could do, was beat them at their game, and take as many of Donny's men down each time as she could, until she grew closer to the man himself.

Betty didn't have to wait long. Two unmarked trucks came along the road, slowly, so as not to leave a telling dust cloud in their wake. They pulled up on the far side of the rail shed, hidden from view of anyone driving past. *This time,* Betty thought, *I've beat them to their own heist.* She had ten minutes until the trucks were due to drive by. If she moved fast enough, she could take them all out before they passed, and let them continue unheeded. Betty tossed the apple core, swung her leg over the bicycle and propped it against the wall. She smoothed her cornflower blue dress, feeling the row of knives circling high around each thigh, warm in their holsters. She only ever wore her knives clean, wrapping them in a towel in her basket to take home for washing, after she'd dislodged them from the ribcage or eye-socket of her victims. Cleanliness was next to godliness, so the saying went. Really though, it was simply a preference to keep her impeccable wardrobe unstained.

Pinzolo's men were out of their cars. There were eight all together, and they positioned themselves in the shadows of the railway shed, ready for the ambush. She took note of where each man was hiding, as she hugged the dark spaces of the hill, making her way down quickly. She was close now, close enough to see their dim faces, but still out of sight. From here, she'd have to cross the grassy space onto the road. A bright floodlight lit the road in front, where the truck tires would be shot to stop them. She would be exposed.

Betty leaned forward, about to stand.

No.

Something's different.

There were two new figures alighting from behind the shed. They weren't Pinzolo's men. They were children.

"What do we do?" called a boy's voice, no more than ten years old. A flurry of cursing and arms waved them away. There was a shuffle and one of the men leapt out of his hiding place.

"Stay back," he hissed to the boys, "I said to keep out of sight 'til I call you in! Get in the truck." Betty recognized the voice. It was Vincent Carelli Junior. She hadn't heard his voice in many years, but it hadn't changed all that much since his late teens. Of all her cousins, Betty would be disappointed to kill him. As a child, he'd been sweet. As a teen, overindulged with family money, attention and a distinct lack of parental moral fiber, he'd soured. His pockets were lined with blood money and his hands were filthy with death. And now he'd dragged children into his web.

The two boys scuttled back around the side of the building, but they didn't return to the truck. Betty could see the shape of them against the back wall, crouching low. Somehow, they'd become part of this terrible mess.

She froze. Betty never left witnesses alive. She never had to. The men she killed were long past redemption. But, *children.*

Her breath caught and she steadied herself against the ground. Her vision blurred and her heart raced. She felt sick as she weighed up her choices. If she took out Vince and his men, the boys would see everything. Under the glaring flood light, they would see her face. Her whole life, unmasked. There was too much at stake. Her perfect life would peel away. Her children, her George, her picket fence and perfumes and painted smile. Gone, all of it.

Inside, Betty felt old scars needling and stretching, threatening to tear apart. This is where she'd begun. As a child on the sidelines of violence, a witness to murder. Hauling stolen goods and selling drugs on street corners while grown men watched from parked cars. Cold, scared, chin up and trying to prove they could do a man's job with a boy's heart. Secretly terrified of the day they might catch a bullet instead of a cold. Her mind stuttered, and she was trapped like a fly in a web of memories that raced beneath her eyelids, dragging her back to a street corner, *her* corner, at only thirteen years old.

***

It was a shabby part of town where the occasional kid stopped for a cigarette on their walk home from school, but there was rarely any traffic. Susie was waiting for one of her regular customers, perched on a low brick fence by the side of a park. Behind her, empty swings squeaked on rusty chains beside a derelict toilet block. A metal climbing frame was skeletal against the darkening dusk sky.

Susie's shoes were wet inside, her feet like bricks of ice. The rain fell intermittently, never letting her alone long enough to pull her precious magazine from the shabby school bag on the brick wall beside her. As usual, Susie had rolled it into a milk bottle and stoppered it to keep it dry for the walk to school. It wasn't worth the risk now to read it though, the glossy smiles and glamorous stories of Cosmopolitan would be ruined, sodden by the rain. And Susie couldn't bear to see those faces fall apart.

Her textbooks would be soaked, and she'd earn the strap from Mr. Carrick for letting it happen, but the man was late and there was nothing to be done. She couldn't go home without the money.

A new downpour began. Susie lifted her school satchel above her head for cover against the rain. She saw two men rounding the corner ahead, walking toward her through the gray sleet. Under the light of the lamp above her, they were silhouettes, like characters from a comic book. One was Jack, who she'd been expecting for over an hour. She could tell by his rounded shoulders and the old wool newsboy that was too big for his skinny head. He'd brought someone else.

Susie could hear them talking. Not across the distance, but inside her own head. She dropped her bag down on the brick wall again and rubbed her face, pushing away the rain and wishing the voices would wash away with it. She was nearly used to them now, the constant violations of her peace. They were just words. Intentions. Invasions. And already, they'd saved her more than once. Selling on the street wasn't safe for anyone. Especially a thirteen-year-old girl.

"That's her? The kid?" the new man was saying.

"Every Wednesday." Jack was edgy, more than usual. As he drew closer, Susie saw that he was pale and hollow, ashen skin circling his

eyes. He shoved his hands into his pockets, then drew them out again, compulsively fisting then stretching his fingers, then shoved them back down. His jacket was threadbare, and he shivered as he drew up close to the brick wall.

"You're late," Susie said, trying to project a bravery she didn't feel. She'd been a year on the street now but still got scared every time someone approached her. Even Jack, who'd never tried to hurt her, either by hand or inside his foggy mind. Susie pushed the fear down and straightened her back.

"Scrapping," Jack said. He gestured toward Susie's school bag with a shaking finger. "You good?"

"Yeah, I got it." Jack's dull eyes would have lit up, if they weren't already dead inside. "Who's this?" she asked.

"Archie. I said you could help him out."

Susie scowled at the second man. He was short and stocky in a gabardine coat, with a red nose and yellow-tinged eyes. His collar was pulled up the back of his neck to keep out the rain. A drunk for sure, but he didn't look like the others. He wasn't addicted yet. That wouldn't take long. Susie caught Archie's eye, then quickly looked away. A prickle of fear caught her neck. There was something in him, not far below the surface. Something off.

"Like I have a choice." Susie looked up the street, in the opposite direction the men had walked in from. A nondescript beige car was parked on the side of the street. The man inside was watching her from behind a newspaper. Ernie, one of her father's goons. He'd been sitting there for the past two hours. Watched as the last four men came and went. The man was dense enough to think that holding a newspaper up might look less conspicuous. She turned back to her customers, intent on getting it over with so she could walk home. Ernie was only there to make sure she stayed to do the work. He didn't give a shit about her being out in the rain.

Jack glanced nervously up at the beige car. He was smarter than Ernie, even with his head a mess inside. Susie noticed that he was skinnier again, barely recognizable from the man she met a year before, when he'd first come to the brick fence. She never knew where they came from, just that they'd turn up at this park looking for her, and that she'd better bring home what was owed, or her father would take it out of her with his belt instead.

"Great. Thanks for coming, kid."

"I'm not doing you any favors. I've been waiting in the rain," Susie said, without much malice. She could tell Jack had spent the day scouring the city junkyards, searching for metal he could sell to scrap dealers to pay for his habit. His filthy hands and scarred face identified him as a 'junkie' as much as his days spent rummaging through the dump for junk to sell. Anything would do, but metal got the highest price. Most of the men Susie sold to were like Jack; young men that fell from the bottom rungs of a working underclass, caught in addiction that grew out of sniffing in alleys and dance halls until they couldn't live without the rush. The euphoric escape from grit and mediocrity. 'Junkies' were the newest wave of addicts on the streets of New York, a social disease that her father, Roy, administered to like a doctor prescribing pills. Very expensive pills that left a trail of track marks and body bags. Including her mother's.

"Sorry. Didn't mean you to get wet."

"Yeah, well, that's what happens when it rains." Susie wiped the drizzle out of her eyes. She reached into her bag and pulled out a small decorative glass jar, holding two remaining rolls of heroin. It was precious. Not because of the contents, which she despised, but for the jar itself. It was made of rose-pink glass with beveled edges and a silver lid. She'd slipped it off her mother's dressing table after the funeral, along with the silver box and a few precious bits and bobs she'd hoped her father wouldn't notice. He hadn't of course, before he'd dumped the rest of her mother's belongings at a shelter. "Pop said eight dollars this time."

"Eight! Shit man, I only got seven! It was seven last time, I swear."

"Pop said it's more now. It's harder to get and he's got plenty of paying customers, so if you don't want it -" She pushed the jar back in her bag, watching Jack's eyes widen. "You're better off without it anyway."

"Kid, please!"

"It's eight dollars or nothing." She knew Jack was lying. He'd made seven dollars fifty selling scrap since Tuesday and stolen another dollar from a lady's bag on the subway yesterday. It was all there, clear as day in his head. The first time she'd believed him, against her own better judgment. Thought he was just mixed up. She'd earned five straps for that missing dollar from Pop's belt. No doper was worth that. Not even an almost nice one like Jack.

"What about you?" She looked up at Archie, ignoring Jack's pleas to get it cheap.

I bet she's up for it. Street kid. Looks like she's been around. Susie froze. Archie still hadn't said anything. Out loud. But inside, he was all talk.

"Might be interested," he said. "What else are you selling?"

Susie shivered, suddenly far colder than she had been before. She took a step back, sinking into a muddy puddle with her left shoe. Archie's eyes were on her dress, searching for a way in.

"I've got money, kid." Archie said, pulling his lips back into what he thought was a smile. "Wanna make some extra? I bet they don't pay you enough to sit out in the rain all afternoon. I'll take a gram of what he wants and a piece of you too. I know a place." His hand flicked out and caught her wrist, still half inside her school bag.

"Forget it." Susie wrenched her hand away. His fingers were slippery with rain.

She looked over at the parked car up the street. The newspaper was just resting on Ernie's face. He was snoring, asleep. Useless bastard.

"Come on. I'm not gonna hurt ya," He slid his index finger under her collar and Susie slapped it away, stepping back.

Again, her eyes shot toward the newspaper-covered face in the warm parked car up the road. Ernie was out of ear shot, too far away and too stupid to help her anyway. She was on her own.

"Keep your grimy hands to yourself."

This new guy, Archie, had a head full of dark thoughts. Each one bore into her mind like a parasite. Filthy and dangerous. Susie could feel the blood draining from her face and her fist clenched around the strap of her bag.

Jack stopped his pleading for a moment and caught up on his friend's intentions. His eyebrows shot up and his hands clenched nervously. "Nah man, you don't wanna do that," he said, "Roy'll have your guts for garters."

"Roy who?"

"Her pop, ya fat-head, who else?"

"Yeah well, who's gonna tell him? We make sure she doesn't talk. Our secret, hey kid? You need money, right?"

Susie's feet burned to run but her head knew there was a belt waiting at the other end if she came home without the cash.

"Just take your fix, man, and let's get out of here," said Jack. He was sweating now, his eyes desperately shifting back and forth between Susie and her school bag where his euphoria was tempting him, stashed inside a roll of paper. "Here," Jack fumbled in his pockets and pulled out a handful of crumpled notes and coins. "What do ya know, I got eight dollars." He tried to shove it into Susie's fist, which was curled tight and ready to strike. She pulled her hand away. Taking it now would do her no good at all. If she set Jack free with his dope, she'd be left alone with Archie.

Susie was biting her lip so hard it hurt.

"Him first. Archie has to pay first," she said. Jack looked desperately to the other man.

"Go on then," he begged.

"And?" Archie pressed.

"I want your eight bucks first."

"You don't have to -," Jack began, but Susie glared him down.

Archie's watery eyes shone with greed.

"Done." He pulled the money from his wallet and passed it to Susie, who counted it, then grabbed Jack's and shoved the cash into her school bag. She pulled out her precious pink jar, unscrewed the lid and carefully retrieved the last two paper rolls. The first one she handed to Archie, who quickly shoved it into his coat pocket, keeping his hands there and bouncing on the balls of his feet. She pulled the strap of her school bag over her head and tightened the lid on the now-empty jar.

"Come on," Archie growled.

Susie looked at him and smiled carefully, then handed the second roll to Jack. The transaction was done.

"It'll kill you," she whispered to Jack, but he wasn't listening.

"What about the rest?" Archie said, his lip twitching nervously. "Behind that wall, that'll do. I don't need fancy for the likes of you."

"I've changed my mind," Susie announced, lifting her chin as she stepped backwards. "Now both of you get lost. And don't bring him again," she yelled at Jack. But Jack had already turned away, clutching the paper roll like lifeblood. He scuttled across the street into the darkness, leaving her. Susie turned toward the beige car, hoping Ernie was awake. The backlights of the car were disappearing around the corner of the street. He'd seen the transaction finish; his job was done. She was alone.

"You little wretch!" Archie sprang forward, grabbing Susie before she could run. Thick fingers dug into the flesh of her arm, burning as she twisted and turned to escape them. She clawed at his hands with her free one, belting his knuckles with her precious pink jar with the other. He was dragging her toward the toilet block. "You owe me one!"

"Get off me you creep!" Susie screamed. Her mary-janes skidded along the dirt, desperately trying to gain grip against the drag. Away from the streetlamp, darkness felt as if it might swallow her whole. "Let me go!" An upwelling of fear boiled inside of her like a volcano. Something exploded.

Susie spun the man toward her, somehow defying his brute strength. She wrenched her arm back with all her might. Her mother's glass jar smashed against the side of Archie's head. For a moment he stood, stupefied, swaying on the spot. Then he crumpled to the ground.

Susie stood, staring. Breathing. Her legs wouldn't move but her ears thumped with the blood rushing inside her veins. She blinked. Cold. Wet. Separate. Like she was standing in a bubble, looking down at the man without being sure what he was. Susie uncurled her fingers from the precious jar, slowly. It was broken. The thick glass had cut her hand and she was cupping blood along with the beveled pieces of her mother's trinket.

At her feet, the man groaned. In a flash, she took off. If she'd been more aware of her own body, she might have noticed that she was running faster than she ever had before. Unnaturally fast. But she didn't. The only part of her mind not terrified into stupidity was the part telling her to run.

To the only person with whom she had ever felt safe.

As she rounded the corner into the street where he lived, Susie slowed down. Her breath was already even. Her mind was clearing. Jacob was outside his house, leaning a gray bicycle against the fence so that he could push open the gate. A pair of boxing gloves hung from the handlebars. A light jumper was pulled over his shirt and long shorts.

Jacob was fourteen now and the past year had changed him. His childish jaw was becoming more defined and handsome. A healthy glow lit his cheeks since he and his friends had begun playing baseball every afternoon on the vacant lot near school, spurred on by their idolatry for Babe Ruth, who'd hit four home runs for the Yankees in last year's season. Jacob was thriving, as any adored, intelligent boy should. But he never for a moment, lost his affection for the girl he'd first come across kicking pebbles by the side of the road outside her house with a bruised eye and a stubborn heart.

"Jake," Susie said quietly, as she met him.

He looked up and caught sight of her, instantly breaking into a wide smile. It just as quickly dropped into horror.

"You're bleeding!"

Susie looked down at her hand still clutching the pieces of her mother's jar. Blood was smeared on the back, where it had run in rivulets between her fingers as she ran.

"Oh." Susie let the shards of rose glass fall gently to the grass. "I'm sorry." For a moment, she stood waiting. Jacob rushed forward and pulled her hands to him.

"You'll need a bandage. Ima can do it," he said.

"No! She'll ask how I-" Susie pulled her eyes away from Jacob's, unable to look at him, but he didn't let go. Jacob's hands felt so warm in hers, and she realized it was the first time he'd ever properly held them. Like, not kids. A rush of warmth and confusion came over her. She liked the feel of his hands on hers. But it wasn't how she'd imagined it would be. With her just standing there, so scared and pathetic. So ugly, covered in blood and scrapes and rain. Tears stung Susie's eyes. There was nothing for it. She let them fall. She reclaimed her hands and covered her face, riding out the waves of shock and misery until at last they subsided. Jacob stood, saying nothing, with his eyes on his shoes. When Susie finally looked up, his mouth was set in a hard line.

"It was your dad again, wasn't it?" Jacob's ears grew red, like they always did when he was angry. When Susie didn't respond, he spun around to his bike again and pulled it away from the fence. "I wanna punch him in the head! I'll get Pop to bring every copper in the city down on him. He's a rat Susie, he should be in jail!" Susie dashed in front of the bicycle, clinging to the handlebars with bloodied hands.

"It wasn't him, Jake! Not this time. I promise. Don't tell your Pop or I'll go to jail too! I was working! Please. You don't know what happened."

"So, tell me, then."

"It was just some man. A customer. He turned up with one of the junkies and tried to hurt me. Wanted me to -" she looked down to the ground, pushing her shame and tears away with grubby fingers, "But I got away."

"Some guy tried to hurt you?"

Susie nodded, then took a deep breath and lifted her eyes back up to meet Jacob's. "But he didn't. I hurt him. I couldn't help it Jake, I just hit him so hard I thought that he was dead." She shuddered. "But he wasn't. I don't even know how I did it."

"I wish he was dead!"

Susie looked at him, horrified. "Don't say that. Then I'd be a murderer! I just needed to get away before he woke up so I ran."

Jacob's ears still burned, but his eyes softened.

"Come here." He took her hand, pulled her gently down to sit on the sidewalk, letting her rest her head against his shoulder. For a while, neither of them spoke.

"I still hate him," Jacob said, eventually.

"So do I."

"If it wasn't for him, you wouldn't be out selling that stuff in the first place. He should be in jail. Or worse."

"And if he's in jail, where am I, Jake? On the street? In some orphan asylum on the other side of town? I'd never see you. I'd have to leave school. Completely on my own. I hate him too, but I'm not ready yet for that - to be on my own."

"Then let me come with you, when you're working."

"No way. The police chief's son watching me sell dope on the side of the road? Pop would kill me. You know I'm not even allowed to see you."

Jacob threw his hands up. "Well, there has to be something I can do! It's dangerous. It's gonna happen again."

Susie shrugged. "Just be my friend. That's all I need Jake. You're the only one who understands."

"Come on Susie-pocket. Please let me help," he implored, draping his arm around her back.

"There's nothing you can do," she whispered, smiling sadly.

Again, they sat in silence. Every minute that ticked by brought Susie closer to having to go home to her father. She wasn't any safer there than she had been on that fence. But at least, here, right now, she was safe.

Jacob suddenly sat up straight.

"I've got it!"

"Got what?! Smallpox?"

"Very funny. No, I've got an idea."

Susie frowned, noncommittally.

"You can't tell your Pop, Jake. You know that."

"That's not it." He twisted around to face her. "I can't stop your dad. Yet," he added, scowling. "And I can't stop him making you work. But I can do something." He jumped up and pulled his boxing gloves off the handlebars of his bike. "My dad is making me take boxing lessons so I can defend myself. In fact, I get to do heaps of sports that you don't because you're a girl: boxing, gymnastics, fencing, even a new type of fighting called karate. Mr. Iwate, the greengrocer, is teaching us that one on Saturday mornings at the scout hall."

"I know you want to defend me, Jake, but you can't come with me-"

"That's not what I mean." Jacob took a big breath, sitting back down on the grass beside her. "I mean I can teach you. I'm learning it all because I'm a boy and you're not, and that's just not fair. You might be a girl, but you need to defend yourself. Way more than me. So, I'll teach you everything I learn so that you can!"

A triumphant smile lit his face and his teeth shone in the dark.

"You'd do that?" Susie said, quietly.

"Of course! It'll be fun too. I'll show you everything you need to know. I'll show you how to fight back. How to stay safe."

Jacob scrunched his nose and lifted Susie's hand to punch the air in front of them. "Pow! Biff! Wham!"

Susie laughed a little and pulled her hand away, knocking him with her shoulder playfully.

"Susie Pocket, Lightweight champion of New York City! You'll be just like Gene Tunney - unbeatable! I promise. I mean, it will take a while, but why not?"

Susie bit her lip. A funny feeling was growing inside her chest.

"When?"

"After school, before your jobs. Anytime you want."

Susie shook her head, resolutely.

"No way. You'll miss baseball."

Jacob rolled his eyes and leaned in, taking her bloodied hands in his own.

"Some things are worth missing baseball for."

He was like sunshine in the middle of the night. Susie beamed.

"Okay, but you're not missing baseball. We'll work around it."

"If you say so," Jacob said, rolling his eyes. "Let's start tomorrow."

"You're sure?"

"I'm sure. Now at least wash your hands before you go. I'll get a washcloth to wrap them in. We'll tell Ima you fell off my bike."

"Thanks Jake."

***

"Ready, kid?" Vince Carelli's voice violated her inner thoughts and the memory slipped back into darkness until it was gone. She'd been lost, for a moment. Betty looked up, wide eyed. Vince and his men were still hidden in the shadows of the railway shed. The ambush was set. Betty felt the warmth of Jacob's arm ghosting across her shoulders. It had been twelve years since that night, but it was a lifetime ago. She was, quite literally, another person now. But it was that night, cold and bloody and terrified, that had sparked the road to retribution that led her here, now. Ready to kill.

"I'm ready," the boy called back. His voice wavered. He coughed and shuffled minutely against the back of the shed. It was a brave front, but inside his head, a different voice was crying out. *What if I get shot? What if I run? I can't - Vince needs me, he said so. He's gonna teach me stuff. Look after me. I have to show him I can do this. I don't want to die.*

Betty had been there, that child on the streets. A pawn.

She couldn't kill him. She'd be killing herself. But if they saw her, she'd lose everything she'd worked so hard to build. Her perfect, terrible lie.

For the first time in many years, Betty was paralyzed. But if she didn't act now, more one-stripers would be dead within minutes.

Too late.

Two trucks came along the bend and she heard a low whistle. Immediately, the boys ran forward onto the road and began kicking a ball back and forth. They stayed in the middle of the road, even as the lorries slowed down, blasting their horn. With a nervous look over their shoulder, they kept playing. The trucks had no choice but to stop in their tracks.

"Get off the damned road," the first driver called. Again, the boys ignored him. The thud of the ball was their only response.

"Bloody kids," the driver sighed, as a security officer opened the passenger side door and jumped out. He jogged forward, cursing at them to move along.

Another low whistle.

And it was on.

The kids dashed behind the building as gunfire began. The security guard on the road was down before Vince was even on his feet. The GI had no chance.

Vince and his men surrounded the trucks. Both drivers were shot through the windows, stalling their screeching tires. Two soldiers jumped out of the first truck and another three from the second. More than usual.

Betty's jaw clenched tight and she squeezed her eyes shut, still hidden in the shadows only meters from the fight. Every inch of muscle rebelled her choice. Her knives felt heavy and cold against her thigh and she slid her hand up her skirt to hold them, desperate to release the fury building inside her. But she couldn't. The children were still there in the shadows, now curled into balls of fear against the weathered panels of the rail shed. But their eyes were wide with fear and the sick thrill of adrenaline.

As the last soldier fell with a hole between his eyes, vengeance roared within Betty's chest. Her head fell back, and she squeezed her eyes shut, not willing to do more than breathe, lest her mind break away from her body and throw her back again to the nights where she was that child. She could hear Vince and his men quickly unloading the trucks, transferring crates to their own vehicle.

"You did swell, Sam," Vince was saying. "I knew you had it in you." There was no response, but she heard the boys shuffling to their feet. Betty opened her eyes and watched the boys help shift crates, stepping over guards where they had fallen. She stole back to her bicycle in the shadows and waited for them to finish. As they drove away, she followed.

The wind cooled the fury in her skin as she rode. *I just need to find another way, that's all,* she told herself. *Eliminate the threat. Get Vince some other way. Keep the kids out of it. No witnesses. A better plan.* Now that children were involved, it was going to be a lot more difficult than she'd expected.

Betty wound through the suburbs a safe distance from the trucks and ended up in an unfamiliar fringe of town where small shops met dark alleys. Loud, lively music pumped from the upstairs window of a bordello. Betty stayed on her bike, camouflaged in the shadows on the opposite side of the street. Silhouettes of burlesque dancers moved behind the glass, accompanied by intoxicated shouts and revelry. A pink stiletto painted on the outside wall read 'Kitty's Kat House'.

Despite the lights and noise of the brothel, the alley running alongside was dim. Vince was coordinating the men and boys, who began unloading crates through a side door.

"Take 'em downstairs," Vince said.

"Shouldn't we be taking this lot to Donny?" asked one of the men.

"Half for Donny, half for me this time," Vince grunted. "I've got some of my own business to take care of before I shack up in his basement of stray cats."

"Won't he notice the difference?"

"Not unless you say somethin', knuckle-head!" Vinnie clapped the man on the back of the head.

"The boss put Felix here, though," the man said. "He'll know somethin's up. I don't trust that guy; he gives me the frickin' creeps."

"Don't worry about Felix," Vince snapped, his hand reflexively touching his nose. "He's out on a job tonight, I heard Donny say so. Anyways, I'll be back tomorrow night to clear it out. He ain't got a key to my office yet. This is still my pad."

"As long as you're sure," his off-sider said.

Felix seemed to remember he was under the watchful eye of the two young boys from the orphanage. "Donny'll get his half. I've just got a few debts to settle here, that's all," he said playfully. "It's our secret, hey, boys? Worth some candy and a few cigarettes to you? What do you think?"

Sam and his friend were quick to nod their heads.

"Sure Vince, we won't tell," Sam said. "Honest!"

"Good lads!" Vince said, and Sam pulled himself taller under the praise. "Right, let's get these crates inside. Donny'll be expecting us back. I'll tell him how good you boys did tonight."

Betty waited until Vince and his crew had driven away again. She sat for a few minutes, considering the latest development. Vince had kids on the street, and Donny was involved. From behind his genial smiles, handshakes and cigars, Donny was *always* involved. It was clear, though, that Donny didn't know Vince was skimming his heist.

Distractedly, Betty tapped her foot to the music spilling from the upstairs window. She'd always liked the blatant celebration of the bordello strips at night, and this establishment was no different. Sure, the pretense of their performance kept their audience sated, but underneath, the working girls held their own independence in hand, and that was something to be admired in times like these. A plan was forming in her mind. An opportunity even, perhaps.

Betty rode away, quite looking forward to her next visit. As the dirty alleys gave way to neat residential streets, Betty's chin lifted to meet the wind. Each house passed on her ride home, with its neat driveway and painted letterbox, clipped lawns and decorative shutters, made her heart feel lighter. Domestic bliss was hidden behind the lace drapes of every window that flickered by. Roast potatoes and meatloaf and peas. Braids and ribbons and bags of colored marbles. Spinning tops and Sunday hats. Betty breathed a sigh of relief. It existed. Despite everything, it was all still real enough to touch.

She zipped along the outskirts of Central Park in the moonlight, and then slowed to toss a small paper package from her basket onto the sleeping pile of newspapers she knew to be Herb, passed out on his usual bench. Betty looked back over her shoulder to wave, but the old man didn't stir like he usually did. Betty frowned and pulled to a stop, then wheeled back to him. She stood astride her bike, toes to the ground and gave him a gentle nudge, lifting a newspaper leaf from his face with concern. Herb snorted, sniffed and twisted to a more comfortable position, then began snoring. Betty smiled. She gathered the picnic rug from the base of her basket and lay it across him, repositioning the brown package she'd left so it wouldn't fall off. At least he'd have a tuna sandwich to fill his stomach when he woke. Betty balanced on her bicycle, ready to take off again, but stopped short. The leaf of newspaper she'd lifted from Herb's face had fallen to the ground in front of her wheel. She hopped off and picked it up. It was a front page, grubby and torn, but the photograph was still clear enough under the lamp light to turn her stomach. An aged but very familiar man commandeered the headlining image, shaking hands with Mayor Sutherland under the headline "Pinzolo's Heart of Gold". She quickly scanned the article. *An orphanage restoration with Donald Pinzolo as the new benefactor. Young boys given a second chance. Offered jobs and training within his business empire. For the good of the city. A local hero.*

No! Betty tore the paper into bits, her jaw set and her eyes stinging. She tossed the shreds of lies into the air like a snowstorm, jumped back onto her bicycle and took off with renewed energy. At least she knew now, where the children with Vince had come from. *St. Augustine's Home for Unwanted Boys.* Where they wouldn't be missed or protected from what lay ahead. Betty set off at a faster pace, eager for a new day to begin. *A woman's work was never done.*

"Here I go again," Betty sang, twirling her blue gingham skirt as she spun around the kitchen to the jaunty notes of Benny Goodman's orchestra through the wireless. She placed a dish of steaming vegetables in the center of the table. Betty danced her way back to the oven, returning with a plump roasted chicken. *"I hear those sweet notes sing again, ring-a-ling again,"* she trilled.

"Twirling in your spell of love!" finished George, in a lovely baritone as he entered the kitchen. He spun Betty into her chair and the children, who were already seated, giggled.

"Oh, George! I'm meeting my ladies tonight," Betty gushed. "I had the most marvelous idea today; you'll never guess what it is!"

George seated himself at the head of the table. His brief frown at her mentioning another night out was quickly quelled by the sheer enthusiasm radiating from his wife's face.

"I won't even try then, Jitterbug. You'd better just tell me - what is this marvelous idea of yours?"

Betty leaned forward, passing George the carving knife, then dishing out the children's meals as she spoke. "Well dear, you know the orphanage that's being all done up in the city – St Augustine's? There was quite a buzz about it in the newspaper -"

"Oh, yes," George said.

"Well, I just thought -" Betty hesitated, her eyes glittering with suppressed excitement, "- why not turn our spring church social into a fundraiser? Ooh, it'll be lovely George! We'll set up in city hall - deck it all out! The Seymour girls have a cousin in administration – they've already inquired for me, it's all set if we want it. Imagine the glamor darling! We'll invite all the glitterati, the local politicians and businessmen, the media - the whole bit! We'll make a real night of it. Just think, George darling - the dresses! The lights! And a big band to dance the night away. You'll dance with me, won't you, George?" she finished breathlessly, jumping up to kiss him on the cheek.

George beamed. He stood up from his dinner, taking her once more in his arms to twirl her about the table, laughing. The wireless was still playing its tune, and George joined the song with good humor.

> 'Things are fixing now, you'll see my sweetheart
>   twirling now,
> We'll have a fairy-tale ending now, dizzy in your
>   spell of love -'

Betty clung to his neck and laughed.

"Gosh, what a big heart you have, love. It sounds like a swell idea," he said.

"You really think so?" Betty asked. "It's all for the children, George. Those poor orphans, just imagine what it must be like for them."

"I couldn't begin," George said. "Just don't overdo it now. You keep some of that big heart of yours for this old dead hoofer."

"Oh, George," Betty said. "You know my heart burns brightest for you. There's no one I love more."

"Better not be, Jitterbug," George winked. He cleared his throat as he sat back in his chair and resumed his dinner. "So where are you off to tonight then?"

Betty turned away and stepped to the oven, pulling out an apple pie and placing it on the top to cool. "I have some colors for Mrs. Sampson," she said, nodding to a bundle of Avon products sitting on the counter. She turned away again, fussing about in the kitchen drawer for dessert spoons. "She's offered to help with the invitations, too, for the fundraiser. She's such a dear."

"I see," said George. "Just don't stay out too late, dear. I was awfully worried about you last night, you got home after ten o'clock! It's not decent, Betty, to be getting about town at that hour on your own. And it's not safe. What if something were to happen to you?"

"I'm sure I could handle myself if it came to it, George," Betty said.

"Of course you couldn't," he said, wiping his mouth. "There's all sorts out there love, you've got such a kind heart you always think the best of people. There are some unsavory types on the streets at night and I'd hate to think of you getting in trouble."

Betty smiled quietly and touched his hand gently. "Of course you would. You're quite right, of course, dear. I'll be home as early as I can get away."

"Right then," George said. "Who's ready for pudding?"

"Me!" cheered the children, together.

Betty pushed her arms through her coat as she walked toward the sitting room, then stopped at the hall stand mirror to pin her hat into place.

"Nancy and George Junior are tucked into bed, dear. I won't

be out too late," she assured George, who sat with his slippered feet up, reading a newspaper. Her husband pushed the mahogany footstool away and dropped the paper on his lap, leaning forward. "Watch your ash on the needlework, George!" Betty ducked across and brushed the embroidered footstool pillow with a gloved hand. Neat stitches of roses and hollyhocks circled the words 'Home, Sweet Home'.

"Sorry, dear," George said, holding his pipe over the side table instead. "Mind you watch the weather tonight love; it looks like rain. Are you sure you don't want me to drop you over there?"

"No really, I'll be fine," Betty said. "It's not far." She kissed George on the cheek and picked up her Avon bag from the front door as she left, closing it gently behind her.

George settled back with his pipe and newspaper, letting the minutes tick by in silence. After a while, he turned to the side table and dumped the ash from his pipe onto a small tray, refilling the empty bowl with folded tobacco flakes. He lit it anew and stood up, stretching his legs.

George wandered into the kitchen, in search of a scotch glass and saw the first spots of rain fall onto the kitchen windowpane. The wind had picked up outside. It wouldn't be long before a storm began in earnest. "Blast," he muttered to himself, remembering Betty was out on her bicycle in the inclement weather. He turned back toward the lounge room. A small pile of Avon products on the counter-top caught his eye. "Horsefeathers," George cursed again. He picked up the pile and returned to the telephone stand in the lounge room, placing them down next to the phone. George flipped through Betty's address book until he found what he was searching for. He dialed the number for Mrs. Marjory Sampson, then shifted her Avon products around vaguely as he waited for the call to connect. There was a glass spray bottle of Crimson Carnation toilet water, an ivory tin of Quaintance body powder, something called Color Pick-up

Cream in a small jar and a handful of powder pots in various shades of brown. Apparently, Mrs. Sampson had a sizable order to pay for tonight and he guessed that Betty would be disappointed at her own carelessness in leaving it behind.

Marjory Sampson was a heavy, bustling type of woman, well known at church for her raspberry jam tarts and outspoken opinions. When any news of interest passed the lips of the parishioners, Marjory could be counted upon to have known about it at least the day before. George generally kept a wide berth from the church social group, as they were the kind of women whose gossiping and babbling about, frustrated him. Betty, however, seemed to bring out the good in everyone, even Marjory Sampson, and she always knew the right thing to say to keep them all in favor, despite themselves. She was good with people, in that way, George mused, as he waited. Betty could twist someone's arm while presenting them with bad news and they'd only thank her for it. He frowned, admonishing himself for the thought. No, she's thoughtful, that's all, and naïve to their gossiping ways. Betty had a heart of gold. Of course, they all adored her.

Finally, a woman's voice picked up the line.

'Good Evening, Mrs. Sampson, this is George Jones. How are you?" He smiled down the phone line, ever courteous, even when no one was there to see it, as the woman responded in kind.

"Oh, yes, I'm fine, thank you, fit as a fiddle," George replied. "I imagine Betty must be with you by now, she left quite a while ago, but I've found the pile of cosmetics here she meant to bring - Oh, she's not? Well, I'm sure that's where she said she was heading. I was going to run them over in the car - tomorrow night, you say? You're quite certain? Yes, of course you are. If she's not there, well, I must have misheard, that's all. Never mind, I'm sorry to bother you. Yes, I will, thank you, good night Mrs. Sampson."

George hung up the receiver with a deep frown. He looked down at the Avon products on the table and scratched his head, then returned to the kitchen to find the scotch glass he'd been originally searching for. He found a glass, poured himself a drink and stood at the kitchen window, watching the rain hit the glass pane. What had only minutes before been a splatter, was now a downpour. George's mouth tightened to a straight line and his brow furrowed with a heavy burden of worry. Then, quite unexpectedly, his eyes flashed with a tinge of something quite unfamiliar to him. Anger.

Just as she had the night before, Betty parked her bicycle under the tree across the road from Kitty's Kat House. She pulled her crocodile-skin bag from the back rack and squeezed the leather handles as she strode across the road with it through the rain, arranging a bright smile on her face. With a look of consideration, she changed tack, and ducked into the dark alley beside the club. A shiny new *blackout special* Chevrolet was parked near the side door that Betty guessed led down to Vince's office. She looked around surreptitiously, then lifted her skirt delicately and pulled her largest knife from her garter. *It would be rather a shame to ruin such lovely paintwork.* With a quick flick of the wrist, Betty stabbed each tire in turn, careful not to scratch the beige finish, then sheathed her knife and continued back to the entrance of the bordello. She placed her cosmetic bag down on the doorstep. Glass jars clinked softly against one another inside. Betty smoothed down her red dress and plumped her hair, then knocked briskly on the door.

The door swung open to reveal a busty woman with a mass of peppered hair twisted on top of her head. A satin burgundy dress with high shouldered sleeves contoured her ample figure to her knees and she had a large freckle drawn above her lip. Behind her, the bordello was in full swing.

"Yes?" the woman said, one eyebrow raised at Betty.

"Avon Calling!" Betty replied brightly, picking up her bag. The older woman rolled her eyes. The door slammed in Betty's face. Betty knocked again. After a moment with no response, she knocked again, then again, progressively louder each time. Soon, the door swung open for a second time. There was no need to read this woman's thoughts, they were written on her face, clear as day. Betty liked her immediately. It was always refreshing to find someone who spoke their mind. All Betty had to do then, was change it.

"Avon Calling!" Betty repeated.

"So you said, cookie," the manageress replied sourly. "You do realize where you are, don't you? My girls are the prettiest in town, I don't need you peddling your beauty products 'round here." Betty wedged her foot in the door, just before it shut again.

"Of course, you're right, Madam!" Betty gushed. "My goodness, no, you don't need anyone to tell you how to dolly up your girls! Why, Kitty's has the finest reputation in all of New York City! That'd be your influence, undoubtedly - an elegant lady like yourself. I can tell when a place of business is well run. Women know these things -" she gave the manageress a meaningful look. "Don't they, Madam...?"

"...Trixie," the woman finished for her, still dubious at Betty's motives, but flattered all the same.

"Madam Trixie," Betty smiled. She looked over her shoulder onto the dark street behind and lowered her voice. "No, it's not your ladies I'm worried about, ma'am. It's the girls at The Harlem Shake! Haven't you heard?"

"Heard what?" Madam Trixie asked, clearly intrigued.

"Oh dear, they're in a terrible fix!" Betty said. "I really must explain! It's just awful." She nudged her way into the brothel with her Avon bag, shepherding the madam ahead of her with apparent purpose. "I'll tell you the whole story, but you must show me to the dressing room at once, I was so worried when I heard! I thought immediately of your lovely girls, I'd heard this was a favorite for shore-leavers and I couldn't imagine a worse predicament for you -" Betty continued her animated volubility as she followed Madam Trixie through the innards of the brothel, taking careful note of its layout. They passed through a series of drinking rooms crowded with rowdy gentlemen occupying plush lounges and card tables under swirls of cigar smoke. At the back of the main parlor was a circular stage with two dancers performing an elaborate shimmy with great sparkling fans made of peacock feathers. A long, polished bar lined with drunken, cheering sailors stood to its left. The area was a hive of activity, with dancing and clinking glasses and customers frequently disappearing with prostitutes up a curved staircase on the far side of the bar. At a large table near the front windows, Vince Carelli and five of his men sat with their heads together. As Betty passed through, still rambling to Madam Trixie as they alighted the stairs, she noticed Vince and his men get to their feet and disappear behind the red velvet curtains of the stage. Betty narrowed her eyes, then took Madam Trixie's elbow with renewed enthusiasm. "It's because of the war, of course," she was saying, as they entered the dressing room. A dozen prostitutes and dancers were bustling around in various stages of costume. Madam Trixie, who by now was completely enthralled, gestured for the women to gather in as Betty talked. "The trading routes have opened up and it's all new ingredients, I'm afraid!"

"From China, you say?" asked Madam Trixie.

"That's right, some sort of powder in the face-creams. And would you believe it? Their faces - they've all turned bright orange! Faces like a turnip and none of them making a dime!" The collective women gasped in astonishment. "And it itches too

- ever so nasty! First orange, then red raw. And after that the sores develop. There's no covering them up, either." Betty shook her head sadly.

"Are you sure?" a small woman asked, with an effervescence of red curls spilling onto her bare shoulders. "I saw some of the girls from Harlem Shake just yesterday in town and they looked fine."

"Well, I hope they stay so, my dear," said Betty, "but I wouldn't hold my breath. Such lovely girls and it'll take weeks to wear off. I saw the doctor calling just this afternoon at the Gentlemen's Club on Hargrave Street and I've seen ladies all over town looking like pumpkins! It's my business to know, of course. That's the trouble with pots from the drug store - you never know what's in them." In less than a minute, Betty had the women entirely won over.

"Good lord!" said Madam Trixie, "but how do we know which cream was to blame?"

Betty looked across to a dressing table and picked up a pot of face-cream. "Why this is the very one! And this!" as she picked up another. Her captive audience gasped in horror and a few women began reflexively scratching their faces. "You just never know where the ingredients come from, it's not all apple-pie these days with rationing," Betty warned, taking the red-head's face in her hands and examining it critically. "We must be extra-vigilant with our skin-care ladies, after all our looks are our best weapon!" There was a muttering of agreement.

"But I used that cream just this evening!" the red head exclaimed, feverishly rubbing her face. "Felix will be coming in later and I'm going to look like a pumpkin!"

"Stop that Tilly!" cried the Madam, pulling the woman's hands from her own face. "Wash your face immediately! All of you girls! Wash your faces and re-do them, then relieve the girls on duty so they can do the same. I will not have a pack of pump-kins working in my fine establishment!" Tilly ran off to the sinks and began scrubbing her face in earnest and the others followed. Madam Trixie turned to Betty, clearly exasperated. "What should we do then? I can't lose my girls to a face-cream fiasco! I have a business to run. Our landlord checks the takings every night."

"Mr. Carelli, I assume?" Betty asked, innocently.

Madam Trixie nodded curtly. "Mr. Carelli for years, but Mr. Felix has taken over of late, and he's not a man to be trifled with." The madam held her shoulders straighter with a grim expression and glanced toward Tilly, still washing her face. "Tilly's the only one that can stand that awful man. I may be the proprietor here, but I still have to pay my way for the rooms and expenses. I'm all tied up. If the girls can't work, I'll be indebted in ways I don't want to imagine. I won't have any harm come to them you know. I may be in the business, but I take good care of my girls."

"I completely understand your predicament," Betty said. "And I'm grateful I thought to stop by. This was just what I was worried about." She looked thoughtfully around the room. "You know what, I'll leave you my samples, I have more than enough - no payment required!" Betty lifted her Avon bag onto the dresser and began unloading small pots of face-cream. Each of the working girls took one with a squeal of delight and raced back to their mirrors to begin the tedious process of making themselves up over again. Outside, Betty heard the rain pick up pace. Thunder cracked and rolled beyond the windowpane with the resonance of a steel drum and flashes of lightning traced the edges of the lace curtain.

Madam Trixie's expression was of sheer relief. "I insist on paying, Mrs. -?."

Betty turned to her, with sincere kindness, gently sidestepping the question. "No, I wouldn't hear of it. It's a community service keeping your ladies looking the part. Work is hard to come by these days and I don't doubt many of your girls have littlies to look after at home. Besides, there's many a lonely man out there with no other arms to keep him warm."

"Well that's the truth," Madam Trixie said. "Those doll-dizzy service boys find a second home here on shore leave -"

"Well of course they do! There's no charge, madam, I really must insist. We women must stick together, whatever the weather!"

"You'll return in a few days with a bigger order, won't you though? I'll need two dozen pots to start and another dozen every week. It seems I can't trust the cosmetics at the drug store, that's for certain!"

"You leave it to me, Madam. I'll bring your order and some catalogs to browse as well," said Betty, delicately pulling on her gloves. "Now, I must get back to my own husband. No, no, you stay right here and deal with this little emergency! I'll let myself out."

Betty picked up her bag and left the room as Madam Trixie began issuing orders to the women in the room. They were hurrying to and fro, preparing to relieve those downstairs from their duties to give them an opportunity to scrub their faces clean.

Betty knew the following twenty minutes would be a fuss of distracted conversation and confusion as word spread of the terrible rash plaguing women's faces in the streets. Twenty minutes was more than enough.

A twinge of guilt hit her. She never liked to deceive people if she could help it, especially young women. Unfortunately, deception was an unavoidable counterpart to murder, which was, of course, what she was about to commit.

5

———

IN FOR A DIME, IN FOR A DOLLAR

As Betty descended the staircase, the lights dimmed. A burlesque singer swept out from behind the split velvet curtain of the stage and walked to a microphone. Her negligée glittered and shimmered under the lights. Cigar smoke swirled from the busy card tables up the open staircase to where Betty paused above the dark room, as the brass band struck up a new tune. The singer lifted her arm seductively and played to the crowd as she sang, hitching the breath of every man in the room.

> "Why can't you be true, like all the other
>   men do?"

She stepped off the stage and wove through her audience singing, tracing her fingernail enticingly down the cheek of one man and leaning into another with a wink. She was altogether bewitching. And her timing – impeccable. Every sailor and suit was spellbound, a stupid smile smacked onto his face as she teased with a shimmy and a fluttering of lashes. Betty's heart warmed in a moment of pride. There was nothing she loved to see more than a woman in control. The room was entirely at her mercy.

How silly of them not to realize, Betty mused, as she quietly descended the remainder of the staircase and stole around the edge of the room unseen.

The singer leaned forward, jiggling her audience into distraction and Betty took the opportunity to slip behind the velvet curtains of the stage with her crocodile-skin bag. A long hallway ran along the back of the brothel with a closed door at both ends. It was a safe guess that one of those doors led down to Vince's basement office. Betty chose the end closest to the alleyway where she'd seen Vince's men unloading the stolen crates. She stifled a yawn against her glove as she walked toward the door, then stopped and closed her eyes for a moment. The pressure of knives strapped around her thigh felt like the reassurance of an old friend. With chin held high and a glint in her eye, Betty opened the door. She found herself at the top of a staircase. She ducked inside and jammed the door handle locked behind her.

As Betty descended the staircase, the brass band and singer faded away, replaced by the sharp clap of thunder and downpour of rain from the alleyway beyond Vince's office. It was a shame. Betty always liked a gay tune to work to. Still, the rain and thunder were a blessing. No one would hear them die.

At the bottom of the stairs, Betty waited. The second doorway was already open a crack. It was Vince's office, not least telling by his obnoxious voice trailing up the stairs. She peeked around the edge of the door, still hidden. Inside the room, crates were stacked up against the opposite wall, beside a plain door. It was a safe bet to lead back upstairs and out to the alleyway.

An argument had erupted between the six men that had come downstairs. Betty hugged the shadow of the door, eyeing them carefully. Each man had the tell-tale signs of a pistol strapped under his jacket, and a Tommy-gun lay upon the table as a deliberately careless threat.

A lanky man sat on Vince's desk in front of the gun, dangling his legs. Betty knew of him. *Sydney Corke.* A made guy, relatively new to the family. The unmistakable shape of a Colt Vest Pocket was hidden in his exposed sock. A backup pistol, only good at close range. A favorite of Donny's crew. Utterly predictable.

"You can't chicken out of the deal now, Jimmy," Vince threatened. Twelve years hadn't aged him much. His mouth was pinched up, the way it had always twisted as a boy when his cousins beat him at mumbley peg with their flick knives. Soon, the pinch would give way to red blotches on his neck and cheeks. Betty had seen it countless times as a child, usually followed by an almighty temper tantrum that sent everyone rushing to placate him. "I pulled this lot from one of Donny's jobs," Vince said, flinging his arm to the side to indicate the stack of crates behind him. "What am I meant to do with it?" His face flushed red under the dangling light fixture in the center of the room.

"Donny's been watching me, Vince," Jimmy argued. "I know it- I got a feeling. If he catches me toutin' for you we're both dead."

"Make 'im take it, Vinnie" a fourth man urged. "No one breaks a deal with us!" The man in question was chewing tobacco with his legs apart and arms crossed, oozing arrogance. His face was freckled and pinched under a shock of scruffy ginger hair. Every move that Vince made was reflected back through the man's eyes in equal parts idolatry and envy. This one was Travis Colby. Betty knew him all too well from her days on the street.

As a kid, Travis had had a penchant for tormenting the stray dogs that loitered near his neighborhood park. He'd latched onto Vince like a leach and was always neck deep in trouble.

Travis was reckless *and* cruel- the most dangerous combination of all.

"You said you have a buyer, just do it quiet-like," Vince pushed. "How's Donny gonna know?"

"I can't! They've gone cold on me, don't want to risk getting caught," said Jimmy. "Jack Sidler did Donny over last month and look what happened to him."

Betty's lips formed a hard line. She knew very well what had happened to Jack last month. Stupid kid. He was in over his head before he'd even set foot on the street.

The last of Vince's men was closest to her, with his back to the door. He was a bear of a man, with hunched shoulders and thick fingers that twitched reflexively over his coat pockets. *The Muscle.* Given he was in her way, Betty decided to dispatch him first.

She considered her options as they bickered. The two extras weren't really part of her plan. They weren't Vince's usual gang, although she knew of them. The smaller man was Jimmy Chan. He wore a white zoot suit and rather splendid hat. *Pity. I do appreciate a man with style.* Underneath the brim, his eyes darted uneasily. Jimmy had a reputation for eating alone, small time jobs, and Betty was surprised to find him caught up with Vince. She tapped into Jimmy's thoughts, curious at his change of heart.

If I don't move this shit, Rex's gonna scalp me. But, Donny – no way, this ain't worth a bullet in the brain for.

Betty frowned. Rex Hatfield was the biggest bookie in town. His empire was built on the backs of whipped thoroughbreds and desperate, addicted fools that bet their kid's meal-money on a stampede of adrenaline at the gate. The races were fixed, of course, and every man that worked for Rex was as crooked as his false walking cane. For the poor bastards that found themselves out of their depth in debt, punishment was hard and fast. It seemed Jimmy was currently under that press.

Jimmy's collusion with Vince now made sense, and if word on the street was anything to go by, so was the recent escalation of his crimes. Only a month ago, Jimmy and his offsider had clipped some New State Bank guards on-route with a transfer truck of greenbacks. They'd never been caught, though Betty would have gladly taken them out herself, had she not been otherwise occupied at the time dealing with a couple of street rats pushing for Vince. Now, it seemed Jimmy's urgency to get his paws on some cash was clearly reaching breaking point. That he'd risk skimming Donny's haul to pawn it with Vince spoke for itself. At least it had. Now, he'd gotten cold feet.

Jimmy's offsider had remained silent throughout the exchange. In fact, Betty realized she'd never actually heard him speak at all. Perhaps he couldn't. She'd come across these two once before. At that time, Betty had had no choice but to leave them to their dirty business, intent as she was at the time, on her own. Jimmy's man was tall, with a red satin tie and a row of gold-capped teeth up front. *I wonder how hard they'd be to knock out,* Betty mused.

Oh well, she decided. In for a dime, in for a dollar.

Betty gently intertwined her gloved fingers and cracked her knuckles. Family reunions were such fun. She lifted her hand to the door.

Knock, knock, knock.

Betty reclaimed her bag and poked her head around the open door, looking in.

"Good evening, gentlemen! I do hope I'm not intruding!" Her eyes were positively gleeful. "You see I followed you down here, I believe I may be of some assistance to you this evening." She clucked sympathetically, at the stunned look on all six faces that spun toward her. "You seem to be in rather a pickle, don't you?"

"What the hell's this?" said Vince, looking to the men around him for some sort of recognition. Betty stepped in and shut the door behind her. A key was hanging out of the door lock, which she clicked satisfyingly into place. *They're as good as dead.* She dropped her bag to the floor.

Finding nothing but confusion on the other men's faces, Vince's frown shifted into a look of bemusement and he stepped forward. "I think you got the wrong office, kitten. Call girls are upstairs." He laughed, then let his eyes sweep her body. "But if you're that keen to help me out, I'll sample your goods first, make sure Madam Trixie is getting a sweet deal for puttin' you on the books. You got a swell herring-cookie-pusher look I could really dig. What do ya' say, boys?"

Sydney and Travis let out a bark of laughter and the burly guard smirked. Only Jimmy and his gold-toothed sidekick stood still and silent, apprehensive at Betty's sudden appearance.

Betty joined the laughter, walking into the room with ease. She placed her hand daintily against The Muscle's bicep, his arms crossed over his chest. She flashed him an endearing smile, then turned back to Vince.

"Oh, yes, you like selling women, don't you Vince? I suppose you're rather pleased your Uncle Donny let you play the big boss here for a few years. Gives you a sense of power to go with that entitlement you've always carried. You always were a rather small man."

"Hey! What do you mean by that?" said Vince, the grin sliding off his face.

"It's just like I said, Vinnie. I rather tired of you profiting from other people's hard work." She stepped surreptitiously away from The Muscle, pointing to the same portrait of Donny on the wall as Frankie had had in his office at Capitol Palace. It undoubtedly hid the safe behind it, as before. "And I think Donny has rather enough money now, don't you?"

Vince's eyes narrowed. There was a shift in the room, and she felt The Muscle sizing her up. He didn't move though. She still, apparently, posed no real threat.

"Who are you?" Vince said. The humor was gone.

"I'm rather astonished you still don't recognize me," Betty feigned disappointment. "Oh well, no matter. You know, I sell something now too, Vincent." Betty pulled an *Avon Calling!* card from her coat pocket. She flicked it at his face. "And I'm rather good at my job."

Vince bent down and picked the card up.

"Cosmetics," he stated flatly. "I'm being threatened by a fucking make-up lady." The other men sniggered. Even Jimmy's silent offsider, gave a fleeting gold-capped smile.

"Throw her out."

"Not yet, Vince, we were just getting reacquainted."

Betty leapt into the air toward the huge guard, snapping her legs shut either side of his thick neck and twisting his head hard to the right. The momentum swung them both around in a full circle, and he lost balance, crashing to the floor in a mass of limbs and confusion as the men scattered around her. Betty wrenched a knife from her garter as she landed on top of him, just for good measure. *Can't be too careful with these large fellows,* she thought.

The Muscle, down.

Quick as lightning, Betty withdrew her blade from between the guards' ribcage as she jumped up again, throwing herself across the table where the Tommy Gun lay. She smashed into Sydney Corke, who was scrambling to his feet as she slid across the desk, collecting the Tommy in her free hand. The lanky man's fingers grappled for his Colt as they fell to the floor behind the table, out of sight. The others had finally caught on. Bullets began to fly. She ducked low as they ricocheted off the steel edges of the table above her.

Betty dropped her bloodied knife beside her. She smacked Sydney's right hand against the concrete floor with her left, knocking the pistol from his fist and letting it spin away behind the crates.

Sitting astride his chest with one knee buried into Sydney's throat and one gloved fist punching his face, Betty flicked the safety catch on the Tommy gun she had collected in her right hand, and locked the bolt, detaching the magazine drum from the firearm. She flung the magazine of bullets into the dark space under a heavy filing cabinet to her left. *Tommy gun disarmed.* She looked down, pleased with her multitasking skills.

It's just like cooking with too many pots on the boil, she thought, and I am a rather fine cook.

Sydney was lying stupefied beneath her, blood on his face. She retrieved her already bloodied knife. A quick flick of the wrist and he'd never get up to kill again.

Sydney Corke, down.

"Stand up," Vince shouted from beyond the desk.

Gladly, Betty did. The floor was a bloody mess and her lovely red dress was getting wrinkled. As she rose to her feet, she found herself the center of attention of four gun barrels.

"What is this?" Jimmy Chan spat. His gun was shaking. "You call me down here into some kind of ambush?" He turned and redirected his gun at Vince instead. "Who is this crazy bitch?"

Vince was fuming. "How the hell am I meant to know? She's insane!" His face was as blotchy as Betty had ever seen it. His eyes were wild. "How do I know you didn't bring her? It's my men she's belted, not yours!" Vince swung his arm around, taking aim at Jimmy instead. Both men drew themselves up, fingers poised.

"I didn't bring her!" Jimmy hissed.

"Well, neither did I!"

Outside, thunder cracked loudly, bringing a rattle to the very bones of the building. The rain was belting down.

"Oh, how delightful," Betty laughed darkly, wiping the blade of her knife against the edge of the desk in front of her. "Please do shoot each other and save me the trouble."

"Who are you?" Vince said, snapping his pistol back to point at Betty's chest. He stretched his neck to the side, trying to see the man that had disappeared over the table to the floor below. Only Sydney's ankles were visible to the men, unless they moved closer to Betty, which it seemed, Vince wasn't willing to do. "Syd! Syd! Get up, man!"

"Oh, Sydney won't be getting up any time soon," Betty purred. "I think he deserves a rest after all his hard work topping GI's down by the East River, don't you think? Too much work is a killer, you know."

"Tell me who you are!" Vince yelled. Beside him, Travis was disturbingly quiet. His hair stood out livid against his pale face. Something was stirring, under the surface of his mind.

Susie Polletti. Could it be?

Betty was surprised. He was smarter than she'd given him credit for. Not a good thing.

"You still don't recognize me, Vinnie? Have I changed so much in twelve years?" Betty smoothed her skirt passively. A small smile flit on the corner of her red lips. "I suppose it has been a long time since you made my life a living hell. I'm sad to say I had expected more from my own cousin though. Even twisted Travis has worked it out."

Vince looked, dumbfounded at Travis.

"It's Susie." Travis said quietly, not taking his eyes off her. He was still, like a ghost. "Seems she's not dead, after all."

"Susie. *Little* Susie?"

"I really do wish you'd all stop calling me that," Betty sighed.

"But – you're dead."

"I'll give you a minute to catch up then, dear. Would you like some thinking music? I heard a rather jaunty little melody on the wireless the other day." Betty began humming a happy tune.

"I don't get it. Why now? After all this time?"

She stopped humming. "I have my reasons, Vince. You really shouldn't have brought children into your schemes though, you know. It just makes my job that much harder."

"No fooling. And what job is that *little* not-dead Susie?" His face flashed with venom and Vince tightened the grip on his pistol. Out of the corner of her eye, Betty saw Jimmy's man give his boss a slight nod. Apparently those two knew each other well enough that words were never needed, inside their head, or out.

"To kill you all," Betty said simply.

Everything happened at once. Betty flicked her knife clear into Travis's left shoulder as she leapt up onto the table once more, this time grabbing the dangling light fitting to hoist herself across the room into the fray. She swung above the men and snap-kicked the pistol from Travis's right hand, kicking-off from his face in an arc to take gold-teeth's gun out as well.

Smash!

Strong hands pulled her down to the floor and she landed in a heap. The stretched electrical cables from the light fitting flickered above her with a strobe flash that seemed to match the crack of thunder outside. A gut-wrenching kick caught her side. Betty curled inward in agony, struggling to breathe as a row of gold smiled at her, upside down. *Nothing. There were still no words in his mind.* Heaving air into her lungs, Betty lashed out, throwing herself onto her back, and pulling her legs into her chest, then flipped up onto her feet, crouching, ready to strike. She spun her leg hard out behind her as she came to stand, hooking the gold man behind the knees and sending him to the floor. In an instant, Jimmy took his place. She knocked him back into the wall, to punch him square in the face, but he ducked, leaving her fist to break plaster instead. As she swung back around, Betty saw a door open at the back of the room near the crates. Vince was halfway out, heading for the stairs that led to the dark alley outside. Squeezing his bleeding shoulder, Travis ran out after him, leaving a trail of profanities in his wake.

No!

Betty grabbed a knife from her garter and flung it hard toward Travis as he disappeared up the steps. She heard him cry out. But his footsteps kept on. Inside, Betty cursed herself for not thinking to lock the back door when she'd had the chance. She had to go after them, but Jimmy Chan and his silent companion had other ideas.

Punch!

Betty ducked under the fist flying toward her and Jimmy's hand caught his offsider instead. She bounced back up between them and smashed her own forehead into Jimmy's. He stumbled back. A roundhouse kick landed in gold-tooth's gut and she jumped up onto his chest, sending him crashing to the floor. Jimmy's body landed on top of them both. These two were good, better than any she'd fought.

Rip!

Betty grabbed the back of Jimmy's white zoot suit, shredding it up the middle and looped each piece around his neck from behind. She wrenched them tight together, choking the life out of him as he fell forward onto the floor. Scrambling to his feet behind her, gold-tooth lifted Betty clean off the floor, and threw her against the wall.

Crash!

A cut above her eyebrow trickled warm blood down her face. Betty froze. A mark. One that George could see. Blind rage exploded and Betty threw herself across the room, striking out wildly as she went. She grabbed gold-tooth's hair and pulled down his head, smashing it into Jimmy's as he came at her from the other direction.

"You're wasting my time!" Betty growled. She jumped across the table, landing on Sydney's dead body. Grabbing the desk chair that had been knocked to the side, Betty flung it, hard at the men. The steel-framed legs caught them in the gut side-by-side, straight through. They stopped, pinned to the spot, like macabrely connected twins.

Then they fell.

Betty was out the back door before they hit the floor.

She belted up the stairs two at a time, her Avon bag forgotten against the closed door on the other side of the bloodied room. She burst through the outer door into the alley beyond, emerging into a deluge of rain. Two dark shapes were disappearing on foot up the opposite side of the main street, turning into a dim alley on the corner of a junkyard nearby. The hood of Vince's shiny beige coupe was now bent around the concrete pillar of a street lamp twenty meters in the same direction. *So much for sparing the paintwork.* Betty was pleased she'd thought to slash his tires on her way in.

Betty raced after the men, her heels clicking against the pavement at unnatural speed. Her red dress and beige jacket billowed behind her in the dark, becoming more sodden with each step. Within seconds, she turned down the street the men had run into. Vince spun around and his face dropped in horror as she pounded toward them.

"The fence!" He yelled.

Vince took a running leap toward the paled wooden fence, scrambling up and over the top. He fell into the junkyard with a screech of pain. Betty stopped and laughed out loud. *Fool.* There was no way out, other than the way he'd come. The junkyard was surrounded by the high brick walls of buildings on two sides, to keep junkies and looters at bay. The only way in was the high fence, and a chained-up gate near the road. Inside, Vince was a sitting duck.

Travis clambered up the fence behind him, falling short. His fingers splintered back down the soaked wood.

"You're done, Travis," Betty said, quietly, behind him, hugging the derelict wall on the opposite side of the alley. "No more nasty tricks for you. No more hurting people. You were always a hopeless case, even from the beginning."

Travis turned around slowly. A cold, vindictive smile ghosted his lips. "And you always were a dark horse, little Susie. Weren't you? Little goody-two-shoes, always skulking around, watching and listening to everyone from the shadows. Pretending to be such a good girl and keeping your nose clean. I always knew there was more to you. Filthy, little whore. That's what you are. Secrets and lies." Travis' eyes gleamed and he spat rain as he spoke. "But you're just like the rest of us, aren't you? Out in the dark, killing. It's in your blood. It's in your soul, Susie. You're a murderer, just like the rest of us."

Betty took a step toward him, slipping away from the shadow of the wall. Her face looked hallowed and her dress sanguine in relief against the watery light of a streetlamp. Water ran down her face, unhindered. She drew closer, slowly, taking in the shock of hair and freckles that now stood livid against his skin from the exertion of the chase. Travis was a dead man walking.

"You think you know me, Travis?" she grinned, her eyes alight with the irony of it. "You think you know me better than I know myself?"

Travis snarled. "You're nothing but a liar, Susie. A self-right-eous little killer, who thinks she's got the dibs on morality because she had a tough start. Well, guess what? We all did."

There was a moment of silence.

When Betty spoke again, the words she used were not her own. They were memories. His memories, stolen from his mind, whispered from another time, and another place.

"Take 'em to the river, Vince, I wanna watch 'em squirm when they drown."

"Who you gonna tell, Levi? You gonna cry to your momma? No one's gonna listen to a little kid. Your word against mine – and if you think about telling, I'll do worse."

"Ajay had it coming to 'im. No one steals my shit."

"Done. He'll be rotten before anyone finds him. You can tell Donny that Mike Conway won't be be fishin' in our lake again."

"Nine GI's in a single night. Reckon' that's gotta be a record, hey Vince? How 'bout you?"

"Trevor's done for. You tell 'im he's about to wake up dead."

"There's a bullet hole where Lenny's brain used to be. Now he really can see out the back of his head."

Betty paused. "You now, I'm beginning to think you aren't a very nice person, Travis. And I don't think your pop running away to the 'sip with a hooker is where it all began." Betty smiled, a little too wide. "I think maybe, somewhere along the line, you made a choice."

There was a gray pallor to Travis now. His mouth was hanging open and fear flickered behind his eyes.

"How do you know?" he breathed. "No one knew about Mike. Only me and Vince."

"I've got a little surprise for you, Travis. I know everything about you."

She stepped forward, close enough to let him feel her breath against his neck.

"I can read your mind."

Smash!

Travis struck out, his fist catching Betty in the shoulder. She spun around and slammed him into the wooden fence.

"Oh, no you don't!"

She threw him back against the palings. The fence rattled all the way up the street. He tried to dash sideways, but quick-as-a-flash, Betty caught his arm and yanked it backward, dislocating his shoulder. He screamed in pain as he swung around, punching wildly and thrashing about. He kicked his legs, dragging her down to the pavement and grabbed her throat, squeezing. Betty gasped, rolling 'im over and smacking his head against the wet pavement, pushing his face into a watery pothole. She pried his fingers from her neck one by one as he gasped for air, then grabbed his wrist, twisting it away. She heard the snap of bone.

Betty got to her feet, straightening her dress.

"You're a killer! No better than the rest of us!" He spat up at her, choking on mud.

Betty leaned forward and tore a paling of wood off the fence with one hand.

"I know," she said, with gritted teeth. "I never said I was doing this for myself."

Crack!

Travis Colby, dead.

Betty stood for a moment, just breathing. The fat raindrops found their way down the neck of her coat, into her heels, underneath her sodden pinned hat. Somewhere in the junkyard beyond her, Vince was hiding, waiting for her. By now it must be past midnight. She couldn't bear to imagine what George might say if he ever saw the state of her. She thought of him sleeping at home, warm in his bed, the children safe and sound.

Travis had been right. She *was* a liar. Betty shifted uncomfortably. *But sometimes, lies are necessary. Sometimes they save lives.*

With a leap, Betty swung up and launched herself over the palings. She let go and landed on the other side with a thump, one foot buried in a pile of metal. As she stepped away, the heel of her shoe snapped clean off.

Bother! Betty pulled off her patent black pump. It was done for. Seething, she pulled off her second shoe, and tore off the heel to match and threw it away, then put the flats back on again. This evening just wouldn't end.

The dark rain swallowed every crack and crevice of the junkyard. The area was about the size of half a city block, piled high with rusting car bodies and bric-a-brac, not two steps clear of rubbish in any direction. The acrid smell of rotting fish wafted over from the far corner.

He was here, Betty could feel him. His mind was quiet but

agitated. Like a child trying to fight his brain into sleep when it was wide awake.

"Let's not play games, Vince," Betty called cheerfully, pulling a knife from her garter. "We both know what you've become. How many guards have you murdered running Donny's heists this month? Fifteen? Twenty?" She picked her way through twisted metal and old wooden crates in the dark, her ears straining for any sound other than the dull wash of nightlife in the streets beyond. "They all had homes, Vince. They had lives you know; children, wives. Good, decent men. Did you honestly think that you'd get away with it? That you'd never get caught?"

Betty stopped still. Breathing, irregular. Coming from the right. And finally, his mind.

"No. No, no. no. Please God, don't let her find me. I'll stop, I swear I will."

"There's no point praying now, Vince. You lost that bet years ago, dear," Betty called.

His thoughts were becoming more incoherent as she drew closer. Rattled by fear, like a playing dice loose inside his skull.

"I'll leave town. No - Donny'll find me. Yes - I'll head to the West Coast. No! I'll join the service! Just don't kill me. Not today -"

There. Crouched in the gutted chassis of a Model T Ford staring through the broken windshield to the darkness beyond. Betty crept closer and silently knelt beside him at the window.

"If only you'd done that twenty years ago, Vinnie, before you had so much blood on your hands," she said. And slit his throat.

It had been an awful night. Betty pulled herself tall as she walked back up the road toward the bordello, but she struggled to find any satisfaction in her evenings' work. She looked a mess. Her shoes were ruined. She'd frayed her lovely satin red Juliet cap on the wet pavement. To top it off, she'd broken a fingernail - she could feel it catching on the inside of her glove.

She despised Travis. Killing him was a pleasure. But the others – they were just another obstacle on her path to Donny.

Another layer of filth to peel away, before she reached the festering disease underneath.

Betty flicked the rain out of her eyes as she walked, wondering if George had stayed up late, waiting for her to arrive home. He rarely did, assuming she was in good company with her Avon customers and perfectly safe. George turned in early of an evening and slept soundly, rising bright and cheery each morning for work. His habits suited Betty's night adventures well.

But tonight, she was much later than she'd intended, drenched to the bone and covered in scrapes. She'd need a ready explanation. A very good one. But the night wasn't over yet.

Betty slipped back up the dark alley beside the bordello and returned a few moments later with her cosmetic bag, neatly packed with the cash from the wall safe behind Donny's painting. She'd gathered her knives, wiped clean on Sydney's jacket. She loaded it all into the basket of her bicycle, which was still propped against a wall in the shadows across the street. She returned to Vince's office three more times, each time bringing with her a stack of crates to tie onto the rack of her bike, stripping a fence paling from the junkyard to rest them on. It was no good leaving the crates behind. If Donny found them before the police did, the drugs would be back on the streets all too soon and lining his pockets soon after. No, they had to be taken. That is, all but one paper package she'd taken from a crate first, and left there, split in a puff of white powder across the desk. Just so there were no misunderstandings, when it came to the police. There were no victims here.

For the second night in a row, Betty found herself wheeling through the backstreets of the city, searching for a new place to stash her unwieldy pyramid of cargo. She hugged the edges of Central Park, intent on checking Herb first. He was sleeping on his usual park bench, a scattering of sodden newspapers over his face to keep the rain at bay. Betty pulled up quietly beside him. The newspapers had shifted as he'd slept, revealing a closed eye and lightly bulbous nose, pink with broken veins. Betty flattened her feet either side against the pavement to keep her pyramid of crates from losing balance, then reached down to unfasten her umbrella from the crossbar underneath her. It was far too late for her to bother covering up anyway and losing it might help explain her appearance if George was cross. The umbrella fitted nicely over the top half of Herb's body.

For a minute, she watched him sleep, stretched out on the park bench. Above him, the American elm which Betty considered to be his, reached its branches out protectively, lessening the shower. She was always quite grateful to that elm. Herb's scraps of possession were shoved under the park bench beneath him, in a puddle.

Betty sailed past Herb often, usually to throw a sandwich or apple his way on route to stash a haul of crates. He lived quite a jolly life, inside his own mind, not quite *altogether* anymore. He drifted in and out of reality, which Betty took advantage of – she could visit him knowing he'd never speak of it again, as he'd either forget or consider it a figment of his own imagination. Besides, if he'd told anyone about the lady that rode through the night with a dozen wooden crates of heroin balanced on the back of her bicycle, who would have believed him? Nobody. He was a wino and a tramp. Pitied, but ignored.

Herb probably didn't even remember his old life, Betty mused. The one he'd had before Donny. He'd lost that reality years ago, after his wife and children fled in fear of the repercussions of a bad-debt he owed to Donald Pinzolo. Herb was forced to repay in dirty service to Donny, and it didn't suit his temperament. He was grief-stricken, out of his depth and developed frayed nerves and a weak mind. Herb had tried to keep clean, but in the end, he'd found solace on the inside of a bottle, and washed away the loss until he could no longer remember it at all.

Even if he had, Herb would never have recognized Betty, and the part she'd once played in his fate. But *she* remembered.

***

"I got a payment coming in next week. I swear!"

"Next week, hey?"

"Sure thing, Donny. I've got a shipload of electric shavers arriving from the coast - real fancy, don't need soap or nothin'. You just plug it into a wall socket and bam! So long, barber. They're gonna sell like hotcakes. I'll get you one - on the house!"

Donny Pinzolo leant back in his chair, took a drag on his cigar. "Santori gives me as close a shave as I need every day." Smoke hung on the air around him, a smell like old barnyards and saddle leather that infused all of their clothing. "This is the third time we've been here, Herb. I was generous. You've racked up quite a sum. Your terms were a month. I've always been generous with you, haven't I?"

"Course you have, Donny." Herb Connell scuffed his shoe against the paisley rug. He sniffed and shoved his hands into his pockets. "I got done over, that's all. It wasn't my fault. Charlie said the horse was good to win, twenty-to-one. Said it was a sure thing. Would've had enough to pay you back, and more, but the bastard took off with my loot and I haven't seen him since."

"Charlie Hopper, you say? From the stockyards?"

"That's right," Herb said. He rubbed his nose.

"Mmmm." Donnie studied him, smiling. He didn't talk right away. Not out loud, at least.

What do you say, little Susie? *Came Donny's voice in her head.* Is Herb here telling the truth?

Beside Donnie's desk, Susie's eyes widened and her head shot up. She sat with her arms wrapped around her skinny legs, which were pulled up onto the chair. If she'd curled up any tighter, she might have disappeared altogether, which would have suited her fine.

She hated Donny. She hated being there. Most of all, she hated her father. An hour earlier, she'd been pulled from her bed and shoved into the back seat of her pop's dusty Cunningham and driven down to the docks, where Donny kept a warehouse.

She was there to work.

It was only a couple of months' ago that Donny learned she had inherited her late mother's ability to tap into their heads. He must have suspected she might have the gift too. She hadn't meant for him to find out but Donny had tricked her.

Susie was mesmerized by a jar of gumballs that appeared on Donny's desk, a treat her father would never have bothered with. Donny knew it. "Take some candy, kid," he'd said one day. It was only after her hand was already inside the jar of gumballs on his desk that she realized her mistake. He'd never opened his mouth.

And so it began. At first, it had only been once or twice a week, but it had grown quickly. Now, she was lucky to scrape together a few hours' sleep before school each morning. Donny used her as often as he liked, just as he had used her mother. Her pop was always pleased to deliver. With his wife gone, Roy was less useful to his uncle's business. And less useful meant disposable. Roy wasn't well built, couldn't hold his own in a fight and was more sour and stupid than his older brother, Frank. His wife had been the best he'd had to offer Donny. He should have guessed Susie was the same. When Donny learned his twelve-year-old daughter's secret, Roy had struck gold. He was useful again, had something to offer. So, whenever Donny called, he dragged Susie to the docks to read the minds of swindlers and dealers as they ran at the mouth, guns at their heads. And Susie told Donny what he wanted to hear. The truth. The truth that, more often than not, got them killed.

Tonight was one more blur between school books and fear.

An uncovered light bulb hung over Donny's desk, stinging Susie's tired eyes. She rubbed them and pulled herself up straight. Her Uncle

Frank knew what she was there for and the two enforcers guarding Herb knew better than to ask questions. They were used to her presence now, as they had been used to her mother before her.

Roy's fist hit the side of her arm. She sucked in her breath, squeezing the pain away with her fingers. Donny was looking at her. Even her father, as stupid as he was, didn't need to read Donny's mind to know he was waiting for an answer.

Susie eyed Herb, who looked quizzically between her and Donny. He'd clearly noticed her in the chair beside Donny's desk when he'd first arrived, but was too nervous then with his own plight, to question it. Now, feeling more confident that Donny seemed to be considering his situation, Herb offered her a smile. Susie automatically smiled back, then faltered and looked away. It was harder if they were nice.

"This your girl, Donny?" Herb said, frowning in confusion. "What's a kid doin' up this late at night? Should be in bed, yeah? My missus gets the little monkeys in bed by eight."

Donny cocked his head toward Herb, then back to Susie. With a sigh, she faintly shook her head. Her stomach hurt. She curled up tighter.

"You're lying to me, Herb," Donny announced. "There is no shipment."

Herb's mouth dropped open. "But - there is! I mean, I might not have set it up yet, but I know a guy who works for Schick. He's gonna get me some off the truck, owes me a favor. I swear. I just have to make a call. One call and it's a done deal."

Susie squeezed her eyes closed, sifting through the desperate pleas in Herb's mind. There was a man. Francis Estelle. Delivery truck driver, fresh out of jail. He knew nothing about swiping the shavers, but - he was crooked. She caught Donny's eye and nodded her head.

"What's going on?" Herb shrieked. "Does the kid know somethin'?"

"Shut him up."

One of Donny's guards kicked the back of Herb's legs, and he crashed to his knees. A tight fist in his hair kept him upright.

Donny rolled back his black leather chair and stood slowly, stretching his legs. He leaned forward on the desk with his head hung in front of the kneeling man, a sorrowful look on his face. Instantly, one of the guards flanking Herb whipped a gun from his belt. It pressed hard against the man's temple as his pleas began anew.

"But -" Susie unraveled herself, almost falling. Her father pushed her back down onto the chair. The small click of the safety was deafening.

"No, Donny, please," Herb shouted, "I can get the money, I swear! I just need a week, is all! A few days!" Herb looked frantically at the little girl, bewildered. Susie curled into her chair again and buried her head into her knees. "It's just a phone call," Herb pleaded, "he'll come through with the goods, I promise."

Donny stood silently, watching the gun barrel bruise Herb's skin.

"You're not gonna do anything rough with a girl here, are ya? She's just a tiny mite. I swear, I'll sort this out. My Rosie, the kids — they need me!" Tears broke from the corner of his eyes.

Donny didn't move. Finally, he sat back down. He signaled to the guard, who holstered the gun.

"I'll tell you what, Herb." Donny said. "I'm going to give you a reprieve. Do you know what that means? It means I don't take it out on your kneecaps. Just this once. Because I think you might know someone worth knowing." Herb's head bobbed like a toy.

"He's good for it, he really is. Owes me a favor."

"And now you owe me another favor," Donny said. "So, you call your guy at this fancy electric shaver company and tell him what you need. Then you tell him who you need the money for and get him to come pay me a visit when he gets here." Donny smiled broadly at his men. "Bout time I got into the barber business, hey boys?"

Herb nodded, furiously. "Sure thing, Donny. Whatever you want."

"And don't you worry about Charlie Hopper. My boys'll go pay the stockyards a visit."

"I didn't mean any trouble for him. I just wanted my money is all -"

Donny waved his hand. "Get out of here. With a parting gift, boys, to remember us by." Herb was thrown out the door with a punch to the gut.

Donny stretched back in his chair.

"Well done, kid. You earned some candy."

Susie took a gumball from the jar on the desk. She knew better than to turn it down.

"Right. Time to get some real business done. I had a visit today from a couple of the hiring bosses down at the waterfront. Sounds like trouble." Donny pulled a heavily bound ledger book toward himself. "Pull up a seat, Frank." He glanced at Susie. "Roy, take the kid home."

Her father pulled her away by the neck of her night gown. Susie's uncle Frank scraped her now-empty chair toward the desk.

She was grateful. Tonight, there had been no blood. She almost didn't mind that her night gown reeked of cigar smoke. Almost.

Herb had been naïve to think Donny would have spared her. He never did. With her mother gone, Susie was Donny's new secret weapon. It didn't matter what she saw.

Frank and Donny's voices muffled as the door slammed shut behind her. Susie followed her father to the car, shivering in her thin night gown but grateful for the fresh air. Behind his back, she pegged the gumball as hard as she could into the darkness. Since that first night, she hated gumballs. She wished every time she left, that Donny would choke on one. The thought almost made her giggle. He wouldn't though. Donny never consumed any of the lures he offered others. And there were plenty.

Donald Pinzolo smuggled heroin from China, among other things. Corruption, extortion, racketeering. He took kickbacks from every hiring boss on the docks so that no longshoremen would find work unless they paid a price. He had a hand in the pocket of every bookie in town and strings behind every bootlegger and thief. All wrapped up in the veneer of a good, family businessman. There wasn't much Susie didn't know, given her unique ability to overhear their private thoughts. Not that Donny cared – a girl was no threat to him.

As Susie curled back into bed half an hour later, she buried her face in her pillowcase and breathed in, deep. Her mother's perfume. She had to use it sparingly now, the bottle was nearly empty. But as long as she only washed her pillow once a month, her mom was still close. She tried to ignore the foul remnants of Donny's cigars that clung to her hair and nightgown but couldn't. She had no other pajamas to change into, to make the smell go away. In the end, as always, an unpleasant aberration of smoke and perfume mixed inside her lungs, poisoning her dreams.

Donny and his men lived on the other side of her bedroom door. Inside, only perfume and pretty pictures were allowed. Night by night, Susie used them to build a wall around her heart, fiercely protecting the memories she kept there. Memories of her mother as Susie wished she had been, in rosy dresses with teacups and glass dishes. Shopping trips and painted faces, pretty hats and full bellies. Her imagination served her better than reality ever had.

On those walls she built inside, Susie painted a freedom that her mother had never been able to find beneath the suffocating pain she absorbed from the world around her. Ethyl's empathic ability had been too heavy a burden. Until the syringe had taken it, and her, away.

But Susie was different. Stubborn. Possessed with an inexplicable instinct for self-preservation and the defiance to see it through. She had lived and grieved too much in her young heart already and sworn that nothing would ever break her like it had her mother.

But first, she had to control it – that power of empathy that had killed her mother.

Susie was learning.

When other people's thoughts came unbidden to her mind, Susie took the emotions that came in alongside and boxed them up inside her head, leaving only words and intentions. It made all the difference. Facts alone couldn't carry guilt or misery or fear.

Only Uncle Donny had that power over her now.

He was fear. Cold, calculated fear, dressed up in a suit with a

***

Betty gently rearranged the umbrella over Herb's face. He was soaked, but so addled by the empty bottle in the brown paper bag beside him, he probably couldn't even feel the cold. The picnic blanket she'd left on him last time she'd come this way was draped over his legs, soaked through. Francis Estelle, the delivery truck driver Herb had promised stolen goods from, had never come through for Donald Pinzolo. Herb's lesson, and price, had been high. As it always was with Donny. Betty whispered goodnight, rebalanced her crates and continued on her way. Soon after, with the crates safely stashed in an unused rail shed, Betty turned for home.

"Under a paper moon," she sang, as the rain finally faltered, letting a silver glow break through the clouds. "Let's make-believe that you believe in me." She hummed the happy tune as she rode, feeling lighter with each passing mile. Her heart soared at the thought of her sleeping children, the weekend bake sale, of her darling George in his tartan slippers. Life really could be a dream. She just needed to keep it that way.

Betty parked her bicycle by the side of her house and carried her

Avon bag to the back door, steeling herself for whatever lay within. She straightened her dress and jacket, re-pinned her sodden hat and slid the knives from her garter. She wrapped them quickly in a towel and hid them under a false paving stone in the garden. There would be time enough tomorrow to clean them properly.

Smile.

Betty quietly let herself through the back door. The house was silent. She slipped off her shoes and jacket and dropped them in the laundry tub. She tiptoed into the sitting room; an apologetic smile ready on her lips. She needn't have worried. George was asleep in his chair, the tendrils of smoke from his cigar, long gone. She watched him snore, with a look of utmost tenderness in her eyes. He'd be cross, when he woke. Angry, even. But even then, he'd never raise his voice at her. Never hit her or be cruel. He would always be a gentleman.

Betty ducked back upstairs and quickly prepared for bed. She washed her face and hid her wet clothes, choosing a high-necked night gown to hide the bruises on her throat. She wrapped her damp hair in a crochet net to conceal it, mussed up her bedclothes and went back downstairs. Pulling a glass bottle of milk from the fridge, Betty poured enough for two mugs and set it to warm on the stove. She walked through to the sitting room.

"George, darling?"

He snuffled and turned on the couch.

"My dear, you really must come to bed now." Betty took his hands but still he didn't wake. She began pulling him gently from the couch.

"Betty?" George said, coming to. "Where the blazers have you been? I was worried sick."

"I've been home for hours, dear. I thought to let you sleep on the couch because you looked so comfortable, but I just can't sleep without you. I've been tossing and turning. I feel so much safer with you by my side."

George pushed her back a little and looked carefully at his wife's face. Betty didn't flinch. He found nothing but sincerity returned.

"I called Marjory Sampson, Betty."

"You did?" Her heart flipped. "Of course, you did. I left her cosmetics on the bench! Only, I wasn't there, of course. I was with Cynthia Westlakes - so you needn't have worried at all. I'm so sorry, George."

"Cynthia Westlakes? I've never even heard of her. And you said you were going to Marjory Sampson, I distinctly remember you said *Mrs. Sampson!*" The color had risen in George's face, and even by the light of the lamp, Betty could see he was more upset than she'd expected. George broke away, pacing. He walked into the kitchen. Betty followed. "I felt like such a goose, Betty! Ringing Mrs. Sampson like that and you weren't even there. Probably got her up out of bed! I was worried about you for hours - thought you'd been taken by the Jerries!"

"I'm so very sorry, George, darling!" Betty gushed. "I just don't know what I was thinking. I was so befuddled yesterday at the thought of the church social that I mixed up my appointments. First it started raining and I got entirely soaked, and then when I arrived to see Miss Westlakes with her new eye shadow, she was in a terrible fix about some boy who she says was a dreamboat to begin with but now he's gone and left her in a terrible state all on her own. She doesn't know what to tell her parents and I feel I really should do something, the poor dear hasn't got a soul she can turn to and I know how terrible she must feel about that – she's already twelve weeks gone -"

George strode over and gently pushed his index finger to her lips.

"Slow down, jitterbug." He smiled sadly. "I just feel a little bruised, that's all. I thought perhaps you'd found somewhere better to be. Or *someone*, to be with, if you want to get technical about it."

"George, no!"

"Well, you're awfully preoccupied these days. I barely get to see you. And don't think I don't see the way other men look at you Betty, they always have. I got lucky; I know that. But if you think I'm going down without a fight, you've got another thing coming. I'd take on anyone that tried to steal you away from me!" George's pale skin flushed. Something within him seemed to spark. Something Betty hadn't known was there.

She reached out to touch his face, earnestly.

"There's nowhere I'd rather be, George. Wherever I am, I'd always rather be here with you. You must know that."

"No," George replied, hesitantly. "I don't think I do anymore, really."

"But I do! Why, George, you and the children are my life! I couldn't bear to think of losing you."

"But we're not going anywhere -"

"I'd fight to the ends of the earth to keep you all safe!"

"Well that's hardly necessary -"

"Do you honestly think I'd throw that away, George? For the sake of a silly dalliance?"

"Well, I suppose not..."

Betty reached her arms around his neck to press her face against his. As she did so, the long sleeves of her nightgown fell back.

"Good lord! What are these bruises on your arm? And these scratches? They look ghastly! Now, come on, you can't tell me you got those from Cynthia Westlakes! You need to see a nurse."

"Oh, it's nothing, George," Betty said, pulling away and grabbing her apron from the cupboard door. "I just fell that's all. The streets were wet -" She busied herself pulling two mugs from the cupboard, thinking furiously. She picked up the warming saucepan from the stove and began to pour. Desperately, her empathic abilities reached out, searching for inspiration. She needed a distraction. There must be someone, somewhere... *Perfect!*

"I fell off my bike, you see. In the storm on my way home. It had been such a long night and I was already so tired! I suppose I wasn't watching where I was going, and I nearly hit - it was sitting right there in the middle of the street – I could barely see

- oh, my goodness, now look what I've done! Oh, I'm such a mess tonight!" Betty exclaimed, as milk spilled all over the kitchen floor and on her husband's pajama legs and slippers. "Oh dear, stay there George, and I'll fetch a towel for you."

Betty rushed out of the kitchen into the laundry, then out the back door into the yard. She listened, her heart racing, desperate to hear that little noise in her head, the one that would tell her where to go. *That way.* Over the back fence. Betty hitched up her night gown as she raced up the yard and took a leap to hurdle the back fence. She dashed through her neighbor's yard, crossed the road and found herself in the park. *Down there.* Caught in a storm-water drain beside the road was her prize. *A mewling kitten.* It greeted her with a cry – the same one she'd heard in her head only a minute before. She fished the little straggled body out of the drain, rolled it in her nightdress and dashed back over the fence to her laundry, collecting a fresh towel on her way through to the kitchen.

"I just fell, that's all," she continued, as if nothing had happened. Betty passed the towel to George, who began to mop up his feet. "I took a nasty turn on my bicycle and scraped myself silly - it was all thanks to this little devil -" She gently unwrapped the kitten from her night gown and placed it on the table. "It sent me head over heels into a ditch! I had to bring it home, of course. I popped him in the laundry earlier, didn't want to bother you with it until tomorrow."

George picked up the black and white kitten. White fur had all but dissolved like wet candy floss on its tiny paws and chest, and the black hair everywhere else clung to its skin.

"Well, how could this be a bother," George beamed, already smitten. "I mean, it's terrible you took such a tumble, but thank goodness that's all it was." He put the kitten on the floor at his feet. "The children will be beside themselves when they see it. And now we have someone to mop up the spilt milk, too."

Betty pulled out a chair. She rubbed her eyes, relieved that

George's concerns had finally been soothed. Every inch of her body ached for the little sleep the morning still offered.

"I'll fetch a hot-water bottle for it to sleep on," she said, yawning, "And visit the veterinarian tomorrow. The children can think of a name -"

💋

"Didn't hear a blessed thing," said the bordello matron, fanning herself dramatically. Sergeant Jacob Lawrence raised an eyebrow.

"Nothing at all? It's quite a scene down there, Mrs. -?"

"It's Madam Trixie, love. And you don't know the half of it. It was a scene upstairs as well! What with a brothel full of turnip-faces and girls running to and 'fro trying to clean up, then a thunderstorm that cracked the roof tiles and flooded the third-floor boudoirs! Lost an entire wardrobe of unmentionables. I hadn't a moment to think straight last night - and now this! Mr. Carelli was bad business, but I never wanted to see him done over!" She blew her nose loudly on a lace handkerchief.

"He was the landlord of Kitty's Kat House?"

Madam Trixie nodded.

"And you didn't see anyone suspicious here last night? No unfamiliar gentlemen?"

"Good lord, Sergeant! This is a brothel! Men come and go like ships in the night, especially lately with the service boys at shore. We have regulars, of course, but I can't keep track of every breeze that blows in. There's not a night goes by suspicious men aren't at my tables. Well, that's why we're here!"

"And what about Mr. Carelli? What kind of company did he keep?" asked Jacob, knowing full well the answer was being loaded into body bags a floor below where he stood.

"All I do is pay for my board and business, Sergeant. He keeps his office and my girls visit him when he wants it, but

200

there's nothing more I can tell you. I run a clean house here and I look after my girls. I never involved myself in his affairs, and I wouldn't wanna know anyhow."

"I understand," Jacob sighed. "Thank you for your time. My officers will be up soon to speak to your girls."

He'd hoped for even a tingle of a lead, but the woman had nothing. Madam Trixie turned away, dabbing her nose.

"Fat lot of good that'll do you," she muttered as she left. "Not one of 'em heard a thing until poor Tilly found that lot down-stairs. They were all in a tizzy and too busy scrubbing their faces to keep from getting that god-awful rash. If it wasn't for that Avon Lady stopping by, we'd have been a right mess -" she trailed off as she left the room.

Jacob froze. *Avon Lady?*

"Wait - "

"Lawrence!" A tall man strode into the room, a flurry of assistants trailing him. Within seconds he had Jacob cornered. "What the hell is this nightmare? Do you realize the media frenzy whipping up outside?"

"Mr. Mayor, Sir," Jacob said, "I didn't realize you were here." His eyes followed Madam Trixie out the front door and he cursed under his breath. Mayor Sutherland stepping into a crime scene meant nothing but trouble. And Jacob had thought his morning couldn't get worse.

"An entire city block is taped off and the place is crawling with reporters," the Mayor growled. "This is egg on my face, Lawrence! I'm out there trying to calm down the storm and you're turning my city into a laughingstock. People don't feel safe on the streets anymore! You've got GI's dropping like flies. And now this – Vince Carelli in a whore house! You know he's related to Donald Pinzolo, don't you? The man giving millions to the city in charity donations and infrastructure? The one who lost his own son last year to yet *another* criminal case you haven't closed? Remember him?" Mayor Sutherland's rage was barely contained. "What am I gonna tell him? That now some whack job has killed his nephew as well? That the police have no bloody idea what's going on? There've been half a dozen of these hits, so far, Lawrence! You haven't even got me a story to spin to the press - what the hell's going on?" The Mayor finished his tirade and drew his hand across his forehead, seemingly trying to smooth away the stress that had ploughed lines in his skin.

"It's a complex case, Mayor," Jacob tried to placate him. "There's nothing random about these killings. They're all inter-connected somehow. Carelli, Polletti, Marco Pinzolo -"

"Now, hang on a minute!" The Mayor hissed. He lowered his voice to a hoarse whisper, each word spat like venom. "Don't you go trying to tie Donny Pinzolo into this mess. He's worth more than your job's worth, you hear me." His eyes were fierce. "Now, there's some group of smart-ass trouble-makers out there, causing havoc on my streets. I don't care what their beef is, or what they think they're up to, just find them and get rid of this infestation."

"These aren't your typical trouble-makers," Jacob argued. "This is organized, someone's sending a powerful message -"

"Let me give you a powerful message, son," Mayor Suther-land interrupted. "Now, I worked with your father for a long time, and he was a fine police commissioner. I'd heard you were going the same way. But if you can't catch these street rats and get the press off my back without costing me a donation big enough to buy town hall a dozen times over, well," he pulled himself up straight, "let's just say writing tickets on the highway isn't going to see you carry on the family tradition.

"Now hold on -" Jacob interjected. "This is a criminal investi-gation. I don't care who you are, you can't just come into a crime scene and start making threats like I'm wet behind the ears! I'll manage this investigation the way I need to."

"Well, you don't seem to be managing it very well so far, Sergeant Lawrence."

Mayor Sutherland looked around. His entourage had made themselves scarce and the only officers remaining were across the room, taking statements from the jazz band that had played the night before. The Mayor lowered his voice to a whisper, his eyes quick. He took a deep breath and forced a smile on his face. It didn't sit well.

"You need to understand the pressure I'm under here. This is a publicity nightmare. I've got a city too scared to go out at night. I've got GI's being ambushed and General Brandway threatening to line the city streets with armed guards just to get his trucks through to Fort Hamilton. I can't shut down half the city! I can't have weapons out on the mall with old ladies and kids running around! I've got reporters camped outside my office door waiting for me to burn on this and an election just around the corner." He looked around the room again, his usual charisma and shine, gone. "Just get me a good, clean arrest and let's tidy this mess up. *Without* stepping on any toes. Look son, you book these creeps and your Pop won't be the only commissioner in the family if I get re-elected."

Jacob stared at the man in disbelief. "I'll do my job, Mayor. And I'll *try* to keep your Darb out of it. But that's all I can promise."

Mayor Sutherland studied Jacob for a moment with a critical eye.

"See that you do." He turned quickly and left again, collecting his assistants by the door with a flick of his hand.

Jacob stood for a moment, gathering his thoughts. There was something altogether sordid about this whole affair, and it didn't begin and end with the bodies downstairs. Or the two in the alley up the street. *Which*, he thought, sighing, *I still need to visit.*

Officer Parker stood waiting for him at the front of the house. As he stepped out into the gray morning, Jacob breathed in the loamy smell of last night's thunderstorm rising from the broken pavement. There was a gritty, neglected feel to the street.

On one side of the bordello was an old drug-store and on the other a rough boarding-house. A few tattered apartment blocks were further up the street near a gin mill and what had turned out to be Carelli's coupe bent around a concrete pillar. Opposite the bordello, were dark alleys that veined between dilapidated buildings and an expansive junkyard that stretched half a city block. The whole place felt cracked and splintered, like the tattered fringe of a city that had forgotten it was there.

Waking up to this mess was a far cry from the pleasant night he'd had before it. Jacob's second date with Adina had gone even more splendidly than the first and he was already keen to see her again. He hated knowing that General Brandway, her hard-boiled boss, had her caught up in this mess, too. And hated even more, the pounding his own reputation was taking by not having solved this case for them already. He only hoped she'd understand. Jacob instinctively put his hand in his pocket and felt the Roxy theater ticket he'd kept there since their first evening out. Adina has kissed the ticket, leaving a pink lipstick smudge, then given it back to him, laughing. *To remind you there are better things than scoundrels to think of,* she'd said. Last night, they'd taken a horse and carriage ride at the lower end of Broadway, before the rain had started. They'd dashed into a restaurant for dinner and shared an umbrella on the way home. It had been a breath of fresh air. He cleared his throat as he fell in step beside Parker. This morning, the air was far less sweet.

"Forensics are just finishing up with Carelli," Parker said, as they made their way up the street toward the junkyard. "Carotid, real quick and clean. No sign of the knife." He flicked through his notepad.

"Can't have been too quick if they chased him all the way up here first," Jacob said. "What about the other guy?"

"Still waiting on a name, Sarge, but it looks like he was hit over the head with a fence paling. Found it next to him."

"Swell," Jacob sighed again. "Well, it's pretty clear what they were up to in the basement, so I guess we'll be expecting another tip-off as to where the crates have been stashed pretty soon."

"You think this is the rail shed heist?"

"I do. Though, I'm surprised to find Chan was in cahoots with this lot. Word on the street is that he works alone. None of this makes sense."

"Maybe someone's trying to frame them for it?" Parker suggested as they turned up a side alley. Ahead, a small team of uniforms were gathered around a body on the ground. Jacob stopped at the gate.

"What do you mean?" he asked. "Trying to implicate Carelli to get to Pinzolo?"

"Well, yeah. I heard he's a bit of a big shot. Got a lot of pull in certain circles."

"You're not wrong there," Jacob said. "Not my circles though."

"Dunno, but it's above my pay grade, I reckon," Parker said, pulling a tall wire gate aside to let Jacob into the junk yard. A chain hung from the handle. "Carelli's in here."

"The gate was open?"

"Not until this morning. The caretaker came in around six. Carelli must have jumped the fence. Found him in an old jalopy."

Parker had been right, Carelli's wound was clean – a professional hit. Jacob left him with the coroner and wandered off to survey the area. There were scuff marks on the top of the wooden fence that separated the junkyard from the alley. On the outside, the second body was being loaded onto a stretcher. Carelli - and the guy that killed him - had certainly jumped the fence to get inside. Not an easy feat.

Crouching down, Jacob picked around in the muddy tangle of scrap metal and wood. An odd shine in the muck caught his eye. He dug his fingers in to dislodge it.

Black, smooth – the high heel from a woman's shoe.

Peculiar, Jacob thought. I suppose someone could have thrown it over the fence. There were plenty of call girls around the area. He rummaged around a little further. About a meter away, he found its pair. What are the chances of both heels breaking off at the same time? And if they did, why not throw the entire shoe away?

Jacob thought for a moment of what Adina might do if faced with a broken heel. Would she break off the other to match? Or keep the first and find a cobbler to mend it? *She'd keep it, I think.* Shoes were hard to come by these days, and not often discarded. *Mend and make do,* he'd heard Ima say. He rubbed some of the mud off to reveal the shiny, patent leather. *Especially something so new.*

"They're ready to take him out, Sarge," called Parker from across the junkyard.

Jacob stood up and waved at him to proceed. Turning away, he pulled a clean handkerchief from his pocket and wrapped up the broken heels. He wasn't entirely sure why he wanted to keep them. There was something about that black patent leather, that unsettled his gut. Just *–something.* And then there was Madam Trixie – hadn't she said an Avon Lady had dropped by? Avon, *again*?

Jacob turned away, tucking the stuffed handkerchief back into his pocket. He didn't notice the lipstick-stained theater ticket fall out as he began to walk, or see it flutter into the mud under his feet as he left.

6

ST. AUGUSTINE'S HOME
FOR UNWANTED BOYS

Donald Pinzolo stood with his back to the room, looking out the window of his second-floor office to the expansive lawn below. A group of teenage boys were running laps around the inside perimeter of the fence, largely ignored by a harried looking nun with a clipboard who was deep in discussion with a colleague. A long driveway separated the front lawn into two halves, which were being attended to by a gardener. It was a glorious morning, crisp and bright. At one end of the long driveway was the gargantuan building in which Donny now stood, recently refurbished and still bearing signs of ongoing construction work. At the far end, beyond the oval, was an iron gate with a brand-new sign arched above it, declaring the property to be *St. Augustine's Home for Unwanted Boys*.

Donny absently stroked the belly of the oversized ginger cat in his arms.

His *benefactory*, as he liked to call it, was going well. There had been no hold-ups with construction as half of City Hall owed him heavy favors, including the Mayor. His nephew, Vince, had begun training the boys in Donny's particular manner of business to great effect, and personally kept an eye out for any kids with what he considered 'leadership' abilities. Overburdened Catholic nuns ran the day-to-day schooling of the three hundred or so boys in their care, with no question as to Donny's motives or the 'apprenticeship opportunities' that took the boys from their beds and classrooms in shifts. They packed crates of amphetamines, sold crack on street corners and ran jobs from one end of the city to the other, each kid on a paycheck of cigarettes, candy and the promise of not being flogged. Donny had used kids as runners for years, but this – having an entire orphanage as a cover and source of labor – was an inspired move. Kids ran under the radar. They could get into places his own men couldn't. They could hear whispers without being seen. They were *useful*.

Donny paid both the church and the Mayor handsomely for their disinterest in his affairs. If anything, this recent opportunity to play up his philanthropy had become a goal in itself.

Yes, the entire venture felt... promising.

With the exception, of course, of that one thorn in his side. The heists.

Donny turned abruptly at a knock on the door. He wasn't expecting Walter Sutherland, the New York City Mayor, until seven. It was only six.

"Come in," he barked. His men knew better than to interrupt him this early in the morning. It spoiled his concentration.

Three men entered, each one with hesitation stitched into his shoes.

"What?"

One man stepped forward with a scowl. The top part of his ear had been ripped off at some time, long past. Despite the violence carved into his scarred face, today he carried fear behind his eyes. And this wasn't a man easily scared.

"Boss. I've – I've got news," the man said.

"Clearly," Pinzolo said, turning back to the sunlight. "Well, it better be good news, Felix, because I've got a king-sized pain in the ass for you, if it's not."

The two men behind Felix swallowed audibly, throwing sideways glances to one another. They'd spent the night shadowing Felix on the street, at his own demand, but now sorely wished they hadn't. The taller one, Carmine, shuffled incrementally backward. The other, Earl, angled toward the open door.

Felix stepped forward again, shaky, but resolute.

"There's been a situation, Donny," he said.

"You tracked down the bastards that are stripping my heists?"

"Not yet, boss, I - " he took a deep breath. "It's Vince Junior, boss."

"What about him?"

"Someone took him out. Last night, at Kitty's."

Donny Pinzolo froze. He turned back around to look at Felix, an unreadable mask on his face. Slowly, he walked to his mahogany desk and dropped the cat onto it next to a glass fishbowl of colored gumballs. The cat leapt off the desk and bolted for the open door.

"What did you just say?" Donny said, his voice soft and unfathomably dangerous.

Felix drew his hand roughly across his own mouth. He pulled himself tall, taking a deep breath. He knew there was no room for weakness. One false move and he'd eat a bullet. The old adage of *don't shoot the messenger* didn't apply to his side of the desk.

"It's Vince, boss. They killed him at the whore house. Vince, Travis, Sydney, The Muscle. Someone took 'em out."

Donny stood, his eyes like flint, as if daring Felix to continue.

Felix waited, terrified his voice might crack, and give away his fear. His ripped ear, itched, as if it were still whole. Phantom nerves that no longer existed. He ignored it.

"I called in early a couple of hours ago, you know – just to see –" he paused, not wanting to mention Tilly. Donny already knew too much about her, "to get set up in the office, like you told me. I thought Vince had cleared out already. When I got there, I found his car up the street, all bent in. Like an accident, but there was no one in it."

He paused, waiting for some kind of sign that Donny wanted him to stop, but none came.

"So, I went in, used Trixie's key. Syd and Muscle were in the office, not Vince though. Someone did a real nasty job on 'em. T – *one of the girls* saw it too and screamed, so Trixie ran and called the cops. I had to hightail it before they arrived, so I went looking for Vince. Couldn't find 'im, I didn't know where he was until just now. The girls called me. Apparently, the brass dug 'im out of a car in the junkyard. Travis, too." Felix braced himself. "Both dead."

Donny didn't say a word. He didn't need to. Felix's eyes widened.

"I'm sorry! I swear I never thought they'd hit Kitty's! So many witnesses, you know. I came straight here when I saw. I'd been out all night, like you told me, chasing down Bugsy's crew. Thought they might have the dope on who's dropping our guys."

"And?" Donny asked, barely audible through gritted teeth.

Felix reflexively scratched his torn ear.

"Cold, boss. They got nothin'."

"So, you're telling me," Donny breathed, "That some wise guy turned up at a whorehouse full of people, killed four men, and then got away without a single pair of eyes on him?"

Felix stared at his shoes. The bile was rising in his throat.

"Six, boss."

"Six?"

"There were six men. Jimmy Chan and that dumb ninja of his. They were there, too. Both skewered with a bloody chair, right through the middle. And dope all over the desk, like at The Capitol, how they found Frank."

"So, the same men have killed my cousin, Frankie. My boy, Marco, God rest his soul. And now, Vince. The only nephew I had left." Donny walked forward and leaned down with both hands on his desk. His head hung, and his eyes closed. "And no one knows who's behind it."

"I'm sorry, boss. I'm so sorry! I'm gonna track down this son of a bitch, I swear to God. And I'm gonna rip his brains out through his asshole -"

Donny was silent. After a long minute, he spoke, restrained, like a hurricane that was being held in check by tissue paper.

"Get out. All of you." Carmine and Earl backed away. Felix turned to leave.

"Not. You."

Felix stopped, rooted to the spot as the two others turned quickly and left the room, flinging the door shut behind them. Within seconds, they were at the top of the stairs, heading for the basement. They paused as an almighty smash came from inside the room. Donny's voice boomed through the walls.

"I gave you one job! I TOLD YOU TO FIND THEM!"

"I need more time," came the desperate reply. Carmine and Earl raced down the stairs.

Inside, Felix pulled himself up from the floor, toppling over the chair that had been launched at his head.

Smash!

Colored gumballs rained across the floor as the glass bowl shattered at his feet. Donny spun around again, grabbing a heavy bronze desk lamp and hurled it at the window, which smashed and fell away in shards. Shrieks of fright sounded from the yard below.

"ONE JOB!" Donny yelled, launching toward Felix and pulling him up straight. He dragged the scarred man to his desk.

"Put out your hand," he ordered. Donny was breathing hard through his yellow-stained teeth, his cigar-infused breath smothering Felix's face. He pushed Felix down onto his knees in front of the desk.

"No, boss! No!"

"You ever want to see that little Kitty Kat, *Tilly,* of yours alive again, you're going to put out your hand. Now."

With tears in his eyes and his jaw set tight, Felix struggled to place his own hand on the desk before him. Behind him, the room was littered with glass and broken furniture.

Slam!

A knife came down, straight through his hand, pinning Felix to the desk. He screamed in agony. Beside him, Pinzolo's face swam into view.

"Find. The. Bastard. Who. Killed. My nephew."

A sweet jazz tune wafted through the house from the wireless, and found Betty sitting on the floor of Nancy's bedroom sewing. Beside her, Figaro, the newly named stray kitten whose rescue had provided a welcome relief against George's misgivings, patted a spool of cotton around the floorboards. Betty sang along with Bob Eberle and the Jimmy Dorsey orchestra as she snipped her scissors, following the love-sick lyrics in a clear and joyful voice.

> "She's got all the boys on the run, and oh! It's the
> sweetest fun,
> How she swings and dances by, to leave them all
> with just a sigh."

She sang as she pushed the last little stack of hundred-dollar bills into the split side seam of her daughter's mattress. The tune picked up into a jaunty jazz beat of brass and percussion.

"Who can catch her heart so gay, when she's
      dancing all her love away,
  I can't believe those eyes of blue, don't see how
      much I love her, true!"

Betty pulled a long loop of heavy-duty polyester cotton from the wooden spool and threaded a needle. Neat stitches began to close the incision she'd made.

The mattress looked a little worse for wear. The contents of Frankie and Vince's wall safes, in addition to numerous other confiscations of drug money over the past several months, had already filled little George Junior's mattress, and now were well on their way to filling Nancy's as well. Of course, it was no good to leave money at a crime scene, ripe for the picking of any miscreant that stopped by before the police arrived, nor in fact, to leave it for the police themselves. Somehow, in some way, it would all flow back to Donny.

"Oops, how did you slip out?" Betty laughed quietly, as she found a rogue bill under her knee. "In you go." She squished the note through the finger-sized hole still left unstitched and closed the gap, tying off her thread with a double knot and a clean snap. She wasn't sure yet what she'd do with the money. Still, inspiration did always seem to strike her at the right time. She gathered her bits and bobs and pulled herself to her feet, straightening the bedclothes as she did so.

"What are you doing, mommy?" came a quiet voice from the doorway.

Betty's head snapped up, surprised. Her twelve-year-old daughter had been standing so quietly, both inside her mind and out, that Betty hadn't even known she was there.

"Gracious, Nancy! You gave me a start."

"I didn't mean to," Nancy replied, pouting. "I just wanted to come and read my book for a while. George Junior is being a tattletale, I'm sick of him." *The Adventures of Pinocchio*, hung from her right hand, her index finger shut inside as a bookmark.

"Georgie's only little," Betty chastised. "*And* he adores you. Just remember that, Nancy. As silly as he might seem, he's still your brother, and that makes him one of the most important people in your whole life. If anything ever happened to your father and I, well, at least you'd have each other. Put up with him every once in a while, darling. Sometimes being silly is the best medicine."

"Alright," Nancy sighed, dramatically, flinging herself onto her bed.

Betty smoothed down her lemon-scalloped skirt, tucking the spool of thread surreptitiously into her apron pocket, glad to have distracted her daughter. It seemed she was, for now, none the wiser. *That child is rather too clever for her own good sometimes.* Betty puffed with pride. *One day, she'll need her cleverness. Not yet, though.* She scooped up Figaro and plopped him onto the bed next to her daughter.

"Half an hour, dear," Betty said, at the doorway. "Then you can come and shell the peas for supper."

"Yes, mother." Nancy flipped open her book, then paused, as Betty turned and began to walk up the hallway. "But Mommy, wait! You didn't answer my question." The girl sat up straight, crossing her legs. "Why were you sewing money inside my mattress?"

Betty froze. She blinked twice. She rearranged her surprise into a kind smile. Then she turned back around. Nancy was sitting expectantly, waiting for an answer.

"Oh, never mind me, dear," Betty said, walking back to Nancy's door. She lowered her voice to a hush. "I'm just saving for a rainy day."

Nancy eyebrows lifted. "But, why?"

"Well, I suppose I might need it to buy a big umbrella. To keep us all safe and dry." Betty winked. "Our little secret, darling. That's why I put it in *your* room. Because you're so good at keeping them. Read your book now. Half an hour." She pulled the door closed behind her and paused, biting her lip. After a moment, Betty continued along to her own bedroom. She crossed to the tall window overlooking the garden and sat down on the window seat cushion. Carefully, Betty pulled the lace curtain back and looked to the sky.

It had begun to rain.

"It's absolutely divine, darling," Betty exclaimed, holding the new lipstick up to the light. Can you see the way it shimmers!?" Several other women around Gladys Eubanks' sitting room gasped. A dainty blonde woman, Fannie Mae, placed a silver tea-tray amongst the cosmetics spread on the coffee table and nodded, enthusiastically.

"I want one all for myself!" Fannie said.

"It's a lovely color," said another woman.

"Yes, I thought so, too," replied a tall woman with camellias pinned to the side of her curls. She turned to Betty, who was still admiring the lipstick. "I know you like to see the new stock before we get it, Betty. Of course, it's limited, you know, so only the highest-selling representatives will sell it to start. That's me, of course," she added pointedly. "I suppose you'll just have to wait until your sales pick up."

Betty smiled, her eyes tight, and handed the sample back delicately. "I wouldn't be too worried about my sales, Gladys, I've picked up a very large order for Heavenly Moisturizing Cream to four separate businesses just this last week. That's over seventy new customers."

Gladys' lips soured and she leaned forward, picking up her cup of tea from the coffee table with a back so straight it might have snapped.

"Four businesses? Seventy ladies? Where do you mean?"

"Oh, just some clubs on the Bowery," Betty said, carelessly, "but needless to say, they're lovely ladies who do like to look their best. And that's what we love to do isn't it, help women look their best!"

"It sure is!" remarked Fannie, her blonde curls bobbing in time with the music from the wireless.

"Not *gentlemen's* clubs?" Gladys stage-whispered. Her eyes were wide, as if she might burst into flames at the mere thought. The other ladies gasped.

"Well, I don't really know," said Betty serenely. "I never thought to ask. Waitresses or usherettes, probably. Darling girls, though. Besides, there's a war on - everybody deserves to take a little time out for beauty, isn't that right ladies?" There was a chorus of agreement and the others turned back to their teacups and cosmetics.

"Yes, I suppose they do," Gladys said. She sipped her tea, clearly disgruntled at Betty's good fortune. Betty sighed. Despite her best efforts, she'd never been able to break through the crust of dislike that Gladys held for her. She had no idea why. Betty could find out of course, but listening in to a friend's thoughts wasn't something she did often – it simply wasn't polite. Then again, Gladys wasn't exactly a friend... *I wonder...*

"Thinks she knows everything." The other woman's mind was broiling like an old ham. "Sitting there with her nose in the air and her ritzy clothes, trying to make a fool of me. Dragging our fine name into ill repute – I should tell the secretary. I've been selling these products years longer than she has but they all hang off her every word -"

There it was then, Betty thought. *Jealousy, plain and simple.* She was relieved. Anything more sinister would have been far too much work to be bothered with right now. But this was easy to fix. In fact, it may even prove to be useful.

Betty poured herself some tea.

"You know ladies," she said loudly, over the chatter, "I

imagine we will all pick up some extra customers over the coming weeks before the Gala Ball Fundraiser at City Hall. I'm organizing it with my church social group for the benefit of the orphanage - it's sure to be swell! All the glitterati will be there, photographers, fancy dresses and champagne. A big brass band and maybe even movie stars! You're all invited, of course, I'll need all the help I can get setting up tables and keeping those dreamboats from Hollywood amused. MGM are going to pass on our invites to Cary Grant and Spencer Tracy! Think of the publicity and money we'll raise for the children!" Squeals of delight broke out and they all began talking at once.

"Will there be dancing?" Fannie asked, her eyes alight.

"Oh, yes, we'll have a gay time!" Betty said. "I'm counting on you to lead the dance floor, Fannie," Betty laughed. "You're such a ducky shincracker, you'll have them lining up!"

The women laughed and Fannie giggled, pink-faced.

Betty then turned deliberately to Gladys, whose lips looked like they couldn't get any thinner.

"Now Gladys, dear. You will come, won't you?" she said gently, taking the tall woman's hand. "I need your help most of all – why, nobody is better at hosting a party than you," Betty indicated the small gathering of Avon Ladies with their scones and biscuits, "and you've been our guiding light for so long and you know the very best products to recommend to our guests should the need arise. I simply couldn't manage the night without your help, Gladys." Betty's voice and heart were sincere. "The ladies at church do their best, but they're rather ill-equipped for such a stately occasion. There are invitations to prepare, supper to co-ordinate and door prizes to draw and dignitaries to greet. I really do need someone with your *talent* for organization by my side." By now, Betty was clutching Gladys' hand with earnest eyes. "Do say you'll help me," she implored.

The other woman seemed to melt. Her face relaxed and her shoulders dropped, and despite what seemed like momentary misgivings, Betty could see the bitterness behind her eyes fade away.

"Well, if you need me -"

"Oh, I really do, Gladys!"

"I suppose I can manage it then. For charity. After all, I am well known for my considerable talents in making sure things are done right. You know, I saved the day at the Spring Fair last year when I discovered one of the workers pouring whiskey in the Shirley Temples! Can you imagine if the children had taken one?"

"That's precisely why I need you Gladys," Betty fortified. "To keep a sharp eye on things."

"Alright then. I'll put my best foot forward."

"Thank you, dear! You're a godsend."

Betty leaned toward her, with a conspiratorial air. "There's one other thing, just between us, if you don't mind. You see, I heard from the Seymour girls who work at City Hall, that Mayor Sutherland's wife has been sporting a terrible choice of foundation powder lately, far too pale for her complexion, looks positively chalky, and I think she really ought to be given some advice."

"The Mayor's wife?" Gladys' mouth dropped in astonishment. She pulled herself even straighter and reflexively smoothed her apron.

"Oh yes, she's an absolute doll, but no sense of color or style, poor love. She really needs someone of your *expertise* to give her some gentle direction. I'm sure the Mayor would be quite appreciative, there's so much publicity following them about, after all. Perhaps you could take some of that new lipstick with you, too - I'd be happy to introduce you at the ball -"

For the remainder of the morning, Gladys was a kitten. The little party of Avon Ladies spent hours going over their latest products and catalogs, sharing techniques for applying cosmetics and tips for making more sales. When they finally packed up their bags and left the house at lunchtime, there wasn't an ill-feeling to be found.

Betty was the last to leave. After assuring Gladys that she would call again in a few days to discuss the particulars of the upcoming fundraiser, Betty sat astride her pale blue bicycle and rode away with a wave. As she pulled from the curb, a dark car took her place.

Sergeant Jacob Lawrence got out of his automobile and put on his hat. He watched the back of a woman disappear around the street corner on her bicycle and looked up to the blue sky. *Nice day for it,* he thought, musing on how long it had been since he'd ridden his own bike. Jacob ducked around the other side of the car and reached through the open passenger seat window to collect his clipboard. He flipped through the pages. *46 Maple Street.* He crossed the road and knocked on the door of a small red brick home. A tall woman with flowers in her hair promptly opened it.

"Can I help you?"

"Mrs. Gladys Eubanks?"

"Yes?"

Jacob retrieved his badge from this inside pocket of his uniform.

"Sergeant Jacob Lawrence, of the New York City Police Department. I just need to ask you a few questions, if I may."

The woman's eyes widened and she stepped back for him to pass. "Of course," she said, "please come in. It's not Henry, is it?" she asked, anxiously.

"Henry, maam?"

"My husband. He's serving with the 165th Infantry."

"Oh, no, maam, this isn't a military matter," Jacob smiled.

The woman sighed with relief as she ushered him to the couch. There were empty teacups and plates of crumbs across the coffee table and misplaced chairs scattered about.

"I'm so sorry, I've just had company," Gladys said, following his gaze. She began to pile cups onto the tea tray.

"Please don't worry, Mrs. Eubanks. I'll only be a minute. If you'll sit down I just have some enquiries. Now, you sell Avon products, is that correct?"

Gladys sat down, surprised.

"Yes, I do."

"Have you ever been to The Capitol Palace in Harlem, Mrs. Eubanks?"

"Perhaps, once or twice. It's not really my thing, but Henry likes the orchestra."

"I see." Jacob scribbled a note. The wooden clipboard had numerous typed sheets pinned to it, each with a long list of names and address. Beside each name, Jacob had scrawled his notes. Many had a line crossed through the middle.

"And your customers live in which area of town?" he asked.

"Well, this area, of course. I cover ten blocks in all directions. That's quite a lot for one representative, but I've been doing this a long time and I'm highly organized."

"I'm sure you are," Jacob smiled, "You don't travel any further then?"

"No, I don't like the bus, so I walk. I draw a good enough income from this area, why would I sell further afield? There are plenty of representatives to look after our New York City customers, I'm only one Avon Lady, as skilled as I may be."

"I see," Jacob said, disappointed. He paused for a moment. He'd already asked his next question twelve times this morning. One young woman had even slapped him for it. "Forgive me for asking," Jacob said, awkwardly, "but there's a call house in the bowery -"

Gladys almost choked. Her face lit up and she looked mortified.

"I'll have you know I'm a good Christian woman!" she cried.

"What are you insinuating?" She stood up and straightened her apron. "I think you should leave!"

Jacob stood, too. He held up his hands, apologetically.

"Please, Mrs. Eubanks. I beg your pardon. I'm simply doing my job." It was clear already, that this woman wasn't the lead he was after.

Gladys sniffed. "Will you tell me what this is all about?"

Jacob smiled politely and tucked his clipboard under his arm.

"I'm investigating a series of incidents that involve the use of Avon business cards. I need to speak to whoever is involved, that's all. Nothing serious."

Gladys looked dubious.

"The bowery, you said?"

"That's right. Do you know of any other representatives that might service that area?"

Gladys frowned. A few hours ago, she would have gladly dropped Betty's name to the officer. But now, something held her back. An odd feeling of loyalty.

"No, I don't," she said finally. "I can't help you."

Jacob's face dropped as he followed her to the door. For a minute, he thought he'd seen just a spark of recognition in her eyes. He pulled out his business card and handed it to her.

"If you happen to remember anything *or anyone* that might be able to help me."

"I'll let you know," Gladys said, curtly. She tucked the card in her apron pocket and closed the door behind him.

Jacob looked down at his list of names and drew a line through *Mrs. Gladys Eubanks*.

The list looked longer than ever.

He pulled away from the curve, heading for the next address.

A few days later, Betty found herself soaking up the glorious sun through the window of George's pride and joy - a gleaming black Chevrolet - as they whizzed along the highway. Her red and white sprigged crepe skirt suit, with its dainty jacket, flared peplum and frothy white ruff at the front was the perfect mix of business and pleasure.

"Eleven cents for a gallon of gas, can you believe the nerve?" George was saying. "Why it's highway robbery. I bet they'll have it at twelve by the end of the week!"

"I imagine it's harder to come by at the moment," Betty said absently. "Say, darling, I was thinking that perhaps we should sow a victory garden? They do say there's no brighter flavor than home-made jams and jellies. We could plant peaches and raspberries and donate them to the church for Sunday luncheons."

"That's a fine idea, jitterbug!" George said, winking at her from the driver's seat. "There's a place in heaven for you."

"I'm not so sure about that," Betty sighed, looking out of the window.

"What's that, love?"

"Never mind." She leaned forward and switched on the car radio. The Nat King Cole Trio burst from the speakers.

> I bought diamonds and pearls,
> To treat you so true,
> Gee, baby, I'm so good to you.

Betty's brow furrowed. She turned back to George.

"Are you sure you want to come to the orphanage with me?" she said, trying to keep her voice light. "Wouldn't you rather drop me off and play a spot of golf with Mr. Williams?"

"And miss meeting the Mayor and Donald Pinzolo? Golly, no! Why, I'll be the talk of the office with their cards up my sleeve - a high profile businessman like that! It was mighty good of the Seymour girls to set this up with their cousin at City Hall.

It's all who you know, Betty. A handshake's worth more than a pot of gold in my industry -"

"Yes, but given what's just been in the papers, about his nephew Vincent, I'm not sure he'll be in the mood to -"

"All the more reason to take out a life insurance policy! Sometimes a man sees things clearer in a shaded room - a smart man like Pinzolo will recognize an opportunity when it comes."

"Yes, but dear -"

"No, I won't have it, jitterbug, you aren't used to dealing with business matters like I am. These men aren't like the girls you dizzy up with your products. You need a man there to get things done properly."

"I'm quite capable -"

"Besides, this fundraiser means an awful lot to you and I want to help. We need to make a good impression; get those high hats in City Hall spinning, hey!?" George winked at her and began to whistle in tune with the radio.

"If you say so, dear," Betty sighed, irritated.

She wasn't pleased at George's insistence on attending. Betty looked out the window and took a deep breath, preparing to fix her smile. It had been years since she had last seen Donny – twelve in fact, and she was nothing like the frightened, scrawny girl she once was. That version of her died, precisely when Donny believed she had. Staging her own death had been a desperate way to escape his empire, but she'd managed it impeccably. Sometimes, she could still smell the smoke of her childhood home engorged in flames. Still see the stunned face of her father, dead on the kitchen floor. His blood was long-washed from her hands, replaced by that of so many more. She didn't fear seeing Donny again now, under the cover of a new life. But she would rather not have ruined a perfectly good Saturday morning by wasting it on him.

She glanced at her husband, who was now singing a merry tune. There was very little danger involved today. This was simply a reconnaissance mission to find out what, specifically, Donny was up to. She had only needed a reason to be on the premises, but now it seemed, she had to contend with George's ambitions as well.

The Chevrolet rolled through an open gate beneath a plaque that read, "St. Augustine's Home for Unwanted Boys". A Delahave luxury convertible was already parked out front. Three men stood beside it, smoking cigarettes. One wore a Driver's uniform, another had an elaborate 35 mm camera slung around his neck sporting a big, fancy lens. The third, a tall man that Betty recognized from pictures in the paper, was the Mayor.

As George pulled up alongside, the men butted their cigarettes, and the photographer took his camera in hand and began snapping shots.

With a grand smile on his face, Mayor Sutherland stepped across to help Betty from the car and turned, posing for the camera.

"Mrs. Jones, I take it?" he said, cordially.

"That's right, Mr. Mayor, please call me Betty. This is my husband, George."

George bounded over and offered his hand.

"George Jones, Mr. Mayor. Mighty good of you to see us today."

"Good to meet you, George," Mayor Sutherland replied. "I hope you don't mind I brought my photographer. Publicity can be a terrible thing, Mrs. Jones, but only if you don't have any." He winked at Betty, who laughed in false delight.

They turned and walked toward the entrance of the orphanage, the photographer hopping around them, taking pictures. Betty tuned in to the Mayor's thoughts, curious.

"Damn do-gooders. This better be worth it."

Betty smirked. This meeting could turn out to be fun, after all.

They entered the building and found themselves in an

expansive room flanked by staircases. The walls had been freshly painted and smelled of plaster. A long line of young boys was being led down one staircase by an austere looking nun. Their solemn, grubby faces disappeared through a doorway to the left.

Betty, George and the photographer followed Mayor Sutherland up the right-side stairs, along a hall and into a spacious office. Two men were busy measuring for a new pane of glass in the tall windows that overlooked the front entrance. There was a box of swept, shattered glass on the floor nearby and one window sported an empty frame.

"Here's the man we want to see!" Mayor Sutherland exclaimed, walking toward the main desk. Donald Pinzolo stood up to greet them. His face looked drawn and irritated. The Mayor laughed nervously.

"Donny, meet George and Betty Jones. They're organizing the big charity do at City Hall that I told you about. Quite a number it'll be, all decked out for your orphans here. Raise lots of money. Good press, Donny, that's what we want, good press!"

The photographer ducked around them, clicking his camera. Betty stepped confidently to Donny, offering her hand, which he took, briefly. His eyes raked her face and dress, discriminately.

"Have we met before Mrs. Jones?"

Betty smiled, coolly. "Oh, goodness no, Mr. Pinzolo. I'm just a housewife, I can't imagine where we'd have met. Have you volunteered at the soup kitchen, perhaps? I'm often there."

Donny looked so confused that Betty had to bite her lip to keep from laughing.

George stepped forward, interrupting their exchange.

"Had a bit of trouble with your window there, did you Pinzolo? I've got a policy to cover that right up for you if you're interested - George Jones, insurance." He thrust his hand to Donny and shook the other's enthusiastically. As George turned away, Betty caught Donny raising an eyebrow to the Mayor, who shook his head incrementally.

"Play along," Mayor Sutherland's mind silently begged. *"We need all the good press we can get after that nightmare with Vinnie."* Betty smiled and looked around the room serenely.

"Had a baseball through the window yesterday," Donny said, nodding toward the broken glass. "Turns out, the little scamps are quite the home-run hitters." He turned to the two men fitting the glass. "Leave it now for a bit, boys." Immediately, the men took off their gloves and left the room.

"Well, it's a mighty good thing you're doing, Mr. and Mrs. Jones," Mayor Sutherland said. "I always like to support my constituents in their efforts to raise money for charities. A city's only as strong as its people, I always say." He shot a meaningful look to Donny.

"It's all for the children, Mr. Mayor," Betty said, genially. "I just can't bear the thought of them on the streets, dirty and unloved, with goodness-knows-who taking advantage of their vulnerability." She looked directly at Donny. "Wouldn't you agree, Mr. Pinzolo?"

Pinzolo smiled, affectedly. "Of course."

Inside Donny's head, his words continued, this time directed to the Mayor, as if willing him to tap into his private thoughts.

"I want these soppy crackers out of my office, for fuck's sake. I don't need this."

Betty's smile widened.

Donny walked around his desk and sat down in a comfortable leather chair. The others followed his lead, taking a seat each in front of the desk, all smiling, pretentiously, with the exception of George, who looked like he was having the time of his life. The Mayor cleared his throat.

"Well, I've been over your list of plans, Mrs. Jones, and I must say, I'm impressed at your ideas. You'd do well to work in my office, I have a number of girls that could learn a thing or two about organization."

George sat forward on the edge of his seat. "She's quite the little steamboat, this one. With the softest heart in New York City!" He winked at Betty with a shine in his eye.

Falsely blushing, Betty turned to the Mayor.

"The ladies at my church social group will take care of the catering, of course. I'll send through more details on that next week. If your girls could send us the final guest list by Friday, I'll have all the invitations printed and sent out by Tuesday next." She turned her attention to Donny. "Of course, Mr. Pinzolo, as the generous benefactor of the orphanage, we hold your opinion on these matters in the highest esteem - if you have any special requests, please do let Mayor Sutherland know and I'll do my best to make sure you get *everything you deserve.*" Betty delivered him her most obliging smile and Donny shifted uncomfortably.

"Thank you," he said, with a slightly confused expression. "Very kind of you."

"Not at all," Betty continued. She turned back to Mayor Sutherland. "I've already notified the press of the date for the Gala Ball and that they're to expect an announcement from your office with the further details. We also already have a number of bids from liquor companies that can manage a refreshment bar for the evening."

"Golly, yes, can't forget that!" George broke in. "Happy to put down a Gin Sour or two, hey, Mayor Sutherland, get those old hoofers burning up the dance floor!" He was positively beaming.

"Well, yes, my wife is certainly looking forward to it," the Mayor said, "I think she fancies herself meeting some of those movie stars we were hoping to entice to the ball- "

Betty delicately rose to her feet.

"Excuse me gentlemen, if I could just step out and powder my nose for a minute. I'm suddenly feeling a little unwell -"

A look of annoyance crossed Donny's face, but was quickly masked.

"Downstairs on the left, Mrs. Jones."

"You'll be alright, Betty?" George asked.

"Certainly, dear, I just need a minute." Betty neatly piled her handbag and coat on her chair and left the room.

She heard George chuckle as she walked down the hall. "The weaker sex, hey gents?" He was saying. "Don't have the constitution for a man's conversation. Where were we? Ah, yes, insurance..."

Betty knew he'd chatter unabated until she returned, which despite being irritating to his audience, was actually very useful. She quickly descended the main staircase and threw a look over her shoulder, then snuck through the building, opening and closing doors quietly. There was no one about, she supposed the children must be in classes with those unfortunate looking nuns she'd seen on her way in. What she wouldn't give to pamper those ladies up a bit.

There was an unmarked doorway near the entrance to the kitchen, which Betty carefully opened. Dark stairs led downwards to a second door. She followed them. Carefully, she opened it a crack, and then, confident that no one could see her, she ducked through, closing it quietly behind her.

She was in a huge basement almost the length of the building above and divided into parts by a maze of stacked crates, each row reaching almost to the ceiling. There were side rooms partitioned off with card tables and chairs, with ammunition and small weapons lying about on open boxes. Betty crept through the room, keeping low. She could hear voices ahead, and shuffling all around, like people were walking back and forth. She ducked behind boxes at each corner. Dust and oiled machinery gave the basement a stifling, stale smell and she swallowed hard, holding in a dry cough that threatened to take her.

Betty followed shadows and hiding places toward the center of the room. Peering out from behind a stack of crates, she found herself in a hive of activity. Long tables were lined up length to length, with empty crates on the floor surrounding them. Beside each crate was a boy, some so young that they stood on upturned crates to reach the table. They were unpacking and repacking amphetamines and weighing and wrapping small bundles of pills and white powder in brown paper and string. Donny's men were milling around as well, shifting crates and checking their cargo. Some of them assembled weapons unpacked from longer boxes, stamped PROPERTY OF THE UNITED STATES ARMY. Beyond those men, at the far end of the room, a garage door was partially open, spitting blinding light behind the shape of a covered cab butcher's truck. A few men were moving to and fro, loading the cab with firearms.

Black market. Betty didn't need to read anyone's mind to know it was all hot. Donny's specialty was moving stolen goods from one place to another. He had willing buyers across states and borders in every direction, even across the sea. But this was the biggest stockpile she'd ever seen. His operation had grown bigger and more extravagant than she'd realized. Betty's heart fell. Her way ahead was going to be more difficult than even she'd expected.

She pulled her attention back to the children. There was no talk down at the table, just the constant movement of hands and an occasional wracking cough. Every click and clatter of the weapons being put together nearby drew a reflexive shudder from the orphans packing drugs. Every child looked bone tired and terrified.

One of Donny's men was standing over them, watching them work. He was an evil looking creature, with half an ear and heavy scars on his face. His left hand was bandaged and a foul temper seemed to seep from his skin. The boy closest to him was trembling as he worked, fumbling over a packet as he tried to unroll it. In a sudden shower of white, the paper split and tiny pills scattered across the desk.

"Idiot!" yelled the scarred man. In one quick movement, he strode forward and hit the boy hard across the head with his uninjured hand, knocking him to the floor.

"I'm sorry!" cried the boy. "I didn't mean it, I swear! I'll clean it up, Mr. Felix."

Betty recognized the boy's voice at once. It was Sam, one of the three that Vince had roped into the railroad heist. The hairs on the back of her neck bristled and Betty felt a chill roll down her spine.

"Get up!" Felix growled. He kicked Sam again as the boy struggled to his feet. Felix left him, pacing around the table. As he passed, each boy worked faster, stood straighter and grew paler.

"You're lucky I don't belt the lot of ya!" Felix spat. "Bloody kids. I got better things to do than babysit!"

Betty tried to calm her breathing. She squeezed her eyes closed. Pulling herself away from the center of the room, back into the maze of crates, she let herself melt into shadow once again. Once, that had been her. She *was* Sam. A memory hit her with the force of a landslide.

***

It was a steaming hot night, the first on her own, selling crack. She was standing at the low brick fence by the old playground. Barely thirteen years old. Her father, Roy, towered over her.

"And don't ya go giving it away!" he growled. "Six dollars, not a cent less or you'll be paying for it with the belt!"

"Okay, okay!" Susie cried, shoving the paper packets in the pockets of her dress. "I heard you!"

"And shut that smart mouth!" Roy yelled again and smacked her over the head. She fell to the ground with tears in her eyes. Up on the

***

Betty's vision swam away. Her insides ached.

Not for much longer, she thought, bitterly. Carefully, she took stock of the area around her, then bit by bit, made her way back toward the stairs.

Nearly there.

Suddenly, she heard a noise close by.

Too close.

She ducked into a narrow gap between rows of crates, out of sight. One of Donny's men pushed past, a crate on his shoulder blocking her from his line of sight. Betty pulled back as far as she could into the crevice. He dropped the crate down onto the floor and turned back, walking straight past, as she held her breath. His footsteps faded and she let out a gentle sigh.

Time to go.

Before she could move, he reappeared in front of her.

"Wait a minute - !" he exclaimed.

There was no time for thought. Betty leapt up, grabbed the man and twisted his neck hard, supporting his body as it crumpled to the floor in a silent, strangely graceful slump. His wide, red-rimmed eyes were left staring in surprise. Betty quickly dragged him backward, stuffing his body into the gap she'd just left. She pushed up his knees, so that only the tips of his shoes could be seen.

Without a second to waste, Betty cracked opened the basement door and ducked up the stairs. She guessed she'd been gone about ten minutes, but that was five too long.

. . .

Inside Donny's office, the three men waited for Betty to return. George had pushed relentlessly on and was now animatedly discussing the War Risk Insurance Act and the differences between government and private life insurance.

"Why, Mr. Pinzolo," he said, "A businessman like yourself could get the best policy a man could buy for only eight dollars a month! Now don't you think ten thousand dollars is a swell endowment to leave your wife if something were to happen to you?"

"I make my own insurance, Mr. Jones," Donny said, unimpressed. His 'good benefactor' persona was slipping and the Mayor was struggling to diffuse the situation. George, however, didn't notice.

"No sense in that, when I can take care of it for you!" George said. "I'll leave you my number, for when you change your mind. Now, let's see –" he looked around, "you don't mind, do you?" Without waiting for an answer, George helped himself to a pen from the top of Pinzolo's desk. He leaned over to Betty's small blue handbag and began rifling through it. "Why, here's the ticket!" George pulled a business card from Betty's purse. It was plain white, with red script on one side, that read *'Avon Calling! Sorry I Missed You!'*. George flipped it over and wrote on the back, oblivious to the aggravated and withering look that passed between the two other men. "My home address," he said, waving it at Donny, who took it resentfully and stuffed it into his top pocket. "If you're interested in taking out a policy, you just drop by now! The missus is always home, she sells those cosmetics to her lady friends, fills the cupboards with them, you know. It's a hobby of course, I'm not too keen on it myself but you know what dames are like, they need their pretty things to fuss over."

Just at that moment, Betty walked back into Donny's office.

"Well, here's the little lady now. Feeling better, jitterbug?"

"Yes, thank you, George, I'm quite well now. My apologies, gentlemen. I don't know what came over me."

George clucked sympathetically then winked at the Mayor. "Women, heh?" he said.

Mayor Sutherland scrambled to his feet.

"Well, I think this has been a fine meeting. Mrs. Jones, you just let my girls at the office know what we can help you with for the fundraiser and it'll all go down a treat. I'll get that invitation list to your church social committee by Friday."

"Thank you, Mr. Mayor," Betty smiled, collecting her handbag and coat. "I must say, I'm so pleased to learn you've got such a vested interest in these orphans. It seems that yourself and Mr. Pinzolo work very closely on this project." She looked between the two men.

"Yes, well, like you said, Mrs. Jones. It's all for the children."

Betty smiled humorlessly. "Of course it is. And I'll make sure your selfless efforts get as much publicity as I can."

"Splendid," Mayor Sutherland laughed, nervously.

George smiled broadly. "The perfect wife, I've got here Mr. Pinzolo! A luckier man, you won't find."

"Outstanding!" said the Mayor, herding them toward the office door. "Right, off we go then."

Within a minute, Betty and George were back in their car, driving home through the iron gates. The Mayor, with his entourage of photographer and driver, shot a look of apology at Donny, who stood in the front entrance of the orphanage, grim-faced. They too, drove quickly away.

Donny walked forward onto the now empty driveway. The morning had been a complete waste of time, all thanks to this publicity scam Sutherland was trying to pull. It was getting out of hand. He knew that bad press was on his ass thanks to the fact his nephew had just been found murdered at a whorehouse, but Sutherland seemed to be doing overtime to cover it up. There was only one thing that Donny was really interested in. Finding the bastard that was taking out all his best men.

Some gang, some *wise-guy*, was on his turf and stealing his shit. And *no one* stole from Donald Pinzolo and got away with it.

"Boss?" came a quiet voice from behind him. Donny turned around to find Felix standing alone, sweating bullets with barely contained terror in his eyes. "We've got a – situation – downstairs, boss."

Donny face burned with fury and his fists clenched. He knew that look. He gritted his teeth. His left eye started to twitch.

"What situation?" Donny asked, painfully slowly.

Felix took a step backward.

"Dimo's been snapped. Some spiv's been sneaking in the warehouse. The boys are still looking but I've searched the place. Can't find a whiff of 'im anywhere." Felix swallowed, subconsciously reaching up to scratch his ripped ear. His voice cracked as he continued. "I think they flew the coop, boss." He covered his bandaged hand, with the other.

Donny's face was like stone. He stood, staring toward the open gate, his breath hard. A small breeze picked up the gardeners' offcuts and fallen leaves, sweeping them across his shoes. When he finally spoke again, Donny's voice was menacingly quiet.

"You're really getting under my skin, you know that Felix? I thought I could trust you. I thought you were the best."

"You can, Donny, I swear it. I promised, didn't I? If I hadn't been babysitting those brats all morning I would've seen -"

"Seen, *who*, exactly?" Donny spat. "How did they get in without a car? Without anyone noticing?"

"That's just the thing! They couldn't have! I don't get it! The warehouse door was barely open, but Stan and Spider were nearby the whole time, packing the truck. They'd've seen! And *you* can see the front entrance from your own window – there's been no one here, just the penguins, the brats and those bluenose visitors of yours!"

Donny stopped still. Something caught him. A thought. An

impossible, *impossible* thought. He reached into his top pocket and pulled out the *Avon Calling!* card that that infuriating imbecile, George Jones, had given him. He flipped it over. On the back, George had written his home address and private telephone number. Minutes passed, while Donny stood, staring at the card, his eye twitching.

"Boss?" Felix said, timidly.

Donny turned and looked at him. He was brick red, sweating and seething from the roots of his hair to his socks. Drilling hard into Felix's eyes, barely able to contain his own anger, he handed the card to him.

"It's the broad," he said.

"A broad? No way!"

"She's the only one that left the room."

"But – Dimo was big. And strong -"

"I knew there was something about her," Donny muttered, his mind racing to recount any word or clue he might have missed. "She looked too smart."

Felix's mind whirred, racing to catch up to this new revelation. "The broad," he repeated, incredulously. "So, who's she working for? Some kinda spy? Military?"

Donny looked at him. The fog in his eyes had cleared and they became as sharp and cold as cut glass.

"I don't know. There's something about her I can't put my finger on." He nodded to the business card, still in Felix's outstretched fingers. "Dog her steps. I wanna know who she is, what she does, who she sees, what she fuckin' eats for breakfast. I don't want to hear from you again until you know everything about this bitch that there is to know. You got it?"

"Got it, boss."

"Go. Now."

7

BEWITCHED, BOTHERED & BEWILDERED

The winter chill hung in the air like a specter, settling into those dark spaces that were first to lose the fingers of afternoon sun. Susie Polletti and Jacob Lawrence were sitting together in one of those spaces, hidden from view, under the front porch of Susie's home. Horizontal slats of timber lit their faces in thin stripes as they talked, crossed legged on the wooden slab of an old door. They'd dragged the discarded door under the house months before, to save Susie sitting in the dirt. Despite the neglected state of her surroundings and clothes that were old and faded, the girl was impeccably clean. Her fingernails were trimmed and rounded and her dark ponytail was tied with a black ribbon.

The last few months had changed her. Susie's fourteenth birthday had come and gone with no fanfare. Her father had forgotten the occasion and she'd spent the night, as always, betraying the privacy of men's thoughts at the docks for her great-uncle Donny. She remembered that night particularly, because the criminal they'd dragged in had looked at her before he died. *Really* looked at her. Like he'd suddenly realized she was there and hated her for it. As if he knew she had something to do with his fate, though she'd never said a word. She didn't need to speak. Just a slight shake of her head would do it. They didn't often see her, not *really* see her, even though she was always in the room. The greasers all knew that if you pushed it as far as Donny's office, you already had one foot in the grave. A kid in the shadows meant nothing when you were pleading for your life. Still, that look had been unnerving. Then a Harlem sunset found the man's throat and that look disappeared along with his worries.

No, Susie's life under the mark of Donny and her father hadn't changed at all. It was *her* that had changed. Inside and out. The last few months had seen Susie grow a few inches taller, her face narrowing and her body rounding out in places that made her pull an extra coat on when she peddled dope at her corner of the old park. She'd had too many grabbers and pervs over the last year to risk looking any more appealing than she could help.

But when she was safe, as she was now, hiding under the front porch with her best friend, that same change lifted her chin a little and quickened her smile. She was more confident. More self-assured. Because she had a secret. One that even Jake didn't know.

"Run through it again," Jacob was insisting.

"We've been practicing all afternoon," Susie laughed. "I don't forget that fast."

"Tell me anyway."

"Okay. Um, distribute my weight across both legs," Susie recounted, frowning in concentration. "Slightly bent knees. Elbows down, hands up."

"Protect your face."

"Protect my face." She studied the cobwebs above her in concentration. "Strong arm back. Pivot off my lead foot, no walking or crossing my ankles or I'll trip over."

"Show me your arms."

Susie held her arms up in front of her face from where she

sat opposite him, knee to knee. She threw a punch, exhaling as she extended. Jacob caught her fist in his hand.

"Again. Palm down."

Susie jabbed again, twisting her arm as she did so. She followed with her right hand in quick succession.

"Right upper cut," Jacob instructed, and Susie complied.

"Left hook. *Ouch!*"

"Sorry."

"I'll live. Okay, right cross." She followed through and Jacob caught her fist in front of his face.

"That's right but always keep your free hand up to defend your own face. Don't let it drop." He leaned over and pushed her left hand into position.

"You're pretty worried about my face, aren't you?" Susie smirked.

A sheepish grin crept onto Jacob's lips. "Yeah, well, I kind of like it the way it is."

He looked at her for a moment, pink-faced and then leaned back on his arms.

"You're pretty strong for a girl, you know."

Susie laughed. "Gee, thanks." He didn't know the half of it.

Every chance they got after school, Jake was coaching her, in secret. If it wasn't boxing, it was karate. He couldn't use any of the proper equipment of course, because someone would notice it missing from the scout hall, but Jacob had given her his new boxing gloves and convinced his Ima to buy him another pair by saying he'd lost them. It had cost him a fortnight of extra chores. They'd even started fencing with switches from the garden.

At first it was just basic instruction, but now that Susie was getting the techniques down, it was hard to hold back her own strength in performing them. And she was fast. For every punch she landed, she could have given two. The sense of power sent a thrill to her heart. But Jacob was smart. Susie didn't know how much longer she could keep it from him.

"You did great today, Susie Pocket," he was saying. "I told you – soon you'll be giving Gene Tunney a run for his money!"

"Thanks, Jake."

"Mr. Iwate showed us a new move last week, I can show you tomorrow."

Susie bit her lip. "I can't tomorrow. Pop needs me."

"Needs you?" A scowl found his face. "You mean needs to make money out of you."

"Yeah, well, I've gotta do it. Besides, you've got baseball practice. I'm not going to let you miss it again. Not for me."

"I told you, coach was sick anyway, I didn't miss much. The boys were just fooling around," Jacob argued.

Susie shot him a withering look. "That's never stopped you before. You'd play underwater if you had to. Don't miss it for me."

"I don't -"

"No, Jake. Besides, your pop is mad keen on you making the team again this year. You can't let him down like that."

Jacob sighed. "Thursday then."

"Okay."

Just then, the roar of an engine hit the far corner of the street. They both knew that sound better than their own heartbeat. Susie's father, Roy, was home. Susie pressed her eyes to the pinstripe gap between the slats of wood hiding her from view. A dusty black Cunningham turned in to the driveway, bouncing over the curb and pulled up near the front porch. Her father got out, shoving his old fedora onto his head and leaning back into the open front window to retrieve a bottle of whiskey. He stood for a moment, scowling by the car, with one hand in the pocket of his grey trousers. His suspenders were sagging and his shirt crumpled. He swayed a little, then took off toward the front steps that led up to the porch.

"Susie!" he yelled.

Susie pulled back from the slats, catching Jacob's eye. He

knew well enough not to make any noise. If Roy found him, there'd be hell to pay.

The screen door above them slammed and Roy's footsteps thudded across the timber floor. "Where are you?" he shouted from inside the house. "Come and make dinner, ya lazy little crumb!"

"I better go," Susie muttered, her lips tight.

"I hate him," Jacob replied. His eyes meant it.

Susie smiled, miserably. She could always count on Jake to tell the truth.

"Yeah, I know." She turned away, preparing to crawl out of the small gap at the side of the house. Jake would take off after a minute or two, when he heard her voice upstairs and knew the coast was clear. They'd done it plenty of times before.

I'll save you one day. I swear it.

Susie turned back to face her best friend. Even in the growing darkness, she couldn't have hidden the adoration that shone in her eyes.

"It's okay, Jake. I can save myself."

"But -"

"Just imagine what they'd do if you tried. I can't bear the thought of you being in that kind of trouble."

But Jacob's expression had changed. The anger had gone. His eyes were wide and his mouth had dropped open in surprise.

"But, I didn't say anything."

"Yes, you did," Susie replied, her heart quickening.

"I mean, not out loud -"

Susie's skin flushed, angrily. *Stupid! Stupid!* Jake's words had been crystal clear inside her mind. *Inside her mind.* She'd been careless. She'd dropped her defenses and tripped up. Just like she had with Donny.

"You must have," Susie insisted, and pushed away, searching for an escape.

"But, I didn't -"

"I've gotta go," Susie cried, "I'm sorry."

"Wait!" Jacob whispered urgently. He fell forward onto his knees behind her and grabbed her hand in the dirt. "Please."

Susie froze. She closed her eyes. It was warm, his hand.

Her heart hammered in her chest as she slowly turned back but couldn't open her eyes. She didn't want to see the look on his face. She was a freak. And now her best friend, her only friend in the world, knew it. Susie couldn't bear the crushing pain at the thought of losing him.

"Please," Jacob whispered, once more.

With a heavy heart, Susie looked at him.

He was smiling, a scared, tremulous kind of smile.

"It's okay," he said. "I don't care."

"You don't care?" Susie's voice was barely audible. She was almost too afraid to breathe.

"No. I don't. And - I should have guessed it. No one understands me the way you do. Like you can read my mind."

"I try not to," Susie said, quickly. "I swear."

Jacob's eyebrows lifted. "Girls don't swear." A teasing shine sparkled in his eyes, which were now almost lost in the falling dusk.

"You know what I mean."

"Yeah, I do."

Susie looked down. She realized that Jacob was still holding her hand.

He looked down too, but didn't let go. His fingers tightened around hers.

All of a sudden, she felt strange. As if she was watching some other girl's dream come to pass, and the warmth from his hand wasn't really for her. Susie's heart pounded as Jacob gently lifted her hand to his lips and kissed the back of her fingers.

"Don't shut me out, Susie Pocket," he said gently, letting it go.

"Okay."

The back of her fingers tingled where Jacob had kissed them and they stared at one another, just breathing, with silly smiles on their faces.

He was like sunshine. At only fifteen he already had a blindingly bright future ahead of him. Opportunities would be created and relationships forged by his adoring family, to build on their traditions and faith. The eldest son. The family name and pride. Jacob would have a happy life. A safe life. And she wanted him to because it was everything she'd ever wanted for herself. But it wasn't hers.

Susie looked down at her fingers, suddenly self-conscious. The tingling stopped. There was no bright future for her waiting at the end of adolescence. Only an invisible chain that kept her tethered to the whims of the most powerful family in all of New York City. Her mother had escaped, but not with her life. It had taken death to buy her freedom. And Susie was far too valuable to Donny to consider any happier emancipation.

She was hiding under a broken home, surrounded by filth she couldn't scrub away. Above her, the heavy footfalls and drunken contempt of her father shouting for his meal gnawed into her like a parasite. Later, after he'd eaten and she'd scratched out as much homework as time allowed, Susie knew she'd be taken to Donny's warehouse at the docks, where deceit and greed would tick the hours away until she was allowed to sleep. *That* was her reality. But not forever. That much, she promised herself every day. Susie took a deep breath, forcing back the tears. They never helped.

"I'll save myself," she said, resolutely. "One day. It'll be like the pictures in those magazines, where everything is perfect and no one ever gets hurt."

"What about me?" Jacob asked.

"Best friends," she beamed, putting on a brave face. It was only in her own thoughts, she truthfully replied, as she crawled out the of gap to go inside.

You're already perfect.

In the early hours of the morning, as Susie finally drifted off to sleep, bone-tired after spending another night in a cold chair, the words drifted into her mind again. *I'll save myself. One day.* But could she, really, she wondered? Would she ever be rid of the terrible game they all played by Donny's rules? *Yes,* she reaffirmed to herself. *Because I have to.*

She recited the words memorized from her schoolbook, that had given her hope and inflamed her courage. *Though she be but little, she is fierce.*

Deep inside, Susie felt a familiar burning beneath her ribs. A *quickening.* Adrenaline stirring up fate, to let her see beyond *now,* into what life could be like *when.*

When she was ready.

When the time was right.

It was only a matter of time.

Because there was something that Donny still didn't know. Something she would *never* let slip, no matter what he put her through. Susie had discovered another secret.

She could do more than just read minds.

Behind her perfumed pillow, Susie's fingers found her mother's precious box of trinkets. Each little object – a wooden clothes peg, a brass bell, a silver hat pin, the Jolly Joker playing card, a tarnished mirror, a tiny carved sparrow, an engraved locket - held memories of the birth-right Susie carried and the women that had come before her. Reminders and promises, both.

Like her grandmother, Peggy, Susie realized she was strong. *Really strong.*

And like her great aunt Rose, she was fast. *Super-fast.*

With every lesson Jacob gave her, and every practice she pushed herself through in the emptiness of her own home, Susie was finally learning how to use those gifts. Every day, her natural abilities were being harnessed and honed.

So that one day, she'd be able to use them.

Donnie didn't know that.

Nobody did.

Susie smiled, and drifted into sleep.

Betty wove through the house, washing basket under her arm, picking up dirty clothes and hanging clean ones, straightening bedsheets and fluffing pillows with breathtaking efficiency. The wireless rang out a jaunty song from the sitting room and Betty sang as she worked. The children were at school and George at work, leaving Betty some much-needed time to herself. She'd waved all three of them off that morning, each with a lunch pail swinging from their hand. Inside each pail, she'd tucked a dried beef and cheese spread sandwich that she'd mixed up from the leftovers of last night's dinner, neatly wrapped in thick wax paper. Two homemade gingersnaps, a boiled egg, a whole tomato finished their rations. George also had a thermos of coffee tucked under his arm and the children each carried a shiny penny in their pockets for a half-pint of school milk.

Another scrap drive was being organized through the neighborhood committee and both Nancy and George Junior had been busy again collecting rubber, paper and tin metal to aid the effort. When Georgie had offered up his beloved toy train, Betty had almost cried. In the end, she'd helped him dig old bedsprings from the shed and aluminum pots from the kitchen and followed him up the street as he knocked on doors filling his little red wagon with old newspapers. Nancy tilled the backyard soil to prepare for a Victory Garden and both had begun collecting pumpkin and apple seeds for planting. Betty was immensely proud of them.

She straightened up the books on Nancy's bedroom shelf and twirled her daughter's ribbons into small loops around her fingers, placing them neatly onto the dresser beside a silver hair-brush and porcelain ballerina. She slowed for a moment and carefully picked up the ornament. The golden-haired dancer fitted neatly in her palm. It was poised, in a graceful Arabesque pose against a rose petaled pedestal support, like a little fairy captured mid-flight. Its painted tutu was accented by layers of powder blue fabric, gathered at the waist and edged in gold paint. The toy was divine. As a child, Betty would have adored such a pretty thing of her own. How different Nancy's childhood had been. In fact, Nancy's childhood, was *perfect*.

Betty set the ballerina back on her lookout and gathered the dirty washing basket from the bed. Figaro mewled from the floorboards at her feet. He'd been scampering along behind her all morning.

"Thank goodness you can't talk," she said aloud to the kitten, "Imagine what you'd tell them." Betty scooped him up, popped him in the basket and carried it to the laundry, singing as she went.

> "My heart is on a blue-birds wing,
> Since your diamond wedding ring,
> Every day, a dream so gay, and shoo those rainy
>   clouds away!"

The jolly melody of a brass band bounced off the walls as Betty busied herself pulling sopping clothes from the washing machine and feeding them one by one through the wringer. Into a rinsing tub the clothes went, first with warm water then with cold, each time back through the ringer to remove all the suds. Betty powered through her work, barely a hair out of place where any other woman would sweat and puff over the steam and heavy handle. Into a basket they finally went, and out to the clothesline in the yard. She pinned them up with wooden pegs, still humming gaily, her fingers working a little too fast to seem right. On days like these, when she was alone, Betty let her gifts for speed and strength lend a hand. It made her chores much easier and if she were being entirely honest, added a little sparkle of fun and mischief to the tedious hours. Besides, there was no one around to see.

Snap!

A sharp noise in the bushes caught her off-guard. Betty spun around. The black and white kitten was behind her again, diving into a pile of leaves. She breathed a sigh of relief, picking him up.

Little scamp, Betty cooed as she walked back inside, shutting the laundry door behind her. *You mustn't scare me like that.*

Next, Betty buzzed around the house with a pink feather duster, dashing cobwebs as if she were a master swordsman in a duel. She mused as she worked, about an article in the newspaper only a week earlier which had reported a man from Alabama had been found beaten to death by his wife with a feather duster after a quarrel. One hundred and fifty strikes had killed him most inhumanely, which Betty had considered a terrible tragedy.

I could have done it in two, she thought, wryly.

"Bother," she muttered, spying a web far too high to reach. She held the very tip of the handle but still had no luck. Shrugging, Betty kicked off her pink peep-toes and shimmied up the door frame, a foot on either side and duster in hand, in an entirely unladylike way that seemed to defy gravity. Finished, she landed gracefully on her feet and looked up, pleased. *Not a cobweb to be seen.*

She carried a basket of odd socks downstairs into the laundry room and tipped them out onto the folding table. In a blur of color and fingers, Betty expertly paired and rolled them. She flung each ball into one of four piles, like a master card player dealing a deck. She held up the orphaned sock remaining. It was one of little Georgie's knee socks, sporting a new hole in the toe. She smiled and tucked it into her apron pocket, to keep for darning later.

Trap! Her hand flicked as quick-as-a-flash, caging a moth that flew out from behind the washer. Betty carried it, caged in her fingers, to the small window, opened it and leaned out, opening her hand. The moth flew away. When Betty closed the window again and turned back to her washing, the man hiding in the garden bed underneath the windowsill, breathed a sigh of relief.

Betty took each family member's pile of laundered socks to the correct bedroom and tucked them neatly away. Back downstairs, she almost felt guilty as she vacuumed the sitting room rug with her Hoover. It was very modern - a model 305 that George had bought her before the war. They'd paid it off in a year at a dollar a week and donated her old carpet sweeper to a family from church. In Betty's mind, her new Hoover was worth every penny and she felt decidedly lucky to have it. In the midst of the war, it was luxury to have any appliance in her hands at all. The Hoover company, in fact, had stopped production entirely for the time being, converting their factory to support the war effort instead. Once a week, Betty carried the vacuum next door to help old Mrs. Parsons with her cleaning. But this morning, she danced around her own sitting room pushing and pulling the long black handle with inflatable gray bag attached, spinning it in her arms as she sang.

> "Throw me a dime and kiss me goodnight,
> I've got a dream to go dancing tonight -"

She unlocked the converter under the bottom plate to pull out the brush and suction tools, whisking her way across the drapes until they were spotless. She didn't notice the fabric of the curtain catch against a standing lamp, leaving a gap open at the bottom.

With a quick glance over her shoulder toward the kitchen (old habits were hard to break), Betty effortlessly lifted the end of the heavy couch with one hand, holding it up high so she could vacuum, underneath. She gently lowered it back down. George had insisted on keeping the heavy couches left to him by a great aunt, despite their needing numerous men to deliver. They were cumbersome, old and a dead weight, but Betty kept them in good condition with a regular polishing of saddle soap. She turned and lifted George's matching, leather-bound armchair with a single hand, pushing the Hoover underneath. A voice suddenly broke into her mind over the music.

"Fuck -!"

Betty dropped the armchair to the floor with a thud and ran to the window. She pulled the drape aside. *If someone had seen her –* She cursed her own carelessness.

The garden bed was empty. Betty pushed the window open and stuck out her head. An empty Chrysler was parked across the road. A few teenage boys were lounging nearby, playing hooky from school, smoking and flicking knives into a wooden mailbox.

"I swear, she had a puss like an angry boil," one boy was saying. "There was no way I'd take her dancing!" The others laughed.

Betty frowned, shaking her head at their dirty language. Still, from that distance, at least there was no way they could have seen her.

Back in the kitchen, Betty assembled the ingredients for dinner. Taking care to pull the curtains across tight to avoid unwanted peepers, she turned up the wireless and soon forgot about the truant boys. Artie Shaw's Orchestra lit her heart with the Back Bay Shuffle and soon her feet were twirling as her hands were whirring. She chopped cabbage at super-speed with her sharpest kitchen knife (Betty was careful never to mix work utensils with culinary duties), flinging the cabbage strips over her shoulder into the sautéing saucepan with perfect aim. The kitchen was a flight of carrots and diced tomatoes, smashed garlic and pinches of curry powder. Raisins, chicken and almonds were sauced together in a blur of skillets and spoons. Betty's hips wiggled and her shoulders bobbed in time with the music as time ticked by.

She dipped her finger into the batter of her chocolate cream pie and licked the sweet meringue off her finger. It was a new recipe, with milk instead of cream and only two ounces of chocolate to accommodate rationing, but she was delighted with result. She pushed the pie into the fridge to set and stored the Panned Curried Cabbage and Chicken with Almonds in the oven to reheat later. Betty sang a merry tune as she washed her dishes. Finally, she sat down at the kitchen table with a well-deserved cup of tea.

Tea towel in hand, Betty dried the wet cutlery one by one as she sipped her tea, making a game of flinging the clean knives into the drawer across the room. *Cling! Shing! Clang!* Betty smiled. Her aim was better than ever. *Flick!* Her carving knife landed neatly in the chopping block, dead-center.

"She's unnatural -" A voice hissed, unbidden into her mind. Not her own.

Someone *was* watching!

Betty sprang to her feet. The kitchen was empty, the curtain still closed.

The back door!

She stumbled over a kitchen chair as she raced for the laundry room, just moments too late. A man had already dashed through, knocking over the iron which had been cooling on its stand. Piles of clean washing were strewn and trampled all over the floor in his wake. He looked over his shoulder as he ran out the door, saw Betty storming after and sped up with a yelp. He was missing half an ear. *He saw everything,* she thought. *And he ruined my clean washing!*

Betty's lips were white with rage. She raced through the mess he had made. On the street ahead, her voyeur was racing for the blue Chrysler parked by the side of the road. The teenagers were still standing around.

"You there! Stop!" Betty shouted as she raced across the road.

The boys scattered as the man dashed through them and jumped into his car. The engine roared to life. Betty sped across the road, her skirt and apron swishing at her knees. She yanked a flick knife that she'd seen the boys playing with earlier, from the mailbox.

"Hey!" a boy yelled.

Rip! She tore a strip of fabric from the bottom of her apron as she ran and spun it quickly around the shaft. Betty threw it with all her might.

Thud! As the man sped off, the padded knife shaft buried deep inside his tail pipe. He wouldn't get far. Betty kept running.

Bang!

On cue, the car screeched to a halt and stopped dead, smoke billowing from the engine. The door opened and the man fell out, scrambling to his feet, and took off. Not fast enough.

"No, you don't," Betty hissed. She grabbed him with both hands and pushed him back onto the hood. With every ounce of restraint in her body to not kill him where he stood, Betty held him tight. She recognized this man. It was the gunsel she'd seen in the basement of St. Augustine's. *Felix.* The one who'd hit young Sam over the head as he forced the children to work. No doubt, one of Donny's closest. *Cruel. Cold. A killer many times over.* The web of scars on his face were nothing to the monster that lay within.

Betty's mind raked through his thoughts, grappling for any information she could use. She shuddered. He knows it was me in the basement. He's seen my *skills.*

How on earth did he find me? Betty had been critically vigilant not to give the Mayor's office her home address. All the Gala Ball arrangements were managed through the church social committee.

"I know what you are," Felix whispered, watching her with narrowing eyes. "Freak."

Betty tightened her fist around his collar. Her body screamed for release. It would be so easy to kill him. Right now. Right here. One step closer to Donny.

The man glanced back to the boys up the street, who were watching wide eyed. "Better be careful, love. You've got an audience." Betty followed his gaze and caught her breath. Delicately, with the utmost resentment, she let him go and straightened up. The scarred man pulled himself off the hood, and stood, eye to eye in front of the stalled car.

"I've been watching you," he said, slowly, with a grin. "Mrs. Betty Jones."

"Mr. Pinzolo sent you."

"That's right." His right hand reflexively covered his left, which was still bandaged.

She peeled strips from his mind, desperate for more direction.

"Donny is not a nice man, you know," Betty said, gesturing to his injured hand.

The man grimaced and lifted his chin. "Neither am I."

Threads pulled together. Madam Trixie had mentioned him at the Bordello on the night she went after Vince. Felix was the new landlord. *"He's not a man to be trifled with,"* she'd said. And Trixie was right. Dark, brooding thoughts swirled inside him. Betty was used to Donny's goons, but this one was different. He was opportunistic and clever and underhanded. Donny's man alright, but deep down, under layers of self-preservation and resentment, he answered to no one. Except, perhaps -"

One woman. *"Tilly's the only one that can stand that awful man."* The memory of Madam Trixie's words now chilled Betty to the bone. That poor, naïve girl had no idea whose heart she had captured. Donny wouldn't hesitate to use her. Surely, Felix knew that – *yes*. He knew. He'd underestimated Donny. And indeed, Tilly was now a pawn in his game.

"She's in danger you know," Betty said aloud. "Tilly."

Felix stiffened. "What did you say?"

"Tilly," Betty said. Her voice was casual, as if they were simply friends having a chat over the fence. "Lovely girl. Gorgeous bangs. I met her not long ago."

"How did you know about - met her where?" he growled.

"Oh, I had some business to attend to at Kitties last week. Didn't you hear?" Betty's teeth shone with glee.

Felix studied her, critically, then finally made the connection. "You chilled 'em all, didn't you? I thought it might have just been Dimo at the orphanage. That you were working for somebody else. Maybe running with some trouble boys. But it was just you, all along." The words came to him like a revelation. "A crazy little skirt with a big chip on her shoulder." He laughed, a callous sounding bark. "Donny's gonna roast you alive, lady."

"I hardly think so," Betty said, her eyes glinting. "Donny's never cooked a day in his life. And I'm an expert with cooking utensils." She nodded toward the back of the car. "As you've just discovered. It's Tilly you should be concerned about, *Mr. Felix.*"

"Smarmy bitch, aren't ya?" he growled. "You don't know anything about Tilly."

"I know that Donny will hurt her to control you. And it will never end. That's what Donny does. She doesn't deserve the life you're drawing her into."

Felix stepped forward, threateningly. "Don't you worry your pretty little head about that, Mrs. Jones. I can look after my own. All I have to do is give him you, and she's safe."

"I see," Betty looked around. "And does she know you're a murderer? Perhaps she ought to."

"Tut, tut," Felix grinned, nastily. "Glass houses, Mrs. Jones.

I'm sure Mr. Jones would love to know what his perfect little whore does every day while he's at work."

"He already knows what I can do," Betty lied. "My *abilities*, as it were. We have no secrets."

"That sap?" Felix laughed. "I don't think so. I've been watching you for days. The only thing your husband knows, is how to wipe his own ass. You've got nice kids, by the way. Pigtails and all." At the look of fury on Betty's face, he added, "Like I said, I've been watching you."

"How dare you!" She growled, a low warning. In her peripheral vision, Betty saw drapes peeling aside. The curious eyes of her neighbors had found them. Betty forced herself back a step, clenching her fists. Perfectly manicured fingernails bit into her palms. Every inch of her skin craved to leap into battle. To twist his neck, to slice his throat. To rid her family of the threat he presented. Nearby, a front door opened. A woman's head popped out for a better look.

What am I thinking? To murder him – here?!

She was standing in her home street, in its quiet, leafy, suburban paradise, surrounded by neighbors and boys with shiny, clean faces and mothers that naively believed them to be at school as they should be. This was no place for murder. Betty covered her mouth. Her hand was shaking. She looked down at it, like the something strange that it was - an impotent weapon. She gathered her wits and squeezed her fist still. Weakness, of any kind, was unacceptable.

No. She couldn't kill Felix today. But she *would* kill him.

For now, there was only one other option. Betty pulled herself up tall, took a deep breath and presented her most intoxicating weapon.

She *smiled.* That cold, cruel smile that she wore like a crown. The harbinger of death. Avon Lady style.

"Well," Betty said, pleasantly. "It seems we have a stale-mate, doesn't it? I can't snap your neck on the street and you can't use that Colt Vest Pocket in your pants to shoot me."

Felix looked down, amused. His hand moved self-consciously to his trouser pocket.

"Far too many witnesses," she said.

Felix raised an eyebrow. "At least we can agree on that."

"So instead, you can give Donny a message for me."

"Yeah? And what's that?"

"The Gala Ball that's being held in his honor; tell him, that *I hope he enjoys the party*." Betty flashed him a wicked grin, then turned boldly away, yanking the knife from his exhaust as she left.

It took every ounce of will power to let him drive away.

And one thing was abundantly clear. She had just run out of time.

"You alright, lady?" one of the teenagers asked Betty as she stood, staring at where the Chrysler had just been. "Did he rob 'ya?"

Betty spun around. She'd almost forgotten they were there. "Goodness," she said, patting her hair. "No – no, it was just a misunderstanding, that's all," she offered, absently, her mind a hive of worry. She unwrapped the flick knife, folded it and handed it him.

"You're a pretty good shot, missus," the boy said.

"Just luck," Betty lied, forcing a smile.

"You need to tell the brass about him! We'll tell 'em what happened, that he was snooping around your house."

Betty put on her sternest 'mother' face. "I don't think that's a good idea. Don't you think the police will ask you why you weren't in school to start with?"

"Oh, yeah."

"I really am fine, boys. Thank you. Now get home, all of you. I know your mothers, you know. If I see you here again, I'll have to tell them you've been shirking."

Betty walked back across the road to begin her washing day all over again.

I need a stiff cup of tea.

It was late afternoon, when Sergeant Jacob Lawrence parked outside a handsome double story house in a quiet, leafy street. His notebook was heavy with dead leads – almost every Avon representative in New York City now bore a line crossed through her name. He'd been offered endless cups of tea and cakes, questioned on his bachelorhood (he supposed in the hopes of securing a new customer in his non-existent wife), scolded for impolite inferences regarding the bordello, slapped and propositioned. He'd found samples of aftershave and toiletries slipped into his pockets (after the insistence that Joe DiMaggio was an avid fan) and he'd even had one lady burst into tears at the sight of him. He was thoroughly fed up.

Not long before Jacob began his morning rounds, he'd sent Parker off to finish the paperwork on the latest stash of drugs they'd found. The usual 'sample' box of heroin and Benzedrine pills along with an *Avon Calling!* card with handwritten note to an obscure address, had turned up on the station steps at noon one day not long after they'd pulled Vince Carelli out of the junkyard. A sizable stash of heisted crates had been left for him in the unused rail shed which turned out to be the place where the heist itself had taken place, confirming Jacob's suspicions. Someone was clearly trying to make his job easy for him. The crates had since been identified as the same ones that had been stolen, though, strangely, only half of the convoy had been recovered. Going on past experience, Jacob fully expected the other half would turn up soon enough, but what preceded that recovery was what he was now trying so desperately to prevent. Another grisly underground homicide was the last thing he needed. Every day seemed to drag longer in overtime and he still felt no closer to cracking this case. He'd questioned bookies and bordello's, snowed up snitches and the skids that filled the cracks of pavement on the streets at night, all in the hopes that someone had seen something unusual. Heck, he'd almost been tempted to put the screws on every hobo in Central Park. Surely, no-one could transport dozens of crates from one side of the city to the other without leaving some sort of trail.

Guilt and disappointment weighed heavy on his heart. Over the past fortnight, he'd canceled every date with Adina that they'd set. She was such a breath of fresh air, smart and witty, always a step ahead of him. But, just as he'd predicted on their first date, his job had already taken a heavy toll on their burgeoning relationship. She said she understood, as busy as she was with her own work, but he knew she'd been disap-pointed. Worse yet, Adina had arrived at his office in a profes-sional capacity only the day before, shadowing the footsteps of her boss, General Brandway, who was the Deputy Port Commander of the Transportation and Overseas Supply Divi-sions for the biggest New York Embarkation Camp. Any military cargo needed by the front line, was sourced, stocked and shipped through his books. Including the trucks of cargo that were being hijacked under Jacob's watch. Brandway had a hard-boiled reputation for running a tight ship, with frequent fits of temper that sent lesser men scrambling for cover.

The meeting hadn't gone well.

"What in blazers is the meaning of this fiasco, Lawrence?" Brandway had yelled as he stepped in the door, causing the entire station to stop and stare. "It's been months! Months of me losing my best GI's, losing resources that our boys depend on at the front line and here you are — sitting on your cracker in a cushy office pushing papers around the desk. I've had it up to here!" His hand hit Jacob's desk, hard. His oiled

gray hair sprung against his pink-face with the vibration and his weathered features darkened like a raging storm.

Jacob, who had been studying his notes, jumped to his feet, spilling papers to the floor. Behind Brandway, Adina stood meekly with her notepad and pen. Jacob shot her a wary smile, but her eyes found her shoes instead. Adina tucked her hair behind her ear and smoothed her A-line skirt, apparently trying to maintain a professional distance and the appearance that they weren't dating, or in fact, it seemed, that they even knew each other at all. Jacob's smile dropped.

"Take notes, Miss Sonberg," Brandway ordered. "I want whatever cock-and-bull story he comes up with written on paper. I've had enough of this department not cooperating with my office."

"Yes, Sir," Adina said, and began to scribble on her pad.

Jacob was humiliated.

"This whole affair has been fouled up beyond all recognition!" Brandway was yelling. "I've got Class Five equipment that is essential to the war effort tied up in red-tape from here to old Aunt Gertie's ass, and Class Eight medical supplies M.I.A! I'm talking millions of dollars here, Lawrence, and I'm just about ready to send armed convoys through the main street to keep this supply line safe. You want grenades and whizbangs on the road every day with a troop of loaded brownings marching alongside shop girls and baby carriages? You think I won't do it?!"

"Most of your crates have been recovered -

"But not by you! And where are these leads coming from anyway? Who's tipping you off?"

"Well," Jacob hesitated. "I'm still trying to establish -"

Adina looked away, clearly embarrassed for him.

"You don't even know who's feeding us this information!" Brandway seethed, through gritted teeth. "It's probably the same hop-heads skimming the rest of my crates. Keeping some for services rendered! Those are military assets, son, and I want whoever is behind these heists to fry!"

"All evidence suggests it was Carelli that pulled that last heist, sir,"

Jacob said, trying to tame his growing frustration. "And Poletti before that. I'd put money on the fact that they killed your GI's too. Both are dead, along with a trail of bodies leading back into last year. Bodies that we didn't see the pattern in until I started pulling this investigation together. Someone's doing the dirty work out there for us. For every heist, we're getting a corresponding tip-off; bodies and crates. If you ask me, our real problem is finding the bait and switch. Somewhere along the line, you've got a weak link. Someone is feeding your transport routes to whoever is bankrolling this operation." If he was angry before, now Brandway looked livid.

Behind her boss, Adina's eyes widened. Nervously, she took a step back. She chanced a look of warning to Jacob, finally acknowledging, to him, at least, that their relationship existed.

"Are you inferring I have a rat in my ranks, Sergeant Lawrence?" he thundered, beating the younger man down with a stare. "That someone is working against the U.S. military from inside my own office! That's a treasonous accusation, sonny -"

Jacob pulled himself straight. He'd had a gutful of tough nuts like Brandway and Mayor Sutherland throwing their weight around his investigation. He was darned well going to run it the way he needed to. The vexation of cold leads and Adina's witness to this disrespect came boiling to a head. He exploded.

"That's exactly what I'm inferring, General," Jacob shouted. "Flushing out that rat should be just as high a priority as finding the killers I'm looking after. But I don't have any jurisdiction in your office, which you know darned well! And then there's the third party involved. Someone is paying for all this. With cold, hard cash. And whoever that person is, they're more dangerous than the others put together. I'm tracking down two of the three, what are you doing?"

For a moment, Brandway was silent. A vein on his temple pulsed as he clenched his jaw, finally considering Jacob's words.

When he spoke, his tone was quiet, but intense. "We've got seventy thousand workers coming through that port every day,

Sergeant Lawrence. Now, how do you I suppose I 'flush out' a single rat amongst them. It could be anyone."

"With all due respect, General Brandway, no, it couldn't," Jacob said, sitting back down. "It could only be someone with high clearance. I'll leave it up to you to figure that one out. In the meantime, if you'll let me get back to my job, I'm trying to catch a gang of serial killers, as well as find out which high pillow in this town has the gumption to steal government assets from the United States Army under our own nose." Jacob lowered his voice further, conscious of the curious ears tuning in outside his door. "This is not some street gang of greasers out for a bit of nose-candy and iron, General Brandway – someone big is pulling the strings here. And I guarantee you, this situation is a lot more complicated than you know. So how about you let me do my job and go take a good look at who has access to your transport data." And with that, Jacob signaled them both out of his office, trying to hide the hurt in his eyes as Adina passed.

Now, Jacob pulled his hands roughly across his tired face. The driver's seat of his car was strangely comforting, and he thought he could almost fall asleep right then and there. But his blasted notebook with its' ever-narrowing list of Avon ladies was still his only lead and if he didn't dig up answers soon, Jacob felt sure there'd be blood waiting for him when he woke. He gathered his wits and got out of the car. He pulled the jacket of his uniform straight, running his palms down the brass buttons to smooth it out, then fitted his hat. Striding across the road with his papers, Jacob knocked on the front door, ready to launch into his usual introduction.

The door opened.

"Mrs. Betty Jones?" he began, head down, reading from the notebook. "My name is Sergeant Jacob Lawrence with the New York City Police Department -". As his head came up, his words broke away, and Jacob's mouth fell softly open. His mind jarred and lost thought. His heart took over, hammering in his chest, and he was immobilized, like a man caught in a storm not knowing where to turn. He stood on the doorstep, gaping. Reeling. Because this woman looked just like her. Like *Susie.*

But it couldn't be, because Susie was dead.

Suddenly Jacob felt cold. He reached out and found the doorframe to steady himself.

"I'm sorry," he mumbled, "you just look like someone..." but he couldn't finish his sentence, because when he looked back into the woman's eyes, he knew.

It was her.

Those eyes had haunted him for twelve years. That face, that mouth. That *ghost.*

Time fell away.

"Susie -?" he breathed.

The woman in front of him smiled sadly. She seemed to be fighting back tears. Somewhere, under the concern in her eyes, was an odd look of relief.

"Jake."

"But you're – I was there, at your house -"

"I know," she said.

"You're dead," he said simply.

"Yes," she replied, "It was the only way I could live."

He stood there in shocked silence, drinking her in like a man lost in the desert, finally given water. She had changed, but to Jacob, barely. Her hair was darker, and longer, curled in victory rolls that swept up from her cheekbones to frame her face and then dropped down over her shoulders. There were tiny lines around her eyes and mouth, as if she'd spent years smiling and couldn't help but show it. The roundness of her fifteen-year-old face was gone and in its place, he found the contours of a beautiful woman. But in her eyes, those depths of dark blue he had known so well, she couldn't hide from him. Twelve years, meant nothing to a person's eyes.

And he knew he had found her.

And suddenly, inexplicably, he was angry.

"Why?" he said, his voice cracking.

"I had no choice, Jake." She held the door open. "Please, come inside."

Jacob stepped resentfully into her sitting room, dragging off his hat. Betty shut the front door softly behind him. Jacob turned to face her.

"This isn't a coincidence, is it?" he asked, knowing the answer.

"No."

He looked down at his notebook and barked out a laugh. The Avon Calling card, poking out from his notebook, caught his attention like a jagged knife.

"You led me here."

"Yes."

"You've been leaving the boxes for me. On the station steps."

"I have."

He shot her a bitter look and slid the Avon card out from his notebook. He turned it over to look at the handwritten address. The writing had always looked strangely familiar. That instinct he had felt, to keep it close, that there was something odd about it, something *unsettling*, now made sense. It was *Susie's* writing. Twelve years displaced.

"Why?"

"Please let's talk first, Jake," Betty said. "You need to understand."

"Understand what? That you left me? That you ran away and broke me into a million pieces?" His voice faltered with emotion that he couldn't disguise. "That you didn't want me?" Jacob was wounded, and every part of his body betrayed him by baring it.

"I knew you'd be angry. And you should be," Betty said. "I realize I owe you an explanation -"

"An *explanation?*" Jacob repeated, dumbfounded. "Twelve

years, I've thought you were dead, Susie! Not allowed to attend your funeral because of who might be there. Barely allowed to grieve because I wasn't meant to know you. You have no idea what that did to me. The thought that I couldn't save you, that I'd been too late to help - I was just a kid! And you - you were alive this whole time? Why didn't you come to me?"

"I couldn't, Jake."

"You could! You should have! You must've known I've thought of you, Susie. Every single day, I've thought of you!"

"It's not that simple, Jake. You said yourself, you weren't meant to know me, from my family's side at least." Betty wrung her hands together. "We spent so many years hiding our friendship, to protect you. My father would have killed you had he known what you meant to me. And even if I ran away from them to you, they would have found me. They're insidious. Nothing is secret from *them*.

"Friendship? It was so much more -"

Tears pricked behind Betty's eyes and she pulled a handkerchief from the pocket of her apron.

"Yes, it was more," she said. "But we could never have been together, you know that. Your parents, as kind as they were to me, would never have accepted me into their family. They wanted you to marry a nice, Jewish girl and bring their grandchildren up with their traditions and loyalty to your faith – it would have broken your mother's heart to see you destroy that, not to mention your Bubbe and Zayde, whom adored you so much."

She took a breath and looked at him, imploringly. Hesitantly, Betty reached out and took Jacob's hand. He caught his breath and felt his anger fade. Gently, Betty led him over to sit on the couch. She looked as if her heart were breaking, as his was, all over again. "I could never have ruined the beautiful family you had," Betty said. "No matter how much I wished I could be a part of it. I loved you all too much."

"It didn't matter to me whether they approved," Jacob argued, "Only what we wanted."

"No, Jake. You're wrong. It never mattered what we wanted. We were just children ourselves. It was far bigger than us, all along."

Jacob sat, lost for words, looking at her. Deep down, he knew she was right.

All those years he'd pushed relentlessly on, trying to bury thoughts of her in the past, suddenly seemed pointless. He'd never buried them at all. He wore her memory, like a coat against the wind, every day he left the house. The ghost of Susie had become part of his skin.

Jacob dropped his head into his hands. He was beyond angry now. He felt foolish to think he'd lost years pining for something that wasn't gone, and that he could never have had anyway. He'd loved her. And she'd loved him. But it was never going to be enough.

He looked down at his crisp, ironed uniform, at his shiny brass buttons. He thought he'd joined the police force for her, and for the years after he won his badge, he'd striven to uphold the family tradition. *Police Commissioner's oldest son.* Jacob's motivation to bring her justice now seemed hollow. Susie wasn't dead. But he still couldn't have her. And in his passivity, he had chosen that path just as surely as she had. It was the same family tradition he worked so hard to uphold that had forced her to disappear from his life, rather than marry him.

It hurt so much that Jacob felt he might have fallen apart, if his uniform hadn't been stitched around him.

Quite suddenly, he realized there was music. He listened to it, strangely detached, playing from a wireless on the telephone stand. Jacob hadn't noticed it before. But now it stood out, so sweet in its merry tune, that it seemed like an imposter in the room.

"So, why now?" he finally asked, feeling entirely defeated.

"A few reasons. Some more urgent than others, I suppose." She looked uncomfortable.

"Why don't you start with this?" He passed her the Avon Calling card and she took it, with an apologetic smile.

Jacob laughed, with chagrin. "You're way ahead of me on this one, aren't you?"

"How much do you know, already?" Betty asked, gently.

"Can't you tell? Just zap into my mind -" At Betty's hurt expression, he said, "Sorry."

"I would never read your private thoughts, Jake. You know that."

"I don't really know anything right now."

Betty nodded. "Alright, I'll start from the beginning. The *criminals*. I know them, of course. As you'll remember from when we were children. I've been watching them for years. You must understand something – I wanted to contact you earlier, much earlier, for many reasons, but the timing wasn't right until now. I've had - *obligations*."

"What obligations?"

"Very important ones. I'll come to that later. In any case, when I first started tracking them down, I just wanted revenge, plain and simple." At the look on Jacob's face, Betty scowled. "Let's not pretend that they don't owe me that." Jacob took a deep breath and waited for her to continue. "In any case, over the last few years, I've discovered the situation is far worse than I'd imagined. I never told you who I was working for, back when I was a girl. I couldn't, you understood that. It was far too dangerous, and I'd never have forgiven myself if anything happened to you. Especially with your father being who he was."

"I never liked your secrets, Susie."

"I know, I never liked keeping them from you." She looked meaningfully at Jacob. "My father was cruel and opportunistic, but he was just a pawn."

"He still deserved to die for what he did to you."

"Yes, he did." She lifted her chin defiantly. "And I killed him, Jake."

Jacob blanched, hearing her say it aloud. Of course she must had done it. He remembered his own father's words as he'd fallen to his knees, coughing and retching by the smoldering house at only seventeen years old.

"They found Roy in the kitchen, what's left of him... There were signs of violence... He was already dead when the fire began."

"I don't care if you killed him," Jacob said, surprised to hear the words coming from his own mouth. Even his respect for the law couldn't stand up against the hatred he still felt for that man, who had so horribly abused his daughter and wife.

"Yes, I've come to peace with it," Betty said, ironically. "Anyway, every night that they brought me in to help them *judge* the men they brought in, not to mention the drugs I sold to junkies, well, I was always working for someone far more dangerous than my father. From the beginning, I was working under the hand of my father's uncle. Donald Pinzolo."

"I knew it!" Jacob stood up, slamming the air with his fist. "I can smell the corruption from here. I've been tracking the ties Pinzolo has with underworld crime for years, but he keeps his nose so darn clean! And every time I get close, it's like he slips through my fingers. Slimy bastard." Jacob looked back at Betty to find her stifling a laugh. "Sorry," he said.

"It's alright. You know I've heard worse. Last week, I heard a nun cuss so bad she'd have made a sailor blush. No one else did, of course. It was just in her head."

Jacob smiled, ruefully. "I suppose nuns aren't all virtue, then."

"Goodness, no."

"I'll keep that in mind. So what do you know about Pinzolo?"

"Everything. I know he has ears everywhere," Betty continued. "In your department, the FBI, at Embarkation Ports all across the country. I started small at first, tracking trouble-makers and hatchet-men with dirty hands - killers, you under-stand, that worked for Donny. Only ever the ones with blood on their hands and innocent blood at that - I don't kill lightly, you know" she assured him. "But when I started intercepting the heists - truckloads of crates too big to dump - I needed someone I could trust to take the stock off my hands *without* passing it straight back into Donny's."

"You dumped crates of amphetamines?"

"I'll give you coordinates, if you insist, but they're better off where they are. The point is, the military's been corrupted, Jake."

"I guessed as much."

"Someone's giving Donny's men access to transport routes to foster the underground drug trade. He controls practically every inch of the city black market, and his supply lines stretch all the way to the West Coast."

"And Mayor Sutherland?"

"A highbinder. It's big business. And to be honest, it's getting to be more than I can deal with on my own."

"This isn't your fight, Susie."

Betty looked away, smoothing her skirt. "Sutherland might not be," she said. "But Pinzolo is. And Uncle Frank and Marco and Vince, Carlos and Tony and every other sludge-feeder they've got out on the streets doing their dirty work. They'll always be my business."

The gravity of her words suddenly hit Jacob. *Marco. Tony. Vince. Frank.* Images of crime scenes flashed through his head. He'd seen the aftermath of every one. Not just a single homicide, but dozens of men - six, even eight at a time.

The blood drained from his face.

"You murdered them all, didn't you?"

"Not all of them. Not yet."

Jacob took a moment to let the words sink in. The woman

opposite him was beautiful. Poised and polite. As unassuming and good-natured as can be. No one would ever guess that beneath the red lipstick and white pearls, was a killer.

"Vince, at Kitty's -?" he began, a question in his eye.

"Had murdered seven men in the last week alone. He had to go."

"You took them all out by yourself?"

"I learned from the best, remember?"

Jacob didn't look amused. "You're insane."

"I am for not wearing a rain jacket that night. Could have caught my death of cold."

"Or just death."

"Yes, well. There's always a price to pay and I think I paid most of mine before I started. I did break a nail though," Betty said, with a twinkle in her eye, "And I ruined a perfectly good pair of patent pumps," She nudged him playfully.

"You broke more than a nail!"

"Perhaps. Everything else deserved to be broken though."

"Hang on, did you say patent pumps?" As if a light had switched on his memory, Jacob began to fish around in the inside pocket of his jacket. He pulled out something black and shiny. "Two high heels," he said, passing them to her. "I found them at the crime scene. Just couldn't figure out what to do with them. They weren't really evidence, but they bugged me all the same. I just couldn't put my finger on how they got there. I never expected Vince's killer was, well, a *woman*."

"No one ever does."

"This is crazy, Susie. You have to stop. I can't – I can't condone this – vigilante mission or whatever it is. Let me take them in, whoever's left. Especially Pinzolo."

"You can't. Donny keeps his hands clean, you said it yourself. He's smart. He has allies way above your pay grade. If you sting him now, he'll just shut down for a while and get himself out of trouble. You'll never get him locked up for long. This situation needs a more – *permanent* – solution."

"But you'll get yourself killed!"

"Good!" Betty growled. "I'm not afraid of death, Jake. You know that. I'm only afraid of how many more lives he'll destroy with his handshakes and dirty men and silver spoons! He has children involved now, lots of them. At the orphanage packing crates of bennies and fet and ammunition that he's moving underground. Good Samaritan, indeed!"

"I'll organize a raid -"

"And the leak in your department will tip him off. The orphanage will be clean before you switch on your sirens. No, this has to be done exactly right. There are children's lives at stake now. Little boys that are terrified and in danger every day being used to sell drugs on street corners and then taking the rap for him if they get caught. Who's going to believe a child against the word of one of this town's most prominent businessmen? He's pulling them into a life of crime they'll never be able to escape from. No one will look out for a bunch of orphans; they've already been cast aside." Betty jumped up in exasperation and began to pace the sitting room. "They're completely alone, Jake – do you know how that feels? Well, I do! And I won't stand for it. Never again!"

"Well, what am I meant to do?" Jacob asked, his frustration wearing thin. "Why lead me here if I can't use any of this information? How am I meant to help?"

"Because you can help me. I need protection. Well, not me exactly, but this house. Just at certain times of the day – or night. An undercover car to keep a watch when I can't be here."

"Why?"

Betty hesitated, looking reluctant to explain. "Well, I had a visitor today. I'm not sure how he got my address, but I'm afraid I've quite run out of time. I'm organizing something *special* for Donny next week, something big. I'll need your help for that.

But in the meantime, I need an extra pair of eyes on this house." Betty sat back down. "Can you spare anyone?"

Jacob considered, glad to have something at last, that he could do.

"I suppose, I can send Parker around. Say it's an undercover assignment, not to ask questions. He's a good officer and a good shot. And trustworthy."

"Entirely off the record," Betty nodded. "Because of the leak."

"I'll get him set up tonight. What are we dealing with, exactly?"

Betty took a deep breath. "Donny knows it's me. And he knows where I live. He sent one of his trigger men around to spy on me today and I caught him at it."

Now it was Jacob's turn to jump up in anger. "Here? He knows where you live?!"

"Yes, and he witnessed my, shall we say, *unusual* skill set. At least the physical aspect of it. I don't think Donny knows who I really am yet, just that I'm the thorn in his side he's been looking for. I don't have much time left to deal with him."

"So why look after the house when you aren't here? Why do you need Parker?"

Betty's eyes were downcast. When she looked up, they were filled with urgency. The soft jazz of the wireless dissolved into something more recognizable and the sweet voice of Helen Forrest began a sentimental melody to compliment the orchestra.

"Because, I have something very precious here," Betty said. "Something I need to keep safe." A single tear slipped over her cheek.

Jacob sat down again beside her. He reached out, gently brushing away the tear with the back of his finger.

Words, not her own, nor his, wafted through the room on the songbird's melody, and for a long moment they both sat silently together in the music, taking each other in, lost in bitter-sweet memories.

> "I'm on fire again, beguiled again,
> A lovesick, lost, little child again,
> Bewitched, bothered and bewildered, am I."

"Susie -" Jake began.

"No, not anymore, Jake. I can't. Susie's gone -"

"No, she isn't. Don't say that." His brow creased in earnest and his eyes were suddenly on fire. "When they told me you'd been murdered, I didn't want to believe it. You're too strong to be taken like that."

"Strong," Betty repeated, ironically. "I am that."

"That's not what I meant. I mean strong," he lifted his hand to touch her temple and Betty drew a sharp breath, "here". His fingers lowered to find her heart and closed over it. "And here."

He pulled his hand away, leaving Betty with the threat of more tears. She quickly wiped her eyes and looked at him.

"I can't lose you again," he said.

"I'm sorry, Jacob. But I'm not Susie anymore. I had to let her go when I walked away from the fire. For my own protection at first, but now, more importantly, for theirs. I'm Betty now, Mrs. Betty Jones."

"Mrs.?"

Betty smiled, pulling herself up proudly and sniffing. "That's right."

"Mommy?" came a small voice from the sitting room door-way. George Junior and Nancy were standing there, school satchels over their shoulders and lunch pails in their hands. They were watching Betty and Jacob with wide eyes.

"I lost track of time," Betty muttered. Jacob heard the distinctive grunt of a school bus rattling away down the street.

Betty got to her feet and Jacob quickly followed, his own eyes wide with surprise. Betty gave him a bolstering look, then turned to the children with a wide smile.

"Darlings! Come in and meet my new friend. This is Sergeant Jacob Lawrence. He's a very important police sergeant. Doesn't he look fine in his lovely uniform?"

"Really?" the little boy exclaimed, "Wow! A real-life police-man? I'm George Junior, I'm a super-hero!" He hopped confidently into the sitting room, beaming.

"A super-hero? Are you really?" Jacob asked. He shot a bemused look at Betty, unsure whether the child was actually playing, given his unique parentage. Betty smiled and shook her head, minutely.

"He's not really a super-hero," said the girl, who seemed twice his age. "He just thinks he is. Superhero's aren't really real."

"Why, yes they are! Mommy said so!"

Betty stepped forward, placating her young son. "Of course they are, Georgie. Nancy don't be unkind to your brother." But George Junior had already lost interest.

"I like your police hat, Sergeant Lawrence," he said, pointing to the hat left on the couch. "Can I wear it?"

"Well sure, why not?" said Jacob, bemused. "You'll look splendid in it." He picked up the hat and put it on Georgie's head. It fell down over the boy's eyes. George Junior giggled and Nancy joined him, taking her turn of wearing the oversized offi-cers hat. Betty and Jacob laughed.

"They're lovely children," he said, quietly, watching them play.

"Thank you."

Jacob caught her eye. "You're happy, aren't you."

Betty held his gaze, earnestly. "Yes, I am."

"I suppose that's all I ever wanted," he smiled, sadly.

The two of them sat down again, chatting with the children as they took turns playing cops and robbers with the hat. It was a minute before they realized, they weren't alone. George stood in the doorway this time, briefcase in hand, with a confused smile on his face.

"Am I missing the party, jitterbug?"

Betty jumped up, quickly followed by Jacob, who looked embarrassed.

"Oh, George! Not at all, not at all!" Betty said, rushing over to him. "This is a new friend of mine, Sergeant Lawrence – Jake, I mean, Jacob – from the New York City Police Department."

"Police?" George repeated. "Well, I see your uniform there, officer. Golly, I hope there's been no trouble!"

From behind George's shoulder, Betty bit her lip and shook her head at Jacob with pleading eyes.

"No trouble at all," Jacob said, offering his hand.

"Goodness, no, no trouble," said Betty hurriedly. I just - I left my Avon bag at the drug store today by accident." She laughed nervously. "My, was I bent! I thought I'd lost it altogether but Sergeant Lawrence here was kind enough to return it to me."

"Mighty good of you, officer," George said. "She's usually stuck to that Avon bag like peanut butter to jelly. I can't imagine what she'd do without it."

Jacob's lips pulled into a tight smile. He cleared his throat. "It was really no trouble." He turned to Betty. "Right. Yes, well. I'm glad that I could be of service, Mrs. – Jones. I mean, Betty." He looked almost pained to say it. "If you need anything, please, call me, directly." Betty shot him a grateful look.

"I will, of course."

Jacob retrieved his hat from George Junior's head and tipped it to Betty and George. Betty let him out the front door and Jacob crossed the road, sliding back into the driver's seat of his car.

He drove away, but only got two streets before he had to pull over to the curb. The shock of seeing Susie after so many years, and the situation he now found himself in, left Jacob breathless. For more than half an hour, he sat, mulling over this new revelation and what it meant to him, to his work and to the murders he'd been investigating all over town.

Before today, the loss of his childhood sweetheart had fueled him like nothing else ever could have done. He'd thrown himself into his job, desperate to feel he could make some kind of difference in a world that had broken the day Susie died. That somehow, he could heal an unhealable wound. And perhaps, he had. His ambition had forced him to push boundaries and there were already countless criminals doing time by his hand. Perhaps, after all, his loss of her hadn't been in vain. But it still hurt. His bones ached with it.

When the shellshock finally eased, Jacob drove directly home, utterly exhausted, but with a single thought resounding in his head.

She's alive.

8

GUNS & GLITTERATI

Betty quietly turned the silver key of her bedroom door, locking herself inside. The children were safe in slumber and George was comfortable with his newspaper and pipe by the sitting room fire. A set of headlights belonging to a nondescript car had pulled up then dimmed, not long after supper. Jacob had come good on his promise to position Officer Parker on undercover watch for the evening.

Betty had excused herself to draw a bath, which she fully intended to take, knowing George wouldn't disturb her. But first, there was something she needed to do. Something that had been aching inside her, touching her very bones, since Jacob's unexpected visit that afternoon.

She switched on the wireless by the window seat and Ella Fitzgerald's soft voice perfumed the room.

> "I'm making believe, just like I used to do,
> That all of my dreams would come true –
> I'm dancing alone, in the shadows of day,
> Where your arms held my waist as I sway."

Betty lifted her cognac crocodile-skin Avon Case from the

floor. Its brass feet sank into her bed cover as she opened it. The bag itself was similar in size and carriage to a doctor's bag, large enough to keep all of her samples and catalogs as she completed her daily rounds of the neighborhood. One by one, each decorative jar, lotion and lipstick case was removed until her bedside table was covered in cosmetics. Scuff marks and patches of dust marked the glossy case and Betty shone the outside with a handkerchief as she hollowed the inside. Just the sight of her Avon case made Betty's heart swell with pride. Every lipstick it held, every scent and pot of rouge was a treasure. With it, she could transform a wallflower into a beauty queen and a plain face to a princess. Her calling was her pride and nothing represented it more soundly than the beloved cognac case she so often carried.

Of course, there were plenty of powders in her bag that brought her no pleasure at all. Half a dozen jars of heroin stood amongst her fare on the bedside table, disguised as bath salts. Betty easily knew which ones they were, though no one else could have guessed. She didn't like to carry them, but for the time-being, it was a necessary evil. This particular lot had been a part of Vince's haul, kept for the purpose of incriminating Donny's goons should the need arise, which it so often did. It was always best to leave the authorities no question of what they were dealing with. A sprinkle of hell dust over a dead body would spell it out nicely.

Betty wiped the inside of her empty case, then ran her polished nail along the inside of the bottom. With a popping noise, the false base came loose. Betty removed it and pulled out a silver box from underneath. Her fingertips traced the shape of it as she sat on the bed, holding it in her lap. It was as familiar to her as her own face. Betty lifted the lid. Inside was an odd assortment of trinkets. A rough wooden clothes-peg. A silver hat pin. A faded playing card. A brass bell. A tarnished mirror. A tiny carved sparrow. None of the treasures in her box were expensive. None glittered or impressed. But they were heirlooms and each and every one had a story. They were more precious to Betty than a thousand diamonds.

Betty's fingers found what she had been aching for. An engraved locket on a chain, rubbed dull with love. She pried it open. Two faded, monochromatic photographs stared back at her. One picture was of a little girl, with ribboned hair and shining eyes. She was only four years old and as bright as a brass button. Betty remembered the day the photograph had been taken. It was a rare Sunday that her father had been in an unusually genial mood. He'd taken Susie and her mother, Ethyl, to Coney Island on the train. She'd skipped along the wooden promenade between them, convinced their adventure was the first of many to come. The little girl had bathed in the sea and ridden the brand-new Wonder Wheel, squealing with delight at the thrill of seeing tiny people far below.

It was late afternoon and Ethyl had changed Susie out of her swimsuit while her father waited down by the beach.

"Quick darling, in here - can you keep a secret?" her mother had asked, looking behind as she pulled her into a photography booth. A man with a curly mustache had shuttered a portrait of Susie and then one of her mother as well, remarking how pretty they both were as his assistant took thirty cents. Within minutes, they were back on the street hurrying to meet her father, with the developed photos tucked discretely into her mother's purse.

The picture of her mother showed an unremarkable oval face, framed with wavy hair escaping from a pinned hat and the ghost of a smile. It was all that remained of what the child had believed was a perfect day. As Betty looked at her mother's photograph now, the tears in her own eyes reflected the sadness she had missed in her mother's on that day nearly twenty-five years ago. At the time, she hadn't noticed the anxious glances or the controlling squeeze of her father's hand on her mother's wrist as they walked. That night was the very first that Ethyl was taken to Donny's warehouse and Susie had been left to sleep on her own.

Betty returned the locket to the silver box and picked up the brass spinning top. She carried it over to her dresser, thinking perhaps she should give it to Georgie to play with. With a quick flick of her wrist, it took flight, spinning across the polished wood. With it, memories spun into her mind like the flickering stills of a cinematographé set in motion.

"Why does it always fall off the edge right before it stops, do you think?" she'd asked Jacob, frowning as the spinning top dropped into a groove along the verandah.

"Dunno, maybe the floor is lopsided," he'd said, as he'd caught it and flicked it anew.

By then, eight years had passed since Coney Island. Her mother had worn a locket, with the photograph inside, every day. That day though, was the last.

Snap! Betty grabbed the brass spinning top and carried it back to her bed.

It had been hard, seeing him again. More than hard, she realized now. Almost impossible. Although she'd felt the inevitability of Jacob burning through her new life to rekindle the splinters of her old one, Betty had still been woefully unprepared.

Then again, how does one prepare for heartache? She supposed that each time that loss flared anew, there were only tears to douse the flame. And tears had never helped her before.

A whisper of music broke through Betty's thoughts and she couldn't help but wonder how things might have turned out if she'd lived the life that had never belonged to her. She sat, listening, with the brass spinning top resting on her knee.

> "I'm making believe, the stars kept you close,
> And the moon shone at night to your door –
> I'll follow the moonlight to the sea of my dreams,

And leave a note for you down by the shore."

With a sad smile, Betty placed the spinning top back in her box of treasures, deciding she wasn't ready to give it up to little Georgie quite yet.

She sighed. Crossing to her dressing table, Betty stared back at the face she found in the mirror. She smoothed her hair then pinned it up, pulling on a pink, ruffled shower cap. With the Charity Gala only one week away, there was no time to be sentimental. She had caterers and entertainers to confirm, *répondez s'il vous plait* to cross-reference with Gladys, decorations to choose, men to blackmail, an underground drug trade to expose, murderers to murder and Donny to bring down.

I have a full plate already, so to speak, she decided.

A twinge of guilt bit Betty at the thought of dragging Jacob into her mess. Especially given she hadn't had the nerve today to tell him the *other* secret she'd been keeping.

"*Secrets and Lies. They really do tarnish a perfect life,*" she muttered. "*He may never want to speak to me again when he learns the truth.*"

With a heavy sigh, Betty placed her silver box back in the false base of her bag and fitted the cover. She layered her cosmetics and *not-bath-salts* inside neatly and clipped it shut, stowing the bag in her closet.

It doesn't pay to dwell, she decided. The right time will present itself soon enough.

Betty slipped off her clothes and donned her bath robe and slippers, then padded down the hall to run a warm bath brimming with lavender-scented bubbles, ordered from her latest catalog.

"She's a freak of nature, boss. A real piece of work! You've got no idea the sort of shit this broad is capable of. I saw her pick up a whole couch with one hand!"

"A couch?"

"That's right. Then she scuttled up the door frame like a bug. And she's fast, too. Chased me out onto the street and flicked a knife dead-on up my tail pipe, like some sort of crazy ninja. Unnatural, she is. And deadly dangerous."

Donald Pinzolo spun around. "She saw you?"

"Yeah. I dunno how she knew I was there, though. I was real quiet the whole time, couldn't barely breathe when I saw her doing that crazy stuff, like some kind of super-woman. Then suddenly, she just turned on me and came running after me out into the street." His voice lowered to a conspiratorial whisper as Donny resumed his pacing. "She knew all about me, too. And you. She's got the finger on us real good, it was almost like she could read my mind."

Donny paused, his back to the man with the scarred face. A creeping chill found his spine.

"What did you just say?"

"I said she came running after me, out into the street. But she couldn't do nothin' because there were a bunch of kids watching -"

"No! After that. What did you say? It was almost like she could -"

" – read my mind," Felix finished.

"Read. Your. Mind." And to the other man's utter astonishment, Donny started laughing. He grew louder, cold and hard. It was a mirthless laugh, like a man gone mad.

"I don't get it," Felix growled. "This bitch killed Vince. And Frankie and Marco and all the others. What's so god-damn funny?"

But Donny just laughed an unrelenting thunder until he

shook. Finally, he made his way over to the newly-mended window and stared out at the grounds below.

"She was right here, all along. Watching me," he muttered. "And I never knew."

Felix scowled, scratching his ripped ear.

"I'll tell you what's funny," Donny said, finally. He turned to Felix with a look in his eye that could have brought an army to its knees. "As it turns out, I know exactly what we're dealing with here. We're dealing with a very smart little girl, all grown up. One who has a few more skills than she ever let on, and one, who until now, I thought was dead."

"Who is it, boss?"

Donny strode behind the desk and sat in his leather-backed chair precisely where Betty had come to see him only a week before. A scam, every inch of it. A brilliantly executed cover story. A plan well in motion that he would never had seen coming.

"Little Susie Polletti, risen from the ashes." He grinned at Felix, who looked utterly perplexed. "And it seems she's got a problem with her great Uncle Donny."

He leaned back, stretching his legs out under the desk with a dark gleam in his eye.

"I know just how to handle this one."

"What do you mean he isn't at the station? I've left three messages over three days for him. Surely he's stopped by at least once!" A vein in General Brandway's temple threatened to explode.

"I'm sorry, Sir, he's on assignment, as you know. I can ask him to call you when he gets in," Parker's tired voice offered.

"But he won't!" Brandway bellowed. "Listen to me, sonny, I need information about this case. For the past three days neither

Lawrence nor yourself have shown hide nor hair in that office of yours. I gather I only caught you by lucky accident today!"

"I've been on night duty, Sir. And Sergeant Lawrence is – unavailable," Parker said. His voice was clipped and disgruntled.

"You have no darn idea where he is, do you?" Brandway growled.

"I'm sorry, Sir. No, I don't," the young officer said, with irritation. Apparently, Brandway had hit a nerve. "I trust he'll be in later though."

"You trust too easily then, Officer Parker! He's avoiding me, and I'd like to know why. There's something fishy going on and you're letting it swim right under your nose." Brandway slammed down the phone.

"Damn it." He stood up from his desk and turned to look out his office window. As always, there was a hive of activity below, as hundreds of soldiers loaded crates of ammunition and supplies on the ships at dock. Brandway shook his head. Fort Hamilton was one of the largest mobilization centers on the East Coast. A multitude of new buildings had been erected since the war began, to house the influx of draftees and recruits for deployment training. With a constant stream of liners docking and leaving port to aid the war effort, there was no room for misstep. Yet, the biggest blunder was happening in his own department.

"Coffee, Miss Sonberg," he yelled, loud enough to be heard through the closed office door. A minute later, Adina knocked lightly, then stepped inside, carrying a silver tray.

"I brought you sugar snaps," she said, quietly. "In case you were hungry."

"Shut the door."

"Yes, Sir." Adina placed the tray on his desk, then walked back to shut the door. She poured his coffee and placed biscuits on his desk, clearing some paperwork for the plate. Picking up the tray, she made to leave.

"Stay, Adina."

Adina stepped to the side of his desk, waiting.

"What do you know about Jacob Lawrence?" Brandway asked, brusquely.

Adina seemed taken aback.

"Sir?"

"Sergeant Lawrence," he repeated. "You've been liaising with the NYPD more than I have and I gather you've picked up a few things. There's something underhanded about him. I've left messages for him over the last few days and I'm getting no call back, which is completely unacceptable. I think there's something going on. So, what do you think? Trustworthy?"

Adina shuffled nervously. She cleared her throat. "I believe he's very well-respected. Newest sergeant on the force, but he's got a long list of achievements behind him already. Many complex operations, I'm told."

"I know all that," Brandway said, waving his hand dismissively. "I mean, off the record."

Adina paused. "Well," she began, somewhat awkwardly, "the office girls seem to think he's very clever. He's been polite."

"I don't trust him," Brandway declared.

"I don't see why -"

"Because he's avoiding me! He can't have missed three messages. He must have made headway on this case by now. I've had two cargo routes pass through this week without incident. No leak. No heist. Something's changed. That means he's hiding something."

"Everybody's hiding something," Adina said, quietly.

"Not on my watch, they're not."

"I'm sure it's nothing to do with our situation here," Adina placated. "He's probably busy, or perhaps there's something personal -"

"Nonsense. Men don't let personal matters affect their work. He's hiding something. It's the only explanation."

"If you say so, Sir." Adina turned away.

Brandway watched his secretary with a critical eye.

"Wait."

She turned back, her face blank.

"You've been avoiding me too. What's the matter with you?"

"Nothing, of course, there's nothing." Adina forced a smile.

Brandway moved deliberately toward her, until his hand was resting intimately on her shoulder. The white utility collar of her dress shifted a little, and Brandway's thumb found the skin of her pale neck. He looked down at her face. Her eyes found the floor and she blushed. *So damn pretty.* "This is about what happened between us, isn't it? I told you that our – *relations* - didn't need to mean anything, Adina," he said, his voice gruff. "You're only fooling yourself, you know. No one knows about it. No one cares."

"But I -"

"You're thinking too much. It's done. Finished. Unless you want to start it up again?" He raised an eyebrow and she looked away, angrily. "We're all doing a job here, aren't we? An important job. Long hours. People depend on this office to keep those ships moving." He stepped back, then turned to sit in his chair, stirring his coffee. "It's only natural when you spend so long in the presence of one man that you think you've fallen in love – but that's not what it was. You're being a sentimental child about it all."

Adina swallowed and took a deep breath, her eyes shining. "I'm not a child."

"Well, stop acting like one," he growled. "A grown woman has nothing to be ashamed of. You're not married -"

"It wasn't right. I'd thought – I didn't realize it meant nothing to you -"

"The fact is, you were a moon-eyed girl and I never promised you anything."

"You did, actually," Adina challenged, her chin raised. "You said it wouldn't change anything and it did. I've spent months trying to forget those - *mistakes* - but whenever you feel like it, you put your hands on me again. It's not fair. Keep your hands to yourself or I'll leave!" Her voice shook with anger.

Brandway looked at her, surprised. She had never spoken with such spark before. Sharp and feisty. He liked it. If he were half his age, she would have made a good wife. More enticing than his own, in any case. He got to his feet, rounded the desk and leant against the front of it. Adina stepped away from him.

"I'm just trying to settle you down, girl," he said. "This is an important job and you're all wound up like a clock when I need you at your best. This job - you're good at it and the office runs on schedule with you around. You get things done. I can see that. If you didn't, I wouldn't try so hard to keep you happy, would I?"

"Keep me happy?" she replied, bitterly. "With all due respect, you wouldn't know what makes me happy."

Brandway chose to ignore her. The conversation was becoming irritating.

"You wouldn't leave us in the lurch, would you, Miss Sonberg? Your country needs you. Surely you have a loyalty to your country? Men off fighting in the trenches and you can't manage to deal with a schoolgirl crush?"

"That's not what it was and you know it," Adina hissed, throwing a glance to the closed door. Her face was pink and she looked utterly ashamed.

"Well, it's done now, so you'll need to think about what you're going to do. There are lives at risk if we make mistakes. We have a leak in this office that's threatening national security. We need to find out who it is! Loose lips sink ships Adina, and I'll be damned if I let it happen again. We don't have time for messing about with bruised egos. It's time for you to pull up your socks and get on with it."

"Is that all, *General*?" she asked, stone-faced.

"No. I'll have another cup of coffee."

Adina collected the empty mug and silver tray and left the room.

It was a risk, following Felix back to Kitty's, but a calculated one. Betty needed very *specific* information about Donny's business affairs and it was far too hot for her to break into the orphanage again. Felix, as loathsome and dangerous as he was, remained her best option. The children were at school and George at work, so she had left the house empty. Betty had even left Figaro with old Mrs. Porter next door for the day, just in case. Officer Parker had been camped outside of her house numerous nights this week and she could hear how tired and strained his thoughts had become. She hadn't the heart to ask Jacob to keep him there unless it was absolutely necessary, so she restricted as much of her preparations to daylight hours as she could.

Betty was quietly confident that her home and its precious occupants were safe, for now. Firstly, because Donny's right hand man was currently in full view of where she was hiding and the other goons were too stupid to be trusted with such an important job alone, and secondly, because it seemed far too crude an offense, even for Donny. She was still an unknown quantity, and for all Donny knew, Betty may have already passed his secrets onto another informant to spill should the need arise. Until he could fully assess the threat she posed, he wouldn't act.

Donny paid well for information. He made it his business to know other people's business, then use it to his advantage. No doubt he was doing his best to unravel her motives right now, all the better to crush her with when he was ready. It was going to be a tough game, but Betty was determined to leave him reeling.

She watched Felix disappear into the side door of the bordello. Leaning her powder-blue Schwinn bicycle into the dark shadows of the alley opposite, Betty ducked around the trash cans and crossed the road to Kitty's Kat House. Her cornflower blue dress matched the morning sky and her eyes sparkled with purpose.

The bordello was quiet, its occupants out living their normal day-time lives, far removed from the roles they adopted under cover of night. The pink stiletto painted on the outside wall of the brothel looked misplaced in the bright daylight. She sidestepped Felix's blue Chrysler in the side alley, ignoring an itch to run her blade through his tires. She was working *incognito* this morning, and as satisfying as it would be to dispense a little well-deserved justice while she was here, it would only hinder her bigger plans.

Betty crouched by the side door, pulling it open a crack to listen. It wasn't sound she was craving, but *thought*. As long as she was close enough, Betty could hear what she needed.

There. Perfect.

Felix's thoughts filtered into her own, like a radio finding a new frequency. He was angry.

I've never met a more miserable man in all my life, Betty mused, glancing around to keep watch. Makes that gold-capped mute of Jimmy's seem like a show-pony.

Numbers flicked through Felix's mind one after the other, and Betty made a mental note as she listened. It seemed he was managing an inventory of sorts. After a few minutes, a second voice came unbidden into Betty's head. He was making a telephone call.

"Rex? It's Felix. Donny wants his share."

"How much?"

"All of it. And I got the figures here, so don't try to shortchange me."

"All of it?! You gotta give me time to pull that shit in," Rex growled down the line.

"No time. He's got a few cops to pull. He wants his lettuce."

"Jeez. Alright, alright. You're killin' me."

"Not yet, I'm not."

"Look, I got double or nothin' on a group of high-rollers that are gonna lose tonight."

"Gonna lose are they?" Felix chuckled.

"Course they are. I've given 'em a long enough rope, it's time to let 'em swing."

Felix laughed. "Crooked bastard."

"Crooked businessman, thanks very much. Come see me tomorrow, I'll get your dough."

"You gonna make Donny wait? Not a good idea, Rex, unless you want a bullet up your ass. I'm sending a couple of boys over at two to collect."

"Two?! Make it four," Rex grunted down the phone line. "I'll call in a few favors. You want me to call Lubach?"

"They'll take care of it," Felix said. "Just make sure you give my boys what they're after. I don't wanna' have to go chasing after you with a gat."

"Come on, now. I'm a professional, Donny knows that." Rex laughed nervously down the line. "Back door at four. And tell 'em to wipe their boots. I just got a new rug."

Felix laughed again as Rex hung up the phone. Betty scowled. It was no secret that Rex Hatfield bought a new rug every other week. Somehow, his old ones kept ending up at the bottom of the Hudson with debtors rolled inside.

Lubach. The name was enough. Betty slipped the door closed again and straightened up. As for the tip-off about the gambling pick-up, they were just pennies from heaven. If she hurried, she would even have time to keep her hair appointment before she relieved Rex of the money. *I'll call Mrs. Porter from the hairdresser,* Betty thought. *She won't mind looking after the children for a few hours after school.* Betty crossed the road. She felt splendidly organized. She already had a delicious supper cooling in the refrigerator, thanks to the new copy of Florence Brobeck's *'Cook it in a Casserole'* that George had given her for Mother's Day.

"Ooh, I like the look of those gams! How much for a bit 'a hoochy coochie, eh?"

Betty spun around, her arm wide, ready to strike.

"Ease up, dolly!" The man said, his eyes suddenly wider than his well-watered belly. He took a step to the side, nearly falling, then righted himself with what seemed like a great deal of difficulty. "No need for rough-housing wi' me! Unless it's the fun sort -"

Betty looked her assailant up and down, then bit back a laugh. He was barely upright, one of his trouser braces fallen off his shoulder and his brown coat collar turned inside out. A drunkard, stumbling home at the end of a very long night. Not a scrap of a threat in him. Betty turned away.

"Come on! Let's 'ave a bit o' whoopee, ay! I gotta' a dollar in my pocket!" The old man called, rustling around in his pocket. In a shower of dimes, his fist broke loose of the fabric.

Betty had half a mind to ignore him but thought better of it. He was already loud enough to bring unwanted attention to the street. Besides, barflys like this one had notoriously loose tongues and she would rather her visit stayed unnoticed.

Betty turned back and gathered up his scatter of coins. She shot him a wink, playfully hitching her skirt a few inches.

"Sorry, love, I've run outta' gas," she said seamlessly, in her broadest accent. "Been a big night, ya' know."

"Aw, not even a little smooch?" he pleaded, falling sideways.

"Nup," Betty said, pulling his arm to straighten him up and shoving the coins into his hand. "It's 'me day off an' I'm skipping out to get me' hair curled. A girl's gotta look keen, you know?"

"You're raggin me," the drunkard said, with a smile so wide, he was all rotten teeth. "You're as pretty as a picture. Don't need no curls -" Betty grabbed his arm again and steered him on his way.

"Sure, I do," she said, "Besides, you're too soused up to smooch a looker like me. Go get some shut-eye and come back when you're sober. Madam Trixie'll find you a squeeze if I'm not 'ere." She gave him a gentle shove along the road. The man stumbled away, then turned back, swaying dangerously, but found her nowhere in sight.

"Gone!" he said, with a look of astonishment. He stood for a moment, blinking like an owl, then turned and shuffled along the road as he made his way home, mumbling to himself. "Poof! Gone! Jus' like the blue fairy. I'll 'ave good dreams tonight..."

From the shadow of the alley way opposite, Betty stifled a giggle. She'd be surprised if he even remembered a fairy when he woke from his addled sleep later that day. She hopped onto her bicycle, ready to take off.

"Oh, I almost forgot -." Betty stepped back off her bike and unstrapped a large box from the rack behind the seat. She hurried back across the road, setting it down on the doorstep of Kitty's Kat House. The latest order for Madam Trixie and her girls had arrived. *There's always time to take time off for beauty,* she grinned, as she rode away.

At four o'clock precisely, Betty parked her bicycle behind some trash cans in a parking lot in Gravesend, removed her Avon bag from the basket and stepped confidently toward a grimy-looking shop not far from the bay. She'd tracked the comings and goings of Rex Hatfield's gorillas plenty of times before and knew what to expect. Donny's shady dealings with him only scraped the surface of the man's lack of decency. Rex wasn't just the biggest bookie in Brooklyn. He was a murderer and thief. Donny's capitol was the hook that caught the wretched creatures lurking the muddy depths of the racetracks. Rex's false smile was the encouragement that lured them in.

Rex played to the ego's of fools and didn't discriminate, rich or poor. Eventually, they all got caught. Addicted, desperate men bet their last ration ticket on a chance to beat the odds and Rex gave them enough line to lose themselves completely, then *snap!* He would reel them in, as they drowned in debt. From there, they were usually passed to Donny. After selling the clothes off their back, and calling in favors to the last, the most pitiful of these creatures paid with their lives.

Rex's empire was built on the backs of whipped thorough-breds and fixed fights. His races brought gamblers from Freshkills Park to Flushing, Fordham to the Flatlands. Dog fights, horses, fists and cards - Rex fixed them all.

The roller door was pulled down tight at the front of the shop, giving the appearance that it was closed. Betty turned down the side of the building instead, then turned left, taking the alley behind. Ahead of her, two men were walking. One was tall and wiry with hair that stuck up at the back like a wire brush. The other was short and fat, with oiled hair that continued down the neck of his shirt. They were arguing.

"What the hell were ya' doing?! Bunkin' off like that. You know the boss wants us to keep an eye on the kids."

"Do I look like a nursemaid to you?" snapped the taller man.

"Who cares? You'll catch yourself a bullet if you don't do it. Besides, you get an extra ten clams a day if they make their quota with them crates."

"Ten bucks? You're all wet, Earl." He stopped walking, suddenly. The tall man pushed his companion against the concrete building. Betty ducked into an alcove to avoid being seen. "I'll tell you what we gotta do," he whispered. "We pick up this lot from Rex and we catch the Super Chief to L.A. Live like movie-stars and drink champagne in a private lounge! We'll order fresh lobster and steak all the way. By Friday we'll be stretching out on a beach somewhere in Cali. Think about it, here we are, bustin' a gut and herding snotty-nosed kids, while

Donny's going under. Some crazy broad is pickin' off his crew and I don't wanna be the next corpse in the drink. So, what do ya' say? Think about it, Earl, we'll never 'ave to work again in our lives!"

"I don't know, Carmine. What – what about Donny? He'll come looking for us, won't he?"

"Course 'e will, but we'll be gone with the wind by then. Sippin' Mai Tai's under a palm tree with a bucket-load of beluga! Well?!"

Earl seemed to hesitate. "I could use a holiday," he finally exclaimed.

"A really long one," sniggered Carmine. "Like, forever."

Betty peeked around the edge of her hiding place.

"And I'm sick o' workin' for Donny," Earl complained. "It's gettin' too hot for me. There's gotta be somethin' better out there." His voice grew whimsical. "You know, I always wanted to run a flower shop. I like seeing 'em grow -"

"A flower shop? What are you talkin' about, ya fat-head?" the taller man said, knocking the dumpy one in the shoulder. "You thinkin' about flowers when we're tryin' not to get ourselves killed?"

"Yeah, well, it was your idea! Doin' the bolt, an' all. If we're startin' again -"

"You're getting' ahead of yerself. Just get the money, alright? Then we'll talk about ya' flippin' flowershop."

"You could help me run it." Earl offered.

Carmine went quiet. "Yeah?"

"Why not? Earl and Carmine's Flower Shop – I can see it now!" the shorter man said and Carmine cracked a smile.

"Yeah! You know, I reckon' I'd be good at somethin' like that. But only if we sold stompers too. Fancy leather ones like the film-stars wear." He lifted the leg of his trouser to show off a shiny two-tone lace-up underneath.

"You're spiffy, for sure, pal," Earl said, nodding.

"Thanks."

"We just need the gravy -"

"So, let's get it. This'll be the makin' of us. Carmine and Earl's flower shop!"

"No, Earl and Carmine's!"

"I'll play you a round of blackjack for it. Now, look sharp, so Rex doesn't suspect anythin'."

The two men broke away from the wall, pulling themselves together. They walked in fits of chortling toward the back door of Rex Hatfield's shop, knocking each other with their elbows. As soon as they disappeared, Betty stepped out.

Idiots. They were so naively stupid she had half a mind to let them go and try their luck. They would barely be out of the station before Donny had them found, drawn and quartered. She'd be doing them a favor by making it quick.

She waited for a few minutes, then rapped sharply on the back door of Rex's bookie den. Without waiting for a response, Betty stepped inside and pulled the door shut behind her. The small warehouse room was mostly empty, with a large stack of boxes toward one end, a card table littered with ash and a long, thin roll of burgundy carpet leading in from the door. She looked down and wiped her shoes on it.

"*You-who!*" Betty called out in a sing-song voice.

Rex Hatfield appeared in an inner doorway. "I'm shut," he growled. In his right hand, he carried a walking stick. Over his shoulder, Earl and Carmine's heads appeared behind him. The safe, and therefore her prize, was probably in there with them.

"I'd like to place a bet, Mr. Hatfield," Betty said, cheerfully. She placed her Avon bag on the floor where she stood and stepped forward.

"I said I'm shut, lady." The man strode forward toward the table, without leaning on his stick at all. "Come back tomorrow."

"I'd prefer now, if it's all the same to you."

"Well it's not all the same, I got business goin' on," Rex said.

"So I see. Still, I'll put a bet on, please. This one's a sure thing."

From the doorway, Carmine's eyes were squinting in concentration. A slow dawning of recognition appeared.

"Holy – that's the dame that Donny's after!" he suddenly yelled. "She's been pegging off our lot for months!" Carmine yelled. He dashed backwards into the room he'd appeared from, dragging Earl by the scruff of the neck to follow. The office door slammed shut behind them.

"What?" Rex's head twisted from Betty to the closed door and back again. "What's this about Donny?" he snarled, eyeballing Betty with distrust. He yanked his walking stick up, and ripped away the handle, unsheathing a long, thin blade.

"Oh, Donny's just upset because I've dealt him a rather bad hand lately," Betty said, pleasantly. "You'd know all about that though, wouldn't you, Rex? I'll admit, I *am* a bit of a killjoy when it comes to racketeering and murder. I just don't like to see the bad guys win. It's so disenchanting."

"That right?" Rex said, his eyes swiveling between Betty who was blocking the exit and the sounds of Carmine and Earl rummaging around in his office.

"And what's a broad like you gonna do about it?"

"Well, I'd like to place a bet, of course. Isn't that what you do?" Betty stepped forward. Rex pulled himself as tall as his stocky body would allow. The knife gleamed in his fist. "For starters," Betty continued, "I'll bet that within thirty seconds from now, you'll be rolled in your lovely new rug like a Continental Twinkie. I had a good think about it over my cup of tea, and I *would* then drop you in the Hudson the way you do to so many of your bankrupted debtors, but I really don't like the idea of your foul corpse muddying up our lovely river."

"Oi! You two! Get your asses out here!" Rex yelled over his shoulder. The knife in his fist was shaking. "This broad's off her nut." The frenzied noises coming from the back office intensified.

"Don't mind them," Betty said placidly. "They're cowards, really. They're currently emptying your safe into their pockets and realizing there's no window to escape from back there. I'll help them out in a moment. First things first though -"

Betty leapt forward.

Smash! Her high heel landed on target in the bobbing center of Rex's throat, crushing his windpipe. His hands flung forward.

Slice. Betty's sleeve tore open as Rex's knife caught it. He stumbled backwards, then heaved himself up, gasping and purple in the face. His expression was a cocktail of fear and rage as he tried to mouth words his lungs wouldn't allow. Bent double, he struggled to breathe. He stumbled sideways to the card table and grasped a chair for support. Betty walked over, dispassionately.

"You made bad choices, Rex."

He stared up at Betty with eyes that threatened to pop out of his face. Suddenly, he lurched himself forward, the knife clenched in his fist, aimed straight for her heart.

Snap!

Her fist met the side of Rex's face in a single blow so violent, she heard the distinctive *crack* of his neck. It recoiled, with no resistance. *Broken.* Rex Hatfield crumpled to the floor. Betty looked down at him, shaking her head.

She picked him up under the arms, and pulled him over to the rug, feet trailing across the concrete. Despite being more beer-belly than bone, his weight was no match for Betty's innate strength. Within seconds, he was rolled tightly inside the middle of the carpet. She grasped the end of the coil and dragged it behind the boxes on the far side, hidden from sight.

"Bother," Betty said, straightening up to survey her torn sleeve. "I don't have the right colored cotton for this. I'll have to stop by the haberdashery." She looked up. Carmine and Earl were standing in the inner doorway, frozen, like rabbits in a headlight. Their minds were running wild with fanciful ways to escape. Betty walked around the boxes toward them loosening her gloves.

"Where's Rex gone?" Earl stammered.

Betty sighed. They were both far stupider than she'd thought. She dug into their minds, searching for dirt. Both were relatively new to Donny's band of thugs. Petty theft, drugs. It seemed Carmine enjoyed a fist-fight in the local gin joint. Oddly though, neither had killed anybody. They were clean. Betty frowned. She'd never once been faced with this dilemma before. Every man she had killed, had almost as much blood on his hands as she did. *What do I do?* she thought. *I can't kill innocent men.*

"Rex left," she stalled. "He's actually - working with - the police." Betty's heart thumped and her mind raced ahead, searching for potential pitfalls. What she was considering was unprecedented. After all, they hadn't actually *witnessed* anything. *Yet.* It was all hearsay.

"A snitch? No way!"

"I'm afraid so. He sold out months ago. We know everything."

"We?" Carmine said, suspiciously. "But you're the crazy -"

"Don't be ridiculous, Carmine," she said, *tut-tutting* him. "Do you honestly think a little doll like me could hurt a fly? The very thought of it is ridiculous. Why, I'd be terrified! All those *big, dangerous* men with guns. Even the idea gives me the jitters."

She smiled disarmingly and batted her eyes. "Goodness, no," Betty continued, as if she were imparting a great secret. "I'm just the *secretary* for the senior detective working this case. In fact, I only came here to pass Mr. Hatfield a message. The Sergeant wanted to see him. He's just left now, to give his statement to the police sergeant -" Betty waved her hand vaguely toward the closed exit, conscious that her Avon bag was still sitting in front of it. *I wonder how stupid they really are...?* "I didn't know he still had company, we thought he was meeting you at two. But seeing as though you're here," she said, "I really feel I ought to warn you -" she looked at them, cagily. "Perhaps I shouldn't though -"

"Warn us about what?" Carmine growled.

"Yeah, what?" Earl said, stepping closer. Fifty-dollar bills were poking from his pockets.

"I really can't say," Betty replied, coyly. She stood for a moment, looking anxiously to the door, as if wrestling with some great indecision. "No, I just can't. After all, this is an *open* investigation and all, and I'm just a *secretary* -"

"What is it? Come on, lady – tell us what's goin' on!"

At the pleading look on Earl's face, Betty relented.

"Well, alright. I think you really should know that the police have been following you two for quite some time. Mr. Pinzolo is buried in some terrible business, I'm afraid, and it's only a matter of time before the police take him down. Just between us," she leaned forward, conspiratorially, "I heard that he's looking to *fry* for it." Betty pulled a fearful expression and made the sign of a cross over her chest as Earl and Carmine exchanged a look. "And every man working for him will too, which I guess includes you two, even though I'm sure you're not at fault, just judging by what lovely manners you have. But still – the chair doesn't discriminate." She made a little buzzing noise and Earl whimpered.

"We haven't done nothin' though! Just workin' for 'im doesn' make us guilty!"

"Actually, I'm afraid it does. He's tied you up in trafficking stolen weapons, drug smuggling, extortion, murder... I've typed the arrest warrants up myself and it's not looking good for either of you. Donny's going down and you'll be there right alongside him. The officers will be here any minute now to collect the evidence, and you'll both be arrested at the scene of the crime." At the look on their faces, she added, "I believe they let you choose a special meal before you die though – perhaps steak and lobster?"

"What are we gonna do?" Earl cried, his suspicion turned frantic. "I don' wanna die!"

"Me neither!" Carmine choked.

"Well, I suppose -" Betty began, looking earnestly from one to the other. "I mean, I really shouldn't -"

"Shouldn't what?"

"Can't you help us?" Earl stammered. "We can turn stoolie like Rex – tell you all about the kids -"

"Yeah, the kids!"

"I'm afraid the police already know all about the orphanage," Betty said. "In fact, they have all of the information they need to bring Donny and all the rest of you down. They don't need another snitch."

"Oh no! What are we gonna do?" Earl stammered. "This is all your fault!"

"It's your fault! You and your flippin' flower shop!" They began to scuffle with each other, and Betty held out her arms between them.

"Please, gentlemen! If anything, it's Donny's fault. He put you up to this terrible business!"

"Yeah! And now the brass are on their way and we're gonna fry!" Earl's lip trembled.

"Oh, I'm such a bleeding heart," Betty sympathized, throwing a glance to where Rex Hatfield's corpse lay hidden. "You both remind me so much of my dear brother, Harold, that's all. God bless his soul."

"Please, lady -" Earl begged.

"As far as I can see, there's only one thing you can do."

"What!?"

"You'll have to leave before they get here. Get as far away from New York as you can and never come back! Catch the first train."

"But you've seen us -"

Betty paused, biting her bottom lip. "That's true. And I really *should* call the Sergeant right away, I mean it's the law and you're neck deep in trouble. Mr. Pinzolo has you right at the end of a noose and you didn't even realize - but I feel so bad for you both -" Betty frowned, a picture of indecision. "I *suppose* I could say I never saw you -"

"Thanks, lady!" Earl made a run for the door.

"Wait!" Betty stepped in front of him. "You can't take all of that money with you. It's traceable! The police planted it on Rex to trip Donny up. They're coming to collect it back as evidence. They'll catch you the minute you spend it."

"Jeez!" Carmine spat, emptying his pockets in fistfuls onto the floor. "Toss it, Earl!" His companion ripped out the cash as if it were burning holes in his trousers.

Betty turned to her Avon bag and retrieved her purse, handing them two crisp fifty dollar bills. "You'll need money though. You'd better take these for the train tickets instead. I hear California is nice this time of year. And remember, never mention any of this to anyone or they'll have you back here in the chair faster than you can say 'blackmail'!"

"Not a soul!" Earl declared.

"We owe you one, lady!"

"Yes, I think you do," Betty said, shifting her bag and ushering them out the door. "Get straight to the train remember, Donny'll have your livers if he finds you first!"

Carmine and Earl ran off up the alley, knocking each other off kilter in their desperation to be gone. Betty chuckled as she turned back inside and shut the door.

She looked around the room. Apart from the littering of cash, the room was relatively tidy. She bent down and shuffled the scrunched money efficiently into a large pile. None of it was traceable, of course.

She replaced the missing one hundred dollars, an entire month of Avon sales, back into her purse for banking. She'd made her final delivery for the new catalog just yesterday morning to Ruth and had been delighted to find poor, wretched Anna there too, still pining for the greaser that had left her bruised. Betty had ultimately repaid him for his bad behavior, though of course, Anna didn't know it. The silly girl simply nursed a tendency for bad choices in men. Betty had left Anna with a perfume she promised was sure to attract a new, law-abiding beau. As she had counted her final takings last night, Betty wondered if she'd given away more products this month than sold. She had topped the earnings up with cash from her own purse and wrote out the deposit slip, ready to be banked Friday morning.

Rex Hatfield, on the other hand, seemed to have no shortage of cash. There was far too much piled on the floor for her bag to hold, so Betty rummaged about the office until she found a sizable box to fill instead, scouring the safe for extras while she was at it. *I made rather a healthy windfall on that bet,* she mused, tucking her freshly curled victory rolls behind her shoulder.

Betty tied the box closed with some twine and carried both box and bag outside to the alley.

Although her stomach twisted with anxiety at the thought of letting Carmine and Earl go free, she couldn't shake the feeling that she'd done the right thing. They were far too stupid to pick up on her game and if need be, she could always kill them later if they showed up to cause trouble. Somehow, she didn't think they would. *Perhaps I'm becoming sentimental.*

Betty walked up the alley, rounding the corner of the building with her baggage in her arms. Soon enough, she'd be on her bicycle again, heading home to the comfort of a delicious casserole and a hot cup of tea.

***

An unmarked car, half hidden at the end of the alley, hummed to life and rolled out slowly from behind a row of dumpsters. It pulled up by the back door of Rex's shop. With a glance up the street to make sure the coast was clear, a man got out of the car and tried the shop door. It was open. Stepping inside, he found himself in an almost empty room. A pile of boxes sat midway to the far wall and a small table and chairs were set up near the middle, spilled with papers. He flicked through them. *Tipping notes and ledgers.* A walking stick sat propped against a chair. It had no handle. *Odd.* The man made his way through the room to an inner door, his hand gingerly framing the Colt Official Police revolver strapped under his jacket.

"Hello?" He elbowed the door open and stepped inside.

The office was a mess, paperwork strewn everywhere and a safe hanging open in the wall. Not a person in sight. Given he'd just seen three leave under highly suspicious circumstances, he wasn't entirely surprised. A flutter of black and white caught his eye. He stepped over to where the boxes were stacked and bent down. It was a slightly scrunched one-hundred-dollar bill. Frowning, the man turned it over in his fingers, then looked to the floor again, in case there was another.

Was that? It couldn't be – but it looks just like -

On his hands and knees, the man dragged a large coiled rug from behind the boxes and set it sailing across the floor. It rolled away, unraveling before him until – *thump.* The man stepped forward, his heart racing. *He was right.* He slipped the gun from his holster and readied it, just to be sure. With the toe of his shoe, he gave a nudge to the shiny patent leather of the shoe he'd seen a flash of inside the end of the roll. *Dead.* An older man, fat and purple in the face lay on the floor, his head lolling from the momentum of being spun. He nudged the man's cheek with the muzzle of his gun. *Broken neck.* A silver knife was still clutched in the man's fist, pressed down the length of his body. It was clean.

Officer Malcolm Parker stood up and holstered his gun, a grim look on his usually cheery face. Every night for the past week, he'd sat dutifully in his car, undercover, watching the manicured house in the flawless street with the picture-perfect family that lived inside. *Protect them,* Sergeant Lawrence had demanded. *But don't tell anyone. Even the department.*

But protect them from what? What crime could possibly be committed on such a faultless home? And the longer Parker watched, the more impossible that perfection had seemed. There were no cracks in the mortar. Not a raised voice or frown to be seen. It seemed a little *odd*.

So, he decided to do some investigating of his own. First, the husband.

Then the wife.

After all, no one is *perfect*.

He scowled at the purple face of the corpse in the rug. *Someone's been lying.*

The dinner table was already laid out with a chicken pot pie and roast potatoes. A trifle was setting in the refrigerator for dessert and the children were under strict instructions to be on their best behavior for their elderly neighbor.

"Now are you sure you'll be alright, Mrs. Porter?" Betty called from the kitchen.

"Fly a kite? It's a bit late for that, isn't it, dear?" Mrs. Porter called back, turning away from the children to shuffle into the kitchen. "But I suppose if the children want to -" Nancy rolled her eyes at the old lady's back. Betty shot her daughter a warning look.

"No kites, just dinner and bed, please. Now, here's the phone number for City Hall," Betty said, passing Mrs. Porter a piece of paper. It might be a late night for you, so do sleep if you need to. George will walk you home when we return."

"My, don't you look a picture!" Mrs. Porter said, admiring Betty's satin evening gown as she pulled off her apron. "Such a pretty dress." She lifted the hem of her own wool day dress and gave a little shuffle. "You know, I used to turn heads too. At the spring dance, back in Bellefontaine I was crowned Belle of the Ball."

"I don't doubt it, Mrs. Porter, you rascal," George said, sweeping into the room and taking the old lady's hand in a gentle spin. "I bet you had them scrapping over your dance card!"

Mrs. Porter giggled. "I did, you know. And I got up to mischief, I can tell you."

"I'm sure you're a terrible influence on the children." He shot a wink to Nancy, who screwed up her face, entirely unimpressed.

"Time to skidoo, jitterbug," he said, turning to Betty and pulling on his driving gloves.

"Yes, I know, I just feel I've forgotten something -" Betty replied, looking around the room, distractedly.

"Forgotten something?" George teased. "Surely you're the most organized hostess in New York City, jitterbug. Down to the very last *hors d'oeuvre*. Those orphaned children will practically have it made after tonight's do with all the high-hats you've invited. But not," he ushered Betty toward the front door, "unless their gracious hostess turns up to empty those silk pockets. So, let's hit the road."

"Honestly, George, when you say it like that, I sound like a criminal!"

"Nothing could be further from the truth, my darling," George winked. "You're the picture of morality and grace."

"Of course I am." She slung a glittery purse over her wrist. It was heavier than it should be. Inside was her favorite ruby lipstick, a powder puff, silver comb and two freshly sharpened boning knives, neatly wrapped in a large handkerchief. *Just in case.*

"Let's skip then," George said, holding open the front door for her. Betty looked up and down the street outside. Apart from the usual familiar cars, there was no one to be seen.

Parker should be here by now, she thought, glancing back inside at the clock on the sitting room wall. She bit her lip with worry. It was just on six o'clock. *Maybe he's running a little late.*

"Perhaps we should wait a few minutes," Betty said, hoping for a sign of the undercover police car she was already used to seeing parked under the red maple.

"Whatever for!?" George exclaimed. "Mrs. Porter is all set and the car's warmed up. The traffic is always wacky this time of evening - you can't be late to your own party!"

"But a few minutes won't hurt -"

George looked at her, with a wry smile. "I think you've got a case of the jitters, jitterbug. It's a big night for you, very understandable. But it's just a party, after all. No need to get yourself worked up over it."

Just a party, she thought with chagrin. If only he knew.

"Yes, I suppose," Betty relented. "Mind your manners, dears." Betty kissed George Junior goodnight, then turned to hug her daughter.

"Please don't leave us with her," Nancy said in a stage whisper. "She can't hear a thing and it's so dull playing Rummy after dinner."

"Just stand in front of her when you speak and don't mumble," Betty whispered, kissing her daughter. "I'm sure you'll manage for one night. I'm counting on you to keep Georgie occupied while I'm out. And remember to feed Figaro before bed."

Nancy sighed melodramatically. "Yes, mommy."

Every time Betty looked at her daughter, the girl seemed to be inching closer to womanhood. The implications of it were too urgent to deny. *It's time,* Betty thought. *As soon as this business with Donny is over, I need to tell her.*

Betty leaned forward and tucked her daughter's hair behind her ear. "I know you're frustrated, dear, but I need you to help me by putting up with it for just a bit longer. Next week, I promise to take you out - just the two of us. We can have a little chat about – well, all sorts of things. *Important* things. I can see you're old enough now to manage the responsibility."

Nancy beamed. "Really?"

"I promise." Betty kissed Nancy's forehead again and slid into the single leather seat beside her husband. "Good night, Mrs. Porter," Betty called as George reversed his gleaming Chevrolet out of the driveway. "Don't forget the trifle!"

"Why do I need a rifle?" the old lady called back.

Betty sighed as they drove away. There was still no sign of Parker. *Perhaps a rifle in the refrigerator would have been more help.*

***

As their car purred its way toward Lower Manhattan, Betty's chest tightened, recounting plans in her head. She was meticulously prepared. *There's no point in fussing over it now,* she told herself firmly. *Besides, if anything untoward should happen, you think best on your feet.* Betty took a deep breath and painted a cheery smile on her face, determined to enjoy every moment of the evening. George was singing along to a jolly melody on the radio, oblivious to her worries.

> "Somewhere out there, music is playing, how
>   sweet the tune,"

He sang in a rich baritone over the gay notes of Helen

Forrest. Betty grinned at him, joining in with a honey-sweet voice.

> "Somewhere above us, heaven is glowing, how
> bright the moon,
> When my love is dancing close to me, I can't help
> but swoon -"

They finished the last notes together, and Betty laughed.

"That's the spirit, jitterbug!" George said. "It's awfully swell to see a smile on your face, you know. You've been a pail of frowns over the last few days."

"I'm sorry, darling, just nerves. I want this Gala Ball to really go off with a *bang*."

"And it will!" George assured her. "If anyone can pull it off, Mrs. Betty Jones is the one for the job!"

Betty grinned as they sailed toward City Hall. He was right of course, Mrs. Betty Jones could do *anything*.

Soon enough, George was handing his keys to the valet as Betty stepped out onto the street in front of New York City Hall. The front gardens were filled with elegant guests making their way inside, swathed in long dresses and dinner suits, hats and gloves. A grand facade of white Massachusetts marble rose in the splendor of a Renaissance revival three stories high with an elegant clock-tower cupola spire rising from the center, alight with a statue of Lady Justice. The ornate balustrade over the front entrance and roof had been decked out with glittering lights. Eight marble columns adorned the front steps, which tonight were dressed in red velvet carpet.

Betty and George handed their coats to the concierge as they passed through the great front doors. Just beyond the arcade, a soaring rotunda greeted them, towering above a grand, floating double staircase, that spiraled each side of the dome's curve to greet the second floor united. Twinkling fairy lights, long-stemmed ivory candles and giant bouquets of summer blooms adorned every surface. Betty allowed herself a small moment of pride. Her church social committee ladies had outdone themselves. The rotunda, already so impressive, was simply breathtaking.

Betty smiled and greeted guests as she made her way up the staircase to the Council Chambers, where the official reception was to be held. On the second floor, elaborate chandeliers hung in the spaces between ten Corinthian marble columns that majestically circled the landing. The columns held the dome itself high above, gilded inside with graduated sculpted roses surrounding the oculus at the very top, where the dark night sky presided over all like a great eye.

Like all other eyes in the room, it found Betty, a vision of elegance in a strapless evening gown that fell to her ankles in a wash of black satin and diamantés, matched with black heels and long, fishnet gloves. Her bright blue eyes were framed by dark, smoky eyeshadow. Tonight, Betty looked every bit as beguiling as she intended.

With a gracious smile to anyone she recognized, Betty took George's arm and they entered the ballroom. The furniture of the Council Chambers had been moved out for the occasion and replaced with dozens of elegantly set dinner tables, all dressed in lace and silver. Hundreds of guests were already inside, laughing and chatting with champagne and cocktails in hand. At the front of the room, was an ornately carved wooden dais that usually seated the most senior council members during session. Tonight, it stood empty, with the exception of a cacophony of decorative flowers, a microphone at the center podium and a single long white and gold banner that hung from the baldachin above. The banner read, 'St. Augustine's Home for Unwanted Boys – Charity Gala Ball' with an underline note in cursive script, *Sponsored by the generous contributions of Mr. Donald Pinzolo'*. Betty chuckled as she read it. It was *perfect*.

Beside the dais, a fifteen-piece military band was playing on a stage. At the forefront stood Glen Miller himself in a United States Army uniform, sporting a gleaming trombone. At his nod, the musicians launched into a new jazz song. *'Doin' the Jive'* filled the room with lively cheer, tempting dozens to flood the dance floor.

"What do you say, jitterbug?" George called over the loud music, offering his hand.

"Why not?" Betty beamed, and they joined the throng of merry-makers. The room was filling fast and the revelry was palpable. New York Times photographers flashed their cameras every which way and high-profile reporters chatted to guests, taking notes. The glitterati were out in force, smiling and posing for the media. Politicians and celebrities competed for attention over Manhattans and Martini's, and at every dinner table, businessmen were grandstanding while society women flaunted their diamonds for all to see. Betty's heart sang as she spun in George's arms. The party was just as she'd imagined it would be.

Betty found a number of her committee ladies on the dance floor, and they chatted as they swung to and fro between their partners, kicking up their heels in triple step.

"Didn't I tell you you're a ducky shincracker, Fannie-Mae!

"I'm almost ready to hang it up," the petite blonde puffed, "but I'm having such a gas, I can't stop! Can you believe it? I think I just saw Cary Grant by that portrait of George Washington. I nearly died!"

"You ought to have gone over and asked him to have a drink with you!"

"In these glad rags? I couldn't!" Fannie giggled, her face pink. "Besides, I've found a keen sheik right here on the dance floor." She glanced at the uniformed GI that had spun her enthusiastically into the fray. "Another glass of giggle-water and I'll be hitched!"

Betty laughed heartily. "You slay me, Fannie darling!"

The girl spun off and Betty turned back to George. The band struck up a new tune.

"Have you seen Gladys, Mildred?" Betty asked one of her church social committee ladies.

"Do you mean the tall lady with camellias in her hair?"

"That's right."

"Yes, I did actually. She was buzzing around the bartenders, looking rather edgy. I think she fears someone is trying to spike the punch."

"I'll go head her off," Betty laughed. She excused herself from the dance floor and made her way to the bar with George. Sure enough, Gladys Eubanks was there, eyeing off the waiters with an air of deep distrust.

"Gladys, dear, there's someone here you really must meet," Betty gushed as she collected the older woman by the arm and drew her towards a group of guests with George trailing behind. *Time for some reconnaissance.*

"Mr. Mayor!" Betty interrupted. "How splendid to see you again." Mayor Sutherland broke apart from his small group, with a well-practiced smile, his young wife at his side. "What do you think of our little fundraiser?" The superficial smile never wavered from his face. *Interesting.*

"Mr. and Mrs. Jones," he said, with affectation, shaking George's hand and looking around. "Brilliant party, a real-humdinger. Great press! You've pulled out all the stops tonight, Mrs. Jones. I've had photographers taking photos for the papers all night. Great opportunity to show what this council is all about, don't you think? The plight of the orphans. Everybody loves a hard luck story."

"Don't they just," enthused Betty, assessing his reaction to seeing her. Besides his false enthusiasm to put on a good show for the press, there seemed to be no reaction at all. *Very interesting.*

Mayor Sutherland turned to his wife, a vacuous little creature dressed in lemon chiffon who seemed as pale and bubbly as the champagne she held. "This is Mrs. Betty Jones, Audrey," the Mayor was saying. "She organized all the bells and whistles here tonight. A real go-getter! It'd do you good to take a leaf out of her book -"

Betty tried to wave off the compliment as Audrey's face reddened. Her maternal instincts flared but Betty smiled through the disdain she felt for the Mayor.

"She's an eager beaver, alright!" George enthused. "Always got pots on the boil."

"Really?" Audrey Sutherland said, her eyes wide. "Well, it's a lulu of a party! Everybody's been saying so. You must be so pleased."

"Oh, I am, dear" Betty said. "I really feel tonight is going to change those poor orphan's lives. Perhaps it's providence so many wonderful guests are here to witness it."

Betty dug into the Mayor's mind a little, to be sure... 'It's that pill of an insurance salesman again. Need to excuse myself. Maybe a cigar in the Governor's room -'

Betty was surprised. *He has no idea who I really am. I wonder why Donny didn't tell him?* Clearly their collusion was biased one way. *Typical Donny,* Betty thought. *Always holding all the cards.* The Mayor clearly already knew about Donny's shady business dealings, including the cargo heists. Taking his gunsels to the street to kill a housewife though, that might be hard for the Mayor to turn a blind eye to. Panic-stricken households. Voter confidence would plummet. *Donny wants to deal with me himself - he's keeping this one quiet.*

"The poor little orphans -" Audrey was saying. "Perhaps I might go up there one day, read to them or something -"

"Now there's an idea!" Mayor Sutherland interjected. "We can take some photographers, put on a good show for the press. The only bad press is no press, that's what I always say!"

"What a thoughtful gesture, Mrs. Sullivan," Betty said,

wedging her way between the Mayor and his wife, to take the latter's hand. "And so bold of you, considering -"

"What do you mean, bold?" Audrey asked, hesitantly.

"Well, those press photographs are terribly unforgiving you know. I can only imagine how much effort it takes, headlining the city newspapers so glamorously, when every shadow and blemish could show up clear as day for all to see! Puffy eyes will add *years* to a lady's face. Tonight's the perfect example - all these camera flashes and bright lights. You must be positively *washed out* from the stress of dealing with it."

"Well, I never really thought -" Audrey began, looking suddenly anxious.

"Surely you have an expert beautician to help you prepare?" Betty insisted. "As high profile as you've become. I imagine your husband employed an assistant for you?"

"No, I don't -" Audrey stammered, "He never did -".

"How taxing for you," Betty exclaimed. "You're the face of our grand city, after all. The Mayor's wife – a pillar of beauty and grace!"

Audrey looked at her husband accusingly.

"Well, we can't have you facing such a burden alone! We must put our thinking caps on –" Betty paused dramatically, then plucked Gladys from the milling crowd behind her. "Oh, what tremendous luck! I've just found you the perfect solution. A very dear friend of mine, Mrs. Gladys Eubanks. Why, she's the most experienced beautician I've ever met! An absolute *god-send* amongst the Avon Ladies in New York City I can tell you, with a *wealth* of knowledge on colors and seasonal trends!" Gladys, who'd been hanging back awkwardly, dashed forward in a kind of odd curtsy.

"Such an honor to meet you, Mrs. Mayor!"

"Oh, Mrs. Eubanks, you really must help me," Audrey pleaded. "I do want to help the children, but I can't face all those cameras unprepared! I don't want to look puffy or blemished!"

Gladys' chest puffed out a little and she gave the woman a maternal pat on the hand. "Now, don't you fret. I'll have you looking like a starlet in no time," she declared. "I have brand new summer colors that will put a glow on your cheeks – only available to the most senior representatives, of course, and that's me."

"Really?"

"Of course! Let's find my table, I brought my Avon case with me, for emergencies you know. I'll do you up now, those nasty photographers are hiding around every pillar here tonight." The two ladies fell into a hushed discussion as Gladys ushered Audrey toward the powder room. Betty excused herself, leaving the confused Mayor standing alone as she dragged George away by the hand.

"Mmm," George said, smirking. "Why do I get the feeling that woman was entirely set up?"

"Whatever do you mean?" Betty admonished, pulling him through the crowd. "Honestly George, it never hurts to add a little blush. And the girl could do with a kind ear."

"You could sell ice to an Eskimo, jitterbug."

"Do you think they need it?" Betty replied, a gleam in her eye.

"Incorrigible."

"Say, George darling, would you get me a drink?" Betty asked, stopping for a moment beside a statue of Thomas Jefferson. "I'm almost done in."

"Anything for you, jitterbug," he winked. "But you owe me another dance before the night is through."

"Absolutely," Betty promised and George disappeared into the crowd. She stood for a moment, enjoying the music and watching the dance floor swell. The Police Commissioner was dancing the *Lindy Hop* with his wife, the Governor General chatting by the bar and an impressive array of highly-ranked military officials were in discussion in small groups around the room.

Betty smiled to herself, pleased her invitations had been so well received.

"It seems I underestimated you, *Mrs. Jones*," came a man's voice from behind her. She didn't need to turn to know who it belonged to. That voice was burned into her memory.

"You've always underestimated me, Donny," Betty replied, meeting his eyes with a bemused look.

"Yes, I have, haven't I? I won't make that mistake again." He looked around at the room swimming with suits and gowns. "You're a fool for doing something like this." Dotted between the guests, Donny's men stood hunched and wary, like gorillas in suits. Up to this point, Betty had been happy to ignore them. She knew that one look from their boss was all it would take. But in the present circumstance, he'd be the fool to try it. "I know everything," Donny declared, with a glint of triumph. "I know *you*."

"You finally figured it out then. Very clever of you," Betty said, her eyes hardening. "I'm afraid you're rather late to the party on that one, though."

"Not too late, though," he smirked. He swirled his whiskey glass. "Go on, then, little Susie. Dig in to my mind, find out how much I hate you. Get a glimpse of how badly I plan to make you suffer."

Unable to resist such a direct invitation, Betty slipped into his thoughts. That same cold, calculating darkness she had known so well as a child came rushing back into her. It was shocking. There *was* fury inside him. A deep, ravenous desire to make her pay. For *revenge*. But she was no longer a child. And Donny was no longer the untouchable force he had once been to her.

Betty peeled away at his thoughts, searching for one thing in particular. And there it was. *Greed.* That same vice that made Donald Pinzolo crave secrets from every desperate soul in the city. The one that made sure victims were lured his way for patronage and then bound tight, trapped in his web like a spider's meal, ready to be consumed as it suited him.

"I'll never work for you, Donny. You can never own me again."

His eyes lit up in dark intent. "Did I think that?" He seemed amused. "You *would* be useful. If only I could kill you first though – I think I could do with the satisfaction."

"You won't kill me," Betty said. "I have too much potential for you."

"Don't be so sure." He looked up, surveying the crowd. "I could have you clipped right here. Right now."

"Of course you couldn't," Betty sighed. "Imagine how that would look to all these lovely dignitaries - a ballroom full of politicians, media, the who's-who of New York City. A scandal like that at a ball in your honor. It wouldn't look good. Mayor Sutherland might have to rethink your little business arrangement. You have your reputation to consider, not to mention Great Aunt Carmella flitting around the room like a primped-up goose with all her hangers-on. Would you have me shot here, in front of her and all these important people? She knows your men. I really don't think you should mix your business with pleasure, Donny. Although at this point, I'm not sure which one is which."

Donny scowled, watching his wife in the crowd. "I could make it look like an accident."

"And I could slit your throat with the fileting knife under my skirt," Betty smiled sweetly. "*By accident.* But let's not ruin the party. Not tonight."

He grunted. "*Little Susie Polletti.* A dark horse if ever I knew one."

Betty flashed him a dangerous look. "You've no idea."

"You're not as clever as you think you are, you trumped up little whore," Donny growled. He stepped closer, standing over her, forcing her to look up to meet his eyes. His skin was red beneath the collar of his dress shirt, like a boiled ham. "You clearly weren't paying attention, all those years ago. I'm not a man to mess with. No one breaks my family and lives to tell the story."

"I'm hurt, Donny," Betty drew even closer and paused, taking the full brunt of his threat with a nasty grin, "after all, I *am* your family." She stepped back casually and laughed for the benefit of anyone who happened to be watching, as if she'd made an amusing anecdote.

"You're sick. You killed my boy."

"Goodness, I don't know what on earth you're talking about," Betty said, blushing with false modesty. "I wouldn't hurt a fly. Ask anyone."

"You killed them all, didn't you?" Donny said, undeterred. "Marco, Frankie, Vince, Emilio, Charlie, Lefty, Joe, Travis and the rest of them. Even Roy, I bet. You vindictive little bitch." He lifted the whiskey glass to his lips and took a sip. "How many men have you murdered trying to get to me?"

"I lost count," Betty smiled. "Time flies when you're having fun."

"Eighty-three men," he answered his own question. "That means you owe me eighty-three lives. Who are you gonna pay me with? Mr. Insurance-Salesman over there? Your pretty daughter?" At the look on her face, he gave a cruel laugh. "Oh yeah, I know *all* about your kids. It's a shame you kept them from me, Susie. I'm a family man, after all." He grinned, maliciously. "So, which one do I start with? How about your apple-pie and star-spangled little mommy's boy? An eye for an eye, and all that."

Betty caught her breath. Her heart roared beneath her ribcage. *My babies!* After all she had suffered to build her perfect life, at that moment, it had never felt in more danger. How *dare* he. Her fingers twitched and Betty flexed them behind her back. At that moment, there was nothing she wanted more than to slip the blade from her garter and stab his heart through his tuxedo. And it would have been *so easy*. Like slicing warm butter. Betty squeezed her fist, forcing herself back from the edge. *Not yet. Soon.* Betty shot a glance to the bar, where George was chatting to a stout man as he waited for their drinks. She looked back to Donny, her face, again, impassive.

"Don't be a bore, Donny," Betty said. She brought her hand forward and studied her painted nails with disinterest. "They're worth far more to you alive, you know that."

"Do I?"

"Of course," she bluffed. "You've no way to control me with them gone. Imagine what I'd do to you then. You know - hell hath no fury... *and all that.*"

Donny grunted, considering her words. "Aren't you a piece of work."

"I like to think so."

"Whatever you think you're going to do to me," Donny growled, looking over her head and across the glittering room, "whatever sick little plan you've cooked up in your twisted little mind – it's not going to work." He leaned forward, his breath warm on her face. "I *own* this town. I *own* everyone in it. And I'm going to *destroy* you, *Mrs. Betty Jones.* Just the way you've tried to destroy me."

"Don't flatter yourself, Donny," Betty replied. She met his eyes with a sugar-sweet smile. "I'm just getting started."

Betty made her way back through the crowd toward the makeshift bar that had been set up under the balcony seating. George was waiting with a flute of champagne.

"Saw you talking to Pinzolo there, jitterbug – congratulating you on a job well done, was he?" George asked as he sipped his gin sour, bopping in time to the music.

"Something like that."

"He never got back to me about that life policy, you know. I might chase him up on it -"

"Not tonight, darling. You're having a night off work, remember?" she curled her finger around his bow tie, straightening it. "You look an absolute dreamboat tonight, George dear," she said, changing the topic. "I think I'd better watch you on the dance floor or someone will whisk you out of my arms."

"What a line!" George laughed, pulling her in close. "But I'll take it. Besides, I only have eyes for you, jitterbug. I am having a gay time though, I wouldn't say no to another spin to that band. Shall we?"

Betty took his glass and placed it with her own on an empty table.

"Let's." She lead the way back to the dance floor.

"Oh, I'm sorry!" Another voice said, as she was bumped in the crowd.

"It's quite al -" Betty began, "right," she finished weakly. Jacob was standing behind her, looking straight-faced and embarrassed. Beside him, a pretty young woman with dark hair and coffee-colored eyes held a glass of champagne. She was frowning and looked irritated by the intrusion, as if they'd just been interrupted from a deep conversation. "Sergeant Lawrence, how nice to bump into you," Betty said.

"My fault entirely," Jacob said. "I wasn't watching my feet." He extended a hand to George. "Mr. Jones."

"Evening Sergeant. Well, this is a surprise! Not here on official business, I hope?"

"No, not at all," Jacob replied, politely, shooting a glance to Betty. "The Police Commissioner received an invite, along with some of my superiors. We got a handful of spares down at the station and I was lucky enough to draw the long straw."

"Good for you, then! And I must say again, I appreciate you coming to my wife's aid the other week with that bag of hers, very good of you."

"No trouble at all," Jacob said, looking to Betty uncomfortably. Beside him, the other young lady looked quizzically between the three of them.

"And who is your lovely companion, tonight, Sergeant?" Betty asked, desperate to take control of the situation. "What a stunning dress, dear, I just love the way it sits on you."

"Adina Sonberg," the woman said, offering her hand. "And thank you, Mrs. Jones."

"Call me Betty, please." Betty studied the woman in front of her. She had dark rings under her eyes and looked like she hadn't slept in a week. Betty itched to know what they'd been discussing but wouldn't have dreamt of delving into Adina's thoughts. It was far too impolite.

"Sergeant Lawrence helped me out of a pickle, you see, Adina," Betty explained, sensing the other woman's vulnerability, nonetheless. "I lost my cosmetic case and he brought it home for me. Very thoughtful."

"I see," Adina smiled back. "Well, he does take his job very seriously." Jacob gave a stiff smile.

"So," George said, rocking back and forth on his toes. "Have you had a chance to get your hoofers buzzing? We're just heading that way ourselves."

"No, actually," Adina smiled. "We've only just arrived – Jacob finished work late. *Again*. I'd almost given up hope of coming." She shot Jacob a look of annoyance. "Besides, he's not the dancing kind, apparently."

"That's not true, I said I would -" Jacob interjected. "Just warming up, you see," he gestured to his shiny black oxfords with a half glass of rum and cola. "I'm afraid I've got two left feet."

"Well, we can't have that, can we?" George said, with a wide smile. "A hep-kitten like this one, standing like a wall flower. I'm no Gene Kelly, but - what do you say, Sergeant, should I take her for a spin on the floor?"

"Certainly, if Adina would like to -"

But Adina had already put down her champagne. "I'd love to, Mr. Jones." With a little too much enthusiasm and a touch of resentment, she followed George to the dance floor.

Betty and Jacob watched them go, lost in their own thoughts as they were jostled by the revelry all around them.

"She's not happy with you, Jake." Betty said finally, under her breath.

"Did you -?"

"Of course not. Call it *women's intuition*."

"I know she's not," Jacob conceded. "But I'm not too happy with her either, for what it's worth. She's been a little unfair lately and she knows it. There's something going on, but she won't talk about it. She's as stubborn as a mule, just like someone else I know." He raised an eyebrow to Betty. "Besides, I have bigger troubles at the moment."

"Thanks to me."

"And my choice in career." Jacob downed the remainder of his glass in a single gulp.

"Come on," he muttered, pulling Betty onto the dance floor.

He pushed his way into the crowd of couples that were pressing apart and twirling back together in glee. Heels flicked up and arms swung wildly as dancers shimmied in the synchronized steps of the jive. Beside them a woman slid between her partner's knees and back to her feet as another couple danced cheek to cheek, their feet in triple step underneath. Betty felt the warm pressure of Jacob's hand at her waist and her heart shifted a little. It had been – *a long time.* He led her in simple steps across the floor away from Adina and George, who seemed to be in happy conversation as they spun.

"Is everything prepared?" Jacob asked.

"Perfectly," she replied. "Thank you for running the paperwork by Michael."

"He was happy to help. Although he's rather confounded by it all."

"Understandably."

"When -?"

"Soon."

The band slowed and a new song began. A clarinet began its melody over the steady heartbeat of a double bass and the vocalist stepped forward again, enchanting the crowd with his smooth voice.

> "All of me, your heart took all of me,
> Honey, don't you know, I'm so lost without you.
> Take my smile, it's lost its shine,
> Take my heart, it's not worth a dime."

Betty slowed to meet the rhythm and felt Jacob do the same.

"It's not too late to end all this, you know."

Betty smiled over his shoulder. "It's far too late. I would lose *everything*."

"Maybe you don't have to," he muttered. She felt Jacob's breath hitch with emotion.

"Please, Jake -"

"I could protect you -"

"No, you couldn't. Not from him."

They were silent for a few moments.

"You don't have to do it alone you know."

She stopped dancing and looked up at him, her eyes shining. "I do. I need this. I need to finish him myself, alone. Besides, I couldn't bear it if he hurt you, or George or the children."

"You don't need me."

"Of course I do."

"Why? Why did you let me find you if you don't want my help?"

Betty met his eyes, dangerously close to telling him. It was a moment, where the truth hung in the air around her, just waiting to be professed.

"It's complicated," she finally sighed, instead.

Jacob's eyes dimmed. "Darn it, Susie. I feel as powerless now as I did when I thought you were dead."

"I'm sorry. That's just the way it has to be. At least, for now."

"And later?"

"That will be up to you to decide."

The song ended, and Jacob gently spun her to finish. As they turned around to wade back through the dancers, they found George and Adina, already waiting nearby. If Adina looked upset before, now she was furious. She lifted her chin in the air, turned, and pushed her way through the crowd toward the door.

"Adina!" Jacob called. He ran after her.

"What was all that about?" George said, his face indignant. "He was making a pass at you, there's no point denying it!"

"George, it's not quite what you think. Please, let me explain -" But as she spoke, the room fell to a hush. Every head turned to the dias at the front of the room, where the microphone had been commandeered by Mayor Sutherland. He stood directly under the ceremonial canopy that fluttered with the gold and white banner declaring 'St. Augustine's Home for Unwanted Boys – Charity Gala Ball, *Sponsored by the generous contributions of Mr. Donald Pinzolo.'*

Betty looked regretfully at George. Explanations would have to wait.

"Good evening, ladies and gentlemen, honored guests and dignitaries," Mayor Sutherland began, wearing his most charming expression. "It's my delight, as the Mayor of New York City, to welcome you all to tonight's Charity Gala Ball."

The room erupted in applause. Every guest tuned in with rapt attention, from the bustling dance floor to the glittering dining tables and above them, where guests crowded behind the wrought iron railing of the spectator's balcony.

"First up," the Mayor said, "I must say it's swell to have the talents of the great big-band composer Glenn Miller and his

Rhythmaires here tonight, to perform one last time before they head over to Europe on their tour to entertain the troops with the Army Air Force Band. He'll be leaving his home in New Jersey to do his duty for our country, but you can still tune into his weekly radio broadcast for that toe-tapping music we all love so dearly. How about a round of applause for Captain Glenn Miller and the *Rhythmaires*?" The audience thundered with applause and cameras flashed. The man, himself, stepped forward with a humble bow.

The Mayor turned back to the microphone. "Tonight, through your generous donations and prize-auctions, we have raised a substantial sum to provide quality clothing and meals to the hundreds of orphans at St. Augustine's. But, it would be remiss of me to let another moment pass without offering our thanks to the ladies of the Marigold Church Social Committee, who have organized this lollapalooza for us tonight! Mrs. Betty Jones, will you please step up and accept our thanks on behalf of your ladies?" Mayor Sutherland gave a simpering smile as he was handed a large bouquet for Betty. With the most endearing display of modesty she could muster, Betty gave George's hand a squeeze and made her way across the dance floor to the raised dais.

"How beautiful!" she said, upon reaching the microphone. Betty stepped sideways, gently nudging the Mayor aside with a clear intention to hold the floor. "Thank you so much, Mayor Sutherland, I must say, it's been an absolute delight and I believe," she lay her hand over her heart, "a mission of mercy, to put our minds and hands to work to create a better future for those poor, destitute orphans. The ladies of our little social committee have been so generous with their time for these children and we are all so grateful to them, but truly," she paused, her eyes glistening with false tears, "nobody has worked more tirelessly, or given so much, as our wonderful benefactor, Mr. Donald Pinzolo. He's been a pillar of strength in our beautiful city for so many years, and generous to a fault."

She looked through the crowd and was delighted to see Donny stiff-backed and tight-lipped, standing by a set of golden drapes near the stage. At the applause of the crowd, he nodded faintly in acknowledgment, eyeing Betty with thinly-veiled suspicion. Beside him, Betty's great aunt Carmella, was fanning herself and loudly accepting the compliments of the sycophants she adorned herself with. Betty beamed. *This was going to be fun.*

"These poor orphans," Betty continued, emphatically, "young victims of misfortune and circumstance, have had no father to put food on their table or clothes on their back or to look up to for the wisdom of experience. *Until now.*" She beamed down at Donny. "We, as a city, must thank you, Mr. Pinzolo, for giving these boys the benefit of you becoming their benefactor at a time while our great nation is at war and their futures looked most bleak." Everybody clapped. She held up her hand to quieten the crowd.

"So, on behalf of the Marigold Church Social Committee, I take the greatest joy in presenting to you, this check of money raised tonight, made out under trust to the Sisterhood of Nuns that work so tirelessly to care for these children on Mr. Pinzolo's behalf." Fannie-Mae, adorned with a glittery-headdress stepped up to the dais, a large novelty check in her arms.

"Step up here, Mr. Pinzolo, please!" The crowd roared and Betty's smile couldn't have been wider. Donny, though, didn't move a muscle.

"Go on, Donny!" His wife exclaimed, prodding his arm. With a look that could kill, Donald Pinzolo shrugged off her hands and made his way slowly to the front of the crowd. Cameras flashed and voices cheered. All eyes were on him. This audience of media moguls, businessmen, politicians and celebrities were far too influential to disregard. A veritable *who's who* of lawmakers and military officials dotted throughout the crowd, and no matter how he played it, Donny's reaction would be center-stage to all in attendance. Betty had made sure of that. He had no choice but to play along.

As Donald Pinzolo reached the mahogany platform under the banner bearing his own name, Fannie kissed him on the cheek. She gave the audience a cheeky wink, setting them off laughing, then handed Donny the giant cardboard check. Donny shot an accusing glance to Mayor Sutherland, who just shrugged his shoulders minutely. Apparently, the Mayor was delighted with the fanfare his proceedings had taken. The press was lapping it up.

Betty took once again to the microphone.

"But of course, Mr. Pinzolo's philanthropy can only be topped by his modesty. I'm sure he won't mind me telling you, that he has prepared his very own surprise for you tonight. These orphans have become such an important part of his life, perhaps to fill that terrible hole in his heart from the passing of his own dear son, Marco," Betty offered Donny a sympathetic smile, "that he has decided to do everything he can to ensure the orphanage continues its vital role in educating and caring for those dear children discarded by society." Betty reached under the podium, retrieving a neat bundle of papers, which she held up for all to see. "As such, Mr. Pinzolo has had documents drawn up by his own personal, trusted accountant, Mr. Stanley Lubach, to ensure that every *asset*, every *property* and every *incy-wincy* little dime to his name will be donated, tonight, into the Sisterhood's Orphanage trust to provide for their future."

Betty was almost giddy with vengeance. She turned to look at Donny. He was ashen, his eyes bulging and his jaw clenched so tight it looked painful.

A knife to Stanley Lubach's throat and the promise of exposing years of his own embezzlement of Donny's accounts had been the highlight of her week. His options were limited. Facing Donny's wrath, Betty's knife or arrest for fraud terrified him equally, and the accountant had crumbled easily, sweating over the figures until every dollar was accounted for. Betty had given the documents to Jacob, who had passed them onto his brother, Michael, to draw up the legalities. The contract was watertight. Mr. Lubach had been given his promised reprieve, far from the grisly retribution he was owed by Donny's hands. By now, he would be halfway to Barbados.

"Mr. Pinzolo has brought this trust deed here tonight," Betty waved the papers above her head as the crowd gasped, "to sign with you all as witness, in the fervent hope that it inspires the people of our city to step up and do what needs to be done, to look after our most vulnerable citizens, each other and our great country in this time of terrible uncertainty. Isn't he just the most honorable and inspiring man! Please, everybody, give him a hand!"

As the crowd roared with approval, Betty turned to Donny. He was frozen, the spectacle of every eye, bursting with impotent rage. He couldn't react. He couldn't deny it. He couldn't step down. In that moment, his entire fortune was being held ransom to his reputation. And Betty knew, with malevolent glee, that there was only one choice he could make. *He had to sign the paper.*

"Sister Mary-Agnes, will you please step up to witness Mr. Pinzolo's signature and receive the trust deed?" The harried-looking nun Betty had first seen at St. Augustine's stepped forward from the crowd. Betty had finally found a way to pamper them up a bit, after all. With a nod of encouragement from Betty, the Sister joined her at the podium. With a flourish and crowd-pleasing shimmy, Fannie-Mae took back the novelty check from Donny. Betty handed him a pen.

"You -" Donny snarled. "You filthy, little- "

"Mind your manners, Mr. Pinzolo!" Betty said, gaily. She leaned forward, placing the paperwork on the desk in front of him. The crowd clapped and cheered wildly at his feet, gushing over the man's generosity as his wife stood alone by the golden drapes, watching in daft bewilderment. Suddenly, the band struck up a drumroll, spurring the audience to a frenzy. A chanting cheer began on the balcony and rolled down through the room toward Donald Pinzolo.

"Sign, sign, sign!"

Betty met his eyes. Sweat was glistening on his brow, and his hand trembled with repressed violence. The man was pure, unadulterated rage. In stiff jerks, as if each stroke was drawing blood from his own veins, the pen in Donny's hand whipped his signature across the line. *It was done.*

The council chambers erupted in thunderous applause which reverberated all the way through City Hall. Betty gathered the papers and thrust them to the nun, who quickly retreated into the crowd.

Betty reached her hand under the hood of the podium. Her fingers found a button that they had itched to press all night.

Click.

Above the dais, hidden behind the ceremonial banner of the canopy, the lids of three wooden military crates that hung upside down from the ceiling, swung open. Each bore a stamp, *"Property of the United States Army."*

Hundreds of thousands of dollars in paper bills, rained from the boxes onto the stage. They fluttered into the audience who grabbed at them like confetti in a snowstorm. Money swirled above their heads, fluttering against the ceiling mural of a beautiful naked woman, the symbol of civic virtues of a great nation. Below, the crowd went wild.

On cue, the band swung into beat, launching the siren of trumpets and trombones of 'Serenade to a Savage' as the bandmaster took main stage once again.

It was blood money, every dollar. Betty had finally found the perfect use for all the money she had stolen from Donny's men. With every murder, came a cash prize. And now, that prize was to be given to the most deserving beneficiary of all, *St. Augustine's Home for Unwanted Boys.*

Up on the dais, Betty leaned forward through the confetti of money as it rained down over Donald Pinzolo. She took him by the shoulders in what seemed for all to see, was a kiss on the cheek. As her lips drew close to his ear she whispered.

"And now, you have nothing."

SERENADE TO A SAVAGE

"Adina, wait!" Jacob broke away from Betty and pushed his way through the crowded ball room as his date ran from the dance floor. He sidestepped a group of women and the jostling revelry of tuxedos by the bar and burst through to the grand atrium beyond. Adina was at the top of the marble staircase, ready to dash down. "Please! Just let me explain," he called.

"I don't want your explanations!"

Her face was set but there were tears glistening in her eyes.

Jacob dashed around the circular landing toward her and stood, breathing hard at the top of the stairs, with one hand on her arm. She shook it off.

"Please. Adina?" he said, gently.

Adina glanced around, her lips tight and shoulders stiff. Several small groups that had spilled from the noisy party inside the Council Chambers were dotted through the atrium and leaning against bannisters, standing in what had been quiet conversation. The couple had caught the attention of every pair of eyes and Adina blushed pink with embarrassment. Lifting her chin with a small sniff, she glared at Jacob.

"In here, then." She spun back around, rattling the knob of

the closest door she could see. It was locked. "Argh!" With an angry grunt she rattled it harder, turning pink with embarrassment as she struggled. Jacob stepped forward, conscious of her failing composure. He gestured her out of the way, then gave the door a hard shove with his shoulder. It broke open and he stepped away.

Adina pushed through, letting the door fall back on Jacob as he followed. Jacob looked around cautiously as he shut the door and was relieved to find they were alone. They were in a long, brightly lit room. Two golden chandeliers hung from the ceiling, each decked with masses of tall, ivory gas-light candles. They illuminated *Verdigri français*-painted walls hung with dozens of full-length gilded portraits of historical leaders. Ancient mahogany armchairs and cabinets lined the walls of the room, and in the center was a long dining table covered in papers. Jacob glanced at them as he passed, following Adina to the low-burning fireplace near a small desk at the far end of the room. A sinking feeling settled in his stomach. Official-looking documents. Military insignia. Maps. Clearly, they'd stumbled into somewhere they shouldn't have.

"This is the Governor's Room, Adina. We're not meant to be in here."

"I don't care!" she said, rounding on him. Her coffee-hued eyes were ablaze. "Who is she?" Adina demanded.

"No one," Jacob sighed.

"No one?" Adina cried, exasperated. "She's *someone*, Jacob. I think, perhaps, she's *the* someone."

"She's not. We were friends, but it was a very long time ago. She's just – a memory – I suppose. I shouldn't have -"

"Well, she's very much *here, now!*"

"You're right. She is here." Jacob drew his hand over his face, wearily. The happy din of Glenn Miller's band had stopped, and instead, the muffled noise of a woman talking through a microphone made its way through the closed door.

Susie. Or rather, *Betty*. Carrying on her plan, despite the difficulty. *As always.* Jacob sighed again.

"I didn't expect to see her again. She needed my help, but that's all there is between us. She's married now, and I'm – I mean, I *was* – stepping out with you."

Adina scoffed, her jaw set tight. "So, you won't need to see her again, then?" she challenged.

"It's a bit more complicated than that."

Adina barked out a hard laugh. "Of course, it is! You must think I'm a real Dumb Dora to brush it off that easily. You're impossible, Jacob Lawrence! You're working day and night, cancelling our dates, and now this. Something's going on, Jacob. You won't talk to me about the case, even though I already know all about the military heists! Who do you think types up the reports?"

"Keep your voice down, please!" Jacob hissed, glancing toward the door.

"...and you're ignoring calls from General Brandway and I'm copping the heat for it. I really thought we had something special, but these secrets and lies..." Adina looked down at the fireplace. The glowing coals reflected in the tears in her eyes.

"You want to talk about secrets?" Jacob said, resentfully. "When you came to my office with Brandway, you pretended we didn't even know each other! There was no harm in telling him we were dating. Why can't he know? You wanted to come here tonight but then you're angry the minute you see me. And you're distant, as if your mind is altogether somewhere else. You've been avoiding my questions for weeks – clearly there's something you're not telling me as well."

A flash of fear crossed her face, but she quickly masked it.

"There's nothing," she said.

"You're scared," Jacob realized, as the words left his mouth. "Why?"

"I am *not* scared. I can take care of myself. And I certainly don't need a man telling me how to live my life! Especially one that lies."

Wiping away spilled tears, Adina lifted her chin defiantly and stormed from the room.

Jacob stood for a moment, staring into the dying fire. He felt miserable.

With the door now ajar, the revelry from the ball room spilled in, loud and clear. The audience was growing louder with each moment.

"Sign. Sign. Sign." They were chanting.

Betty's plan was working. *As always.*

Jacob leant back against a small desk that sat alone by the fireplace. There was no question that Adina was lying. Something was wrong. Very wrong. He wished for just a second that he had Betty's gift, that he could simply reach into Adina's mind and lay bare that darkness that was growing between them, holding their new relationship to ransom.

Selfish, he thought. *To want to steal her thoughts without sharing my own.* There was no way he could ever reveal the extent of his relationship with Betty to Adina or tell her why he couldn't break ties with Betty now. This business with Donny, the heists, the orphanage – he was in far too deep. And a twist in his gut told him, he didn't want to give her up anyway. Not again. Not yet. For years he'd felt as wane as the dying fire glowing in front of him, but now, despite his anger and frustration at the mess he found himself in, he was aflame. Adina had sparked that fire. But now, was someone else keeping it alight? *Little wonder she doesn't trust me with her secret.*

Jacob took a deep breath and straightened up. He turned around. The wooden desk he'd been leaning on was old and well-worn. There were too many drawers, polished silver feet and narrow shelves that stepped up on either end. It was piled with neat, hand-labelled folders. By any account the desk looked old and well-used, but Jacob had a niggling feeling about it that he couldn't place. A plain leather chair sat on the opposite side to where he stood, the seat cushion shaped from constant use. *Someone sits here every day.* He glanced at the folders. Every one of them was stamped with military insignia. *Someone important.* Jacob shook his head, trying to clear unhelpful thoughts, then turned to go.

No.

He spun back around and looked again. Even reading it upside down, the name on one folder was unmistakable. Jacob's heart pounded as he reached for it, slowly turning the folder around to face him.

Betty Jones.

Sweat pricked the back of his neck and he shot a glance to the door. He flicked the folder open. A single typed page. A dossier. A photograph of Betty, taken from a distance. Someone knew what she could do. Someone important was *watching*.

Jacob's fingers found his shirt collar. He pulled it away from his throat. For a moment, he stood, paralyzed. The air in the room seemed to have been sucked out.

Then, on an impulse he knew he would regret, Jacob grabbed the folder. He shoved it inside his jacket, up under his left arm. Pulling his jacket straight, with his arm pressed to the side of his body to keep the folder from slipping, he walked briskly to the door, turned the handle and opened it a crack. The atrium was deserted. Every guest was now inside the ball room and their applause and chanting had reached fever pitch. It was deafening. Without another thought, Jacob stepped out and closed the door behind him. He reached into his top pocket with his right hand and pulled out his handkerchief. He rubbed the door handle clean, then stuffed the handkerchief back into his pocket. In less than a minute he was out of City Hall, heading for his car. As the cold night air cooled his burning face, guilt and concern hit him in equal measure. Adina had fled before he could offer to drive her safely home. Betty was expecting him to stay for the proceedings. It seemed he had disappointed them both.

Adina was angry, her steps quick as she made her way back toward City Hall. Her vision was now clear of the tears that had been swimming in her eyes when she'd left Jacob. He'd been right, of course, about that room – they shouldn't have broken in. It was only now that her head was less muddled that Adina remembered why. Through quiet discussion between General Brandway and his colleagues at the Transportation and Overseas Supply Division, Adina had overheard that the room had been converted into a military command center for the war. She'd seen security milling through the crowd when they'd first arrived, and looking back now, was surprised it had been left unguarded. Perhaps the revelry in the ballroom had pulled the guards away, or maybe nothing of consequence was ever left out overnight.

Adina felt a fool. After she'd run out of City Hall for the subway, she'd realized her coat was still in the cloak room. She was shivering but didn't want to go back. Not only for the risk of running into Jacob again, but in case she saw *him*. It had been a mistake to come here tonight, though she hadn't known it when Jacob had mentioned the invitation. Now, she regretted every minute she'd stayed.

Adina had watched for nearly ten minutes by the subway stairs in shadow, waiting to see Jacob leave. When he finally did, she turned back to collect her coat, hoping fervently that *he* would be gone too. Adina couldn't even bring herself to think his name. His name made her stomach churn. He was just *him*. The man intent on destroying her. The one who had ruined her life.

For the second time that night, Adina stepped through the entrance to City Hall and made her way to the Concierge desk.

Self-conscious of her tear-battered eyes, she passed her coat ticket to a neatly groomed man in uniform and he disappeared with a smile, returning a minute later with it draped over his arm.

The concierge stepped around the counter toward her, holding the coat up for Adina to shrug into.

"Miss," he said, graciously.

"Thank you," Adina replied. The thick wool felt heavy and reassuring on her shoulders.

"If I may be so bold, Miss," the man said. "A face as pretty as yours, should have a gentleman who'll put a smile upon it." His eyes crinkled, kindly. "Not one that casts such a shadow." Adina felt her face burn with embarrassment. No doubt the man had seen her run by him with tears in her eyes, not ten minutes before. *If only it was that simple.* She couldn't blame Jacob entirely for the unfortunate turn of events this evening. At the moment, every step she took felt plagued with dark, unforgiving consequence. *And I brought it all upon myself.*

"Thank you." Adina said, quietly. "But I'm not sure I deserve to smile right now." She offered him the only smile she had left, one tinged with sadness, and passed the man a tip. "Have a good night," she said, turning away.

"You too, Miss," he said. "Keep your face out of those shadows."

Adina stepped down the red carpet again and into the cool air. There were a few people leaving now, waiting for valets or heading toward the bridge on foot. Although she could hear the band playing upstairs, it seemed that the formalities were over.

Adina quickly crossed the garden again to reach the sheltered subway station entrance opposite the main doors. Walking inside it felt rather like entering a telephone box to descend into a cathedral. The City Hall subway had been opened to great fanfare at the turn of the century. It was an icon to illustrate the power and importance of a rising city. Adina stepped down the concrete steps quickly, the tapping of her shoes echoing off the tiled walls. From there, the station opened up into a breathtaking display of Romanesque Revival architecture that housed a Ticketmaster's booth. The conductor had long gone home for the evening. Adina followed a second flight of stairs down to the ornate Guastavino tile vaulted ceiling surrounding a sharply curved platform. Aesthetically, it was a sight to behold – a place of majesty. It should have felt welcoming. Inspiring even.

But it didn't.

The platform was empty. Not a soul was waiting. Green and gold tiles glowed an odd yellow hue under the light of the chandeliers and Adina looked up to the three great skylights, which had been brilliant with leaded glass mosaic and sunshine the last time she had seen them. Tonight, they pressed sinisterly in, bleak and blackened-out with paint, a new precaution against air-borne enemies after the Pearl Harbor attacks. Shuddering, Adina drew tighter into her coat. Underground, the air was colder. She'd travelled from this station occasionally in the past, but never at night. It felt abandoned, eerie. She wriggled deeper into her coat. Adina was no stranger to a late-night commute, her work often required it, despite her father's insistence it wasn't appropriate or safe for a young lady to be out on the streets alone. But she'd never felt *scared* in her solitude. She never felt vulnerable. Until now.

Forget it. With a turn on her heel she began to leave. *I'll dash across to Brooklyn Bridge station instead.*

Suddenly, the familiar drone of a train rattled up the line toward her. Adina turned back and let out the breath she hadn't realized she'd been holding. She adjusted her handbag and coat, moving forward to the platform's edge, ready to step onboard.

Whoosh!

The train came into view, rounding the steep curve in a jolt and sped through the station in a cacophony of noise, leaning dangerously close to where Adina stood. It didn't stop. The lit carriage windows flashed like a strobe light as it passed, throwing her face into sharp relief for the few dozen commuters onboard who failed to look up and notice her. Within moments, it was gone again, leaving nothing but a trailing rattle and her pounding heart.

Overhead, one of the chandeliers flickered and died. Its buzz echoed up the empty archways of the line.

"For goodness sake!" Adina muttered, once again on the verge of tears. She bundled her arms around her handbag and began to run. Disappointment and fear coursed through her and she was suddenly desperate for the cool night air above. Her heels clapped on the first set of stairs and rang from the walls under the great vaulted ceiling as she reached the ticketing platform. There were shadows all around her, dark corners and alcoves that suddenly seemed to be closing in.

And from one of those dark corners, stepped a man.

Him.

"Good evening, Miss. Sonberg," he said quietly. Adina skidded to a stop with a cry on her lips, not ten meters from her escape. The blood drained from her face. *He* was in her way.

"Please, not tonight," she whimpered. If she was cold before, now she was frozen.

"I trust you enjoyed the ball?" he said, apparently amused by the reaction he had elicited. There was an edge about him tonight. His eyes were sharp and menacing and his overcoat seemed to confine a barely restrained rage inside it's stretched fabric. Adina had already learned that at the best of times, Donald Pinzolo was dangerous. At the worst – she didn't want to imagine.

"I – I didn't stay."

"Good for you. Turns out, it was a flop. To say the least." Donny looked around, taking in the architecture. "Nice place, isn't it? Barely gets used anymore. Didn't anyone tell you they close it at night?"

"No."

"Dangerous. For a young lady to be out alone at this hour."

"Yes," Adina breathed. "I should probably go."

Donny stepped forward, into her path.

"Not yet, doll. We need to talk."

"Please, Mr Pinzolo. Don't make me do it again. People are getting killed because of me –" she stifled a cry.

"We have a deal, Miss. Sonberg. Surely, you're not skipping out now, when we're so close to the end? I'd hate for your *Aba* to have this little number turn up in his private mailbox." Donny reached into his coat pocket and pulled out a black and white photograph. He waved it, tantalizingly, in front of her face. She was laid bare in the image, her body naked and entangled with Brandway on his own office desk. It had been taken without permission, from somewhere far away, through the split drapes of a window. Nevertheless, it was her. Her mistake. And now, her downfall. Adina reached out desperately to grab the photograph from his fingers, but Donny snapped it out of reach. "Think of the shame, Adina," he growled, softly. "Your father such a well-known man. Such a *good* man. A pillar of family values, a respected member of the synagogue. Imagine. *Retired Associate Justice Amos Sonberg,* raising a chippy for a daughter. And with a married man, no less. Twice your age. The shame might just kill the old geezer."

"No!" Adina begged. "Please, Mr. Pinzolo. Just let it be! I did what you want –"

"He'd have to turn you out, girl," Donny said, with a critical eye. "And that job of yours? *Gone.* Brandway won't want you around causing trouble. Nor will his wife, and I'll make sure she knows all about it. *Mrs. Gloria Brandway* – benefactor of the New York Women's Morality and Temperance League, isn't that right? Quite the dried-up old gasbag, from what I heard. What a lot of damage she could do. Think of the talk. You'll be shunned, girl. You'll. Have. Nothing," he finished slowly, with a cruel hiss.

Adina looked aside, her face and eyes burning. She couldn't bear to see him. It had been this way for months. Every time he loosened the chain and she thought she might finally be rid of her regrets, Donny called in another favor. Her heart was so wracked by the burden of what she'd done, she could barely think straight. All those transport guards, sent to their death to pay the price for her own indiscretion. It was killing her.

"You've towed the line, Miss. Sonberg," Donny said, matter-of-factly, all trace of malice suddenly gone. "I'm not an unreasonable man. You've given me all the transport routes I wanted so far. In my book, that makes us just about even."

Adina looked up, her pulse racing with the promise. *You've heard this before,* she screamed inside.

"One more job. Tomorrow night. I don't care what part of town."

Nausea rose into her throat. *He's lying. It'll never end.* Every cell in her body screamed her lips to just agree, to make the call and give him what he wanted. The price to disobey was too terrible to risk. He was right. Her father would die of shame. Her job would be lost, she would be shunned from society, Brandway's wife would see to that. But to stay complicit in these murders, was murder itself. It was killing her, day by day. And Pinzolo's 'favors' were never-ending. *Unless I end them myself.*

"No," Adina said quietly. "I'm done."

Donny stepped in, chillingly close.

"What did you just say?"

"I can't do it."

"Think about what you're saying, Miss. Sonberg. Let's not forget that what you've committed here is *treason* against the U.S. Government. Leaking classified information that got soldiers killed. They'll lock you up for years if you confess. And there's no point trying to implicate me in all this, you won't even get me to the courthouse steps. I *buy* protection, Miss. Sonberg. The very best."

"But I can't live with myself," she whispered.

"Sure, you can, doll. Or your life will be over anyway. It's not a choice."

Adina squeezed her eyes shut to block out the paralyzing fear that had been growing inside her for months. Slowly, she breathed out, then opened them once more to meet Donny's cold stare.

"It was always a choice," she said, in the strongest voice she could muster. "And I made the wrong one. But I'd rather be punished for it forever than let you kill any more of those men." Without waiting for a response, Adina dashed past him up the concrete steps into the dark night beyond.

A few minutes later, Felix came down the stairs. Donny hadn't moved.

"What'd she say, boss?" Felix asked, cautiously, taking in the unnatural line of Donny's shape under the yellow tinge of the chandelier. "Where's it gonna be? Rail shed again?"

Donny didn't look up. The lines on his face seemed carved, deep, like cracked stone. Felix took a step back, covering his left hand reflexively. His eyes darted to the concrete steps he had seen the woman leave by from across the park.

He knew that stance. The last time he'd seen it, Donny had pinned his hand to the table with a knife.

"She didn't -?" Felix croaked, dumbfounded.

Donny looked up at him with unfocused eyes. He walked to the ticket booth. Suddenly, he raised his fist, smashing it down onto the wood paneling. A shower of splinters hit the air.

"*Two. Women. Defy me in a single night!*" he roared. "I'm god-damn done with these crazy broads."

Felix flinched and stepped back. For a moment, he said nothing. Some dark scheme seemed to be playing through in his mind as he scratched his ripped ear.

"We don't need another heist," he finally said. "I can get your hands on the freak-show, boss. I got another way. Trust me. I'll bring her right where ya' want her."

Donny turned sharply to face him. "You're damn right you will. I'm going to end that bitch if it kills me. By tomorrow night."

Felix nodded. "What about the chippy?" he asked, nodding to the empty stairs that led up from the subway.

Donny's eyes narrowed, maliciously. "She just signed her own suicide note." He threw the photograph onto the ground. "And you can leave this for her daddy."

The car ride home was silent.

Betty watched the houses flash by, from tall city apartments to brownstones, and finally the cookie cutter lawns of suburbia. She should have been elated. She was *so close*. Donny was on his knees, his head in the guillotine. He was bankrupt, his assets robbed from him, his accountant fled, his crooked business partners and best hitmen taken out. All she had left to do, was release the blade.

But none of it seemed to matter right now.

George's stony silence was breaking her heart. Finally, he spoke, but so quietly, she almost missed it.

"Who is he, Betty? *Really?*"

The question stung. There was no point telling him the truth. It was far too complicated and incriminating. Instead, she thought it, as if she were speaking aloud, wishing George could hear and understand, and never ask again.

I've known him since I was a child. He helped make me who I am. Who I really am. A murderer.

Perhaps a half-truth was the best she could offer.

"I met Jacob a long time ago, George. I suppose – I never expected to see him again. But then he returned my bag and I suppose it sparked some memories, that's all." It was a dilution of the truth, and the best she could do.

"Sparked some memories," George repeated.

"Yes. I knew him as a child."

"You've never spoken about your childhood before."

"There isn't much to speak of. It was all perfectly normal until my parents passed away, just before I met you. I told you that."

"And *Jacob*?"

"Lived nearby, a few years older than myself. We walked home from school together and rode bikes on weekends."

"Just a chum, was he?" George growled.

"Well, perhaps I was sweet on him for a while – but George, this is silly! It's been years. I was a child then and you know how devoted I am to you now."

George looked at her apprehensively. He fell quiet again and they rode the distance home with silence an unwelcome third-party, prickling the space between them. As their black Chevy purred into the driveway alongside the white picket fence, Betty was desperately relieved to see Officer Parker's car sitting in the darkness under the red maple tree opposite. He had simply been late, after all. Without a word, George gathered his coat from the back seat, stepped around the car, and stiffly held the passenger-side door open for his wife.

"Thank you, dear," Betty said, with an infusion of warmth in her voice, as if nothing had transpired. If her weak explanations couldn't melt his unnaturally icy demeanor, Betty could only hope to chip away at it with her usual unbridled optimism. George was jealous and it was entirely her fault for making him so. She didn't need to read his mind to be sure of that. Her husband had always been simple and honest, wearing each mood like a hat, clear as day for all to see. It was one of the things Betty adored about him. No searching for ulterior motives, no secrets or shadows. And he'd never had cause to wear anything but good humor. George was like a breath of fresh air.

Until recently. Now, Betty felt his inner thoughts may be changing. He seemed angry and confused, and every so often, a shadow of darkness flickered behind his eyes. Her heart roared with a need to protect him from it. From *her*. But she had never, *would never,* take the privacy of his own thoughts away from him by reading his mind.

What's she hiding? came a sudden voice in her head, not her own.

Betty stopped still, almost stumbling into her husband who was now twisting his key into the front door. The voice was unexpected and unfamiliar, and it took her a moment to realize where it had come from. *Not George*, she breathed a sigh of relief. Even inadvertently, she would be devastated to break her oath. But someone – a man. Betty turned around, her eyes searching the darkness.

Across the road, under the red maple, Officer Parker was stirring in his car. Betty and George were home, and his undercover protection was no longer needed. But he wasn't leaving. Without a moment's hesitation, she reached into Parker's thoughts. *Bother.* He'd been following her. He *knew*. An image of Rex Hatfield's corpse sprang into her mind from his thoughts, the body uncoiled and sprawled on the rug with a purple face and lolling head. Parker had seen Carmine and Earl too, dashing up the alley in a bid to be gone. He'd seen *her*, leaving Rex's office afterwards.

Bother. Bother. Bother, Betty frowned. This is a fly in the ointment I really don't need.

"Oh dear, I've left my purse in the car," she said cheerfully, stuffing her glittering handbag under the coat hanging over her arm. "You go in, George dear. Mind not to wake Mrs. Porter in the spare room. I'll only be a minute." George stepped through with a nod. As soon as he'd set foot on the staircase, Betty pulled the front door gently closed behind him.

Within seconds, she was tapping at the window of the unmarked car.

"Good evening, Officer Parker," she said, briskly. The man inside startled. Apparently, he'd been lost in thought. He quickly opened the door and stepped out into the chilly air.

"Ma'am," he said, tipping a hat that wasn't there, by force of habit. He let his arm fall, embarrassed.

"I don't believe we've been formally introduced." She held out her hand and he shook it lightly. "Mrs. Betty Jones. For what it's worth, my husband George doesn't know you've been watching the house," she added. "I'd prefer it stayed that way."

"I never intended to -"

"You've been following me," Betty cut him off. "It's alright, I don't blame you. I should have assumed you would. I'm normally quite careful with these things, but I've been a little... preoccupied, lately."

"How did you know?"

"I saw you, of course."

Parker frowned, his eyes narrowing under the dim light of the streetlamp.

"You found Mr. Hatfield, then?" she said, getting down to business, with a glance to the still-closed front door.

Parker's mouth fell open.

"You knew he was there?" Parker said. "I wondered if perhaps you didn't see him. A nasty thing for a lady to see."

"Yes, I'm afraid I saw." Betty unfolded her coat from her arm and pulled it on against the cold night air. "You're a good man, Officer Parker," she said, studying his face under the streetlamp. "Rex was a bad one. I don't think anyone will mourn him." Betty looked around again, conscious not to take too long. The last thing she needed was for George to come out looking for her.

"Was he dead when you arrived, then?"

"I suppose he must have been," Betty said vaguely.

"Who bumped him, then?"

"That I can't say."

"Those two fat-heads I saw skipping off?"

"No, it wasn't them. They don't know anything, so don't bother chasing them. Barely a wit to rub together between them, to be honest."

"So, who then?" Parker crossed his arms against the night chill.

Betty smiled but didn't answer.

"Alright, then why were *you* there?"

"I just stopped by to collect a debt," Betty said, cagily. "Which has now been returned to its rightful owners. Sergeant Lawrence can attest to that."

Parker looked shocked. "The Sergeant already knew about this?" His eyes narrowed and his mouth drew tight in irritation.

A flicker of concern caught Betty's throat. In the rush of the Gala Ball preparations, Betty had forgotten to mention her latest outing to Jacob.

"Of course," she lied, trusting Jake would cover for her well enough. "I suppose you reported it to him anyway?" Betty asked. "Of course, you did, it's only right. We can't leave bodies lying around in rugs for people to stumble over. The smell would be terrible."

"Actually, no," Parker said, testily. "I reported it to Sergeant Lovett instead. Sergeant Lawrence has been – *preoccupied* – lately as well. I couldn't get a hold of him on the telephone."

Bother. The last thing I need is another shadow on my tail.

"– and before you ask, Mrs. Jones – *no*, I didn't mention your name, out of respect for Sergeant Lawrence asking me not to at the beginning of this detail. But that's not to say I won't." He bounced on his toes, looking agitated, rubbing his hands together to keep them warm. "You know Ma'am, I'm not one to question the virtue of a lady, but I don't think you're telling me the whole truth. Women don't just 'stop by' to pick up packages from dead bookies."

"The whole truth is never the *whole* truth, Officer Parker," Betty sighed. "But if you insist on investigating me, please talk to Sergeant Lawrence about it first." Betty turned to leave, then paused.

"For what's it worth," she added quietly, "thank you for protecting my family over the last few weeks. I'm sure it's taken precious time away from your own loved ones and I'm very grateful for your help." She turned away.

Parker shook his head and looked around. The street was deserted, the lights of every house extinguished in slumber. A backdrop of idyllic suburban ordinariness. Not a hint of danger lurking anywhere.

"But why do they *need* protection, Mrs. Jones?" he called after her.

Betty stopped in the middle of the road. Creeping shadows settled in the creases under her tired eyes. It was well past midnight, and if tomorrow was anything like today, she would need more than beauty sleep to get through it. She turned around again to face the young policeman.

"If Sergeant Lawrence feels you should know, he'll tell you," Betty replied. "I trust his judgement implicitly. Goodnight, Officer."

As Betty walked back to the house, she didn't notice the light flicker above her, as George let the corner of the curtain slip back down against the window frame in the bedroom upstairs. Before she closed the front door, he was already in bed, feigning sleep.

Tiny specks of dust flew up, twinkling and suspended in the air all around Betty as she made her way through the house, feather duster in hand. Despite the urgency that begged her to begin the final phase of her plan against Donny, her family and housework came first. They were, after all, the reason she had so determinedly fought against him until now. Preservation of some semblance of normalcy, even at an inopportune time such as this, was paramount in keeping a cool head. Besides, she would hate for George or the children to think she was ruffled.

George had been unsettlingly quiet. This morning he'd simply uttered a thank you when she'd placed his hot breakfast on the table, barely said a word at church, and had since retreated to the front porch with his newspaper. No doubt it was a continuation of his silent protest at the goings-on at the Gala Ball the evening before. His unhappiness pained her. She'd been a fool to allow such an intimate conversation to take place on the crowded dance floor. *I lost my head. And I can't let it happen again.*

Betty was bone-tired from over-thinking and wished for nothing more than a nice, warm bath to soak all her worries away. But there was still washing to be hung, beds to be made and Donny's murder to plan before she could really put her feet up.

And plan it she had. Months of conscientious observation was on her side. Betty knew every movement Donny made, his vulnerabilities and his routines. Bankrupting him was never going to be enough, it was just the icing on the cake. One step closer to revenge. She had taken down all his best men, his business partners, his puppets. She had taken his money and his assets. Now, it was time to take *him*. Tomorrow morning, on Donny's drive to the orphanage, she had a little detour for him in mind. Tonight's filthy cigar would be his last.

Betty hung her feather duster on its hook in the laundry and walked through to the kitchen. A row of empty glass jars were lined up on the kitchen bench, ready for pickling the beets she'd collected from the church victory garden. Small circles of floral fabric with scalloped edges were neatly piled next to the jars, along with a spool of red ribbon to tie the fabric cover onto the lids. Nancy had painstakingly cut the fabric days earlier and neatly handwritten paper labels, ready to glue onto the jars before selling at the church market. She planned to teach Nancy how to boil up casein glue for the labels, using milk and vinegar, after the pickled beets were jarred. Before the war, scotch tape had done the trick of fixing the labels on nicely, but now, as with so many other factories, all adhesives were being used for the war effort instead. Home-front patching jobs couldn't hold a candle to the importance of sealing up blood-plasma cartons or labelling weapon parts. *Mend and make do*, Betty had trilled to Nancy, who'd been miffed at the inconvenience after all her hard work writing out the labels.

Nancy would turn twelve years old in less than a month. Flashes of that same fiery determination and stubbornness that Betty claimed herself were now beginning to show up in her daughter. But, without the terrible experiences that Betty had endured in her own childhood, the girl was far more naïve and easily tempered. She used her imagination most effectively in playing out stories from her books, instead of plotting the murders of those who abused her, as Betty had done at Nancy's age. *Reading is a far healthier pastime for a young girl to entertain,* Betty mused. *She really is growing up terribly fast, though.*

George Junior's sing-song voice rang in to her through the open window. Betty leaned forward, pushing aside the daisy-laced curtains. Beyond the white picket fence, her elderly neighbor, Mrs. Porter was shuffling around with a garden rake in hand. Closer to home, George Junior was playing with a ball in the driveway, his shirt hanging out under his knitted cardigan, one sock pulled up to his knee-length knickers and the other fallen down to his ankle. His little cheeks were ruddy with effort as he dashed around, singing.

"Ball, ball bouncy, Bingo's in the bath,

Bunny's eating lettuce seed, up the garden path!
Mouse is in the larder, Geegees rather lame,
Ball ball bouncy, let's have a game!"

Betty's heart swelled at the sight of her five-year-old son. He was a dream come true, from his freckles to his toes. Grass stained the palms of his hands and one bare knee. His nutmeg hair flecked with sunlight as he danced around without a care in the world. *Anything,* she said to herself, for what must have been the hundredth time in as many days. *I'll do anything to keep them safe.*

A shrill ringing broke through her reverie. Betty let the curtain fall back and walked through to the sitting room, picking up the telephone receiver from the side table.

"Hello?"

"Mrs. Jones?! Oh, thank goodness! Please, help me! I don't know what to do!" The voice on the other end of the line was hysterical, spluttering and gasping in shallow bursts. "They took her – they took Anna!" the woman cried.

"Ruth?" Betty said, "Is that you?" Her heart skipped a beat. *No, no, no. Not yet.*

"Yes! It's me," the girl sobbed. "Please, you have to help! He broke into my house just now – said they've taken her to some rail shed... that they're going to kill her!"

"Who came, Ruth?" Betty pushed, her eyes darting around the room. Her mouth was dry and a cold wash of dread doused Betty from scalp to toes. "Who was it?" As if she needed to ask.

"I don't know. He had a gun and ... and –" The girl paused, and Betty heard a shuddering cry. "Please, no. Please," she whimpered.

"What did they look like, Ruth? You must tell me."

There was a quiet choking sound. "Scars," Ruth whispered and Betty knew.

Felix. Of course. He must have followed Betty on her sales rounds – he as good as admitted it himself when she had chased him from her house. And when Donny couldn't get to her family, he hit the next best thing. Her Avon customers. Her work. Her dream. And she'd never seen it coming. *What a fool I am.*

"He knew Johnny," Ruth was sobbing. "That dirty spiv Anna was so sweet on that got himself done in last month – he said Johnny got himself in trouble – that he stole something from them and they were going to take her as payment unless I – I …"

"You *what*, Ruth?"

"– call you," the young woman burst again into tears. "I don't understand," Ruth whispered. "Why am I calling you? You're just an Avon lady –"

Desperately, Betty tried to reach out and grasp Ruth's memories, to see what happened for herself. But it was no use. Betty had never been able to reach another person's thoughts from so far away. Betty's fingernails bit into her palms in frustration.

"Did you call the police, Ruth?" Betty pressed, desperately hoping she hadn't. Betty's meticulously laid plans were being unraveled by the moment and Donny wasn't a prize she was willing to share.

"I can't!" Ruth hiccupped. "He said if I call the brass, they'll kill me." Ruth's voice lowered to a hiss. "I don't know what to do." Betty imagined the girl balled up in a corner, terrified and tear-stained with the cord of the telephone wound tight around her fingers.

"Do nothing," Betty said, forcefully. "You rang me like they asked, you did the right thing. Go and make yourself a cup of tea, Ruth. I'll take care of Anna."

"But they're going to kill her," Ruth choked. Her voice cracked down the telephone line.

"I won't let that happen, dear," said Betty, soothingly. "You have to trust me. Tell no one what has happened, I know just the person to fix this problem. Anna will be fine, you'll see. I have to go now."

Betty hung up.

💋

Twenty blocks away, on the second floor of an old brownstone apartment building, Ruth listened to the disconnection tone with puffy eyes. Her face was a mess of bleeding mascara and her rag curls were pulled long and messy around her face. She held out the telephone receiver with a trembling hand.

"There," she said, dissolving into tears. "I did it."

"And a good job you did too," Felix said, chuckling darkly as he replaced the receiver on the cradle in his hands. "Time to get yourself another Avon lady, doll. This one's about to go out of business."

Ruth shuddered and pulled her knees up closer to her chest. She was curled on the sitting room floor against the wall. A spilt cup of tea was dripping from the coffee table onto the carpet and magazines that were scattered across the floor.

"Please, you said you'd let Anna go if I called Mrs. Jones," Ruth begged the man. "You promised -"

"Well aren't you the pretty-patsy," Felix sniggered. "I never had her to begin with. You broads'll believe anything."

He stood up, stretching his legs and yanked the telephone connection plug out of the wall then strode to the kitchen window. He pushed it open and tossed the entire telephone outside. A second later, Ruth heard it smash on the sidewalk below. Shouts of surprise rose from the children playing in the street and a woman yelled.

Ruth shoved her knuckles into her mouth to stifle a sob. A moment later, the man was leering over her again, his torn ear only inches from her own.

"I *will* kill you though, if you call the brass. That wasn't a lie,"

351

he said. "And I'll be leaving a trigger-man out on the street to keep watch. If you set foot out of this house, he'll throw lead at ya pretty little curls." Felix tousled Ruth's hair roughly and then stood up again, towering over her. "You keep your kisser shut."

He stepped over the ruined magazines and let himself out the front door, leaving Ruth trembling on the floor.

It was a trap. There was no question about it.

And I have no choice but to fall in, Betty decided. *I can't let Anna die. I was careless. I should have guessed Felix would follow me on my rounds. I should have taken him out last night, after the Gala Ball.* But last night, she'd had George by her side at almost every moment and more witnesses than she could manage. Now Donny had the upper hand and Betty's meticulous planning was wasted.

With a quick glance to check that George was still reading on the porch, Betty ducked into the laundry. She pulled the inner door closed behind her and walked through to the open back door leading out to the garden path that stretched the side of the house. Using her garden trowel, Betty levered a large, false paving stone out of the dirt and retrieved a bundled towel from the hole underneath. She set the paving stone back to rights, then carried the towel into the laundry. A collection of gleaming silver knives glinted as Betty unraveled the towel across the top of the washing machine.

Fileting knives. Boning knives. Cimeters. Paring knives. And a meat cleaver for good measure.

Betty lifted her dress and strapped them efficiently into the garters around the top of her thighs.

A half dozen each leg.

Cold and heavy.

Familiar and reassuring.

Betty smoothed her petticoat and red polka-dot tea dress back down over the top, hiding the knives from view. Slowly, as if in a trance, she untied her apron strings and folded the apron neatly onto the laundry bench.

She stepped quietly up the stairs to Nancy's bedroom, avoiding the stair that creaked. She wasn't ready to face George. Not yet.

Her daughter was lying on her belly on the bed, reading. Figaro, the little black and white kitten Betty had plucked from a stormwater drain only a few weeks before, was purring in the crook of Nancy's waist. The girl's hair gleamed like spun gold under the haze of afternoon sun streaming in the window.

"Nancy, darling," Betty said, trying to keep her voice on an even keel. "I have to pop out for the afternoon. Will you be a good girl and keep an eye on little Georgie for me? Daddy's downstairs but he's in rather a grump, so I don't want to bother him too much."

Nancy looked up with a frown.

"Where are you going?"

"Just to see a customer about some cosmetics, nothing exciting, dear. There's some leftover pot-roast in the refrigerator for dinner in case I get held up. Just put it in the oven like I showed you." Anticipating the objection that was forming on Nancy's lips at the thought of doing extra chores, Betty quickly added, "I know I can trust you with this, because you're so much older and cleverer than little Georgie. And you're far better at cooking than your father is, so I trust you to look after him kindly for me, just this once."

Nancy sighed, melodramatically. "Alright." She shut her book and rolled off the bed.

"Thank you, darling." She pulled her daughter in for a tight hug at the doorway. "Never forget how much I love you." With a tight chest, Betty turned away from her daughter.

She walked along the hallway to the top of the staircase, her black oxford lace-ups tapping each step as she descended. Betty pinned on a hat with a black net veil from the stand near the front door. She shrugged a black coat over her dress. It felt appropriate that she be cloaked in black today. After all, someone was about to die. She went back into the laundry and out through the side gate, collecting her bicycle on the way past.

"I'm sorry, George, I must run," Betty called out, avoiding her husband's eyes as she pushed her bike across the front lawn past the porch. "I have an appointment with Mrs. – um, Mrs. Findley." *Don't look at him. Don't look back, you mustn't falter.* Betty's heart leapt into her throat. For the first time ever, she wondered if she'd make it home tonight. She could hear little Georgie, still chasing his ball and singing merrily at the top of the driveway. Despite the warning in her heart, she couldn't help but allow her eyes to find him. Her joy. Her perfection. The personification of everything worth fighting for in a bundle of five-year-old-boy.

No more looking back. Betty tore her eyes away, her breaking heart hardening into immutable resolve. *I can't let Donny ruin any more lives. I need to protect my own. I need Donny dead.* She'd reached the end of the driveway.

"What do you mean you have an appointment?" George yelled from the porch, throwing his newspaper onto the tabletop and jumping to his feet. "It's Sunday!"

"I'm dreadfully sorry, darling! I forgot entirely, but I really have to go." Betty paused for a moment, breathing hard, staring resolutely at the road in front of her. *Don't look back.* "I might be late tonight, please don't wait up," Betty called, her voice wavering. "Look after the children for me."

Throwing one leg over her bicycle, Betty took off down the street. "I love you, George," she called over her shoulder.

"What the blazes –?" George shouted after her. "Since when –?"

But it was too late, Betty had rounded the corner and was

gone. George's eyes narrowed as he stared down the empty street. His heart sank and his eyes burned.

Lies. Secrets. Intimate conversations with men she claimed barely to have known. Mixed-up appointments. Rendezvous with parked strangers at midnight. Dark nights out alone, doing goodness knows what, with goodness knows who.

No. George thought, resentfully. *I do know who.*

Sergeant. Jacob. Lawrence. Even in his own mind, the words were dripping with vitriol.

His suspicion had been growing for weeks, and there was no denying it now. Betty was having a love affair with another man. George hadn't known who, but after the events of last night it was obvious.

His shackles raised.

His jaw set.

His pulse began to race.

And a lion awoke within his chest and roared.

Well, I'll be darned if I'm not going to fight for her!

George dashed inside the house, scrambling for his car keys.

"Blast!" Unable to find them, he raced upstairs to their bedroom. The keys were still sitting on the bedside table, where he'd left them the night before. As he grabbed them, he noticed Betty's crocodile-skin cosmetic case sitting neatly in the wardrobe, door open wide. Betty would *never* go to an appointment without her bag.

"Mrs. Findley, my eye!" George growled, dashing past Nancy who was now sitting back on her bed patting Figaro.

George burst through the front door and jumped inside his black Chevrolet.

"Mrs. Porter!" he called through the open window over the roar of the engine as it sprung to life. "I say, Mrs. Porter! Watch the children for me for a while. I have to dash off – it's very important!" His elderly neighbor straightened up with her rake and turned to the sound of the revving engine as George backed out of the driveway. She waved as he sped off, up the street after Betty.

With a vacant smile, the old lady gave a deep sigh and tottered back to her front door, sidestepping the pile of fallen leaves she'd gathered on her lawn. She leant her rake against the stoop, in favor of a hot cup of tea and a biscuit. Twiddling one finger in her ear to try to clear it, she stepped inside and shut the door.

She hadn't heard a thing.

Betty sped through the streets toward the old train shed, barely aware of the buildings that grew more industrial and neglected as she got closer. She was near the metal factory, where so many young ladies had taken up the mantel of industry in the absence of men, and now spent their days working on the great hydraulic press under the approving eye of Rosie the Riveter posters. Today though, being a Sunday, saw the streets still and silent.

Soon enough, Betty came to that desolate place beyond the bricks where she'd first encountered Vince Carelli Junior and his goons heisting a convoy of Army supply trucks. That time, she'd been disarmed by the shocking discovery that they'd brought young boys from the orphanage into their violence. A dozen soldiers had died defending their cargo that night. This time, a young woman's life was at stake instead. But this time, Betty was prepared.

Betty leaned her bicycle against the concrete wall of an empty building on the hill that overlooked the shed from above. Down below, two cars were parked on the dirt road that ran parallel to the train tracks. The cars were in full view, they hadn't even tried to hide. She assumed that Anna was held in one of them. That meant ten men at the most, unless there were more cars behind the long, decommissioned railway shed, but she doubted it. Why hide some cars, but not others? Ten men. *Easy.*

Betty looked around, assessing the situation for advantages. There really weren't many. The sun was still making its way down the afternoon sky, so it was too bright to hide. A surprise ambush was out of the question as Felix had forced her hand to come here in the first place. There was no place for pretense or shadows.

So, it's straight up feminine charm then, she decided. Betty took a steeling breath, then walked boldly down the hill toward the cars. She tapped on the window of the first in line. Slowly it wound down to reveal a face she knew only too well.

"You got my invitation, then?" Felix smirked. He opened the door and got out of the car as Betty stepped back to give him room. As he did so, the passenger doors of both cars opened, and another nine men stepped out to join him. Donny's gorillas.

"I'm flattered you feel you need such an impressive entourage, Felix. I'm just one lady, after all."

"I wouldn't call you a lady," he growled.

"Well, that's rather rude of you. In any case, I'm here for the girl you took. Where is she?"

Felix grinned maliciously and looked around at his men in mock confusion. "I ain't seen a girl around here," he said, loudly. "Any of you seen a girl?" The goons laughed. Felix turned back to Betty. "Looks like you've come fishing in the wrong pond, sweetheart. Nothing here, but a group of eager gentlemen."

Betty felt the blood drain from her face. She needn't have asked. There was no sign of Anna in either of the cars. Inside his own mind, she could read that Felix's intentions were clear. *Get her alone. Take her to Donny.*

Time for a change of plan.

"I wouldn't call you gentlemen," Betty said, without missing a beat. "But I'm not one for semantics. Let's get to it, shall we?" With a gleam in her eye, she stepped backward, lifting her petticoat and preparing to unsheathe her first knife. The ten men around her stepped forward, closing in. Betty felt her senses heighten, critically aware of every breath and shift of muscle within them. She'd fought more men and bigger and come off unscathed before.

"Don't be frightened boys," Betty teased, grinning as they cracked their knuckles, "it only hurts for a minute."

She heard the sound of a gun cock beside her head.

"Why fight," Felix snarled. "When I can just pull a trigger?"

Betty turned her head slowly to look him in the eye.

"Because it's nowhere near as fun," she said. A familiar tingle spread throughout her body, the rush of adrenaline surged through her, and she tensed, like a coil ready to spring as the men inched closer.

"Betty!" a voice yelled. "Betty! I say, get away from her!" Betty spun around. George was racing down the hill toward the cars, his eyes wide and face pale. "He's got a gun, Betty," he was pointing at Felix, while his other hand clutched his hat to his head. "You there, step away from her!"

Betty's stomach turned to lead. *Oh, lord, no.* Of all the nightmarish situations she had ever found herself in, nothing compared to this. Her darling George. *Here.* In more danger than he could ever comprehend.

"George, no!" she cried out. "Go home! Go home right now!"

Slam.

Felix's fist found her gut and Betty doubled over in searing pain, gasping for breath. *What do I do?* Her mind raced through the options. If she fought back, he would know. Her perfect life shattered.

"Betty!" George shouted, frantic. He reached the dirt road, pushing his way through the smirking men to get to her as Betty fought to push him back out. She had no air in her lungs to warn him. *Run.*

"Well, isn't this a nice little surprise," Felix jeered. "A knight in shining armor. I don't think this little princess needs your help though, chump."

George spun around, throwing a misaligned punch at Felix but hit only air. The men around him stepped back, laughing cruelly at his humiliation.

"Now that you're here though, how about you stay for a while. Sticks," he called to a lanky man closest to the car. "Get the knock-out juice." The man called Sticks grinned and ran to the trunk of the car.

"No!" Betty yelled, sucking the air back into her bruised lungs. "Let him go, he's nothing to you!" She pulled herself up tall, pushing George behind her. "Donny can have me, just let him go."

"Oh, he'll have you alright," Felix scorned. "With a bullet between your eyes at the bottom of the Hudson."

"How dare you threaten my wife!" George yelled. "What is this? Some kind of mugging? Attacking ladies in the street are you boys? I'll have you all thrown in jail for this!" The men around him laughed harder.

Betty could smell the sickly-sweet scent of chloroform the moment Sticks had opened the bottle.

"No!" she yelled, twisting viciously toward Felix's gun. Beside her, two of his goons had already moved, kicking the back of her knees in.

"One more for the road," Felix said and punched her gut, as she fell.

A hand came from behind, smothering her face with the rag until Betty's vision swam before her eyes. From somewhere far away, she could hear George yelling. And then it all went black.

When Betty came to, it was to the sound of scraping chairs and the smell of acrid cigar smoke filling her lungs. The skin around her mouth and nose stung like it had been burned. Her mouth tasted like copper pennies – the chloroform had left its mark. So, apparently, had Donny's goons.

Bruises were blooming on her cheek and collarbone, the telltale tightness of her skin suggested they were already swollen and darkening. Before she opened her eyes, she listened.

Shuffles found her ears from every direction. Heavy breathing close by, on her right. A whimper from her left. The crackling broadcast from a wood tube radio playing somewhere behind her. The hollow notes of a jazz clarinet piped from the speakers, echoing off a surface not far in front of it and bouncing around, distorting her sense of space.

A big room then, full of obstacles. Betty knew before opening her eyes where Felix had brought her. She had murdered here before.

Betty opened her eyes. She was in the basement of St. Augustine's Home for Unwanted Boys, Donny's most recent cover story. As of the night before, when Betty forced his hand to pass its ownership to the nuns that ran the orphanage, he was no longer the benefactor he once was, but it seemed they had yet to force him out. They wouldn't dare. Betty knew the only way to get him out would be to drag his cold, dead body from the building. Something she was perfectly willing to do. But now, George's appearance had all but ruined her plans and it was her own body, not Donny's, that could end up cold.

Betty didn't struggle against the chains that bound her hands behind her back. Just a gentle tug was enough to know that her wrists were securely attached to the chair. There was no need to move. *Yet.* Now was the time for cold strategy, not reaction. She'd let her emotion get the better of her when Ruth had called, and it had landed her here. But as much as she tried to clear her head, to be the dispassionate killer she had trained herself to be, it was almost impossible. Her beloved George, sweet, simple, naïve George was bound as she was, but in ropes, rather than chains. His head was lolling onto his chest, unconscious. *The heavy-breather to her right.* Seeing him like that, and knowing she was to blame, was agony.

Betty looked up at Donny. He was sitting opposite her on a chair similar to her own, with nothing in between them. Betty's eyes were like shards of ice.

"You will die," she said quietly.

Donald Pinzolo smiled and raised an eyebrow, his cigar in hand. His thoughts though, screamed with anticipation. He wanted revenge. To have been outwitted so many times, and by a woman no less, set his teeth on edge.

Felix stood by Donny's right hand, his scarred face gloating. As far as he was concerned, the game was already over.

The basement itself was all too familiar. A maze of heisted Army supply crates, old furniture and bric-a-brac were piled to the roof in all directions leaving no space bigger than a few meters wide, with the exception of the center of the room, where they currently sat. Although she couldn't see it for furniture and stacked crates, far ahead of her, at the opposite end to the stairs, would be the double doors that led outside to a second driveway, where Donny's heist trucks delivered their stolen cargo. The doors were undoubtedly locked and chained to impede her escape. Donny would have taken every precaution.

To Betty's left, was the long table the orphans used for re-packaging the stolen military supplies of amphetamines that had been destined for the front. Wake up pills for pilots and soldiers. A dozen unkempt boys had been disrupted from their work, no doubt by her arrival, and now they stood behind the table, their eyes to the floor, too terrified to look up. *The whimper on her left.*

There was a movement in the maze of boxes somewhere behind her, and Betty closed her eyes. With a huge effort against the pounding inside her head, she pulled the thoughts of the room in from around her. *The shufflers.* How many?

Seven – twelve – nineteen – thirty – thirty men hidden in the shadows of crates and makeshift furniture around her, all brought in to make sure she never made it out alive. Thirty-two, including Felix and Donny himself. Some were Donny's usual crew, but others he'd found further afield. Betty felt a swell of vindication in her chest knowing that she'd made such a mark on his soldiers over the past months. His army was dwindling. He was getting desperate.

This time though, he'd pulled out all the stops. Filth. Murderers. Mercenaries. Every one of them deserved to swallow his own bullet.

"Let them leave," Betty said, nodding toward the group of orphans cowering behind the packing table. "They don't need to see this."

Donny's eyes grew tight in thought and he looked to the boys.

"Maybe they do," he said, provocatively. "This lot are my finest and smartest – the *heirs to my empire*, so to speak. You take my own boys away from me – I take *them* instead." He stood up, letting his cigar hang from his mouth with his hands in his pockets as he turned toward the orphans, bouncing on the balls of his feet. "Pay attention kids," he called out to them, his voice laced with dark humor. "Listen to your Uncle Donny. I'm your family now, ain't I? You had nothin' before I took over this joint. I've been good to you, given you clean sheets and hot dinners and kept the penguins on their toes looking after you. We're family now, ain't we?" He swung back to smirk at Betty. "Today's lesson is about trust, boys. There are consequences for betraying trust in a family like ours." He lifted his hand and reclaimed his cigar from where it dangled at the side of his mouth, leaving a trail of smoke as he gestured to the boys. "And I'm the only family you've got!"

There was a sprinkling of laughter from around the room, but not from the orphans. The gunsels were listening to every word, and apparently found it all very entertaining. Donny smiled broadly, pleased with his unseen audience. "Family is everything, *Mrs. Betty Jones*," he said. "Shame. I always thought you had potential."

Beside Betty, George groaned.

"George?"

He opened his eyes and tried to shift in the chair. Betty saw the moment the panic hit him. He began to struggle against the ropes, his eyes wide.

"Stay still, darling," Betty hissed. His head turned to her and the blood drained from his face. She could only imagine what a fright she must look, in a crumpled dress, covered in bruises and chained to a chair.

"Betty!" He shouted, jarring against the ropes and rocking on the chair to the point it's legs might break. "What the blazes is going on?" His head twisted wildly until his gaze fell on Donny.

"You? Pinzolo? What is this!?" he demanded. "Let us go at once!"

Donny watched him, amused. "That won't be happening, Mr. Jones."

George's face turned purple. He was incensed. "Well, you'll be hearing from my lawyer! This is illegal!"

At this, Pinzolo and his men laughed outright. George turned and twisted, searching for the men whose laughter mocked him, but unable to see them beyond the tall crates dividing the room into pieces.

"Who's there?" he called out.

"Your lawyer?" Pinzolo repeated. "Boys, he's gonna call his lawyer." Again, they laughed, their taunts reverberating off the walls like a cruel echo. Donny drew close to George's face; his eyes suddenly void of mirth. "I own your lawyer, Mr. Jones."

"Let him go," Betty said, dangerously quiet. "He's nothing to you."

"Ah, the good wife speaks." Donny turned to Felix with a

nasty grin. "She cooks, she cleans, she gets down on her hands and knees…" Felix sniggered. "A luckier man you won't find – he told me himself."

George struggled, full of rage.

"How dare you! Don't you ever speak about my wife that way!"

"Your wife?" Donny said, playing dumb. "You mean this woman here? Let me ask you something, George the insurance salesman, how well do you know your wife?"

"What are you insinuating?" George growled.

"Should we ask Betty? Or should I say, *Susan?*"

"Don't you dare," she spat at Donny. Betty's face was white, like marble, but her eyes betrayed her.

"Betty?" George asked, angry and confused. "What does he mean?"

"He doesn't mean anything," Betty said, through gritted teeth. "He's a madman. A killer."

"That's true," Donny said, thoughtfully. "But I'm not the only one, am I little Susie?"

"What is he talking about, Betty?" George looked between them, bewildered.

Betty strained at her chains, then turned to George with a false smile, "Please don't worry, darling. This is all just a misunderstanding."

"One heck of a misunderstanding!" George spluttered. "You barely even know him. What's all this he's saying?"

Betty took a deep breath and tried to control her voice.

"There are some things about my past, my childhood, that you don't know. I'll explain it to you, but not now -"

"I think now is a fucking good time to tell him, Susan," interjected Donny, walking past her, tauntingly close. "She's a clever one, this wife of yours," he said to George. "I figured it out, you see, what this pretty bit of ankle did all those years ago. Impressive, Susie. Making it look like a hit by the Castellano boys.

Setting fire to the house – that's their style. The brass bought it. Until now, we bought it too."

"Shut your face, Donny," Betty warned.

Donny ignored her.

"But stabbing your old man in the back? Slicing his throat? That's fucking sick, sweetheart, even for one of us. Not that I ever liked Roy – he was a boozer and a sap. But still, he was family, right? *Our* family."

As he spoke, Betty turned ashen, all pretense of her new life draining away. She began to struggle violently in her chair, yanking her wrists apart in a tremendous effort to stretch the chains that bound them.

"You are not my family, you sadistic bastard!" she spat at him. "I will *never* be like you – spreading powdered death across the country, getting rich on blood and ruined families."

"I had my eye on you from the beginning, you know," Donny continued, ignoring her outburst. "Roy never saw it, he was too stupid. Even Frank never clued in. But I did. You were smarter than the rest, even my own boys, God rest their souls. When they told me you got hit, I wasn't pleased, Susie. You had potential. You were *useful*. Like your mother was, before she broke."

The memories flared up inside her mind, raw and aching, as if only a day had passed since her mother slid down that kitchen bench to the floor, white poison in her veins to replace the voices inside her head. He spoke of her as if she were a used car. Replaceable. Inconvenient. *How many more had Donny murdered since then?* Betty looked over to the table where the boys were watching them, wide-eyed.

"Well, you'll find I'm not so easy to *break*." Behind her back, Betty felt the metal of the chains stretching as she strained against them. She caught Felix's eye, and his own narrowed, critically.

Donny tossed his burnt-out cigar on the floor and leaned over her, one hand on each side of her chair, his thumbs pressing against the outside of her legs. When his face was only inches from her own, he spoke again.

His breath was hot and dank on her face and every pore on his skin glistened with sweat.

"And you've had the curse on me all these years," he murmured, with a dark grin. A tiny nerve under Donny's left eye twitched.

So close.

Betty stared back, unflinching.

"Yes, I did. And I'm going to murder you today, in this room."

From his chair next to her, George whimpered, an appalled look on his face, as if he was seeing her for the first time.

"Is that any way to speak to your great uncle, Susie?" Pinzolo growled.

Betty took a deep breath and straightened her shoulders. There was nothing for it now. No use trying to hide what George already knew. The damage was done. There was only one thing left to do.

Save him.

A deliberate smile spread across Betty's face, like a skilled artist painting on a mask.

Radiant. Charming.

Betty's eyes flashed, a little too bright, as if something inside had suddenly come unhinged.

"I hope you're ready for that family reunion, Uncle Donny," she said. "Because I'm ready to give you one."

With an almighty smash, Betty slammed her head forward, cracking Donny's skull with her own. The chains from her wrists clattered to the floor.

❧

"I'm hungry," George Junior pouted, folding his arms across his stomach melodramatically. "I wish momma was here to make us some cookies."

"If wishes were fishes, we'd all have a fry," Nancy recited, with an air of superiority, from behind her open book. They were both sitting at the kitchen table with empty milk mugs in front of them. "You can't just have whatever you like all the time, Georgie, you're such a baby."

"I am not!" the little boy cried, indignantly.

"You are. If you want something, you'll just have to grow up and manage it yourself. I'm nearly twelve, I know these things."

"Well, I don't know how to make food yet," Georgie complained. "And my belly is making funny noises."

"Mommy and Pop will be home soon, I'm sure of it," Nancy said, non-committally. She looked up at the crystal clock on the shelf. It was half past five in the afternoon. Her mother had mentioned that she might not be home in time for dinner when she'd left a few hours earlier, but Nancy hadn't expected her father to leave as well. She supposed he had some urgent business to attend to. The children had occasionally been left alone before, but not recently, and never for this long. Nancy did her best to ignore the gnawing feeling that she should tell someone. After all, her mother had specifically asked *her* to look after Georgie, so perhaps she'd anticipated they might need to make do alone for a while.

"I'm bored," Georgie complained again, dropping his head down onto the table with a *thunk*.

"Read a book," Nancy said, wisely.

"I'm too hungry to read," he groaned. Nancy rolled her eyes. Small children were such a bother.

"If you're so grown up, then you should make the cookies for me!" Georgie said. "Please, Nancy? Or I'll go and tell Mrs. Porter that no-one's home and she'll come over and make you play rummy with her all afternoon."

"You wouldn't!" Nancy said, closing her book and jumping to her feet.

"Sure, I would. If it meant making cookies," Georgie grinned.

"My stars!" Nancy exclaimed with her hands on her hips, in a manner almost identical to her mother. "You're such a little tattle-tale!" She scowled at her brother for a moment, pondering her options. Nancy had used the oven plenty of times before, but only under the watchful eye of her mother. Still, mommy *had* said she was getting older and more responsible. *And* that she would start trusting her with important things. The anticipation of a promised day out in the city discussing those important things, whatever they were, drifted to the front of her mind. *If I look after Georgie by myself, she'll definitely see how responsible I am,* Nancy decided.

"Alright, I'll make you cookies," she said. "But you can't eat them all at once or you'll get a belly-ache and I'll get in trouble for it."

Georgie beamed, pushing his nutmeg hair out of his eyes. He dragged a chair across the linoleum toward the bench.

"Can I lick the spoon?"

"If you behave," said his sister, trying to hide a small smile. She was beginning to like her newfound responsibility. Nancy walked through to the laundry and returned moments later, tying her mother's apron on over her dress. She pulled a cooking book out of the kitchen drawer and began to flick through the pages. "We'll leave some extras for dessert so mom and pop can try them, too," she said. "Shortening cookies, here it is. We start with a cup of flour –"

Nancy set about the kitchen, pulling out a mixing bowl, sifters and ingredients and piling them on the bench next to her brother. George measured a cup of flour and dropped it into the sifter, shaking it through ungracefully until as much ended up on the bench and floor as in the bowl.

"Now you've wasted it, silly," Nancy sighed, in a vain attempt to dust it from the benchtop back into the bowl. "And you dropped it all over the floor. Here, let me do it."

"I'm the boss, applesauce," sang Georgie to her, trying to take the sifter back while simultaneously dancing on his chair.

"Don't be wise, bubble-eyes," Nancy trilled back, returning his playground ditty with a laugh, "or I'll cut you down to peanut size!"

After a minute of stirring butter and rescuing an egg that first fell onto the floor, the sifted flour was added. Nancy retrieved the sugar castor.

"Empty!" she said, disappointed. "Oh no. I should have checked it first." Sugar rations had recently been cut to only eight ounces a week, and Nancy was sure her mother had been saving up the ration coupons for canning jellies instead of trading them in.

"I know where mommy keeps sugar!" declared George Junior. "I'll fetch it." He dashed off as Nancy measured out some Watkin's Vanilla Extract from a small glass bottle.

"Here it is!" Georgie said, holding up two jars of white powder. "Mommy keeps some in her work bag." He set them down on the bench.

"That's bath salts, silly," Nancy said, frowning.

"It isn't," George insisted, opening the jeweled lid of one. "It doesn't smell at all, see. Bath salts smell nice." He dropped the lid on the bench beside him and bent down over the jar, taking a great, big sniff. The powder puffed inside the glass and George stood up on the chair again with a wide smile, white powder sticking to the end of his nose. "See, doesn't smell like anything!"

"Alright then," Nancy said. She poured it into a small cup to half full, leaving the glass jar almost empty, then tipped the powder into the mixing bowl and began stirring again. She began to sing cheerfully.

"What are little boys made of,
Snips and snails and puppy dog's tails,
And such are little boys made of -"

She turned to her brother, expecting him to counter the words of the nursery rhyme, as he always did.

"Georgie? Georgie, what's the matter?"

The little boy was still standing on the chair beside her, but he was swaying slightly and his skin was suddenly drained of color. He slowly reached out his hand to grasp at Nancy's shoulder, then fell, backwards off the chair and thudded onto the linoleum floor.

"Georgie!" Nancy screeched, dropping down onto the floor beside him. "What's wrong? What happened?" She grabbed at his face, but it lolled like a rag doll on the floor beneath her touch. His eyes were open but his pupils tiny and glazed. Nancy shook him, but there was no response.

"Help! Someone, please help," she screamed. "What do I do?" His lips were turning blue. The rise and fall of his chest was so slight that it seemed he was barely breathing at all. "Georgie!" she shouted again, shaking him on the floor.

Stumbling to her feet, with tears streaming down her face, Nancy ran to the front door and flung it open.

"Help me!" she screamed, but there was nobody about. Nightfall was creeping, and there were only shadows to hear her.

Mrs. Porter was inside her own home and too deaf to hear, and the Sanders family, who lived on the other side of the fence, were out for the evening. Nancy rushed back inside for the telephone. The handle fell off the cradle onto the floor as her fingers trembled to spin the rotary dial for an ambulance. Suddenly, she heard a loud thud.

Nancy ran back into the kitchen. Georgie was still on the

floor, but he'd rolled into the base of the cupboard. His body was rigid now, and convulsing in spasms, hitting the linoleum with stiff arms and clenched fists. His eyelids were fluttering and his mouth hung open, a smudge of white powder still on the end of his nose.

"Please help!" she screamed again. But no one came crashing through the door. No one heard.

Suddenly, the little boy went still. His limbs relaxed and he lay unconscious, tinged with blue, his eyes closed.

"*What do I do?*" she begged, desperately, in great heaving sobs.

The answer came from inside of her.

Nancy's body reacted.

Offered her a solution.

It changed.

A great rush of adrenaline coursed through her veins.

Within her girlish frame, every muscle stretched and contracted with unrealized potential.

Her heart raced, her senses heightened.

Every beat that passed felt like a lifetime of opportunity, as if she could catch the dust dancing in the air and use it, before it swirled away. Time slowed. Her mind sped up.

An innate power built up inside, desperate to break free.

There was no thought.

No decision.

Only action.

Nancy scooped up her five-year-old brother in her arms and clutched him against her chest like a sleeping baby.

And she *ran*.

Fast.

Out the door, leaving it creaking in her wake.

Up the leafy streets.

Faster.

Beyond the corner where a *closed* sign rattled on the green-grocers' window as she passed.

Faster.

Faster than she'd ever run before.

Faster than any girl should be able.

Faster than any ambulance could have sped.

Nancy wove and ducked past blinding headlights, barely aware of them against the growing dark.

Suburbia broke into city center where the subways rumbled beneath the roads under her feet.

Buildings whipped past, almost too blurred to see.

And on Nancy raced, without thought or pause.

To where the hospital glittered on the far outskirts of the city.

Because there was only one thing that mattered anymore.

Save him.

Smash!

The chair flew out from under Betty as she kicked it, dragging the broken chains along the cement floor as it travelled. Donny reeled, falling backward as Betty's forehead ricocheted off his own. He lay stunned for a moment on the cement floor, and in that micro-second of stillness, Betty looked up. Felix's eyes grew comically wide as if in slow motion, and then he grimaced and threw back his head.

"Kill her!" he screamed.

There was an outbreak of noise and men poured in from their hidden places in the maze of crates.

"Get out!" Betty screamed at the cowering boys behind the packing table. They didn't need to be asked twice. The orphans scrambled in a dozen directions at once like mice from a broken cage. They dived under boxes and scuttled between the legs of the goons running toward Betty, heading for the staircase that would take them up and away from the basement.

"You're not going anywhere," Felix yelled. He'd leapt after the children, grabbing one by the scruff of the neck, and dragging him painfully back into the center of the room. It was Vince Junior's little tag-along, a boy of about nine years old, Sam. Felix had a gun in his other hand. "You're stayin' with me, kid," he growled as he pushed away toward the back of the warehouse. Betty knew she'd have to get through Felix to save Sam. *Collateral.*

Thump!

The first fist landed against her jaw and Betty heard a roar of protest from George. She grabbed the goon's hand and forced her left arm through their embrace, then wrenched her elbow back into his face, snapping his neck. *One down.* As he crumpled to the floor, she caught the foot of a second man as he kicked out. Betty twisted, spinning him around on the spot, holding two other men at bay with his floundering arms and knocking the gun from one's hand as he aimed. A bullet flicked by her and caught the metal screw of her upturned chair, sending it skidding it back another foot, and narrowly missing George, who was still bound in his own. With a mighty flick of her wrist, she sent the spinning goon crashing into a pile of crates.

Donny was scrambling to his feet, pale in the face. The basement was bedlam.

Through the shouts and stampede, Betty could make out the music of the wood tube radio somewhere up the back of the room, now piping a fast-paced swing. *Serenade to a Savage* was pulsing through the air with Artie Shaw at the helm of a brass orchestra. Betty let the jungle drums swell inside her as she punched and kicked through the onslaught of men piling toward her to the beat. A whining trumpet siren sang out and she caught a glimpse of her husband through the bodies. His mouth was hanging open, slack with disbelief. He wasn't even struggling anymore. *Oh dear.*

Betty's head snapped back as a well-aimed hit caught her cheek. She recoiled, stumbling back. She grabbed the throat of its source with one hand while the other lifted her skirt, searching for the familiar warmth of metal in her garter. Her heart skipped a beat. Her knives were missing.

"You don't think I'm that stupid, do you?" Donny jeered, above the din. He was over behind the packing desk now, where the orphans had been before, content to let his trigger-men take their turn first. But a twitch of his eye gave him away and Betty pulled what she needed from his mind. *In a lidded crate, with my coat, behind the table.* That's where he'd thrown them before they'd chained her to the chair. Betty shuddered reflexively at the thought of Felix's filthy hands frisking her and peeling off her jacket as she'd lain unconscious. His filthy fingers pulling her knives from her garters. She'd make sure he regretted it later. Her fingers found a ladder at the top of her nylon hose and Betty's eyes glinted furiously. Stockings were a precious commodity these days, thanks to the donation drives to collect them for the gunpowder boys and parachute silk. In a cry of rage, Betty swung at a hatchet-man heading her way and cracked his jaw, sending him sprawling to the floor in a spray of blood and teeth.

"That's for ruining a perfectly good pair of stockings!"

Betty ducked her head at a hurl of intention inside the mind of someone behind her. *Bang!* A bullet flew over her head. The smell of cordite caught her, as she twisted to the side, dislodging his gun that was now pressed to her shoulder blade. Throwing herself forward into the arms of a lanky black-haired thug closing in, she redirected his knife with his arm still attached until the blade sank deep into the gun-wielder's heart. He fell to his knees with a scream of surprise. *Two down.* Betty round-housed her right leg to kick his Colt from his hand as he fell. It clattered to the floor. She dropped to her hands under the lanky thug as he stumbled forward, skidding through his open knees. Betty's fingers found the gun. Before he turned around, she had rolled onto her back and shot him up through his gullet. *Three down.* An empty click. Betty detached the box magazine and let it spin away under the maze of supply crates as she scrambled to her feet.

She heard a strangled yell of anguish from behind her. George was struggling again, rocking back and forth on the legs of his chair, still tightly bound. A string of near-obscenities were tumbling from his mouth.

"Confounded son-of-a-sea-cook!" George spluttered, as the chair rocked too far backward. He fell with a thud, smacking the back of his head against the concrete floor.

"My poor darling," Betty gushed, breaking away from the fray. She grabbed the chair with one hand and pulled it to rights with George still tied on. He looked dazed, but despite it all, tried to yell over the din. His eyes were as wide as silver dollars.

"How did you – ? I don't understand –" George was frantic, his face red with exertion and a tinge of betrayal behind the fear in his eyes.

"I don't – I don't know what to do – or how, how you can – ?" he stopped midsentence, lost for words.

"I can't explain it, darling, not now!" Betty pleaded. "Please leave, George. You must get out now!"

"I'm not going anywhere without you," George huffed, as Betty wrenched her arm backward into a goon's chest and sent him smashing onto his back beside her.

"I'm so sorry, George." The thug was at her feet, a knife in his fist. As he stabbed it toward her calves, Betty grabbed his wrist. She heard the sickening crack of his bones as she twisted the knife from his grip. With tears in her eyes, she looked down at the hitman, then back up to meet her husband's eyes. The hitman grimaced and lunged toward her with his good fist clenched. With a shuddering sigh of resignation, Betty stabbed the man directly into the heart. *Four.* Droplets of blood spray stained the perforations in the beige leather of George's two-toned spectators. Betty tried to smudge it away with her hand, but only made it worse. "I'm so sorry," she said again, climbing to her feet. "I never wanted you to see any of this." With a quick slice, Betty cut through the ropes that bound George to the chair and they fell away to the floor.

"Leave. Now," she demanded, unable to look him in the eye.

"But I think –" he stammered, "I think you just killed that man –" George gawped at the body by his feet, a bloody knife protruding from the man's heart like a monument, his eyes wide and glassy.

George's face was almost as ashen as the dead man.

Words tumbled from his mouth. "How did you know to do that?" George got unsteadily to his feet, trying not to step on the corpse sprawled in front of him. He was trembling, one hand over his mouth, as if he was going to be sick.

"Girl Scouts," Betty growled impatiently, knowing full-well how ridiculous she must sound. "It's a long story, my darling, but you really have to leave. *Now.* There's a door that way that leads upstairs," she nodded toward the entrance she'd found on her reconnaissance visit weeks ago. "Behind all of the crates. Please, go!" She cracked her elbow backward in a sharp blow and caught a balding ginger in the Adam's apple. He fell backward, choking.

"I just – but I feel like I don't even know who you are –" George stuttered, clearly in shock. "What Pinzolo was saying – and all this fighting – and this dead man –" George stumbled backwards over his chair, trying to put distance between himself and the body.

"I'm sorry, darling," Betty said, kicking the ginger over and picking him up by the seat of his pants then smashing him headlong into a wooden crate. "But I had to do it, dear. He was an absolute scoundrel – shot two railway guards last month after he held up a woman on the subway!"

"How on earth would you know that?" George asked, weakly.

"Well –" Betty began, distractedly. It was no good trying to explain that she had read the criminal's mind before stabbing his heart, or in fact, that she could read the stains that every man in the room wore on his soul before she killed them. Betty suddenly realized she still had the chance to keep at least one of her gifts a secret. "I saw his picture in the newspaper!"

A spray of bullets ricocheted off the cement and Betty threw her husband to the ground behind a pile of crates.

"The newspaper?!" George spluttered, from the floor.

"Please!" Betty begged, "Just leave, George! Go home." She couldn't bear to hear where his naïve questions would take him, or where they would leave her. She couldn't bear to let her heart break. *Not here. Not now.*

"But I can't leave you!" George growled, obstinately, getting to his feet. "I'm not going anywhere until I know what the blazes all this is about!"

"Then I'm sorry, George," Betty cried, as another wave of men hurtled toward her, "but you'll have to keep out of my way!" She leapt past the men and grabbed an empty ammunition crate. She tore the hinged lid from its frame, leaving a meter-cubed hollow inside. She heaved it up onto her shoulder. "Get down!" she yelled to George and he fell back to the floor in fright as she ran toward him and brought it down over his head, trapping him inside on his hands and knees.

Betty turned to another crate, nailed closed and full of ammunition. Wincing with effort, Betty picked the full crate up onto her shoulder and stacked it on top of the one George was trapped underneath. He'd be furious, but at least, for now, he was safe.

"Let me out of here!" George screeched through the small

hole cut into the side as a handle, his fingers poking through in a ridiculous attempt to grab hold of something.

"It's for your own good, dear" she yelled back, turning away into an oncoming horde.

Betty threw herself down onto her hands and kicked her legs out violently behind her, knocking a pistol from a thatch-chested thug as he ran in, bullets flying ahead of him. She kicked out again in a swish of petticoat, wrapping him in her outstretched thighs and pushed her arms up and away from the floor with all of her strength. They both crashed back down, Betty's legs still wrapped securely around his fat chest. She grabbed the gun from the floor and shot him straight between the eyes. *Five.*

Flecks of blood sprayed her face, staining her red polka-dot tea dress with spots that didn't belong. She shoved the gun into her garter with gritted teeth as two more men came running toward her, firing. Betty jumped up, her eyes ablaze with fury.

"This. Dress. Was. From Macy's!" she yelled.

Betty grabbed the first, a rotten-toothed beer-belly, and threw him over the wall of crates into the maze beyond with a scream. Her fist found the second man's jaw, hard, in a spray of blood. This one was scrawny, with dark hair and an ill-fitting pin-striped suit.

"The hound? Is that what they call you, dear?" Betty breathed, grabbing him by the tie and wrenching it up in the air. The Hound's toes dragged on the ground and his mind spilt murder like a broken pail. *Arson. Aggravated Assault. Rape.* Like some of the others hidden in the shadows of the basement, this one was a contract killer for the Chinese mafia on the other side of town. Donny had recruited further than ever before. Smelling his desperation was satisfying. Betty narrowed her eyes, considering the man in front of her with distaste.

"Well, Qing, *darling*," she said darkly, as he spluttered, face turning purple. "I happen to think that you give dogs a very bad name. You should have worked in the fish market with your brothers, like your good mother wanted. Such a disappointment."

Betty dropped him onto his feet then pulled him up straight, finding the man's gut, hard, with her fist. He doubled over, groaning and gasping. Betty sent his meagre weight stumbling back into the goon coming up behind, sending them both sprawling. She whipped the ginger's gun from her garter. *Six. Seven.* She spun and gave a bullet to the unconscious redhead while she was at it. *Eight.*

Betty looked up. Felix had long disappeared into the chaos with Sam. Fat splinters of wood exploded from the edge of the crates to her right as a new wave of bullets hit. Betty dove, throwing herself behind a wall of crates, desperate to redirect the flow of ammunition from where George was trapped.

"All together!" Donny was yelling from somewhere ahead. "Attack together, you imbeciles! Don't let her pick you off!"

"What's the matter, boys?" Betty goaded, crawling between the piles of crates, machinery and supplies. "You're not scared of a little housewife, are you?" Her dress was torn now, and blood-splattered, her petticoat filthy under her knees. Cautiously, she stood up and poked her head out from her hiding place. A barrage of bullets flew in and she ducked back out of sight. The crate that Donny had stashed her knives in was only meters away. A thick-necked gunsel stood beside it, eyes keen, with a Tommy gun at the ready.

Betty slid back down to the floor, her back against the stack of crates. Bullets flew hard and fast. She slid the magazine out of the Colt she still held. *One bullet left. I really need those knives.*

The chaotic actions and intentions of Donny's men streamed into her mind from every corner of the room. There was dark amusement from some, uncertainty from others. A handful were only here for the money, others for revenge of their comrades she'd cut down in the past. Most though, were just blind fools, ready to die for a man that moved them like pawns on a chessboard.

Somewhere in the darkest corner, Betty could sense Felix waiting, calm and detached, his mind a hive of cold strategy. His ambition had led him here, but Betty knew Felix held only disdain for Donny and his business. It was the promised reward and the threat to Tilly that kept the fire burning under his skin. Felix saw himself in Donny's shoes. In control of a pulsing city and the network of arteries underneath that kept it alive. Donny's closest were already dead, his *caporegimes* diminished. Betty had done that dirty work already. Felix now saw himself as Donny's right-hand man, ready to step sideways into his shoes as soon as Donny himself had been dispensed with. Felix's thoughts were confident and quick. He had faith that Betty would complete the inconveniency of Donny's murder for him tonight. If not, he would continue to play the loyal *consigliere* until he did the honor himself. Letting Betty rid him of Donny, then ridding himself of her, was now Felix's play. And the orphan boy, apparently, was his insurance to see it through.

Her head felt stifled. Overflowing.

Too many voices all at once.

Betty closed her eyes for a moment, blocking them all out. The shouting and gunfire fell away.

Silence.

She pictured her silver box with its small treasures inside, each one an embodiment of its original owner's super-human skill.

Strength. Telepathy. Speed. Agility.

Her birthright.

Each woman had carried a blessing and curse in her gift. All had borne it in secret.

Mothers. Sisters. Grandmothers. Daughters.

They had fought with their gift. Nurtured with it. Protected with it.

My blood, Betty thought, with gritted teeth.

The desire to live up to their legacy caught aflame and burned inside her chest like a raging inferno, until even the tips of her fingers felt ablaze. But there was one more gift running through her blood. The one that had brought others' secret thoughts and pain inside her mind. An Achilles heel that could douse that flame.

Empathy.

The source of her mother's greatest strength and agony.

The two-headed snake.

It was Donald Pinzolo who had taken that gift and twisted it into something terrible. He'd raped compassion to breed deceit and murder and built his empire on an abomination of love. Turned strength into weakness. Into hopelessness.

Donny.

Betty opened her eyes. Bullets ricocheted off the crates all around her. She got to her feet, unflinching.

Tonight, empathy would find no home inside her mind.

It was filled with revenge.

With an almighty yell, Betty launched herself away from the shelter of crates and over the refuse of boxes and equipment that separated her from the thick-necked gunsel guarding her knives. Her polka-dot dress streamed out behind her as she landed with a *thump* on the packing table where the orphans had been forced to work. She slid along it, twisting and turning, smashing paper packets of bennies and fet onto the floor where they split open in a confetti of white powder and pills. Around her, all hell broke loose, as Donny's men shot up the room in a trail of shattered furniture and raining glass that followed her across the table.

Bang!

The single bullet left in Betty's pistol found its home between the eyes of the guard and he fell backward as she leapt off the table. *Nine.* His index finger, already poised on the trigger, spasmed as he fell backward, sending a shower of bullets into the roof as an endless stream of metal shells sprayed from the barrel and rained back down on his face. The bullets shattered industrial hanging lights and supporting columns, rebounding off metal chair legs. Two men fell as they ducked for cover. Betty swept underneath the rain of fire as she landed in a crouch and wrenched the Tommy from the dead man's arms, replacing his trigger finger with her own.

She finished off the fallen two and a third as he threw himself behind a table.

Ten. Eleven. Twelve.

The Tommy stuttered. *Empty.* Betty leaned over the packing table and brought it smashing down onto its side with her free hand, sheltering her and the dead guard from fire. She released the magazine from the gun. It clattered to the floor. Betty bent the metal barrel over her knee, snapping the timber fore grip into a nest of splinters. She threw it aside.

Betty swung her leg high and kicked the crate holding her knives from atop another with a sweeping foot, letting it smash down onto the dead guard. The lid swung open on its hinges, spilling her precious knives across his body. As she slid them into her garter, a surge of icy familiarity bit her bones. The music from the wooden tube radio caught her veins again from over the din and Betty grinned.

"Now we can play fair," she yelled.

With an almighty surge of adrenaline, Betty rushed toward the upturned table that was shielding her from gunfire. It slid across the floor as she pushed it from behind, toward the barrage of attackers coming at her. Three were caught behind the tabletop as it swept them backward. With a quick change of direction, Betty sandwiched the stumbling men against a wall of crates on the other side of the open space. Whipping her cimeter from her garter, Betty spun in a wide arc with her arm outstretched, slicing their throats as one, as they stood pinned in a Harlem sunset. *Fifteen.* She spun around and ran for cover as five more closed in. Betty dodged bullets, kicking and fighting like a demon as Donny's hitmen swarmed in.

Smash. A side table crashed to the ground underneath her, as Betty dived onto it, her hands around the neck of a hep cat swimming in a white zoot suit. His red-rimmed eyes and excoriated skin gave him away as one of Donny's pushers, no doubt paid in the bindles he sold. Betty searched inside his mind as her hands held him down. *Lorne Wright.* One of Frank's button men at The Capitol, selling crack in the alleyways of the jazz club district, before Betty put him on ice. This one deliberately overdosed trouble-makers with toxic cutting agents on Frankie's watch, instead of selling them clean fet. A killer then, like all the rest.

"Sorry, sugar. Got to be quicker on your feet to Lindy Hop with me." Betty forced him further into the rubble as he gasped for breath. With a sharp move, his fist split her lip and dislodged her hands, as he tried to roll over.

"I saw what ya' did at Frankie's," he hissed, "all them bodies you left for the meat wagon, ya' crazy broad!"

"You should have taken the hint then, dear," Betty admonished, as she punched him again. "Now look at the mess you're in." She brought her knee up into his groin and the man groaned and curled away. Betty threw him off, fighting the next as Lorne staggered to his feet and made a run for it.

"No more dancing for you!" she yelled, ripping the meat cleaver from her garter and flinging it over her shoulder after him. *Sixteen.*

The heavy-set man she was wrestling a gun from seemed to ignite with renewed energy at the sight of Lorne's fate. He caught Betty's arms as she pitched his gun out of reach and they broke away from the rest, falling over furniture in a fierce battle of strength. Glass shattered and crates smashed. He was relentless. The man beat her soundly as they tried to best each other, his sheer momentum almost a match for her super speed and strength. Heaving with labored breath, Betty finally sent him crashing across the basement floor in an explosion of broken wood. She knew it was a temporary fix. He wasn't yet dead. She raced back toward the main group, searching for Donny. If she could just get her hands on him, hiding wherever he was now behind his armor of henchman, it could all be over sooner. Without Donny's allegiance, these filth-mongers would scatter back to the holes they crawled out of.

Betty fell as her legs were kicked out from underneath her. Furiously, she sprang back up to her feet. In retaliation, Cutthroat Charlie dropped with a paring blade between his ribs. *Seventeen.*

The smell of urine caught her as another cocked his pistol behind Betty's head. She spun and ducked before his finger pulled the trigger. The barrel clicked, empty. With comically wide eyes, Wallis Morrish let his gun clatter to the floor at Betty's feet. He turned to take flight. *Too slow.*

Wrenching him backwards, Betty pulled Wallis in close, a human shield against the bullets of a lanky greaser with a loose tie and a penchant for souvenirs. Dropping the deserter to the floor, she punched the greaser's jaw and heard it crack over the staccato of bullets and shouts.

Swing. Rip. Spin. Betty moved in time to the drum of her own heart as the radio dipped beneath the suffocation of yells and gunfire.

Nineteen. Salvatore Hill, the ice-pick punisher.

Two men grabbed her arms and pulled them behind her back.

Slam!

The butt of a semi-automatic found her gut and Betty curled inward, dangling from her arms, her head swimming.

"No bullets left, Leo?" she choked out, trying to find her grip. Betty wrenched her arms forward with as much strength as she could find, dragging the two men around her in a strange dance that smashed their skulls together in front. They fell backwards to the concrete and mess.

Betty dropped to the ground under the line of incoming fire. A fileting blade from her garter found a warm home in one man's throat as she scrambled back to her feet. Rufino the Rat, a filthy creeper that made the rodents he kept house with at the flophouse with look well-bred. *Twenty.*

Knee. Elbow. A shatter of teeth across the floor.

Betty's breathing was strained. Every part of her body ached and her skin was a lacework of bruises and blood. Her hair had pulled out of it's neat curls and her black-netted hat was long lost to the fight. Through the staccato of bullets and yells, she could hear George still banging on the inside of his wooden prison.

"I'll just be a minute, darling," she shouted, not quite loud enough to reach him as she hurled a crate at Rufino's comrade before he could regain his footing. *Giovanni Greco,* a dock walloper gone rotten under Donny's influence, not above settling bar-brawls with a bullet. He disappeared beneath the crate with a crunch. *Twenty-one.* Betty fell forward onto her knees, then scrambled back up.

She ran at Leo, collecting him as she came and ramming him into a wall of crates. They collapsed, crashing across the floor, releasing a fresh supply of ammunition to Donny's remaining men, who scooped them up around her and took cover to begin anew. Once more, Betty dove out of sight.

Her muscles screamed in protest. It was getting harder to keep them at bay.

The fist of a Chinese mafia underling caught her jaw and Betty fell back, reeling and disoriented. She stumbled, trying to find her footing. Her black lace-up oxfords were now blood-red, the heel catching in uneven debris on the floor. A crowbar, used for prying the lids off crates, had fallen amidst a jumble of smashed supplies. Betty leapt over a mound of spilled ammunition to reach the end of it. *Stomp.* The crowbar flicked up into her hand in heavy obedience. Betty turned back. *Yun Fen Chu.* A nasty little scarecrow who'd worked clean-up crew for Jimmy Chan. Betty ran him through, impaling him against the wall. *Twenty-two.*

Ten men remained, including Felix and Donny. *Only ten.*

She was exhausted. Her gifts had never been pushed so hard. Betty reached for her garter and found only two small paring knives left. She ducked behind some rubble.

There was a shout.

The remaining men fell back.

And suddenly it was quiet.

No gunshots. No screams.

No shuffling.

Nothing.

The wooden tube radio near the stairs could be heard once more. A sentimental croon rose over the hollow strings of a jazz standard, sweet and melancholy like a soft hand soothing her pain.

> "Love is the sweetest thing,
> Blue birds sing, since you wear my ring,
> Never forget the memories we hold so dear,
> They'll keep us safe now year by year."

The words shattered her heart. Betty shook her head and tried to block the music out. She flexed her muscles, feeling a sharp pain ripple down her side and up the base of her neck. A cut on her leg was weeping blood. Every inch of her felt tender. She blocked out the pain as well.

Focus.

Then she felt it.

A typhoon of anticipation began building in the room around her.

Betty closed her eyes, reaching out in her mind for a voice she knew too well. But she needn't have bothered. The voice came loud and clear without her help, from somewhere beyond the pile of bodies.

Donny.

"How much do you love your husband, *Mrs. Betty Jones*?" he called.

The cock of a pistol echoed off the basement walls.

Cold dread crept down her spine. Betty stepped out from behind the rubble. At the far end of the basement, where the double doors leading outside were chained shut behind him, Donald Pinzolo stood with a gun to George's head. George whimpered, wide-eyed, as two of Donny's goons held him up under the arms from behind. In her efforts to keep Donny's soldiers at bay, she'd left George too long unprotected in his makeshift cage. He was safe no more.

"Get over here," Donny yelled.

Betty walked forward, in full view of the ten men left standing with her husband. Her fingers were twitching against her dress where the knives were hidden underneath.

Nine.

Felix was missing.

A hard blow caught the back of her head and Betty fell to the floor, reeling. Felix kicked her again, leaving her prostrate on the ground. Betty allowed herself to take it, knowing there was only one bullet between George and his life. She hated Felix. But Felix wasn't about to kill George. Donny was. Betty knew she'd have to get closer for any chance at saving him. And she was willing to die. But not without fighting to her last breath to keep him safe.

Felix reached down and grabbed her hair, pulling Betty roughly to her feet. Betty felt her face burn beneath the blood stains as Donny's remaining men laughed. George was standing stock-still, his face gray. He looked as though he was barely breathing. Felix put his own gun to Betty's head. She and Felix stood, opposite Donny and his men, about fifteen feet apart.

"So, who's first?" Donny jeered.

"I won't let you hurt him," Betty said, as calmly as she could. She grimaced as Felix's pistol pushed harder.

"Sorry sweetheart, but you're in no position to stop me," Donny said. Again, his sycophants guffawed. "Your good husband gets a bullet to the head, all because you couldn't keep your mitts off my boys and my business. You should have learned your place, Susie, like everyone else. It's all a game, see, and you weren't invited to play. There can only be one winner in this room. And nobody beats Donald Pinzolo at his own game."

"Let him go," Betty warned, her voice dangerously low. "The game is over, Donny."

"What? And let him waltz out that door, as if you didn't try to tear down my empire? Like you didn't murder my boys? Ruin my business? Sacrifice all my years of hard work? You know me, Susie, I could never let him go." Donny smiled, a cold and ruthless promise. "No more playing *happy families* for you."

Jacob pulled up outside the white picket fence of Betty and George Jones' house. It was the last place he wanted to be. He had tried calling first, but the phone seemed perpetually engaged, so instead, he'd driven over. Now, he was sitting in his car under the streetlamp, unwilling to go inside.

It was almost dinnertime. His car radio crackled as an advertisement ended, *"everybody needs the real zip and zing pep that delicious Sunbeam bread gives you!"* and Al Bowlly's somber voice began to croon through the speakers.

"Love is the sweetest thing,
Blue birds sing, since you wear my ring -"

Jacob switched the radio off, annoyed. If he had any more sentimentality in his life, he might just go insane. The last few months had been a mess. The last few days, a catastrophe.

In truth, he hadn't even wanted to take Adina to the Gala Ball, knowing the potential danger Susie's stunt on Pinzolo could incur. But when he'd stupidly mentioned his 'invitation' to Adina while trying to justify his inability to see her, yet again, of course, she'd insisted on coming along. Then, due to his own foolish behavior, she'd stormed out, convinced of his romantic involvement with Susie. Now, Adina wouldn't return his calls.

He didn't blame her. Truth be told, no matter how hard he had tried, his heart furiously clung to the childhood sweetheart he thought he'd lost for so many years. As a boy, he'd idolized her. As a young man, pined for her. Most recently, he realized just how much he had missed her all those years he'd believed her dead. But Susie, or Betty, rather, had changed in time gone by, and so had he.

Jacob loved Adina too and he knew it, clear as a sunlit sky. She'd awoken a spark within him that had so long been dormant that he couldn't help but be thankful for it. She was lively and bright, and undeniably beautiful. She kept him on his toes and had made him finally relinquish the sheath of excuses he had wrapped himself in for so long. Jacob had felt free with her, at least for the short time before things had become so complicated.

Now new life and old love warred within him relentlessly and to Jacob it seemed he was the most indecisive, or perhaps, cursed, man on the earth to have been captured by two such formidable and stubborn women in one lifetime.

They'll be the death of me, he thought grimly, shaking off his bad mood with a touch of dark humor.

Reluctantly, Jacob got out of the car, determined to speak to Betty about the two most pressing issues on his mind. The first, was an unpleasant but not-altogether-unexpected confrontation he had had with Malcolm Parker that morning at the station. It seemed he'd been more thorough with his undercover detail than Jacob had hoped. A more pressing issue though, was the dossier he'd found in the Governor's Room after Adina had fled the ball. Betty was being watched by someone far more important, and potentially dangerous, than an over-enthusiastic police officer.

As he let himself into the front gate, Jacob noticed that George's black Chevy was missing from the driveway. *At least that makes my visit a little less awkward,* he sighed to himself. Jacob walked up the porch steps in darkness to knock on the front door.

It was wide open.

"Good evening?" he called out, rapping on the open door and removing his hat. "Betty, are you home? It's me, Jake – uh, Sergeant Lawrence," he added, for the benefit of the children, who might have been listening.

There was no answer. He called out again. Still no response.

Why on earth would they have gone out but left the front door wide open? Anyone could walk straight in.

Jacob took a tentative step inside. The lights were out, as if no one had been home since the sun had gone down.

An uneasy feeling prickled the back of his neck, and he unclipped his police issue Colt from its holster inside his jacket.

"Betty?" he called out. "George?" He stepped through the sitting room carefully, and made his way to the kitchen, where the only light from the house seemed to shine. "Nancy?"

The kitchen was in disarray. An upturned chair was by the bench, and the remains of what he assumed were the ingredients of a half-battered cake were spilt across the kitchen bench. The oven was glowing brightly and buzzing, radiating heat throughout the room. It was empty, as if someone had begun to bake, then left in a hurry and forgotten to turn it off. Jacob stepped over spilt flour on the floor and clicked off the oven dial.

"Betty? Nancy?" he called, but the house remained silent.

He turned back to the bench.

With a steady hand and a racing heart, Jacob picked up a small jewel-lidded jar that sat on the bench by the batter. It was filled with white powder. He unscrewed the lid and gently sniffed inside. No scent. *Pure heroin.*

He knew it, this jar. It was identical to those delivered to his office after every heist for the past six months. Most recently accompanied by a small white card, signed "Avon Calling!" in cursive script. Betty's calling card.

Her coded message for him to figure out. A clue to the truth that she alone, was taking vengeance on the murders and atrocities committed by Donald Pinzolo's crew.

And here it was. *Heroin.*

Sitting in plain sight, in a dark house that had been abandoned at a moment's notice.

It could only be a warning.

She's in trouble. They all are.

Betty was vigilant, above everything else. Her home was her fortress. She would never have left the oven on, or the door cast open to the street. Unless, she had not fled herself, but been forcefully *taken.*

By Donny's men.

Jacob grabbed the jar and raced to the telephone in the living room. It was askew, the receiver dangling on the floor. He picked it up and shuttered the cradle to reset it. His finger trembled as he dialed his own number at the station, desperately hoping he would find Officer Parker on the receiving end before his shift finished for the evening.

The line picked up.

"Parker!" Jacob practically yelled. "Betty Jones is in trouble! All of them are!"

"Sir – ?"

"No time to explain. Gather as many officers on the street as you can find. Armed but *no sirens*. I'll meet you there –" Jacob nearly dropped the phone in his desperation to be gone already.

"Where, Sergeant? Where are we going?" Parker asked.

Jacob looked grimly at the jar of heroin in his hand.

"St. Augustine's Home for Unwanted Boys," he said. "The basement."

10

LULLABY TO A JITTERBUG

The orphanage basement crackled with the heavy weight of anticipation. Death seemed to permeate every inch of the concrete floor and crept, festering, beneath the peeling layers of paint on the walls.

Not fifteen feet in front of Betty, Donny held a loaded gun to her husband's head. George himself, was sickeningly pale, his eyes wide and lips trembling as two goons held him up under the arms from behind. He was like a mouse in a den of lions. Absurdly easy prey.

Donny's face was red and gloating. His eyes held the malicious glint of a man who saw himself already the victor of a grueling opponent. Betty stared right back at him, every inch of her body aching beyond reason. There was nothing that Betty wanted more desperately, than to eviscerate the man where he stood and watch his life dissipate in the throes of the savagery he had nurtured for so many years. The cold muzzle of Felix's pistol pushed harder against her neck. Betty didn't move. It seemed she was out of options.

"I'm not the only one, you know," she said, quietly. "If I don't bring you down, someone else will. It's inevitable, Donny. There's a price on your head."

"A price on my head?" He sneered. "And what am I worth to the fools that don't like the way I run this city? Thousands?" His eyes flashed in dark humor.

"Oh, you're worth thousands, alright," Betty replied. "Thousands of foolish young men kept safe from your poisoned powders. Thousands of families who won't have to beg for mercy from your debt-collectors. A thousand tears saved from every widow whose husband is dragged from the Hudson with your name on his dead lips.

A dark cloud drew across Donny's face. "Is that right? And what am I worth to you, little Susie? What's the price you'd pay to see me die?" He shot a look at the goon behind George, who jolted his captive to attention. George whimpered as the gun dug deeper into his temple. "Is this the price you'd pay? Your perfect husband? Well," Donny looked over Betty's shoulder to Felix, "at least we know he has life insurance." The nine gunsels surrounding Donny, laughed.

Betty took a deep breath, steeling her resolve. She willed her broken body to submit one last time to the fight, despite the pain it knew was coming. There would only be this one last chance to save her husband. And if death was coming for her, at least it would be swift. *One more fight.*

"Oh, no," Betty smiled, as the laughter died down. "George doesn't need any life insurance – he has *me*."

Snap!

Betty threw herself around, cracking Felix's arm with her elbow as she spun. She tried to wrestle the pistol from his hands, but his grip was too tight. Felix struggled against her as Betty maneuvered him forward instead, taking control of his aim and forcing his finger down onto the trigger.

Bang!

Donny's own gun flew into the air as a bullet caught his fingers, so close to George's head that his hair ruffled.

"Fucking bitch!" Donny screamed. He cradled his bleeding

hand as the others dove for cover. Donny ran at Betty, incensed, as the others reappeared from behind broken crates and chairs, bullets flying. George had dropped to the ground and scuttled out of sight.

Betty threw her full weight against Felix, smashing him backward onto the concrete and rolling them both across the floor as she tried to wrestle the gun from his hands. Felix forced himself on top of her, his gun securely lodged under her chin. He pulled the trigger.

Click. No bullet discharged.

Betty grinned maliciously. She smacked the pistol from Felix's grip.

"Looks like you're out of luck," she spat, forcing him underneath as she rolled again, determined to keep moving to avoid the rain of bullets that ricocheted off the concrete all around them. Felix fought violently as they rolled, blood spraying the grey concrete in equal measure from them both. She whipped a paring blade from her garter and stabbed it down hard. Felix rolled again, and the blade snapped against the concrete instead of his flesh. Betty swiped with the broken handle, slicing his arm. Felix cursed and scrambled to his feet. He dodged and ran, disappearing behind the detritus of the room. Betty pushed up to follow. A hard blow knocked her back down. Donny had thrown himself at her, falling on top like a paunch, dead weight. He pushed up and away, to his feet.

"You stupid, little – " *Slam!* His gut swung as he kicked Betty hard in the middle. She heaved on the floor, forcing oxygen back into her lungs and struggled to pull herself up. *No air.* The room swum dangerously. Again and again, Donny kicked her as she tried to rise, sending her crashing back to the floor.

Betty rolled far enough away to find a moment's relief and staggered to her feet. She turned to face Donny, blood running down her chin and the metallic taste of it in her mouth. With a screech of fury, she rushed headlong into him.

Smash!

Together they fell back over an upturned crate, landing on one of the goons shooting lead from his hidden shadow. It was Guanting Wang, one of the Chinese triad Donny had drawn in on a favor. The others stuttered their gunfire to a halt. The risk of hitting Donny was, apparently, too high.

I'll take that risk, Betty thought, rearing her fist high for a punch. But the Chinese had other ideas. Guanting recovered his footing. He rounded back and belted her from above. Infuriated by the interruption, Betty twisted around from her place on the ground.

Smack! With an upper cut to the jaw, Guanting's head snapped back. He hit the concrete with a blow that knocked the lights, and life, from him.

Betty turned her attention back to Donny, who was still writhing underneath her. His arms were pinned either side of his body by her knees. Betty looked down at him, every synapse of her mind crackling with memories, years of hate welling up inside her heart. She smiled, that cold, cruel smile she had worn so many times before. Donny's eyes grew wide with sudden fear.

"You're a very unattractive man, you know, darling. I think it's time for a makeover."

Betty pounded Donny's face, feeling a rush of vengeance flood her veins. Her fists were relentless. Soon, his struggles became weak and his head began to loll. Betty reached inside his mind. His thoughts had begun to fade. He was barely alive. Death was at hand. She smashed him one more time and heard the back of his head resound on the concrete. A half-dozen hands grabbed and pulled at her, dragging Betty backward off his body.

"Oh, no you don't!" she yelled, kicking out. The three men holding her fell back as she spun to face them. A split-second assessment before she moved.

One. Vito Negri, *the chef*, known for his meticulous butchery skills when disposing of Donny's 'leftovers'.

Two. Raoul Serafini – a big-name jazz player whose double-bass was often rehoused to hide a Tommy that served up bullets instead of a tune. Both enforcers for the family business.

The third. Another ring-in, Tao Li. He was unfamiliar, so Betty dug into his mind as all three launched themselves at her at once. She fought back hard. The Chinese was ambitious, barely aware of the other two alongside him, attacking Betty as new shots rang out from the cowards left crouching behind the broken crates. Exhausted, she pushed further into his memories. *This must be personal.* She ducked a roundhouse kick aimed at her head.

"You're good darling," Betty gasped, countering his blows, her suspicions confirmed. "Almost as good as your brother was. Nice to see you've taken better care of your teeth too." Her mind flashed back to the mute with a golden smile in the basement of Kitty's Kat House. Tao grimaced and struck again with renewed enthusiasm. "Pity you won't need them anymore," she added. Betty whipped the final knife from her garter and dragged it across his throat. Tao sank, gurgling, to the floor. "Your poor mother," she sighed with chagrin, as she swung back around and tore a pistol from Vito's hand, snapping his wrist in the process.

Vito fell back with a cry. Leaping forward to grab him by the shirt before he scarpered, Betty hauled *the chef* across the room, using his body as her own shield, straight into a fresh rain of bullets pelting from the far end. Betty tossed Vito's body over the crates, sending the trigger-happy goon crashing backwards under his comrade.

Serafini had fallen back to become another discordant note within the nightmarish clamor of the basement. Every nerve in Betty's body was screaming. Every thump of her heart throbbed down her spine, sending jolts of pain into her fingers and toes.

Her gifts were waning. It was becoming *so hard* to keep fighting. But still, she struggled on, ducking and rolling against the tirade of ammunition. Only six ring-ins left to kill.

"Let him go!" a man suddenly shouted, over the din. "Right. This. Minute!"

It was George. He was standing unsteadily behind a mess of broken furniture, pointing a trembling pistol – Donny's – over Betty's shoulder to the room beyond. Betty spun around, following his aim.

Felix was making his way across the room, shuffling slowly backward. He was only meters away. Sam was clutched in one arm, in front of his own chest. There was a knife at the boy's throat. Felix's eyes snapped to Betty. His lips were closed tight, but his thoughts were practically screaming.

"I know you can hear me, you crazy broad," Felix screeched inside his mind. His pupils drilled into her own. *"I want out. You're gonna let me leave this room, or the kid gets it."*

He was inching his way toward the internal stairs that led back up to the orphanage. Sam's face was white and tear-streaked, his little mind whirring with terror. He looked up at Betty helplessly.

"I'm warning you," George yelled, "you low-life scourge on society!" His brow furrowed in resolve, even as his nerves and hands shook.

"Let me deal with this, George," Betty yelled back, desperately grateful to see him alive but devastated he'd made himself a target once again by standing up. The six remaining hitmen were still dotted around the room, hidden. They fell quiet, watching as Donny's newest right-hand man, his coldest dispatch, stood alone against the woman Donny had paid so dearly to see killed. Now, it seemed, that Felix was trying to run. The thought *traitor* echoed throughout the room, filthy and dripping with resentment. No one moved.

"You kidnapped my wife," George yelled again, "and now

you're threatening an innocent boy! You should be ashamed!" George lifted the gun higher, apparently searching for a clear shot. Felix bent closer to the ten-year-old, his knife pressing into the boy's skin. Sam gave a whimpered cry and squeezed his eyes shut.

"You won't shoot, ya nancy!" Felix shouted back. "I know all about you, George Jones. You've never had your hands dirty in ya life! You don't have it in you!"

George's face burned. "I may be out of my depth here, in – *whatever the devil is going on*– but I'm not a coward! I won't let you hurt him."

Felix sneered and began to drag Sam backward once more, never dropping Betty's eyes.

"Help!" Sam squealed. His little fingers clawed at Felix's arm, but the scarred hatchetman was immeasurably stronger. Behind Felix, Betty saw a shadow flit between the crates. She smiled.

"Well, I think you've underestimated me, old boy!" George cried. "Like I – " he looked at Betty with a nervous smile, "like I think I underestimated my wife." Betty returned his smile like a beacon. Felix looked between them. He dashed backward, dragging Sam.

Bang! Bang!

The pistol in George's hand echoed through the basement and he jolted back from the unexpected kick.

Chaos broke.

Felix fell to the floor, clutching his leg. George rushed forward and heaved Sam from beneath the man's sprawling body. The torrent of gunfire began once more. Bullets sped toward Betty as she ran at Felix who was scrambling to his feet, still clutching his knife. George bent down over Sam, dragging the boy away from the gunfire toward the last pile of supply crates left standing in the center of the room. The bullets suddenly changed course. A new target burst into the fray.

Jacob leapt from behind a mass of smashed furniture. Now

fully exposed in the vast room, his Colt boldly picked off the remaining gunsels.

"Betty!" he shouted.

Betty jumped a low lunge from Felix's blade as she closed in on him. Jacob was yanking Betty's carving knife from a body beside the broken chair George had been tied to. With one hand still shooting, he aimed the knife directly at Betty's heart and flung it hard. The carving knife flew across the room toward her, spinning as it went.

Betty stepped aside.

In one swift move, she forced Felix's arm down and spun him around. Betty caught the flying blade by the handle and redirected it, slamming it between Felix's shoulder blades.

He fell, dead.

"Move!" Jacob yelled, as he took down a gunsel triggering for her head. Betty ran for cover. A great yawn of buckling timber shuddered through the room. Betty spun to follow the noise.

"George!"

An avalanche of crates was crumbling above the spot George was crouched, shielding Sam from the gunfire. The crates lurched precariously. George caught Betty's eyes and realized, too late, the danger they were in. He grabbed the boy and threw him forward, clear of the crates, as they came crashing down. A heavy wooden corner caught George's head and he disappeared underneath it. Betty was already running.

"George!" Betty cried again, heaving crates out of the way to make a path. With a desperate effort, she dragged her husband free. "My poor, poor darling," Betty hushed, cradling his unconscious body and stroking his bloody forehead. She leant over him, tears running down her cheeks as Sam watched silently from beyond the rubble. She looked up. The child was terrified. Betty held out her arm, and Sam scuttled over to her.

"You have to help me, Sam." Carefully, she moved George's head from her own lap to the boy's.

"It's nearly over, I promise," Betty said, wiping Sam's face with the back of her hand. "Will you stay with him for me? Just a little longer? I'll make sure nobody hurts you."

Sam nodded, his face as white as a sheet.

"Just stay quiet," Betty whispered.

Somewhere, Jacob was fighting hard. A man's body crashed into the space where the packing table had once been. Above the staccato of gun shots, fewer now, there was a deafening bang, as if someone was battering the chained garage doors at the end of the basement from outside. With each thunderous crash, the walls rang out and plaster dusted from the ceiling like snow.

"Jacob!" Betty yelled, running back to the center of the room. She dropped to the floor as a bullet whizzed over her head. Anticipating another, Betty ran straight for the shooter instead. *Serafini, the musician.* Betty leapt over the refuse he was hiding behind and landed in a crouch behind him.

"Play this!" she grunted and snapped his neck with both hands. He rolled to the floor. Close by, a man yelled in pain. Betty jumped to her feet.

"Jacob!" Betty dodged debris, searching for him. He was on the ground, clutching his arm.

"Over there," Jacob winced, nodding to his left. "There's only one left and I'm out of bullets."

Betty nodded grimly and stood up. A single bullet ricocheted off the concrete by Jacob's leg. The crashing sound from outside was getting louder. Beyond the carnage, the garage doors were straining inward with each thud.

"Time to come out, little mouse," Betty sang. She heard a shuffle. "Is that you Keenan Carey?" she said softly, tapping into the fugitive's mind. "Are you scared, dear? Are you regretting your life choices? Perhaps if you pop out here we can talk about it – see if we can come to some kind of understanding?"

There was a scraping sound and the man suddenly stood up, his hands above his head.

"I wanna talk about it," he said with an Irish lilt, against the pounding background din. He stumbled forward, over the debris at his feet. "I'm out. I don't wanna do it no more."

"Mmm," Betty said, lightly, stepping toward him. She knew she looked utterly atrocious. Her clothes were torn, her hair disheveled and her body bruised, swollen and splattered with blood. "You know, I've been told I'm a very understanding person."

A flicker of cautious relief crossed the man's face. Betty drew closer, until she was only a foot away. She lay a reassuring hand on Keenan's bicep. He was at least a foot taller than she, and well built.

"I'm quite understanding, in fact," Betty said, gently. "You know, I see things a little differently to most people. I understand their motivations – why they do what they do. Take you, for instance. I understand you needed a job. I understand Donny thought highly of your connections with the IRA. I understand you wanted to use your hard-won skills – make a name for yourself here. After all, there's no harm in a little pride in one's accomplishments, is there?"

Keenan furrowed his brow and offered a nervous smile. "That's right. It's my job, innit?"

"Of course, just a job," Betty purred. "And I understand you killed six men in your first year working with Marco. Impressive. Then another five, out on your own. Six if you include the *collateral*. Just doing your job, though, of course."

Keenan's smile wavered.

"Interestingly," Betty continued, "one of those men was a dear old vagrant from the docks. His name was Charlie. I'm friends with all the tramps you know, they make wonderful informants. Always willing to share information if you offer them a kind ear and a ham sandwich. But he got in your way, didn't he? Charlie was just in the wrong place at the wrong time."

Keenan took a step back.

"I suppose that's what happens sometimes, isn't it? People end up *in the wrong place, at the wrong time*. Like you, here today."

Keenan nodded emphatically. He stumbled backward over splinters of wood and tiny white pills spilt across the floor.

"Well, I for one am glad you came today, Keenan," Betty smiled. "It means I can thank you for all of your hard work." Betty hitched up the tattered remains of her polka dot dress and snapped her leg out. With a fiercely high kick, she knocked the Irishman from his feet, grabbed his gun and fed him his own bullet. Donny's final man was dead.

"Betty, you have to get out of here," Jacob warned, squeezing his arm as he limped up beside her. An almighty smash came from the chained door. They were almost through. "I've got the full cavalcade outside. I told them not to come through the front on account of the children upstairs, but that garage door won't hold them for much longer. As soon as they see this mess, they'll start asking questions. I can't cover for you if you're caught in here."

"I know," Betty said. "But Jake –" she looked around. If she was indeed caught in here, no amount of womanly wiles would explain it away. The basement was a catastrophe of gore and stolen drugs. Betty's eyes were wide in earnest as she looked at her best friend, the only man who had always known who she truly was. "*Thank you.* I was nearly at the end of my tether. I couldn't have gone much longer."

"You did a better job of them than anyone else could ever have done," Jacob panted. "What happened to Donny?"

"Dead." Betty reached out her fingers to touch Jacob's arm. "Finally."

"Well done, then," Jacob smiled, grimly. "I know what that means to you."

"You're the only one who does," Betty said, quietly.

"Maybe not, anymore." Jacob nodded to the mess beyond, where George was still lying hidden.

"I suppose not," Betty sighed. Her heart sank at the conversation that was coming. She'd lied to George, for years. Her past and present had finally collided and placed him directly in the danger she'd so long tried to keep him safe from.

Jacob stepped forward, intensely close. Behind them, another shuddering crash almost tore down the doors. His fingers found her cheek. He leaned in. *So close.* Jacob's eyes spilled hope and understanding from their depths. Because he *knew*.

What she had been through.

What she had suffered.

How hard she had fought to be rid of them all.

Suddenly, the noise seemed to drop away. The bodies and bloodshed were nothing and there was only the two of them again, a boy, striving to follow his father's footsteps and make his parents proud, and a girl, desperate to wipe her life clean of her family's crimes and cruelty.

"Betty – *Susie* – you don't have to keep living a lie, you know," Jacob breathed. "It's all a charade. You're living *half a life*. He doesn't really *know* you. He never *can*. It kills me to see you pretend." Gently, he wiped some blood from her chin with his thumb. "You'll never have to pretend with me, you know that, don't you? Because I know you, the *real* you. In a way that no one else ever can. I *love* you, Susie. I always have – you know that."

Betty looked up at him, tears in her eyes. "Of course I do, Jake. And you know that I love you too. I always will. But," she bit her lip to keep it from trembling. "They make me *happy*, Jake. And *ordinary*. And that's all I've ever wanted, to be happy – to have a family of my own, a *real* family, you know that. You know what that means to me. They're my everything now."

"But they don't understand you –"

"They don't need to," Betty said, her eyes shining. "*I understand them.* And that's enough for me."

Jacob swallowed, his face miserable. "Then you better go, or you won't be able to keep them."

"Yes."

"Please - just once. *Susie-Pocket.*" He leaned forward and kissed her softly on the lips.

Betty pulled away sadly. "I'm so sorry, Jake."

"Go then," he muttered.

Betty ran her hand gently down his unhurt arm, her eyes shining. Then she turned and raced through the mess to find George standing now, leaning against an upturned crate, looking pale, with Sam by his side.

"It's over," Betty said, taking a hand of each. "But we need to leave, straight away. The police are here."

"Am I in trouble?" Sam asked, his voice wavering.

"Of course not, sweetheart. But you'll have to come with me for now. This was far too traumatic for you to deal with on your own. You need to be kept safe while I sort this whole thing out. In case there are repercussions for you –"

"Really?" Sam looked up, hopeful. "I can leave?" Jacob had followed her and Betty looked to him as she spoke, searching for confirmation.

"You'll have to. For now, at least. I know a lady, a dear friend of mine, who will care for you with the utmost kindness, Sam. She'll be thrilled to help. Sergeant Lawrence will see to the paperwork." Jacob gave a nod.

Betty pulled them toward the door, but stopped, when she realized George had stopped moving. She turned around. He was standing perfectly still, a dazed look on his face.

"George, darling. We have to go. I know you're upset, but I can't explain it all here. Let's get home to the children –"

"The children?" he said, wincing and touching his forehead, which was blooming an enormous bruise. "The children? Where are they? I can't remember – jitterbug, why are we here?" He looked around, with a mixture of abstract curiosity and repulsion at the carnage, then jolted at the smash of the doors being rammed once again. "Are these men dead?"

"Oh no," Betty cried, stepping over and gingerly touching the stretched skin. "It knocked you senseless, didn't it? My poor George – what do you remember?"

"I don't – remember – you left and I followed – the children were –" He stopped, apparently unable to find any more words.

"Your children aren't at home," Jacob interjected, his eyes frantically flicking between Betty and the pounding, splintering doors. "I went there first to see you about, *something else* - your house is a mess. No lights on, food all over the kitchen, the front door was wide open – that's why I came here – I assumed Donny had taken you all by force." Jacob rummaged in his pocket and pulled out the small glass jar of heroin with the bejeweled lid. "I found this on the bench. Nancy and George Junior definitely weren't there –"

Betty's face drained. She heard blood rush from her eardrums. Her knees buckled. After all she'd dealt with in the last few hours, it was this, that faltered her. The ground swam beneath her feet.

"What do you mean they weren't there?" She whispered to George, desperately. "What did you do? Surely you asked Mrs. Porter to watch them when you left?"

But George only looked more confused. His eyes were raking the bloody havoc of the basement, his hand over his mouth as if he was going to be sick. "I don't know," he whispered. "I don't remember –"

"Just go!" Jacob urged. Light was breaking through the doors where the cracks were growing wider. It was only a matter of one more hit, two at most. "Leave!" he hissed. "I can't explain you being here, you can't risk being caught involved in this. You're already being watched!" Betty looked up at him, questions in her eyes, but Jacob was already dragging her with his uninjured arm toward the internal staircase.

From somewhere behind them, came a dark, deep laugh. Betty froze. She wrenched away from Jacob.

"You!" she cried, spinning around.

Donald Pinzolo was leaning back against rubble where Betty had left him. His face was a bloody mess, but he was most decidedly, not dead. A strange glint of satisfaction flashed in his eyes at the sight of her fury.

"What have you done with my children?" Betty cried, advancing on him with Jacob dragging behind her, as another thundering crash threatened to tear the garage doors off their hinges.

Donny smirked, his mouth lopsided under bruises and split skin. "I'm no fool, Susie Polletti. You think I'd pluck such valuable fruit before it's ripe? I don't have them. *But someone does –*"

"Liar!" Betty dug into Donny's fractured mind, throwing herself toward him to finish him off, as Jacob yelled and heaved her back toward the staircase with all his might.

But it was the truth. Donny had no memory of where her children were tonight. He hadn't taken them. Instead, his thoughts swirled with dark ways to *use* them and find out which latent powers might lay inside their young bodies.

"You'll never get your hands on my babies," Betty seethed, as a final crash reverberated through the basement. A flood of flashing headlights swept the dark room and Jacob hurled Betty away from Donny with every ounce of his strength, forcing her behind the crates near the internal stairs with George and Sam at their heels.

"Get out of here, now!" Jacob hissed, furious.

"I have to *kill* him –"

"It's too late! They're in. If they find you here, you'll never see your children again." Shouts and exclamations of alarm were rising from all over the basement as officers raced through, guns at the ready. "Go!" Jacob hissed again. He pushed them all ahead of him, up the internal staircase. With a huge effort, Betty turned her back on the final murder she so desperately craved, grabbed George and Sam by the arms and raced with them up the stairs. As promised, Jacob had kept the cavalcade of law away from the front entrance of the orphanage. The halls and entrance were deserted, no doubt in lockdown from the terrifying racket below. Betty dropped Sam's arm, confident the boy would follow and ushered George through the front doors and into the pitch-dark night beyond. They traced the spectral contours of the garden and passed back through the front gates of St. Augustine's Home for Unwanted Boys.

In the grimy shadows of the industrial area beyond, Betty collapsed on a gravel road. She was trembling. The gritty surface cut sharply into her knees. Her splayed palms grasped the filth, and within it, some distant, intangible force.

"Lady!?" Sam's voice seemed miles away.

A pounding *whoosh* of blood-filled Betty's head and ears. Every other sense was draining away, disappearing to some other place.

Someone was tugging on her arm. *George.*

Betty squeezed her eyes shut. An unbearable pain tore through her heart.

Where are you? She screamed inside.

Every spark of her consciousness warped and stretched out into the darkness.

Searching.

For something to grasp. Some*one* to grasp.

Who's taken you?

Betty pulled her body inward, in agony, drawing every strength she had left to reach out with her mind.

Searching for someone too far away, further than she'd ever been able to reach.

Someone whose own gift was too inchoate and unfledged to respond to her, barely an inception of what it one day could become.

Desperately searching.

Calling.

For that twelve-year-old girl with Betty's bloodline of gift and curse.

For Nancy.

Her daughter.

Her children.

Where are you?

Like a crack of lightning, Betty's back arched and her head was thrown back to face the sky. Far away into the night, her gift found it's mark. She connected.

Mommy!

A series of visions flooded the darkness behind her eyes.

She saw the world through her daughter's mind, far beyond the boundaries of distance she'd ever reached another mind before.

Alone at home. Cookies.

Her cosmetic case. Sugar, no – that's not sugar!

Heroin!

Georgie!

The little boy, Betty's pride and joy, fallen, *broken.*

Help me!

But no one came.

What do I do? He's turning blue!

Convulsing, barely breathing.

Please help!

His body limp on the linoleum.

And then, *a miracle.*

An explosion inside. Latent powers unleashed. A decision.

I will save him.

Through Nancy's memories, Betty saw the streetlights flash by.

Speeding cars.

A blur of apartments and shops and noise.

Rumbling subways beneath the soles of her feet.

The heavy softness of a little boy held tight in her arms.

A great red cross in the distance that lit the sky like a beacon of hope.

I'm coming, Betty cried desperately into the void between them.

And she knew that Nancy heard.

Betty opened her eyes to the dark night, her mind suddenly crystal clear with purpose.

"They're at the hospital! Come, George, Sam. We need to run!"

Betty pulled George along behind her, guiding him through the dark streets with the orphan following behind. George's pale face grew more robust as he ran.

"My children," he cried, as purpose took hold. "What have I done? I left them alone."

Betty grabbed his arm and pulled him to a stop under the shadow of a peeling iron smelter.

The realization was devastating. In her desperation to create a perfect life, she'd put them in more danger than they should ever have been.

"You did nothing wrong, George," she said urgently, finding his hands with her fingers under a sliver of moonlight. "I did this. I brought this danger into our home. This is all my fault."

"I don't remember what happened, Betty –" George began anxiously. He seemed on the verge of tears.

"But you will," Betty said, "and when you do, I'll explain it all to you. And there's every chance you won't forgive me. Which, perhaps, is what I deserve."

"But Jitterbug –"

"Please, not now, darling, we can't. We must get to the children."

It was only minutes later, as they left the industrial park and found themselves on the city fringe, that Betty saw a cab and hailed it down.

As they sailed toward the bright lights of the hospital, she willed the cab to fly above the traffic and deliver them faster than she knew it could. If she'd been alone, Betty's feet would have brought her there quicker.

As they drove, Betty tried to wipe the blood from her face and hands with the inside of her dress. She tucked her hair back into place and re-pinned it as best she could. She looked a mess, blood and bruises all over, her petticoat torn and nails broken, with George sporting a bruise on his forehead that seemed to be swelling more obscenely by the moment. There would be questions, undoubtedly, but right now they were far from her cares.

As the cab pulled into the emergency bay, Betty burst through the hospital doors and ran at the nurse in the reception station.

"A little boy, and his sister, please - he was terribly ill! Where can I find them?"

"Good gracious, ma'am," said the nurse, in her spotless starched apron and stiff white mob cap, "what's happened to you? I'll fetch the doctor -"

"No, please," Betty urged, "we are perfectly alright, we just had a small – automobile – accident on our way in, rushing to find the children. Really, I know we look a fright, but we really are quite fine. Please, our neighbor told us our children were here - a little boy of five and a girl of twelve, they arrived on their own -"

The nurse's eyes opened wide in recognition. "Oh, goodness,

I'm so glad we've found you!" She bustled out from behind her desk and lead Betty and George up a corridor, Sam trailing behind. "No one knew where they came from, the girl wouldn't say." She looked down at the fob watch pinned to her top pocket. "They've been here nearly three hours. The boy went straight to emergency. You'll find your daughter waiting outside his recovery room with a police officer. This way, please, Mr and Mrs –?"

"George and Betty Jones," said George, finally finding his voice. He'd been disconcertingly quiet during the taxi ride, staring at his own hands in his lap, miserably. Betty's heart wrenched at the sight of it, knowing she was unforgivably at fault, but her heart and mind so desperately pulled her toward her lost children that she couldn't allow herself to deal with it, yet. Besides, Sam had been sitting between them, wide-eyed and shaken, and Betty still needed to organize a suitable arrangement for him. For now, that too, would have to wait.

The astringent scent of chloramine burnt their nostrils as Betty, George and Sam followed the nurse into a brightly lit waiting room. Nancy was curled in a metal chair in the corner, a young police officer sitting beside her. He had a notebook flipped open and was flicking the pencil against its cover with a frown on his face, apparently having given up on trying to cajole the facts of the situation from the silent girl. Nancy's face was white and pinched. Her arms were wrapped around her knees. At the sight of her parents, Nancy jumped up and ran across the room, into their waiting arms.

From her daughter's thoughts, Betty knew she hadn't said a word to the officer of how they'd come to be there. It was time for some very fast thinking.

"I'm so sorry," Nancy cried, bursting into sobs. "I didn't look after him properly, like you asked. He fell over and stopped breathing and I didn't know what to do!" As if she had been holding her emotions in check for days, Nancy's body suddenly wracked with sobs and she fell limp into George's arms. Gently, her father picked her up and carried her to an empty chair, hugging her on his lap, offering soft words of placation under his breath. Betty had never seen such grief on his face.

Betty walked toward the young officer, who had risen to his feet, but was instead intercepted by a doctor who appeared from a nearby doorway at the summons of the nurse who'd accompanied them. As the door swung shut behind him, Betty saw a small room beyond, sparse and clean, with the white metal rails of a bed.

"He's alive," she breathed in relief, taking the knowledge from the doctor's mind before he had even opened his mouth to speak.

The doctor's face was stern and tired. His mustache twitched in agitation as he surveyed the room. "You're the mother of this boy?" he asked, grimly.

"I am," Betty said. "His name is George Jones, Junior, and he's five years old. How is he? Do you know what happened?"

"He's very unwell," the doctor said, reproachfully, moving closer to George Senior instead, who was attempting to extricate himself from Nancy's arms to get to his feet. "Something you could have circumvented if you'd kept a closer eye on your children, Mrs. Jones. From what I can gather, they found a jar of an illegal opiate in the streets or some such place, and the boy ingested some of it. He had a severe reaction and would have died, had his sister not managed to bring him here in time."

"Oh, my poor baby!" Betty wiped her eyes, penitently. Her tears fell true with regret and shame. Although she had already known the truth of the situation from Nancy's memories, the words spoken aloud cut through her like a blade. *It's all my fault.*

"And now?" George asked, quietly. The police officer had moved alongside, his pencil scribbling furiously. Sam found himself a chair and the nurse hovered for a moment, then, deciding they were taken care of, left again, through the corridor.

"I gave him an injection of Nalorphine," the doctor replied, lifting his chin. "It's an experimental drug, an opioid antagonist we're developing here at the hospital. It counteracts the effects of heroin on the respiratory system, gets our patients breathing again, like your boy here. Not strictly standard practice yet, but it was that or nothing. Oxygen had no effect on him and all his symptoms pointed to one thing. *Heroin overdose.* Accidental, I assumed. Since the beginning of the war, we've had an exponential increase in the number of deaths by overdose, it's becoming an epidemic, here in New York City more than most places. I imagine something is driving this problem, criminals selling it on the black-market and taking advantage of desperate addicts, I'd say, but that's not my area of expertise." He looked pointedly at the young officer, who cleared his throat and jotted something down in his book. "In any case, the problem is getting worse. We've been working on this antidote in our labs and can only try to save people from their own stupidity." He looked over his shoulder at the closed recovery room door. When he spoke again, his voice was less abrasive. "Of course, in this case, as he's just a small child, it's clearly accidental. At least that's what the girl implied."

"Is that so, Miss?" the officer interjected, turning to Nancy, who held George's hand.

Nancy looked over at her mother, her eyes burning. The truth, that the heroin had been found in her own home, would have tipped an avalanche of enquiries, leading down the complicated involvement of child welfare agencies. Despite it, Betty didn't prompt Nancy to give anything but the truth. In her efforts to protect them from the evils of a world where Donny and his murderous empire reigned supreme, it was she, their own mother, who had delivered the most danger into their young lives. Whatever punishment lay ahead, Betty was willing to take it. As if she knew this, and perhaps she had heard it inside her own mind with the burgeoning gift of her mother's line, Nancy turned and spoke evenly to the officer, never dropping her gaze.

"We were playing in the park and found that bottle under the hedge," Nancy said. "Georgie thought it was sugar. He fell over and stopped breathing. It all happened so fast I didn't know what to do, so I brought him here. I'm sorry, Officer Hall, I was too frightened to tell you before."

Betty's eyes widened at her daughter's smooth lie. Despite herself, a flicker of pride flared in her chest. Nancy was indeed, true to her gifts and the curse she would carry with them. No doubt the child's head was swimming with questions and confusions. Her reality had already changed so much.

The officer snapped his notebook shut with chagrin.

"Well, that's all I need for now, then," he said, "now that your parents are here and the boy is recovering. There will be an investigation of course, and I'll need a copy of the boy's medical report."

"Well," the doctor growled, "you can tell your superiors that if we don't get this black-market heroin problem sorted out, there will be more deaths on the streets than they'll be able to handle. Addicts leaving drugs in parks for children to stumble across! This was a close call, but mark my words officer, there'll be more children at risk unless you find who's at the center of this epidemic and bring them to justice!"

Betty bit her lip. For the first time since she'd left Donny in the orphanage basement, she thought of him. He was alive, unfortunately so. But his empire had indeed fallen, at her own hand. His men were dead, his warehouse of stolen drugs and weapons now under the jurisdiction of the New York City Police Department, and his reputation irreparably broken. He was incriminated in the biggest scandal to hit the city in decades, and no amount of buying favors would get him off the hook this time. Besides, she had bankrupted him into the ground. She took a deep breath, desperately glad for Jacob's help in covering her trail. From here, it would be a matter of law and strategy to keep Donny behind bars. Violence was no longer needed. She caught Sam's eye, as he listened from his chair.

"I'm sure the NYPD will be able to assist you on that front, doctor," Betty said, as the young policeman scowled. "From what I've seen here, we have the finest officers we could ask for." She offered a grateful smile to the young man that had sat in frustrating silence with Nancy awaiting their arrival. "Nancy and I will bring a batch of freshly-baked cookies to your station on Monday, officer, to thank you for your trouble."

The policeman shifted uncomfortably. Apparently, Betty's usual charm didn't work so well when she was covered in blood and bruises.

"That won't be necessary, ma'am, I'm just doing my job," he said. He tucked his notebook into his pocket, tipped his hat, and left the room.

"What in the devil's name happened to you two, anyway?" the doctor asked, his brow furrowing at Betty and George's bloodied and disheveled appearance.

"An automobile accident," she explained. "We were in such a hurry to get to the children when we heard. Spun right over into the gutter. Hit a maple tree." The doctor raised an eyebrow but said nothing. Betty had lost all her knives to the bodies in the basement. She had no bag or personal effects on her, and nothing to indicate she had been involved in anything more sinister that evening than an accident on her way to the hospital, or that she had been anywhere but her own home before so. She was just a mother, albeit, a negligent one, who had allowed her children to play too long in the park after dark, where they had stumbled across the poison that brought them into dire straits. Such accidents, in the days of children's unrestrained freedom to play in the neighborhood streets until dinner time as they waited for mother's call, weren't unheard of.

Shaking his head, the doctor sighed. "You can go in, only you two for now. He's asleep and mustn't be disturbed. The nurse will be in to monitor him every fifteen minutes." The doctor left through the corridor.

💋

Hours later, after Nancy had been delivered to Mrs. Porter for safekeeping and an astonished, but determined Gladys Eubanks had been called in to the hospital to pick up her new charge, clucking over Sam like a mother hen as she shuffled him home, Betty and George sat quietly on either side of Georgie, holding his hands as he slept. He had awoken briefly, then returned to a deep sleep, still suffering the effects of the antidote.

Betty sang to him softly, smoothing the hair back from her little boy's forehead with her free hand.

> "Little Jitterbug, sweet dreams,
> You're in safe hands now, sweet pea,
> You're just a tiny tot, but soon you'll grow a lot,
> and the world will see you shine like a moon-
> beam – "

"Ten years, we've been married," George said quietly, "and I feel like I don't know you at all."

Betty looked up. Her eyes were glistening with tears.

"You know my heart, George, you've always known my heart, from the very first moment you met me."

"Have I?" He looked away. "I thought I did."

The air in the room crackled uncomfortably between them. The walls suddenly seemed much closer, the beeping of machines louder.

"You loved me from that first day, and I you," Betty said. "Even though I wasn't perfect. You knew I had a past. That there had been other – *people* – in my life before. And unhappiness. You knew I could never be entirely yours because of those memories. You didn't want to know. You were *happy* not knowing."

George looked up at her, his eyes shining with tears. "But I trusted you."

Betty nodded. "Yes, you did. And I took it for granted. I'm so sorry, George. It breaks me to know how much I've hurt you. I never meant to."

"I just don't understand how you got caught up in all of this. That orphanage, what I saw there – and I don't remember what happened before this blasted pain in my head and it riles me – " he gingerly touched the swollen lump on his forehead, which was now wrapped with gauze, " – but I'm not sure I even *want* to remember. It's beyond me, Betty. That's not the life for us."

"I don't want that life, I swear." Betty got to her feet and walked around the bed, falling to her knees beside him. "I never did. I only ever wanted a happy life, a safe life, for all of us."

Safe," George scoffed quietly. "Yes, well, that's me, alright. The safest ticket around." He stared, humiliated, past Georgie's sleeping face to the black wall beyond. "I'm not the man you want me to be, Jitterbug."

"But you are! You always were. But – I'll never be the perfect wife you want *me* to be, George. As desperately as I try, I'm beginning to wonder if there's any such thing."

For a moment there was silence. The second hand of a clock ticked by on the wall, the metronome broken only by the soft breathing of the child that lay in the bed beside them and the noise of the machines that monitored him. George rose, and stood dejectedly by the closed door.

"I don't remember how we got to that place, or what you did to get out of there, but I do remember something." He turned to look at Betty accusingly. "He kissed you. *Sergeant Jacob Lawrence.* He was never just an innocent childhood friend, was he? Or a good Samaritan that returned your lost bag that day."

Betty's ashamed silence spoke volumes.

"It's him, isn't it?" George said. "The one who - the one you ran away from?" George studied her face, searchingly. "The one who gave you Nancy." He closed his eyes, and Betty didn't need to read his mind to know what memory George had found. She had been honest with him about her daughter, from the very first day he'd come blustering into the drug-store to escape his flu, and fallen head-over-heels in love with her.

"I have an illegitimate child," Betty had warned him from behind the gleaming counter of perfumes and cosmetics, at barely eighteen years old herself. Although she'd be disappointed to lose the affection of the handsome young man who brought his optimism and adorable good humor to her counter, Betty held her heart at bay for the inevitable rejection she was accustomed to. This was not the first man to woo her since she'd run away to start her new life, only to then be appalled at her lack of moral character when they found out. To be a young woman, with no respectable family, with a bastard child of *"father unknown"*, was tantamount to social suicide.

It was a stigma, and burden, that Betty willingly carried. By the time George had met her, Susie, now Betty, had already spent two years working her fingers to the bone to protect her dearest treasure. The baby daughter she had escaped her old life for, to save from it.

"She's an absolute little doll, mind you," Betty had said kindly, "but to love me is to love her as well, Mr. Jones. And I don't care what any man thinks of me for it." She'd lifted her chin proudly and packaged up his medicine in a brown paper bag. George had stood there, clearly taken back, then left the store, only to stand in the snow and stare in at her through the sleet-covered windows until his nose had turned quite blue and he was shaking with cold. To the astonishment of the other counter girls, he had finally come back in, bedraggled and sneezing and fallen directly to his knee with a look on his face of earnest determination.

"Then I have no choice," George had replied, sniffling into his handkerchief. "I'll simply have to love you both equally. Because you're the prettiest girl I've ever seen, and gosh darn-it, I'm not sure I'll ever forgive myself if I can't tell you so, every day for the rest of my life!"

And love them he had.

He'd been the father to Nancy that Betty had always dreamed she might one day have, and when George Junior was born four years later, her husband's pride had seemed to have given him wings. If not for Betty's past, and the ghosts that plagued her every waking moment, life would have been idyllic.

But those ghosts had never left her. And Betty's own memories held demons that no amount of perfume or bath-salts could drown.

Particularly the memory of that fateful night when she had finally taken her freedom, only sixteen years old as she stood over her father as he lay dead on the kitchen floor.

A knife hard in his chest.

Blood on her hands.

Revenge burning in her heart.

The smell of gasoline trailed through the house.

The cold comfort of the silver box held tight in her arm as she lit a match.

The blazing inferno of her childhood home behind her.

The warmth of her own small hand supporting her pregnant belly as she walked away.

Her eyes like steel as Susie looked ahead, to a new life. A safe life. A *perfect* life.

With ghosts still fading from her mind, Betty wiped away a

tear. The clock kept ticking. Georgie's soft breath seemed to keep the beat of her heart in check.

"I wasn't running from Jacob, George" she said. "I was running from my past. Jake was the only part of my life that was good and kind. He was the only love I had. But there was simply no way he could be part of my future. That wasn't his fault. Even at sixteen I knew that."

"Does he know about her?" George asked.

"No. He never knew."

For a while they sat in silence. *Breathing. Watching.* Each lost in their own thoughts.

"You'd be better off with him, Betty," George said finally, finding her through some unfathomable fog. "I think he knows you. The real you."

Betty walked over and took George's face in her hands.

"Then you'll just have to get to know me too, George. The *real* me."

George looked at his wife, a spark of hope flickering behind his tired eyes.

"I made my choice a long time ago," Betty said. "We're yours now, George. We're a family."

💋

"I won't bother asking how you know where I live," Jacob grinned, as he opened his front door to find Betty on the stoop. His arm was in a sling.

"A wise decision," she smiled, following him inside, glancing surreptitiously at the quiet street before doing so. Even in the modern times of 1943, it wasn't considered entirely appropriate for a lady to enter a bachelor's house alone. Still, it couldn't be helped. There were important things to discuss.

Jacob's apartment was small and neat, with minimal furniture and comforts.

"You need a woman's touch here, Jake," Betty smiled. "I'm not sure this vase has seen a spot of polish in its life."

"You know me, all work, no play," Jacob said. A touch of regret marred his voice. He shifted some papers and gestured to a couch for Betty to sit, then offered her some tea.

"No, thank you, I can't stay long," she replied, as he sat down opposite. Betty offered a kind smile. "How is she?"

"Adina?"

"Yes."

Jacob sighed, leaning back with his good arm against the armrest, his hand supporting his chin.

"Managing," he said. "They're considering a plea bargain. She'll give them everything she's got on Donny and she won't do time for her part."

"Good." For a moment, Betty considered. "He'll try to stop her, you know," Betty said, darkly. "He still has connections, inside and out. As a key witness, she's not safe."

"I'll protect her."

"As will I."

There was a moment of comfortable silence as Betty picked some lint from the cotton cushion beside her.

"And you?" she finally asked. "Can you forgive what she did?"

"I don't know. I can forgive her indiscretion with Brandway, although I can't for the life of me understand what she saw in him. But, as for the affair itself, well, who am I to hold that against her? It was before my time and we all have our skeletons in the closet." He offered a tight smile, "Don't we?"

"Some of us more than others, I think."

Jacob nodded, sadly. "But still, she was a fool to let Donny blackmail her. Photographs or not, surely her reputation, or her father's, was not worth the sacrifice and torment she went through."

"A young woman's reputation is everything, Jake."

"I would never have let it go so far."

"You're a man. You would never have been judged to begin with."

Another moment of silence.

"I should have known," Betty said, ruefully. "If only I'd read her thoughts at the ball. It was so clear that something was wrong."

"I told you not to."

"I should have anyway. You know, my mother always said it was unladylike to impose on another person's thoughts. I try not to unless I can't help it. Sometimes though... "

"Mmm. You know if I had your talent my job would be a lot easier."

Betty laughed. "But your life would be a whole lot harder."

"That's true," Jacob smirked. "Less complications. I'm a simple man with simple tastes."

"Hardly," Betty laughed again.

"I'm going to Ima and Aba's for dinner tonight. They've invited Adina and her parents. Trying to show support for what they're going through, although I have to admit, my mother's opinion of her as the perfect 'beryeh' for me has severely dimmed since she found out about this entire mess. Adina's own parents are devastated, of course. Barely speaking to her, from what I hear. It will take a long time to move past a scandal like this. If they ever do."

"And your father?" Betty asked. As a young girl, she had always found Abraham Lawrence to be a kind man, the sort of father she wished for herself as her own brought the stench of violence and alcohol home each night after taking care of Donny's business.

"Aba? He believes that good people make mistakes," Jacob sighed. "I don't think anything could surprise him anymore, after his years on the force. He's just glad I got out of that basement with only a bullet to the arm."

"And I'm the one that put you in there," Betty paled, imagining an outcome very different to that which had come to pass. Jacob, George, Sam, even Georgie could have died at her own hand. Guilt weighed heavily in her heart. "Does Aba know about me?" she asked. "I wouldn't blame you if you told him and I really don't mind. In some ways, it might be nice to stop hiding. From some people, at least."

"Nice, but dangerous. Especially now that Donny knows. No, I'd rather keep it quiet for now. Donny hasn't mentioned you yet, but I don't doubt he's working on some diabolical plan from his cell. I don't think we've seen the last of him, but at least we have a reprieve – for now. Besides, Aba knows enough to know you never really died, for me, at least. I think his nerves need a break. He was so keen on me courting Adina, too. It's hard to believe it's only been a few months since I met her. It seems like a lifetime ago."

"I've rather scuttled your life, Jake. I *am* sorry."

"I know." Jacob looked critically at Betty. "You know I'm not sure you ever needed my help though anyway," he said. "With Donny. You certainly never wanted it. So, *why*? Why did you leave that trail of *Avon Calling* cards for me to trace? You had to know I'd find you eventually."

"Well, I needed to return Donny's contraband to the authorities somehow," Betty said.

"Any officer could have picked them up and dealt with them."

"You were already working on the military heists."

"And Sergeant Frakes was working on that case before I was appointed. You never contacted him with the cards. You said yourself, you dumped those early crates."

A slight smile twisted on Betty's lips.

"You wanted me to find you, Susie."

"Betty."

"Sorry. *Betty.*"

Betty sighed heavily. There was no point beating around the bush. It was *time*.

"I needed you to know what I was doing," she began, uncertainly, "in case it all went horribly wrong. I mean, if something happened to me and – well, I just thought you deserved to know. About my family. *Your family* – as well, I suppose. You have every right to know, Jacob and I'm just sorry I could never tell you before. It was far too dangerous."

"My family? What do they have to do with – ?"

"No, I don't mean *your* family. I mean – " Betty took a deep breath. "Our family. *Nancy*." Betty's dark blue eyes dropped. Her hands twisted nervously in her lap and her heart skipped a beat. For twelve long years, she'd held the truth of Nancy's birthright locked away so tightly inside, she felt as though she might explode simply saying it out loud. But now that she had to tell him, she couldn't find the words.

"*Nancy?*" he said. "What do you – ?" The confusion in Jacob's eyes drifted into something else, a memory far away. From another time. Another life. And Betty remembered too.

He was all of seventeen, smashing his boxing rounds into a dusty punching bag that hung in the community hall, his trainer shouting instructions from behind. Nearby, two dozen teenage boys paced their routines under the watchful eye of a strong-jawed cornerman.

With sweat stinging his eyes, Jacob looked up to the clock on the wall. *Fifteen minutes left.* The thought of escaping the fetid, stale air of the hall imbued him with enthusiasm, and he punched the bag with renewed effort.

Shouts and cheers suddenly hailed throughout the large room. Jacob spun around, catching his bag in one arm as it rebounded toward him. Down below, a sparring match between a new recruit and a well-known trouble-maker had turned into a brawl. Spit, blood and gangly limbs were tangled in a mess on the wooden floor of the hall.

"Hey, you two! Knock it off!" Jacob's trainer jumped the ring ropes and pushed his way through the cheering crowd of boys to pull them apart.

Glad for the moment of relief, Jacob wiped his brow with the back of his glove and looked out of the dirty window ahead of him. He grinned and waved. As always, Susie was watching from the opposite side of the road, perched outside the general store, waiting for him to finish. She waved back at him with a smile that seemed to suck the foul air from his lungs and fill them with a cool breeze instead.

Jacob snuck a look behind him to his trainer, but the man was still preoccupied rebuking the boys. He pulled off his glove and held up his hand, fingers wide, three times to let her know he was nearly done. *Fifteen minutes.* He couldn't stand the boxing lessons that his father had insisted he take. If it weren't for the fact that after each session, he taught all he had learned to Susie, he would have asked to give it up already.

At first, she'd been awkward and uncoordinated, unsure how to direct the speed and strength that seemed to be growing inside her week by week. They spent hours after school down by the docks practicing, with Jacob recounting all of the lessons he was afforded as the promising eldest son of a police sergeant. Lessons that only boys were invited to join. Boxing, fencing, gymnastics, even the karate lessons he took at the scout hall with Mr. Iwate, the greengrocer. And Susie absorbed them all as if her life depended on it. She didn't just memorize the moves; she was *good* at them. For fun, as they talked afterward, Jacob and Susie always played flick-knives too, hitting chalk targets on empty grain barrels left down by the water. She was a crack-shot.

Using Jacob's old gloves, Susie had already progressed far beyond his own skill in boxing. A dozen stolen pillows had exploded in a blizzard of duck down in the alley before Jacob realized Susie's strikes were much harder than his own. For a time, he wouldn't admit that his pride was bruised by how quickly a girl had out-skilled him. There was no competition. But then again, Susie wasn't just any girl.

She was faster and stronger than any boy in his classes. As she learned the strategies to direct her movements, so Jacob had finally realized that she still needed him despite her strength, as an instructor and encouraging friend. After all, it was Roy, Susie's father, that she was really fighting against in her heart, and Jacob *wanted* her to win that fight.

So, he kept up with his own lessons to help her learn. It was nearly three years since they'd begun training. Susie now moved with the fluidity of a ballet dancer and an unnatural speed that almost seemed like precognition, which of course, Jacob had come to realize over time, it was. She was almost unstoppable.

Jacob beat the next five minutes half-heartedly into his punching bag willing the time to pass quickly. With one eye on Susie out of the window, and the other on the trainer who was now berating the scrapping boys in the nearby storage room, he saw Susie's smile drop. A loud catcall had caught her attention. Someone was approaching her.

Instantly, Jacob's shackles raised. His ears grew red as he imagined some sheik schoolboys trying to sweeten her up while he was stuck in his lessons, watching from afar. *They'll try to take advantage of her,* Jacob told himself, *drop her a line and try it on.* A swell of jealousy hit him. The part of his brain that knew Susie could read any boy's intentions better than they could them- selves, and the knowledge that she could easily defend herself if she needed to, refused to be acknowledged. It wasn't the first time that she'd caught the attention of admirers. In fact, it happened far too often. The truth was, that every day saw Susie grow prettier and more desirable. Even with her well-worn dresses and plain, old shoes, she was undeniably attractive.

Susie's shiny eyes and quick mouth revealed a lively mind, and although she never seemed interested in letting any of the boys court her, she had a curious ability to send them on their way without bruising their egos as so many other girls did. Deep down, Jacob could no longer lie to himself that it was simply brotherly protection that kept his nerves on edge.

He was *in love* with her.

It had hit him two years ago, before he even understood what it truly was. That first, bone-crushing, unrelenting, all-consuming ache that takes hold of a young person's heart and never quite leaves it again. As each day passed, it grew stronger and he, more protective of her. Jacob pushed his feelings as far from his conscious mind as he could, terrified Susie would read them and feel betrayed. After all, Jacob was her best friend, her only *real* friend, and the only person she could trust. He couldn't bear the thought of losing her if she didn't feel the same.

As the catcallers came properly into view, Jacob's stomach flipped. But not for the reason he'd anticipated. They weren't local cats trying to sweeten her up as he'd first thought. The opposite in fact. Susie's older cousin Marco and his stocky cohorts, Ernie and Mack, were well known bullies in the neighborhood. Unlike the other boys, they loved to torment her.

Without warning, Marco shoved Susie backward, hard. She crashed onto the concrete pavement.

"Hey!" Jacob yelled. A few boys training in the hall stopped to stare at him, but outside, Marco and his thugs didn't hear. Susie did though. She scrambled to her feet, stony faced and red. Her arm was scraped and bleeding. She glanced across the road and through the window, directly into Jacob's eyes and shook her head minutely. A warning.

"But –!"

She glared at Jacob, then turned away from him. Theirs was a hidden friendship, even from her own family. *Especially*, from her own family.

Jacob clutched the punching bag, seething.

Marco was saying something to her, a smarmy look on his face. He gestured up the road and shoved a packet into her hands. Quickly, Susie shoved the packet into her satchel. He pushed her once more in the direction he'd pointed, then turned away and left, laughing and jostling his friends.

Susie looked back across to Jacob. He didn't need an explanation. Jacob knew what this was. A *job* from her father. She offered a humiliated wave and walked away. There would be no training tonight.

Jacob slammed the bag with every ounce of anger inside him and it swung violently on its hook. He smashed it again and again as it rebounded, beating his hatred and frustration into every inch of the canvas. His ears burned and his heart pounded. The sweat that had stung his eyes, only minutes before, now dripped unheeded. His whole body was aching for justice.

Despite her abilities, Susie still let her father beat her and use her as a drug mule. She still let her cousins torment her into submission. And she *still* let someone else, that unnamed man she worked for each night, keep her tethered to the life of crime and violence she so desperately hated. It was stupid. It wasn't fair. And there was absolutely nothing he could do about it.

"Good form, Lawrence!" barked his trainer, springing back into the ring. "That's what I like to see, no pulling punches. Give me five more minutes of that!"

***

It was the following day, after school, that Jacob had managed to track Susie down at the docks. It was an easy guess to find her there, at least for him. This was their training ground, a largely ignored spot on the edge of the Hudson which had become a jumble of timber cast-offs and decaying barrels, old fishing line and concrete pilons rising from the water like ugly birds. Behind, derelict warehouses served as storage areas for the freighters whose cargo spilled over from the newer modern buildings upriver. By day, only the poorest fishermen moored here and on rainy afternoons, the dim warehouses made the perfect place to practice fighting. Now, at dusk, it was deserted. Except, of course, for Susie.

She was sitting alone outside on the dock, flicking knives. A crude target had been chalked onto an empty mooring post. It had a man's face.

"Why do you let them do that?" Jacob growled, plonking himself down on to the concrete beside her. "You could beat the blazes out of those fat-heads if you wanted to. You're dead stronger than any boy, and faster with a punch. Teach them a lesson, or at least, let me do it!"

Susie cocked her head to the side, seriously. "Can you imagine what would happen if Pop found out how strong I was? Can you imagine what he'd make me do? Or, that *man* he works for –"

"*Who is –?*"

"You know I can't tell you," Susie muttered, angrily. "It would only put you in danger, Jake, especially with your Aba being who he is. If they even knew we were *friends –*"

"But this is stupid."

"I can't fight back," she said, definitively. "You know *he* already uses me to read the minds of the filthy criminals that work for him. Not to mention the poor sods that end up on the wrong side of them." Susie shuddered. "*He* takes my gift and turns it into something cruel and terrible. Something I'm ashamed of. What do you think he'd make me do if he knew how strong I was, or how well I could fight?" She looked expectantly at Jacob, who just scowled back. "He'd use it, that's what. He'd turn me into something that he could hurt people with. My body wouldn't be my own anymore. It would be *his*, just like everything else." She looked away, staring across to the dirty water through the eyes of someone far older than her fifteen years. "So, I can never let them find out."

"Surely they'll guess though, at some point? You're not exactly... an *ordinary* girl." Jacob's face flushed with pink.

"They've got no reason to suspect me, as long as I don't fight back. Mom never had this gift, the strength or the speed, or the, *whatever* it is that I can do. So, they aren't expecting it from me, either. Just the mind-reading. And it's years too late to keep that a secret."

"Well, how long are you going to put up with them treating you like rubbish?"

"Not forever. Just, as long as it takes."

Jacob's eyes narrowed, critically. "What does that mean?"

Susie just shrugged, her lips tight.

He sighed and let his eyes follow Susie's out to the Hudson. "Well, when you're ready to fight back, let me know. I'll be glad to give that cousin of yours a box around the ears. Dirty, rotten git that he is." Jacob nudged her shoulder and was pleased to see her frown drop slightly.

There was a pause in conversation as they sat, both lost in their own thoughts, watching the dark tide draw away from its concrete pilons, leaving a gungy stain where it had been.

"I *want* to be an ordinary girl, you know," Susie said, quietly. "A *normal* girl. With a nice house, one day, and some pretty things – not lots of things – " she quickly quantified, "just a few things. Like, lace curtains and maybe a red dress with fancy shoes. The things other girls have. Ordinary, *pretty* girls."

Jacob raised an eyebrow. *Pretty girls?* Susie rarely spoke like this, even to him. She was proud, never indulging herself in resentment toward the other girls at school for having what she so clearly did not. Jacob looked at her, frowning. *Besides, how could she be so blind?* Shabby clothes and scuffed shoes couldn't hide what the world saw every day she stepped out of her door.

Did she really have no idea? He suddenly wished she *would* read his mind for once, if only to save him having to speak the words aloud. His skin tingled and he rubbed the back of his neck. Hesitatingly, Jacob found his voice, despite himself.

"You'll never be ordinary, Susie," he muttered, now staring intently at his own hands. "Or even *pretty* –"

"Gee, thanks –"

"– because you're already the most beautiful girl in New York City. And you don't need fancy dresses or shoes to show it. Everyone can see. All the boys at school are keen for you, and Edwardo, the grocer's son, and Jimmy at the pier. And it's not just the boys, either. Grown men call out as you pass. You don't even seem to notice."

Susie looked up at him, her eyes unreadable. "And do you – *notice?*"

"The other boys looking at you?" Jacob's face burned. He ran his hand through his hair self-consciously. There wasn't a part of his body that didn't notice the way other boys puffed up as she walked by, boasting and dropping lines in her wake. "Of course I do," Jacob scowled. "And I want to knock their blocks off!"

Susie tipped her head, amused.

"Not just – I mean to say – well, they're just preening heels, aren't they?" Jacob said. "I mean none of them *really* know you. Not like I do."

"So, if they *really* knew me they wouldn't try?"

"That's not what I mean," Jacob said, his face growing redder. When he realized Susie was smirking at him, he glared. "You're just trying to razz me up."

"Sorry, Jake. I can't believe you think I'd take notice of any of them though," she said smiling, "When I have you."

"You'll always have me," he promised.

"I know that." Susie looked away, out at the water again.

Jacob watched her. Her dark blue eyes seemed to suddenly lose their humor. Now, they reflected the tempestuous mood of the river as it caught the late North-Westerly wind. Her brow was furrowed, imperfecting the youthful lines of her face. Susie's shoulder-length hair, whipping in the breeze, was rolled off her forehead and pinned on one side, falling away behind her, as was the latest fashion. Shabby clothes and scuffed shoes had never stopped Susie looking as put-together as those girls in her glossy magazines. But Jacob knew the haunted look that so often stole her smile could never be rid of entirely. He wished, more than anything, he could save her from it.

Susie turned back to him and forced a smile. Jacob mustered all of his courage.

"Susie-Pocket?"

"Yeah?"

"I need you to know something," he said, his heart pounding. "It's just that, well, we've known each other forever, it seems like, and I understand if you think of me like a – a *brother* – or something, because you know you're my best friend –"

"You're my best friend too, Jake –"

"But you should know, that even though we've never *gone steady* or anything," Jacob paused, his voice catching in his throat. *Was he about to ruin everything by saying it aloud?* "I just –" he looked away again, feeling hopelessly out of his depth. "I just want you know that I adore you. Actually, Susie, I *love* –"

But before he could finish, the words were stolen from his mouth. Susie's lips, warm and sweet and trembling, found his own. Whatever misgivings had been in his mind before, dissolved. With a sigh, Jacob fell into her kiss, and returned it, enthusiastically, until all other thoughts were gone too. It was as if no one else existed.

"I love you, too, Jake," Susie said. No other words were needed. And she kissed him again.

The moment stretched into minutes. The ache only seemed to grow. Their young hands found one another, away from the cold concrete beneath them. The smell of salt and wet, rotting timber seemed to swell, and they fell back, lying together in the jumble of discarded crates and barrels. Hidden from view, the distant rumble of trains and automobiles snaking their way into the city frayed at the edges of their thoughts, then disappeared, leaving only the quiet lapping of water behind, as the great river licked itself away from the dock and out toward the sea.

Jacob's fingers sparked with fire. This love, this *need* had been growing inside him for so many months. His fingertips found her face. Her hands. Her waist. And Susie seemed to fear nothing. She wrapped herself around him on the cold concrete until the heat of their bodies broke through the thin fabric they wore.

The night grew cold around them and the deserted dock overhung with the specters of empty buildings and discarded crates and barrels. Long shadows cocooned their moving form until the darkening sky matched the inky black of the pilons and the tide had drawn out as far as it could go. This was the place they had spent years learning to fight together, suddenly softened by the promise of love.

Their passion was not quick to burn out, but rather, had been tempered by years of silently watching the other grow into their body. Her kiss was shaped by years of learning to trust the only friendship that brought her happiness. His touch embodied months of peeling away his own fears to inspire the courage that would shape both their adulthoods, looming so close.

Muffled cries and kisses rose and fell. Fingers entwined, clasped and broke away again. And the dark night kept their secret safe.

"I promise I'll look after you," Jacob said, raising his head from her chest as they lay breathing in the dark. "One day, you'll have everything you want. Dresses and lace curtains and – we'll get married. When we're older and we've finished school. You'll have a *real* family – my family. Aba and Ima will love you too."

Susie's face paled and the radiant smile that had been there only seconds before dropped away. The thought of Jacob's parents, despite their enduring kindness to a poor girl from a violent, godless home their son befriended, shattered the façade of his promises.

Abraham and Golda Lawrence were proud and traditional in their beliefs, and no one but a Jewish girl of outstanding moralities would be acceptable as a wife for their first-born. Jacob carried their pride like a mantle. As the eldest, he was expected to carry on the family name, their hard-earned social standing and precious traditions and his father's profession as one-day commissioner of the New York City Police Force.

"They'd never let you marry me," Susie said, tears slipping down her face. "I'm not the right kind of girl. I'm not *their* kind."

Jacob kissed her tears away, tracing the salty lines with his lips.

"You're *my* kind," he said, earnestly. "And in a few years, I'll be a police officer, and I'll be able to keep you safe from your father. From *them*."

"They'll never let me go, Jake. Not while I'm alive. I'm too valuable to them."

"You'll be married to me. They'll have to."

"But they won't. They'd kill you first."

"We'll figure it out," Jacob growled under his breath. "Besides, we have years until then."

Years.

But once Susie realized what it was, that nausea that kept finding her in the morning and night, the tiredness that plagued her as she tried to scratch out her homework after being dropped back from Donny's warehouse at midnight, the tenderness of her body and the aching of her stretching belly, there was only one choice she could make.

To leave.

Disappear.

Before her weakness showed.

Before they used it against her.

If her father, Roy, found out she was pregnant, Susie knew that he would track Jacob down and kill him. She was too valuable to lose. Susie was Roy's only insurance against Donny turning on him and he had threatened her too many times, for Susie to be naïve. Roy may have been stupid, but he was violent and unpredictable. A hired thug. A killer. And Susie was his *property.*

She was left with no choice.

Susie had to rid herself of her father before he recognized the child within her.

She had to rid herself of Donny and his insidious web of cruelty and manipulation.

Because if she stayed, her baby wouldn't be safe. Donny already knew that Susie's gift had passed down from her mother, Ethyl, to her. He would recognize the potential Susie's baby held, as insurance against her fighting back, and eventually, as another weapon in his own arsenal. Donny was a patient man. He would wait. Then use them both.

And Susie could never allow him such an advantage.

No.

She had no choice.

Susie needed to *die.*

Only then, would she be free.

Only then, would Jacob be safe.

Only then would her baby have a chance to live an *ordinary* life.

A happy life.

And so, with nothing but her silver box, her mother's locket and a kitchen knife, Susie made her first hit.

She lit a match.

She walked away.

And Betty began.

"She's mine?" Jacob whispered in disbelief.

"Yes."

"That's why you ran away, after –"

"Yes."

Jacob sat in stunned silence.

"To protect her from Donny?"

"And to protect you from my father. He would have killed you, Jake. Like he killed so many others. I loved you both too much to stay."

For the longest time, Jacob stared at the sitting room window, not seeing past the lace curtains that hung there.

"I just - I don't know what to say." His face was pale and his hands were trembling. "I would have looked after you, and her - my - *our* - Nancy. But I - I never even had the chance."

"I know you would have." Tears stung Betty's eyes at the heartbreak on his face. "But they would never have given you that chance, Jake. My father and Donny - they would have had you killed before they let me live a normal life with you. I was too important in their game to relinquish and as the son of such a high-ranking police officer, you weren't someone they could ever have brought into their insidious business to make us both comply." The very thought of Jacob becoming caught in Donny's web made the bile rise to the back of Betty's throat. "Your father made you untouchable. He was one of the few people who would never have fallen under Donny's spell, he couldn't be blackmailed or bought. He was irreproachable, both in his work and his personal life. So your Aba was too dangerous to have close, and that means they could never use you, either. You were all too *good*, Jake. Imagine the damage I might have caused Donny if I got too close to you - to your father. What a threat that might have been to him. They would have murdered you, rather than lose me to your family."

"They ruined us. Every chance we might have had of happiness together!" Jacob got to his feet and paced the small sitting room. "We could have taken him down, years ago! Had a life together!"

"We were just kids, Jake. Still in school. We could never have escaped Donny's clutches alive. It's taken me years to break his empire, you know that. And years for you to be in a position with the police force where you finally have the power to see it through." Betty shook her head sadly. "There was no other way, don't you see?"

"But I - "

"No Jake," Betty said getting to her feet. She led him back to the couch, where he sat, angry and pale, staring at his hands. "There was *nothing* you could have done. I had to leave, with our unborn child before they found out she existed, and make it seem to them as if I could never return. I had to die, in everybody's eyes. It was the only safe way that you both could live."

He looked up at her. Sadness had replaced the anger, but regret still lingered. Perhaps it would never fade.

After a long minute of silence, he spoke. "I think I finally understand," he said. "And I'll be doing everything I can to make sure that man never sees the outside of his jail cell again. But - I'm just so sorry you were alone."

"Only to begin with," Betty smiled, gently. "George has been a wonderful husband."

"Yes." Jacob swallowed hard. "I'm grateful for that. He's a good man. Does he – know about me?"

"He does now."

"And Nancy?"

"No. In time, though, if you want her to."

"I see. I think – I need some time myself. To think about all of this. To get my head straight."

"Of course you do. You know where to find me when you're ready." Betty stood up with her handbag. She knew when he was ready, that he would have more questions. But now, there was a lifetime ahead to answer them.

"Wait," Jacob said, getting to his feet. "Before you go. There was a reason I came to see you at your house that night. I stole this –" He strode out of the room, and Betty heard a timber drawer slide open and then shut again. A second later, Jacob returned with a folder in his good hand. On the front was the insignia of the U.S. military. A neat, hand-written name was below it. Her own name. Jacob passed her the folder.

"It was on the desk of a high-ranking official at City Hall. They're using the Governor's Room as a base for operations during the war – classified, of course. But this," he flicked the folder, "has been read by someone very high up in the chain of command. No one saw me take it, but I assume it's not the only copy."

Betty flipped it open. Inside was a monochrome photograph of herself, taken from a distance, atop a single sheet of typed paper. Underneath was a dossier.

BETTY JONES (Mrs)
Current residence: Whitestone, New York.
Of unknown origin. Approx. 28 years old.
Unusual and extraordinary speed, agility.
Unnatural strength.
UNDER SURVEILLANCE.
Implicated in Grandville Bank Robbery, Military Heists. Possible connections to Chinese Triad, Russian Bratva and Five Points Gangs. Potential underworld figure. Unknown allegiance. Mrs. Jones has significant influence on local informers.
Possible connections to NYPD law enforcement.
HIGH SECURITY RISK.

"You're being watched," Jacob said, grimly. "Closely."

"So it seems." Betty sighed and handed the file back to Jacob. "To be honest, I'm not surprised, although I tried my hardest to cover my tracks. I've been killing people for so long now –"

"Well not anymore," Jacob warned. "Now you play it safe. Let me take care of Donny from here. *Legally.*"

"It says *'Possible connections to NYPD law enforcement,'* Jake. It seems they're watching you too."

"Apparently so."

"Well then, I suppose this will keep me on my toes. Don't worry, I'll figure out who's watching us." Betty winked. "You know I like to keep busy."

She turned to leave. "Thanks, Jake. For – *everything.*"

"Always."

Jacob opened the door and Betty walked out. She turned back at the threshold and smiled.

"Adina will love it, by the way."

"Love what?"

"The lapel watch hidden in your desk drawer. With the little bow. Practical *and* fashionable," she winked. Jacob shook his head, grinning.

"Keep out of my head."

Betty laughed. "Almost always."

As Betty rode the elevator to the sixth floor of an elegant New York City building, she took a deep breath and smiled. It was familiar and thrilling, all at once. She'd once followed her spark of passion and independence to the revolving glass doors and found within it the spark which inspired her new calling in life. Her world had flourished since that day.

She wasn't entirely sure why she had been called into the Avon head office, and hoped it wasn't due to the unfortunate return of a number of cosmetics she'd sold to Mrs. Clara Belvedere the week before. Admittedly, Betty had been rather preoccupied during her visit, planning Donny's imminent murder at the time. Moreover, the poor woman had come down with a nasty case of hives that had changed her skin tone quite drastically. After picking up the refunded cosmetics and offering a very cranky Mrs. Belvedere a jar of home-pickled beets in apology, Betty had written to her superiors explaining the unfortunate situation. Minus the homicidal distraction, of course.

Betty stepped out of the elevator into an ivory waiting room.

"Welcome, Mrs. Jones," greeted a stylish young receptionist with a blonde up-do.

"Hello, Margaret, dear. My, I do love that eyeshadow on you today!" Betty trilled. "Forget-me-not blue, am I correct? With a touch of frost?"

"You are indeed! I don't think anyone knows our latest catalog as well as you do."

"Well, that shade suits you just beautifully, Margaret. You really should convince them to take your photographs for next season's catalog, you're an absolute dish, darling."

"Oh, I could never!" the girl blushed.

"Well, I'll suggest it myself," Betty winked. "We can't keep a beauty like you hidden behind a telephone, all day." She settled herself with the latest copy of *Vogue*, as a red-faced Margaret busied herself with a ledger, barely containing the smile on her face.

After a few minutes, a sharp buzzer sounded. Margaret sidestepped a long vase of pink tulips on a stand beside her counter and held her arm out graciously toward an office door.

"Mrs. Birchman will see you now."

Betty followed Margaret into a bright, crisp boardroom. The tasteful décor and large, printed product displays paid homage to the modest beginnings of the Avon dynasty before the turn of the last century, to modern times, an icon of women's empowerment and self-sufficiency. Painted advertisements boldly claimed their place in the evolving history of the United States women's movement.

"Our Pledge to Loveliness, since 1886."

"We support our suffragettes – Votes for Women!"

"Enchanting perfection that's kind to your purse - Good House-keeping Approved!"

"The Fair and the Brave – join The American Red Cross effort today!"

As the door shut behind her, a hearty round of applause came from a dozen ladies standing around the table. Betty recognized all of them. A handful of corporate administrators and sales staff were beaming at her, along with local representatives from her own district, including Fannie-May, Dotty Morris, Toula Apostolou and Mrs. Gladys Eubanks, who was clapping most enthusiastically of all. The table had been laid with an arrangement of crumb cakes, sweet biscuits and pots of tea, each sitting on a starched white doily. Given wartime rationing, it was an impressive spread.

"Goodness me, what's all this?" Betty cried with delight.

"A celebration for you, Betty," said Gladys, stepping forward to embrace her. Betty gave her a meaningful look.

"And how's Sam?" she whispered as she kissed Gladys' cheek.

"Perfectly well and an absolute delight. I've written to my dear Henry to explain the boys' predicament. He has a few days leave before he ships out, and well, as we were never blessed with our own children, we've decided to adopt the lad. Sergeant Lawrence is pushing all the paperwork through for me with the Sisters." Gladys's eyes were shining with tears.

"Henry says he'll feel better knowing I'm not alone while he's off fighting."

"That's wonderful, Gladys," Betty said, truly overjoyed. With just a flicker of suggestion and a little mind-reading to make sure her intuition was flying true, she'd managed to spark the perfect outcome to both parties' privations. Sam had a home, and Gladys a new purpose.

Standing behind the director's chair, a copper-haired woman held up her hands in an attempt to quiet the room.

"Mrs. Jones," the woman said, in a voice loud enough to carry over the trailing applause, "we must congratulate you on your recent efforts. You have not only surpassed your own sales record this month, but made this season your highest ever, as well as lending your support to numerous new recruits in their efforts to learn our range and practices. You really are an asset to us, dear." She stepped forward, lifting a small porcelain statue of a lady in Victorian Dress from the table and continuing around the other women to pass it to Betty. The statue was exquisitely hand-painted with gold embellishments, complete with parasol and handbag. "In honor of our very first Avon Representative," the woman continued, "we present to you, the Mrs. PFE Albee Avon Sales Award for 1943, for your dedication and outstanding sales!" She pinned a small gold brooch to the front of Betty's red coat dress. "We've put on this morning tea today, as a small gesture of our appreciation, in the hopes you'll continue your most excellent work!"

"Oh, Mrs. Wheeler," Betty said, blinking back tears. "I never imagined such a delightful surprise. For once I – well, I don't know what to say!" Betty dabbed at her cheeks with a lace handkerchief from her purse. Her heart was singing.

"We would have held this little ceremony earlier," Mrs. Wheeler said, "but we felt it rather inappropriate timing with your recent automobile accident and that unfortunate mishap with your son. I trust he is well again now?"

"Oh, yes, fully recovered, thank you."

"Well, I'm relieved to hear it. As much as we appreciate your devotion to your work, I do worry about keeping our ladies from their families when they're most needed. Our children are our most precious treasures, aren't they? A mother can spread herself too thin, especially in these busy, modern times. Do take some time out for yourself too, dear - we aren't superheroes, after all!"

Betty smiled in quiet delight at the unintended irony of her words. But, perhaps it *was* time to slow down a little. "I will, Mrs. Wheeler. But as we like to say, there's always time to take time off for beauty too!" The other representatives laughed.

The little party broke into cheerful clusters to enjoy the platters of food and tea that had been laid out on the boardroom table. Betty chatted to several of the ladies before noticing something was amiss. A tall, long-faced woman was nervously watching her, hands clasped, and wearing a somewhat forced smile on her face. It was one of the company's senior account managers, Maud Franklin. At that moment, she had the appearance of someone who had swallowed a rather large fly and was unsure whether to spit it out or pretend nothing was wrong. With a furtive look to the other women in the room, now occupied with cake and conversation, she stepped over and touched Betty's arm, then ushered her to the window so they wouldn't be overheard.

"Mrs. Jones," the woman began, apparently having decided to come out with it. Betty bit her tongue and fixed a disarmingly naïve smile on her face. Betty knew that Maud Franklin oversaw her personal sales ledger, and although the woman had no authority to question her clientele, she could read the woman's disfavor as clear as day. "I don't mean to cause any ill-will of course," Maud said, "especially with today's celebration and all, but as the supervisor managing your sales ledger for inventory purposes, well, I must bend your ear for just a moment." She hesitated. "I'll admit you have a certain flair for selling cosmetics, Mrs. Jones, but – " the woman exhaled in a sudden flurry of words, " – a monthly order of Heavenly Moisturizing Cream for a half-dozen bordello's in East Harlem? Heaven's above, my dear! That's not the kind of clientele we want to be associated with. What's next?" she lowered her voice to a hiss, "Greasers and dope fiends?" She leant back, her lips pursed in disapproval. "If Mrs. Wheeler knew about this – "

"Goodness, I didn't take you as one to discriminate against sporting girls, Mrs. Franklin," Betty said, in feigned surprise. "Surely all women deserve to look lovely, even those with less favorable working opportunities?"

"We are a proud company, Mrs. Jones, with quality products. Our customers expect a certain decorum and *savoir faire* by our representatives!"

Betty looked thoughtful for a moment. "Yes. You are quite right, of course. I've been awfully remiss."

Maud stepped back, looking slightly mollified. "Well, I'm glad you see my point of – "

"You've inspired me, Mrs. Franklin," Betty interjected, beaming. "Given their difficult circumstances, I think they really do deserve a little more attention than most, a little *savoir faire* on my part, as you so eloquently put it. Perhaps I should offer these ladies a special discounted rate to accommodate their meagre wages. The Madam's take half every night, you know, and it's not always easy work, as you might imagine. I'm sure many of the women have little mouths at home to feed that could do with those savings. I'll discuss it with Mrs. Wheeler straight away, she's always had a charitable heart. I imagine that's why she's such a wonderful ambassador for our beloved company."

"Well, I'm not sure that's what I –" Maud stammered.

Betty leaned forward, conspiratorially. "Thank you so much, Mrs. Franklin, for your *délicatesse* in this matter. I'm so glad you brought it to my attention. What a thoughtful woman you are!"

Betty patted her on the arm in a bolstering show of affection. She inclined her head slightly before she stepped away. "One little thing though, as a fellow proud representative of our brand, I must give you a spot of advice. I don't mean to cause any *ill-will* though, of course –"

"Advice?" Maud repeated, astonished.

"Oh yes," Betty said, looking as sincere and contrite as she could. "You see, the foundation you're wearing is a shade too dark. You're a winter hue Mrs. Franklin, so you really must be sure not to overstate your complexion with the wrong blend. Try a crimson lipstick to brighten up your tone instead, it will detract from the many imperfections of your skin. I believe there's a lovely shade in our latest catalog."

Maud's mouth fell open.

"And one last thing, you might like to consider one of our own products for your scent, I'd recognize a *Dior* perfume anywhere." Betty flashed her a charming smile. "I think I'll have some of that lovely spice cake now, if you don't mind." Betty walked away, her head held high.

> "Love is the sweetest thing,
> Kiss me all through the spring,
> As the days grow longer and never end,
> We'll dance on a cloud, always together!"

Betty tucked the crisp white sheets expertly under Nancy's brand new mattress and sang gaily to the song piping through the radio. She was as light on her feet as ever. Georgie and Nancy's old mattresses had been finally retired to the junkyard. Without the thousands of dollars of stolen cash inside to bolster them, they'd been left somewhat deflated. Besides, she felt it was high time for some fresh new beginnings. Betty spun happily, tossing Nancy's pillow onto the bed and smoothing the covers, then picked up her daughters washing basket, sidestepping Figaro, who was curled up sleeping near the dresser. Dancing her way to the utility room, she tumbled the soiled clothes into the washing machine and set it on.

"Sponge cake, my darlings!" Betty called, whirling to the kitchen to pick up a platter of sweets and a jug of homemade lemonade. She stepped out onto the front porch, where George sat reading his newspaper, smoke from his pipe curling away into the breeze.

"Good gravy!" George exclaimed, folding his paper onto his lap. "Two days in a row?"

"Nancy made this one, darling. Icing and all. She made a roast for dinner, too. Isn't she clever? It was quite an adventure, wasn't it, Nancy, dear?" Betty winked at her daughter, who was sitting on the porch with little Georgie, playing marbles. Nancy grinned back.

"The best adventure," Nancy's reply came into Betty's mind. She hadn't opened her mouth.

"And more adventures to come, dear." Betty replied silently. *"Did you remember to save the waste fats for Mr. Timms, the butcher? The war office says they need them to make explosives. We must all do our part for the boys at the front."*

"I scraped them into the bucket, like you said," came Nancy's silent reply.

"Well done, sweetheart."

Since Betty had begun training her daughter to use the gifts she could no longer hold back, the girl's behavior had greatly settled. She was an avid student. Betty wondered if, one day, Nancy might surpass her own abilities.

George looked quizzically between the two of them at their extended silence, then raised an eyebrow.

"That's rather unfair, don't you think?" he said.

"I was just complimenting Nancy on her cooking skills,

darling," Betty said. "It's good practice for her." She shot a quick look at her youngest, but Georgie was happily distracted playing on the porch floor.

"Mmm," grumbled George, warily. Although he was now aware of Betty's mind-reading ability – her telepathic connection to Nancy after they escaped St. Augustine's was impossible to explain otherwise – he was still unnerved by it. Betty had since given him endless assurances that she not only had never read his own mind, but never intended to. Given their recent escapades, he'd taken it as well as could be expected.

Picking up her silver handled cake knife, Betty gently cut through Nancy's sponge. Her wrist movements were as inconspicuous as possible, endeavoring not to trigger any memories from George, whose amnesia of her *skills* with a blade seemed to have held – *so far*. It was inevitable that he would remember, of course, and Betty *was* ready to talk about it. She'd already explained the truth of her childhood, and family to him, and their reconciliation was progressing. It would take time though, and Betty didn't want to push him past his capacity to cope. The day would come soon enough.

"Georgie?"

"Cake!" the little boy cried, jumping to his feet in a scatter of marbles.

Betty served the cake and lemonade, humming happily along to the radio, which crackled through the open window. The newspaper, still folded on George's lap, caught her eye.

"What's this, dear?" she asked, leaning over him. She lifted the paper and unfolded it. A bold headline practically leapt off the front page.

"Disgraced Mayor Scrapped from Race."

A black and white photograph of Mayor Sutherland emblazoned the cover. He was bound in handcuffs on the steps of City Hall, surrounded by an entourage of reporters and police. A wave of satisfaction swept over Betty.

"Not quite the butter-and-egg man anymore, is he?" George said, darkly. "And to think, that all that time he was taking money from Pinzolo and turning a blind eye to what was going on with those orphans. He seemed such a decent fellow!"

"You just never know, do you?" Betty said.

"He'll be put away for a long time for this," George said. "Blackmail. Collusion. Misuse of public funds. When Pinzolo goes down, he'll take Sutherland right along with him."

"I certainly hope so," Betty sighed. "It will be a long and complicated road to get there though. I certainly hope Jacob is up for it."

George shifted uncomfortably. "Yes, well. I imagine if anyone can keep them locked up, it's him. He's clearly the right man for the job." He cleared his throat. "Look here, jitterbug, you'll get a tickle out of this." He leafed through a few pages to find what he was looking for. George held the paper up, showing her a short article. "That woman we met at your Charity Ball, Sutherland's wife, it seems her husband's public disgrace has put a bit of a fire under her. Given her a bit of gumption. She's starting a literacy group to help those orphans. Reading to them and such. What do you think of that?"

"I knew she had it in her!" Betty exclaimed, delighted. "Well, I'll just have to talk to the church social committee about raising some money to buy books for their school library. There are plenty of children there to read them!"

"What a swell idea," George said. "You've got such a big heart, jitterbug."

George lay the paper aside and Betty pulled up a chair beside him at the table, helping herself to some cake and lemonade. The children ate and then ran down to the grass to play. George gave Betty a contented wink.

"We're alright, aren't we, love?" he said.

"Perfectly," Betty replied.

For the longest time, they sat, a scene of domestic bliss,

watching the children play. It was nearly lunchtime when a Ford delivery truck pulled into the driveway with a screech. A man got out and walked toward them.

"Hello, Cliff," Betty said, as the man drew close. A sinking feeling was growing in the pit of her stomach. "It's not a postal day, is it?"

"Sorry Betty, George," he said, tipping his hat to Betty. He passed a letter to George, who rose to his feet. "Official delivery today." He stepped back, looking concerned. "I'll leave you with it, then. Best of luck."

"Oh no," Betty cried, miserably. Her heart was racing. As the postmaster drove away, George ripped open the letter. It was a telegram. The official insignia declared it to be from the United States War Office. With a tremulous voice, George read it aloud.

"ORDER TO REPORT FOR INDUCTION
The President of the United States"

"To GEORGE W. JONES
You are hereby ordered for induction into the Armed Forces of the United States and to report to Fort Hamilton on October 5th, 1943 at 6.30am for forwarding to an Armed Forces Induction Station."

Betty's knees collapsed under her, and she fell down into her chair.

"The lottery! You've been drafted."

George stood, rigid and blank-faced, holding the telegram. His hand was shaking. He seemed to be having an internal struggle, and as Betty watched him with tears in her eyes, she felt more helpless than ever before.

"So I have," her husband finally said. "And there's no getting out of it. I must play my part, as we all have to." He looked up at her, resolutely. His mouth was a hard line. All at once, George seemed both stronger and more defenceless than ever before. "I'll manage, Betty. It's time I protected you, for a change. I'm not afraid."

"Well, I am!" Betty cried. She fell into his arms in a flood of tears.

An age seemed to pass as they stood together, sheltered from the afternoon sun, commiserating. Eventually, George placed his finger under Betty's chin and lifted it gently, so she could meet his eyes.

"Be ready when the brave, new world is ready for you," he recited. "Isn't that right, jitterbug? Besides, I'll have three months of training before they ship me out anywhere. And I'll still be home for Christmas."

"But it's not enough –"

"Then we'll have to make it enough. Dry your eyes now, I can't bear to see the prettiest kitten in New York City looking so glum."

Betty dried her eyes, determined not to make it any harder for him than it already was. Her husband hadn't the fortitude of a soldier, but like so many other men, he had been thrust into a future that was both unfair, and terribly dangerous. The injustice flamed Betty's heart and her mind whirred into action.

There *must* be a solution to this devastating turn of events, she simply needed to determine it. Suddenly, so much needed her attention.

Donald Pinzolo and his threat to Adina, the key witness to his crimes.

The unknown government agency that seemed to be tracking her every move.

And now this. George was no fighter. Not like he would need to be. Not like *she* was.

He would need her protection. Whether he knew it or not.

Another deadline. Urgency threatened to overcome her.

Betty's thoughts fell back to her little celebration at the Avon head office only the week before. Her life then, had seemed so utterly rebalanced. Surrounded by the women who had given her empowerment. The brand that so perfectly embodied the future she desired. The lipsticks, the perfumes, the posters on the wall.

A flash caught her mind. An image. It was a poster in the Avon board room, displayed among others on the wall. An advertisement of corporate support for the war-effort. *Patriotic. Beautiful. The very essence of selfless devotion.* The poster was of a young woman wearing a white, long-sleeved dress and starched nurses cap, with a royal blue cape flying out behind her. *"The Fair and the Brave"* the poster had declared *" – join the American Red Cross effort today!"*

Not quite a soldier, but certainly a necessity on the front line. *And I've always been rather partial to capes,* she mused.

Was there some way forward then, in which she might yet fight to keep George safe? Betty tucked the thought away in her mind for another day. George was right. For now, they still had much to be grateful for. She must embrace the time they had together. Keeping her chin up and hands busy was the best course of action. George needed her, the children needed her, and Betty's beloved work was waiting patiently in an alligator-skin cosmetic case by the front door.

Life, it seemed, planned to bustle her along as always. And Betty was up to the task.

A woman's work, *really was*, never done.

💋

WANT TO BINGE-READ BETTY?

HayleyCamille.com/ladyvigilante-seasontwo

JOIN MY READER'S CLUB

There's more murder to come... can you keep up with Betty?

HayleyCamille.com/subscribe

LOVE IT? PLEASE REVIEW!

Your reviews are vital to the success of each book. Each book takes me months to research and write, so I'd really appreciate a few moments of your time if you enjoy reading them.

HayleyCamille.com/ladyvigilante-seasonone

THE LADY VIGILANTE PODCAST

Listen at HayleyCamille.com/podcast

A multi-cast radio drama is under production. We invite you to be part of the fun. Experience the sights, the sounds, the music and adventure of WW2 New York with Betty.

Episodes are available on Spotify, iTunes and GooglePlay.

LADY VIGILANTE COLORING BOOK

The Lady Vigilante Companion Coloring Book is big, bad fun for grown-ups.

If you're a fan of the Lady Vigilante crime series, or you just want to dip your coloured pencils into the murky underbelly of 1940's New York, then this is the coloring book for you. The boldest, baddest housewife you've ever seen is ready to take on gangsters and thieves and bring the mafia to it's knees - all while keeping her perfect double-life hidden.

It's time to get out your felt-tip pens and markers.
Sharpen those coloured pencils. Draw down the curtains.
Because Mrs. Betty Jones is going to paint the town red.

Find your copy at:
HayleyCamille.com/LadyVigilanteColoringBook

ABOUT THE AUTHOR

Hayley Camille is the author of the *Ivy Carter* adventure series and multi award-winning *Lady Vigilante* crime series, as well as *The Ultimate Players Guide to Skylanders* gaming guides for kids.

Hayley loves dinosaurs, jazz, animals and all things vintage. She lives in the beautiful hinterland of the Sunshine Coast, in Queensland, Australia with her family.
www.hayleycamille.com

Connect with Hayley at:
Facebook.com/HayleyCamille.author
Instagram.com/HayleyCamille.author
Goodreads.com/Hayley_Camille
Bookbub.com/authors/Hayley-Camille
Amazon.com/Hayley-Camille/e/B01C27M2KE
Tiktok.com/@hayleycamille.author

ALSO BY HAYLEY CAMILLE

The Ivy Carter Series

HUMAN

Archaeologist Ivy Carter holds the fate of humankind in her hands.

Ivy Carter is no stranger to losing the people she loves. She keeps everybody at arm's length, even Orrin James, the brilliant young astrophysicist falling for her.

But when she is stolen through time, and trapped fifty thousand years in the past, Ivy is tasked with the greatest challenge of her life; to prevent the extinction of a primitive human species against overwhelming odds. Determined to save them and desperate to find a way back home, Ivy reaches out across time and space, to the only person in the modern world who remembers her.

As Orrin uncovers Ivy's trail of archaeological clues to prove she existed, the modern world around him spirals into destruction. Every move Ivy makes in the past, puts future Earth in danger.

Each alone, they battle demons, inside and out, to prevent a genocidal war that could change the course of human evolution forever.

In a thrilling adventure that flips between modern world catastrophe and primitive survival, Ivy Carter holds the fate of humankind in her hands.

Available at: HayleyCamille.com/human-novel

EXTINCT

Two species of Human. Only one can survive. The choice is hers.

In the stunning sequel to HUMAN, modern-day archaeologist Ivy Carter begins a perilous journey across prehistoric Indonesia, at a time when volcanic eruptions, mass extinction and a genocidal war are tearing it apart.

Available at: HayleyCamille.com/extinct-novel

The Shadows and Light series

Judgement

In the shadow of Mortwood Forest dwells the most prolific murderer of the Kingdom. The curse he carries, however, may also make him their saviour.

In a world where magic has been lost and innocence is stolen, a prophesy begins. The darkest intentions hidden within every man's soul are exposed, as Shadows and Light, and only one has the power to Judge them.

But he is not what you expect.

Free short story available at:

HayleyCamille.com/judgement

Mrs. Betty Jones: Lady Vigilante is the Amazon best-selling crime series that readers describe as "An EXPLOSIVE laugh-out-loud story!" with the indomitable protagonist, Betty Jones, as "a female Jack Reacher", "powered as all hell" and "Sassy, Smart and Deadly!"

"Lady Vigilante takes on the tropes of femininity in the 40's- the dutiful wife, gals who just want to look pretty letting their man do all the heavy lifting and thinking - and flips them on their head." - *ScreenCraft*

If you love ruthless revenge, kick-ass action and unforgettable characters, then you'll love Betty Jones.

SEASON ONE

As WW2 rages, a lone vigilante takes to the streets of New York to wage war against a powerful crime syndicate. She's the antihero the city needs, hidden in plain sight, with the perfect double life. Meet Mrs. Betty Jones.

Betty Jones has a dark past, which she paints away each day with Avon cosmetics and a bright smile. She has created a new life with her picture-perfect family, but old scars are beginning to itch.

When a series of heists leave a trail of dead soldiers and missing military cargo, Betty recognizes the calling card of her past demons. Blessed with gifts that make her more than human, Betty is unable to live with the continuing existence of the people who once ruined her, so she embarks on a cold-blooded vigilante mission to be rid of them once and for all. But the past is catching up to her, and Betty's perfect life is beginning to crack.

SEASON TWO

A gang war is raging in the underbelly of 1940s New York as a mysterious femme-fatale, known only as the Boudoir Butcher, leaves a trail of bodies between the sheets. When NYPD Detective Jacob Lawrence turns to Betty for help tracking down the serial killer, she can't refuse him. After all, Betty has always been drawn to old flames and open fire...

But will Betty's perfect life be engulfed in the raging blaze she stirs up?

Season Collections available at:

HayleyCamille.com/lady-vigilante-season-collections

LADY VIGILANTE COMPANION COLORING BOOK

This Lady Vigilante companion coloring book is big, bad fun for grown-ups.

If you're a fan of the Lady Vigilante crime series, or you just want to dip your coloured pencils into the murky underbelly of 1940's New York, then this is the coloring book for you. The boldest, baddest housewife you've ever seen is ready to take on gangsters and thieves and bring the mafia to it's knees - all while keeping her perfect double-life hidden.

Can Betty bring the head of organised crime to justice?

Can she keep her blissfully oblivious husband and children safe?

Can she resist the temptation of her long-lost childhood sweetheart?

Can she save an orphanage full of innocents from the clutches of evil?

Sharpen those coloured pencils. Draw down the curtains.

Because Mrs. Betty Jones is going to paint the town red.

Find your copy at:
HayleyCamille.com/LadyVigilanteColoringBook

Non-Spoiler Alert: The colouring pages and story excerpts within, loosely follow the highlights of Season One in the Lady Vigilante crime series. You won't find all the secret twists and turns of the story on these pages - some are left hidden, so that you can discover (or re-discover!) them through the pages of the novel instead.